CAULDRO

by

JENNIFER JANE POPE

CHIMERA

Cauldron of Fear first published in 2001 by
Chimera Publishing Ltd
PO Box 152
Waterlooville
Hants
PO8 9FS

Printed and bound in Great Britain by
Omnia Books Ltd, Glasgow

CAULDRON OF FEAR

Jennifer Jane Pope

This novel is fiction – in real life practice safe sex

Author's Preface

The seventeenth century was a time of great change in Britain. The Elizabethan Age came to an end at the century's beginning and a Scottish King, James VI of Scotland, son of the ill-fated and tragic Mary Queen of Scots, came to the English throne as James I.

When the autocratic and headstrong Charles I succeeded him, it quickly became clear that the country was heading for confrontation of the worst kind – civil war. The eventual victory of the Parliamentary forces and the subsequent execution of a king who refused to concede one iota of what he considered his God-given rights, brought to power Oliver Cromwell, who, although he refused to accept the crown, ruled the country with a rod of Puritan iron.

Eventually, following Oliver Cromwell's death and the short-lived period of hapless misrule under Cromwell's son, Richard, the late King's son would return from exile in Europe as Charles II, and a new age of enlightenment and scientific reasoning would begin.

However, at the time our story begins, the country and its inhabitants are still steeped in superstitions and lore that even the Church has been unable to penetrate fully; in fact, with its witch hunts and executions, particularly the excesses of Matthew Hopkins, the notorious Witchfinder General, the Church played more than a small part in ensuring that fear and ignorance continued.

Some might say that this was deliberate and that the Bishops and their minions had a vested interest in ensuring that the largely uneducated populace remained as unenlightened as it had for centuries; certainly, Britain was a country of largely two extremes: the rich and powerful were very rich and powerful, whilst the poor were generally little better off than the animals they tended.

As for the rights of women, they simply did not exist, but then the same could be said of the rights of at least nine out of ten of the male population, too.

Few people will not have heard of the Great Plague and of the Great Fire of London that is generally accredited with finally cleansing the streets of the capital of the virus that was responsible for decimating the population, but the Great Plague of 1665 was nothing more than what many had been predicting would happen over many years previously.

Sporadic outbreaks, mostly in London, but also in Oxford, Derby and in one or two other large cities, had been killing people for decades, though the authorities did little about this. In fairness, there was probably little they could have done, short of levelling entire cities and rebuilding them on a far more modern and hygienic scale.

The 'Commonwealth' period, as the years of Cromwell's virtual dictatorship are generally referred to, was the worst period of flux in an age when the so-called civilised world was evolving at a rate faster than at any time since the days of the Roman Empire.

It is easy, with the precise science of hindsight, for us to look back and see how easy some of the answers could have been. However, for those who lived in the times, efforts towards progress were fraught with seemingly insurmountable problems and the fact that the government of the country had now fallen into the hands of a man who brought new depths of meaning to the word incompetent.

The privileged minority, looking down from the top of the pile, saw only the potential seeds of revolution and their own, eventual, deposition. 'Give them an inch, etc' was never more soundly an echo of blinkered insecurity than it was then. Fear at the top, fear at the bottom – a guaranteed recipe for a society in which the avaricious, particularly the truly cunning avaricious, could wreak their own particular brand of havoc and insanity. The whole country had become a cauldron – a *Cauldron of Fear*.

The girl was fresh and virginal, even her shaven skull unable to disguise her basic, innocent prettiness. Jacob Crawley, standing in the shadows at the far end of the vault from where she hung chained against the rough stone wall, licked his thin lips in anticipation.

Quietly, with a lightness of step that belied his fifty-something years, he moved closer, until he hovered at the very edge of the pool of orange torchlight that illuminated the captive wench, his black hair and the long black cape he held about his tall frame blending with the darkness behind him and rendering him all but invisible. He saw her eyes were closed and guessed that she was probably fallen into a light sleep of sheer exhaustion, despite the pain her enforced position would be growing in her shoulders and arms, and in the stretched muscles of her calves and thighs as they tried to take some of her weight via the tips of her toes that barely touched the cold floor.

Her breasts, distorted somewhat by her stretched posture, were small and firm, the nipples prominent and deeply coloured, as yet unmarked, per Crawley's strictest instructions. He grinned maliciously to himself, knowing they would not remain thus for much longer.

Between her taut thighs, her shaven pudenda pouted alluringly, the chains at her ankles holding her legs apart just sufficiently to prevent any attempt at modesty, and Crawley felt a cold shiver of lust crawl slowly up his spine. This one, he thought, was far too good to waste on the scaffold, far too sweet a fruit to plant in the chill earth beyond the consecrated ground of the churchyard. No, he chuckled, this one would not be broken, though he knew she would probably require a taste of his own peculiar skills and more than a modicum of bending before she would be totally satisfactory.

Not that the process would take that long; it seldom did. Two days, three at the most – three days that would to her, however, pass like a millennium, so that when Crawley finally granted her even the smallest measure of relief and the chance to avoid the fate to which she would by then have consigned herself and probably even craved, she would take it gratefully, no matter to what level of degradation she must surely know she would sink.

Crawley shuffled his position, the muscles in his right thigh having stiffened in the damp air, and the slight sound brought the girl immediately awake again, her wide brown eyes flickering from side to side in alarm.

'Who – who's there?' she cried, her voice thin and wavering in her terror of the unknown. 'Please,' she wailed, when Crawley made no reply, nor moved to reveal himself, 'please, whoever you are, take pity. I am no witch; surely you must all know that by now. Ask in the village, as I said, everyone will tell you.'

'Oh, people always tell me what they think I will believe,' Crawley replied, breaking his silence at last, though still remaining back from the light, 'at least, in the beginning.' His voice betrayed his north country roots, though many years had softened the harsher edges of his accent. 'Satan woos his brides to proliferate his evil lies, but the Good Lord has bestowed on me the gift of cutting through them.'

'Sir!' Tears welled up in the girl's eyes and began trickling down cheeks that were already stained. 'Sir, I am no bride of the devil, nor do I lie. I fear God and worship our saviour and a more devout girl you will surely never find.'

'You are Matilda Pennywise, of the Parish of St Jude?' The girl nodded, swallowing hard. Crawley inched forward, so that his outline was now visible to her, but only as a deeper shadow. 'Speak girl,' he commanded. 'Are you, or are you not, Matilda Pennywise?'

'Yes!' Matilda gasped. 'Yes sir, indeed I am… sir,' she added, as an afterthought.

'That's better wench,' Crawley cackled, 'you seem to be learning something at last.' He coughed, clearing his throat. 'Then, Matilda Pennywise,' he continued, after a carefully judged pause, 'you stand accused of several counts of witchcraft, sorcery and consorting with unholy forces.'

'No!' Matilda shrieked. 'No, it's all lies, as God is my witness—!' Without warning Crawley leapt forward, his right arm swinging in a wide arc, the open palm of his hand slapping into the girl's unprotected cheek with such force that she would have been knocked off her feet, were the chains not holding her upright. She let out a howl of pain, not least because the full weight of her body had momentarily been transferred to her already tortured upper limbs.

'Silence!' he roared. 'Heresy, to invoke the name of the Lord God you have betrayed.' Matilda was struggling to regain her balance and clearly scarcely heard him, but Crawley knew his words would sink in eventually.

'You are all the same, you Devil's spawn harlots, every single one of you,' he intoned. 'Yet I shall save your unholy soul, mark my words. You will return to the arms of the heavenly master cleansed of your foul wickedness, else my name be not Jacob Crawley!'

Harriet Merridew pushed the small window of her bedroom as far open as the creaking hinges would allow and leaned out over the cill, breathing in the crisp, early morning air and looking up at the pale blue sky above. She smiled, shook her tangled mane of fair hair, and let out a deep sigh. The fourth fair day in succession and the harvest now three-quarters gathered in. If the weather held another forty-eight hours…

The previous year's harvest had been a near disaster, half the crop ruined by rain and unseasonable hailstones, so that Harriet had been forced to sell off from an already dwindling livestock in order to pay bills and taxes and to keep herself and her almost permanently bed-ridden father through the ensuing twelve months. It had been a close-run thing, especially after four of the remaining cows had taken sick and died from the rot disease, rendering them worthless as meat and fit only for burning.

And when one of the sows died giving birth to a troublesome litter, only many weeks of salted pork and Harriet's grim determination to retain their independence prevented her from finally accepting yet another of Thomas Handiwell's proposals of marriage. She shivered at the thought now, for the prospect of a lifetime sharing Handiwell's bed was more than she could believe she had ever contemplated, no matter how desperate their situation might have been.

Not that the man was unpleasant to look at: he was, after all, a fine figure, with broad shoulders, strong back and good legs, his black hair long and thick, if slightly greasy. And he had means that might attract many another female, for his inn, the *Black Drum*, stood alongside the main highway between London and the busy naval centre of Portsmouth, down on the south coast, and he had twice built extension wings to it in order to accommodate the constant influx of weary travellers seeking rest and replenishment for the night.

He was also not an unpleasant fellow. Slightly terse and given to the odd oath at times, true, but not unkindly and with an even disposition and definitely in love with Harriet, as his eyes and gauche manner betrayed whenever he was in her company. No, Harriet reflected, as she withdrew back inside the room, Thomas Handiwell would make a good husband again, as he had clearly done for his long dead first wife, but for someone other than Harriet herself.

Ye gods, she chuckled, he was at least as old as her own father, if not perhaps a year or so older, and his own daughter, Jane, had been at least three years old by the time Harriet had been born, as Jane herself had been quick enough to point out on more than one occasion when the two young women met.

'He's becoming a silly old fool,' the sallow complexioned innkeeper's daughter had remarked, shrewishly, when Harriet delivered the last pig carcass to the *Drum* back at the beginning of June. 'Marry you indeed. He'll make himself an even bigger laughing stock and probably kill himself into the bargain.' Her thin lips curled maliciously and there was no disguising the hate in her eyes.

'If the stupid oaf must take himself another wife,' she had continued, her narrow nose wrinkling in distaste, 'then he should look to someone more his own age, someone who'll keep his feet warm in bed and not tempt him to racing around the bedchamber.'

'Someone who will possibly die before he does, you mean?' Harriet suggested, and immediately regretted her words, though she knew she had hit the nail squarely upon its head. Jane Handiwell did not want her father dying and leaving his well-gotten gains to a wife who might outlive her. She had not remained at the inn, cooking, cleaning and managing just for some flighty usurper to march in on her pretty heels and snatch away her inheritance.

'Poor Jane,' Harriet whispered, as she opened the top drawer of the oak chest and began rummaging through the clean underthings there. 'Poor plain Jane with your twisted humour and silly jealousies. Why you won't believe me when I say I have no intentions of marrying your father, heaven knows, but then a mean spirit bleeds itself hardest, and no mistaking.'

Her name was Miranda Parkes, but the people here persisted in calling her Kitty, not just refusing to acknowledge her real identity, but actively punishing her with their cruel whips if she dared try not responding to the name they had given her, let alone when she tried to insist that they use her correct title.

'Here you are, Kitty,' the young overseer had told her, gripping her jaw between a powerful thumb and forefinger and jerking her face up towards his own. 'You're Kitty here and you'll be Kitty from now on, unless your new master decides to rename you.'

'But I'm not a slave,' Miranda squeaked, defiantly. She clenched and unclenched her fists in desperate frustration, but her wrists remained strapped to her hips as they had been when she first recovered consciousness in this awful place. 'I'm not a slave,' she repeated, futilely.

The overseer, Adam, released his grip and pushed her away. 'Is that so?' he smirked. 'Well, you look like a slave, right enough, for no free woman I ever knew would stand before men shamelessly showing off her titties like you do.'

Miranda felt her cheeks redden, for she had almost managed to forget that she was kept so terribly near naked. 'It's not my choice to be like this,' she whispered, lowering her eyes, grimacing as she saw how hard and extended her nipples appeared. 'If you would permit me, I'd cover myself suitably.'

'I think your appearance is suitable enough,' Adam laughed, 'for a slave girl.' He slapped the short leather crop against his high boot, making Amanda wince. 'And that's what you are, Kitty, whether you like it or not, so the sooner you start learning how a slave should properly behave, the easier it will be for you.' He flexed the crop meaningfully.

'So,' he said silkily, 'what's it to be, or shall I add a few more stripes to those rosy little bottom cheeks?'

Kitty winced again, for if the immediate pain of the

whipping he had given her that first evening had faded, the memory had not, and she did not have to try too hard to recall each of the six burning stripes he laid across her buttocks. She let out a long breath. 'I don't want to be whipped again,' she said, quietly.

'Master,' Adam reminded her.

She sighed again. 'I don't want to be whipped again, master,' she corrected. 'What is it you want me to do?'

'Whatever I tell you,' he said, smiling now. 'It won't be that hard to learn, I promise you. Now, step up closer and present those slave girl titties for my inspection.' Swallowing hard, Amanda took a pace forward and forced herself to draw her shoulders back, thrusting her generous mounds into even greater prominence. Adam's free hand reached out, hefting the left breast carefully, kneading one side gently with his thumb. To her chagrin, Amanda felt a tremor run up and down her arched spine and an involuntary squeal escaped her lips before she could check it.

'Very good, Titty Kitty,' Adam purred, evidently pleased with the reaction to his touch. 'Look down now, see how your teats swell to my caresses. Why, I swear that if you weren't wearing your slave harness you'd throw yourself wantonly upon me, you brazen little trollop.'

He let the whip drop at his feet and his left hand began to explore, but this time much lower down, pushing between the stiff leather strap between her thighs and searching, first for her recently denuded mound and then for the swollen lips that had begun to throb as though developing a will of their own.

'Ah, naughty Titty Kitty,' he breathed, his mouth close to her right ear. 'What's this then, are we all wet down here? And so hot, too. Would you like me to take care of this hungry little cunny, Titty Kitty?'

'Yes, master.' Amanda could not believe she had said that, and was on the point of drawing back when

14

commonsense and self-preservation interceded. To resist, even to object, could only bring one inevitable and painful result and after all, she told herself reasonably, she was no virgin. Besides, she had to admit, he was handsome, even if his manner was brutish.

Slowly, she raised her face until her eyes met his. 'Yes, master,' she repeated, quietly but surprisingly calmly, 'I think I should like that very much.'

Matilda hung awkwardly against the unforgiving stone blocks, shifting her position every now and then, at least as far as her chains would permit, in an effort to bring a measure of relief to a few different muscles in turn. However, with her toes barely touching the floor, there were few options and gradually her limbs were beginning to feel numb through their agonies.

'Dear God,' she whispered, half opening her eyes to peer into the gloom, suspecting that the gaunt, black-garbed man was there somewhere, watching her ordeal, 'dear God, why is this happening to me? You know only too well that these are nought but foul lies.' She closed her eyes again, groaning and trying to draw more air into her lungs.

Was this, she wondered, what it felt like to be crucified? She had heard, somewhere, that it was not the nails through hands and feet that killed, but the position of the condemned, whereby the chest finally collapsed and no air then reached the head. James – James Calthorpe, the miller's son – had told her that, hadn't he? James had been educated, sent away to London, his father's money buying him a future that wouldn't involve humping heavy sacks of grain and flour and long hours toiling to keep the unreliable mill machinery grinding.

James Calthorpe knew many things, Matilda knew. He knew about other countries, Europe, the new cities in the new world across the ocean. He hadn't visited them personally, of course, though he had assured Matilda that he would – and soon – but he told her of the books in the universities and libraries, shelf upon shelf of learning and knowledge, where a man could spend a lifetime of days reading and still not have touched upon one tenth of what was there.

And James knew of many things much closer to home, especially of those secret places that Matilda thought were known only to her, and just how and when to touch, caress, kiss these places and invoke in her sensations that drove her to forget everything her mother and aunts had ever told her. Perhaps, she reflected mournfully, this was her punishment; the wrath of God unleashed upon her for those stolen moments of passion in the various small barns behind the watermill.

They had done things that Matilda knew were wrong, sinful, against the teachings of the Church, things the pastor had told the entire congregation would be certain to condemn their eternal souls to the fires of everlasting Hell. She had been wicked and now she was being punished.

'No!' she cried out, her eyes snapping open. 'No!' It was not right, she was not right. The Crawley man had said she was a witch, that she had consorted with devils and imps. James Calthorpe was no angel, to be sure, but he was no devil, that much Matilda knew beyond doubt. No man could be more flesh and blood than he.

'Please!' she cried into the echoing darkness. 'Please, you must believe me. I'll swear on the good book, I am no witch. Let those who accuse me do so to my face and swear their oath likewise and in the church itself, before the altar!'

Francis Calthorpe regarded the old woman quizzically. Everyone in the village knew Hannah Pennywise, but no one could ever really say they 'knew' her, as he was want to tell his wife on frequent occasions. Of course the majority

16

of the locals, little more than ignorant peasants in Francis's eyes, regarded her as a witch and openly said so, though never, naturally, within her hearing.

Francis did not subscribe to this point of view, though he had to agree that Hannah was slightly odd. She was old – very old – though nobody could say her exact age and nobody dared ask her directly, and she looked stiff and frail, though she walked briskly everywhere, banging her cane into the ground as she went. Moreover, though the passing of the years had taken its inevitable toll, enough remained to indicate that, in her younger days, Hannah Pennywise had almost certainly been a handsome woman.

That evidence was also reflected in her granddaughter, Matilda, a fine looking young woman, if also slightly unconventional in her ways, a trait that Francis proscribed to her earlier upbringing in London, where women, so he heard, were beginning to behave slightly more independently, despite the supposedly strict Puritan regime of the Protector, Cromwell.

This combination of beauty and wilfulness was doubtless what had attracted Francis's son, James, to the girl – that and her obvious intelligence and an education far better than the average village female was ever likely to have benefit of. Given her character, Francis could see his son was quite possibly courting trouble for himself in the future, but then James was a strong character in his own right and was of an age whereby he was entitled to make his own choices – and mistakes.

'Mistress Pennywise,' Francis said at last, dusting down the front of his apron, but simply creating a further cloud of flour between them, 'my son left for London yesterday, to the best of my knowledge. Of course,' he added with a wry smile, 'you may be in a more privileged position than I.'

Hannah sniffed and leaned on her long staff, shaking her

head.

'He may have left for London, Master Calthorpe, but he was supposed to be calling in to see my lass before he travelled,' she said. 'They were to meet at the crossroads and dine at the inn, but I am told that neither of them ever arrived there.'

Francis raised his eyebrows. 'I see,' he replied slowly. 'Well, perhaps he decided to delay his departure. Perhaps, well, perhaps many things. Young people today do not necessarily observe the proprieties of past ages.'

'Yes, well I know what you're thinking, Francis Calthorpe,' Hannah growled, 'but in this particular case you're quite wrong, I think. Besides, where would they go? They would hardly ride to London together on the one horse, would they – unless you're going to tell me your lad had a spare mount with him?'

'No, that he did not, I can say for sure,' Francis said, shaking his head. 'Though he could, perhaps, have hired another mount at the inn.'

'No,' Hannah said, 'I already told you. He never went to the inn.'

'Then I don't know,' Francis admitted, holding up his flour-covered hands. 'But I shouldn't worry overly much. It was a warm night last night, so they could – well, they could easily have fallen asleep somewhere.'

'They could, aye,' Hannah said, 'but I'm damned certain they didn't. Something is very wrong and I can feel it. Trouble is,' she added, turning to leave, 'I don't know what and I don't know where. Not as yet, anyways.'

'That young woman could do a lot worse for herself, I'm telling you,' Thomas Handiwell grunted. 'There b'ain't so many eligible fellows around these parts, in case you hadn't noticed.'

From the other side of the well-worn oak bar counter,

Ned Blaine tried not to smile. Ten years younger than Thomas, Ned had been happily (for the most part, anyway) married to his childhood sweetheart for getting on for two decades, a union that had brought forth nine surviving offspring, six of them male, and the eldest two female children were now both around marriageable age and themselves not that much younger than the object of Thomas's desire.

'Fair enough, Ned,' Thomas continued, 'there's a difference of more than a few years—'

'More'n a few, Thomas,' Ned interjected, but Thomas appeared, or chose to appear, not to hear him.

'A few years, I'll grant you,' he said, 'but I have good health and a good home to offer here.'

'Wench has a home already,' Ned pointed out. 'Barten Meade's a fine house.'

'Once, mebbe,' Thomas grunted. 'Place is going to rack and ruin now, or ain't you been over thataways lately? Hardly surprising, really. Girl like that can hardly be expected to keep a place like that in good repair.'

'Well, that's right enough, I suppose,' Ned conceded. He stared down into the bottom of his pewter tankard, regarding the dregs quizzically. 'Maybe one or two on us could go over and offer the odd helping hand, just to be neighbourly and Christian, like.'

'Place'd need more than an odd hand, I'm telling you,' Thomas snorted. 'Hasn't seen a lick of wash these past five years, I'd wager, not since Oliver Merridew took properly to his bed and Harriet paid off the Walden lad.'

'Aye, well, that's another thing, ain't it?' Ned remarked, scraping his pot pointedly along the bar top. 'Wench ain't goin' t'leave her father now, is she? Thinks the world of him, and no mistakin' that.'

'Wouldn't expect her to leave him,' Thomas grunted. He reached across and took the tankard, turning towards the nearest of the ale casks behind him. 'Told her plain enough, I did. She can bring her father here and I'll bring in a proper nursemaid to take good care of him. Not only that, I can put up the money to hire on enough hands to have their farm up and running again as it should be.

'There's fifteen acres at least should have been under the plough this season, 'cepting they couldn't afford to keep a ploughman on long enough to turn it all. That's a devilish waste, and no mistaking.' He turned back and placed the brimming pot back before Ned, who seized it greedily.

'If'n they had any sense they'd sell off what they can't till regular,' Thomas went on.

'Or sell off half of it and use the money to bring the other half under the plough,' Ned added, wiping the thin froth from his upper lip with the back of one less than clean hand. 'Tried suggesting that, have you?'

'Tried,' Thomas replied mournfully. 'Tried and failed. She won't listen, that one. Wilful to a fault. T'ain't right.'

'She be female,' Ned chuckled. 'Females ain't right, not like men. Got udders instead o' brains and—'

'That's enough of that sort of talk, Ned Blaine,' Thomas snapped, cutting the younger man short. 'I thought better of you, a married man with girls of thine own not that much of an age different.' He looked up and down the deserted bar, as if fearful that someone might have overheard his companion's words, but it was still very early and the place deserted.

'Aye, well, then there's little you can tell me about the so called fairer sex, is there?' Ned grinned. 'Think your self lucky thou've only got the one female to contend with.'

'I'd think meself luckier if I had the two,' Thomas mused. He reached beneath the bar, brought up a heavy glass and a bottle of brandy, uncorked the latter and poured himself a generous measure. Ned took another gulp of his ale and wiped his mouth again.

'T'ain't going to be, Thomas,' he said. 'Sooner you accepts that as the truth, easier it'll sit on you. It'll ride easier with your Jane, too.'

'Jane will do as she's told and accept whatever I decide,' Thomas said bluntly. 'She's not too old, nor yet too big not to get my belt across her backside and I'm still master in this house, if none other as yet.'

Adam Portfield cinched the second breast strap tighter and stepped back to admire the results of his adjustments. The girl, Kitty, was certainly well endowed, but now the tightened leather about the base of each bosom thrust it into even greater prominence, and the cuffs he had added above her elbows, drawing them closer together by means of a linked chain, forced her to stand with both magnificent globes thrust enticingly towards him.

He reached into his pocket and brought out the miniature cat-o'-nine-tails. Unlike it's bigger sibling, favoured so much in the navy, this implement did not have little lead pellets braided into the tips of each thong, nor were the thongs themselves more than flat strips of soft hide, for this whip was intended for purposes other than simple punishment. Adam had seen slave women come to orgasm under these flailing fronds and, for all his youthfulness he liked to think he had perfected its use.

'Tit whip, Titty Kitty,' he laughed, seeing how the helpless girl's eyes had grown round at the sight of the little cat. 'I'm going to punish those provocative melons of yours and punish them till you cry for me to tup that pretty little cunny instead.'

'But, master,' Kitty whimpered, 'I've already asked you to do that, haven't I?'

'Yes, but too easily, Titty Kitty,' Adam sneered. 'I like my wenches to be hot and writhing, so they dance on they end of my cock like wild demons. Now, stand still and hold

21

your ground, else I'll kneel you down and truss you there.'
He stepped forward and, with a flick of his wrist, sent the
nine strips humming through the air. They landed about
Kitty's left nipple, already engorged from the stringent
bondage of her breasts. She let out a high-pitched squeal
and jumped backwards, but there was really nowhere to go
inside the barn stall.

Again the flails snaked out, this time at her other breast.
She gasped and groaned, staggering back against the timber
partition and Adam saw her eyes roll, before she screwed
them shut. The third and fourth blows landed with equal
precision, reddening the area around each pouting teat and
Kitty writhed against the rough wall, growling and mewling.
Her eyes opened again, slitted now as she peered at her
tormentor through a haze of tears.

'Bastard!' she hissed, but Adam noticed how she was
pressing her firm thighs together. 'Noooo!' she wailed, but
now stood more erect, making no attempt to lessen his target
area.

'Brazen little bitch,' Adam taunted and added two more
blows, one to each side. 'I do believe you're starting to
enjoy this as much as I am.'

- II -

The two men were the same who'd brought Matilda to the cellar dungeon originally, how long ago now she could only guess, though it seemed like a lifetime since she last breathed fresh air.

Neither of them was local and she guessed they must travel about with the Crawley creature, for he would need his own men to assist in the execution of his dreadful duties. Not that Matilda knew anything of the man personally, but she had heard of his kind; feared figures who travelled the land, searching out witches, terrifying entire areas with their awful retribution. There had been one name that instilled terror throughout half the realm, but Matthew Hopkins was reputably dead, ten years ago at least, maybe more, and with him had gone the worst of the fear that his name and those of his ilk had represented.

Witch finding, James had assured her, lost all credibility since the death of the old king. This was a new world now; a world where superstition would have no place, swept aside by a tide of knowledge and education. Yes, there were still a few backwaters where the successors of Matthew Hopkins could still ply their deadly trade, but they were few and far between, isolated pockets of ignorance in an otherwise much better informed society.

Matilda had never considered Leddingham to be a backwater, however. Standing alongside one of the main highways to London, it was only a small rural village, admittedly, but the newssheets from the capital arrived only one day late and the talk in the inn was as informed as any she had heard, save when in James's company, of course, and during those days when she had lived in London herself.

So why here? And why her? Why had Jacob Crawley come to the village and just who had made such ridiculous allegations about her? And where was James? If only James were here, surely he would put an end to this nightmare? Surely someone from the village would tell him what was happening?

For the moment, however, it seemed obvious that James remained in ignorance of her situation and the whys and wherefores were unimportant. For the moment she was here, naked, her head shaved, her wrists chained and facing two men whose dull eyes offered little comfort.

'Don't know why he always insists on cutting off their hair,' the taller one said, shaking his head. 'This one had such pretty curls. Seems a dreadful waste if'n you ask me, Jed.'

His companion looked darkly at him. 'Hush your mouth, Silas Grout,' he hissed. 'If his eminence hears you I'd not want to be in your shoes. Ours ain't to question the likes of him and well you should know that by now. His moods are bad enough o' late, so don't give him any reason to act worse.'

'Just saying, that's all,' Silas muttered. 'Besides, I should worry what his high and mightiness thinks. I'm startin' to get a bit fed up with all this travellin' about. We've hardly bin three days in the one place this past twelve months. I reckon this witch huntin' business is near on finished. Don' reckon half the ones we catches is really witches anyway.'

Watching the two men through slitted eyes, Matilda saw what she thought was a glimmer of hope. 'That's right, sir,' she gasped, astonished at how cracked and dry her voice sounded. The two of them stopped, looking at each other and then back at her. Swallowing and trying to moisten her lips with her tongue, Matilda pressed on. 'You're right,' she croaked. 'I'm no witch and there will be plenty of people in the village who'll bear me witness. If one of you would just go and fetch Mr Calthorpe the miller, or his son, James. They'll tell your master the truth.

'Or my own grandmother,' she added hastily. 'Her name is Hannah Pennywise and she lives in the third cottage along from the mill. She's lived in this village all her life. Everyone knows her.'

'Probably knows her for a witch herself,' Jed, the shorter man growled. 'Witchin' runs through entire families, everyone knows that. Maybe honest people would be too afeared to say ought agin her.'

'Then who's accused me?' Matilda demanded. 'Surely I have the right to know at least that much?'

'You have the right to whatever Master Crawley decides,' Jed replied blandly. 'Master Crawley holds papers from three bishops and from Parliament itself. He's an official witchfinder with the best reputation a body could want. He knows a witch when he sees one, so it don't really matter who first testified as to what you really was, does it? He's got all the evidence, all writ down proper, according to the law, plenty enough to hang you right now, but he's decided to have one last try at saving your soul first.'

'He has?' A flicker of new hope sprung up in Matilda's breast. 'Then please, take me to him. I'll swear my love to the one God.'

'That I'd bet,' Silas grinned. 'But then anyone'd swear anything, with the shadow of the noose over their pretty necks, wouldn't they?'

'Then what?' she protested. The two men exchanged looks again.

'You'll soon see,' Jed retorted, grinning, though with little humour in the expression. 'And so will your grandma. Master Crawley has a special penance for witches he thinks he can *save*.' The way he laid emphasis on the last word made Matilda's flesh crawl and suddenly, despite her pain – perhaps because the pain was focussing her thoughts – she thought she understood quite clearly what this nightmare was really about.

The statements against her, if they really existed, had probably been obtained with promises of reward, and any 'evidence' against her merely fabrications initiated by Crawley himself. Grandma Hannah had lived all her life simply enough in her cottage, which had belonged to her father before her. Nathan Pennywise had been aptly named, for he saved, invested money in the watermill with James Meldrew's grandfather, sold his share in that some years later and bought land, little pockets of acreage all about the area, all of which were then, as now, rented out to local farmers.

His careful investment was not worth a great fortune, not by any means, but the rents that came in every quarter day mounted up and neither he, nor his daughter after him, ever had profligate tastes. Matilda never questioned Hannah about money, but she knew there must be a small nest egg somewhere, and what she knew surely must be fairly common knowledge in Leddingham and the area about it.

Somehow Crawley had gotten wind of this; an aged woman, her young granddaughter and no other living relatives that anyone knew of – they offered themselves as easy prey to anyone unscrupulous enough to take advantage, especially if that advantage could be taken, at least to all appearances, by using the law. The hysterical witch hunts of Matthew Hopkins's day were a thing of the past, but witchcraft was still a crime in England and news still filtered through of another unfortunate being hanged, probably for no greater sin than living on her own, or having a lazy eye or deformed hand. Ignorance, Matilda knew, was a terrible thing, even more terrible all the time people like Crawley existed to exploit it.

And in this case, she, Matilda, was the easiest route to whatever money Hannah had salted away. Undoubtedly, Crawley would offer the old woman her granddaughter's life in exchange for gold. It was blackmail, but he would not be crude enough to state it as such. No doubt he would tell Hannah that it was a tribute to God, paid to his servant, who would then intercede with the Almighty on behalf of Matilda's soul.

Meantime, however, the way she had been treated thus far and the way in which Jed had spoken suggested that Crawley might see this situation as the chance to avail himself of more than just pecuniary rewards. Matilda pictured the hawk-nosed man's cruel eyes and thin lips and shuddered at the prospect…

The warmth of the late summer sun was fast fading as it dipped towards the far hills with what seemed to be growing speed, and the shadows of the trees and the huge barn structure stretched far across the deserted meadow, as the heavy timber-sided wagon lurched unsteadily up the rutted dirt track behind two disinterested looking cobs.

The driver, a thickset fellow of indeterminate middle age, dressed simply, though in good quality cloth, pushed his floppy hat to the back of his head, scratched behind his right ear and then hawked up a huge glob of spittle, which he expelled towards the bushes with surprising velocity. Like his horses, he seemed little interested in his surroundings and looked tired and dusty, evidence of a long day's journey.

As the plodding horses drew close to the barn they slowed and stopped, both without any visible or audible sign of instruction from the man. One snorted and tossed its head, but even this seemed a half-hearted effort, whilst its companion remained motionless, only the occasional twitch of its ears distinguishing it from a statue.

The driver hawked and spat again, studied his unused whip with the air of someone who has just remembered something, and placed it tidily on the bench seat at his side. He stretched his shoulders back, arching his neck and just caught in time the hat that was too loose fitting to stay in place under such duress. Then, with a sigh and a grunt, he began to climb down from his perch, landing heavily on the hardened mud as the door at the end of the barn swung open.

'You're nearly two hours late.' The speaker was a younger man, perhaps not yet thirty, with dark hair cut close to his skull, in the Puritan fashion. He wore polished leather breeches and a stiff leather waistcoat, over a loose-sleeved shirt of pale lemon silk, and moved as languidly and easily as the older man moved stiffly.

The driver grunted and gave him a look of contempt. 'Military had the road blocked half the morning,' he said, without any hint of apology. 'Wagonloads of cannon going down to Portsmouth, along with a few hundred casks of powder, so I heard. They don't like the likes of us getting too near that sort of convoy, so all other travellers have to wait up till they're well clear. Not that I'm complaining, mind. Wouldn't want to be anywheres around that cargo if'n a stray spark from a pipe went the wrong place.'

'You could have looked for another route,' the younger man suggested. 'I don't like the idea of you and this wagon just standing around, especially not in a crowded area.'

'Master Hawkin,' the driver said flatly, 'if there were another road I'd have taken it. As it stands, the only other way would have been around the back of Harting Hill, which be about twenty miles off the beam. These two nags are willing enough and they'll plod all day and all night if'n I ask 'em, but you're talking another four hours, maybe five, so if'n I'd gone that way I'd not have been here much afore ten tonight, if then.'

'And your cargo has been well behaved?' George Hawkin said, ignoring the driver's explanation as if it were totally unimportant.

The older man nodded. 'Quiet as four little corpses,' he said. 'Sleeping like innocent babes and unlikely to wake afore midnight, if'n I'm any judge. Swallowed their medicine good as gold and out like lights not ten minutes after.' Sam Perkins did not like George Hawkin very much, but then that was not really surprising, as Sam did not like anyone really, himself included when he was in his cups.

But in addition to Sam's general lack of sociability, there was the fact that George, in his opinion, had ideas far above the station of a man whose father had been a swineherd all his life and whose mother had worked in the scullery of a country house that had not even been very grand. Quite how Hawkin had risen to become Roderick Grayling's steward at Grayling Hall, Sam had no idea, but then the nobility were a rum lot at the best of times, and the Graylings among the rummest.

Still, he reflected as he trudged around to the rear of the wagon, they paid him well, both for his work and for his ability to keep a still tongue in his head, and the job had occasional little perks, just so long as George Hawkin never got to find out. He reached up and inserted a heavy key into the formidable lock that secured the equally formidable door, turned it and swung the thick oak section to the side, revealing a sight that most anyone else would have found remarkable, if not bizarre, but to which both men had long grown accustomed.

The three young women lay side by side, a thin layer of sacking between their near naked bodies and the rough hewn planks that formed the floor of the wagon. They lay on their backs, their faces, eyes closed in drugged sleep, facing upwards, arms by their sides, wrists cuffed there to the thick leather belts that had been laced and locked about their slender waists and from which further straps, roughly elongated triangular in shape, descended to cover their sexes, passing between their thighs and locking again to the lower edges of the waist belts at the small of the back. They would, Sam knew, remain in these chastity-enforcing devices for several days, with further humiliating refinements yet to come.

'Pretty little trio, b'ain't they?' he chuckled. In the pocket of his breeches the other key, much smaller than the one he had used to unlock the wagon door, seemed to grow larger and his hand went inadvertently to where it pressed against the thick woollen material, as if to satisfy itself that the bulge there was only in Sam's imagination. He wondered what Hawkin would say if he knew that Sam had that particular key, or how he frequently made use of it during stops in the journey down from south London.

He chuckled again, but this time to himself, as he wondered how many little Sams there might now be, running around somewhere out beyond the seas, in the Orient, or maybe in the New World, for these girls, despite their initial rigorous training and 'breaking in' period would always be well on their way to their new masters long before any evidence of what he had been up to might show.

'Papers all in the box there?' George Hawkin said tersely, leaning in to slide the small walnut-veneered portfolio towards him and not deigning to comment on the physical attributes referred to by the older man.

Sam sniffed and wiped his nose on the back of his hand. 'What d'ye think, George Hawkin?' he snapped. 'Think I'm beyond seeing to a few simple details, is it? Don't you forget, lad, I remembers youse when you was runnin' around barefoot and damned nearly bare-arsed, and I bin runnin' this damned wagon up and down for his lordship and now his boy maybe twenty-five years in all now. Never lost a wench and never lost a scrap of the damned paperwork in that time, neither!'

'And never learned to read any of it, either,' Hawkin rasped, tucking the box under his arm. 'Well,' he said, turning on his heel, 'don't just stand there, start bringing them inside.'

'Me?' Sam cried, feigning indignation. 'Where's that good-for-nothing lad William then? I'm a bloody driver, not a porter.'

'Then you'd better start keeping better time,' Hawkin grinned evilly. 'I sent the lad off for his supper an hour since, so there's just you.'

'Supper?' Sam echoed. 'Some of us ain't had bleedin' dinner yet.'

'The sooner they're inside, the sooner you get fed,' Hawkin pointed out. 'And there's a little extra treat for you tonight. Master Roderick has picked out a nice bed-warmer for you, very handsome little blackamoor wench we bought a week or so since. Ladies maid, she was, and great big eyes.'

'Big eyes and small teats, I'll wager,' Sam replied sullenly. 'All the same, these black wenches, and they jabber away all the time you're tuppin' them, all in their heathen tongues. What about the lady she was maid to?'

'Hah!' Hawkin made a wry face. 'You don't think the young master would waste quality like that on the likes of me, let alone you? No, that one is already heading east and a good bounty she's fetched. Fair-haired, sweet-faced and tight-crossed legs – at least, when she first got here. Not a day over twenty and probably a virgin, but she seemed a quick learner and there's only one stiffness she'll have from now on.'

Jane Handiwell wriggled into the tight breeches and began lacing them even tighter about her generous hips, finally drawing the wide belt about her waist and fastening the ornate cat's head buckle and cinching herself as tightly as possible.

Turning, she studied her reflection in the tall mirror and pursed her thin lips. Yes, she thought, ruefully, with her hair tied back and the masculine shirt, she made a more than passable male – better than she made a woman, she added bitterly, and her thin nostrils flared momentarily, but her anger had no time to grow, for a quiet knock on the bedroom door heralded the arrival of her maidservant, Beth.

The seventeen-year-old orphan already boasted a larger bust than her mistress and wore tops that plunged away to reveal plenty of it, the laced bodice pushing the twin globes into prominence. Her hair was red, a deep gingery mane that steadfastly refused to obey even her most ardent attempts to control it, and the freckles on her cheeks ran their own riot in sympathy.

Jane considered her own thin, straight black hair and her lips twitched again, but she knew she should not take it out on Beth, for the poor girl could not help her innate prettiness and only displayed so much cleavage as she did on Jane's specific instructions. Those breasts, Jane knew, were as much hers as they were the younger girl's, and Beth worshipped her mistress with a devotion that bordered on fanaticism.

'Nearly ready, miss?' Beth whispered, closing the door quietly behind her. 'The master's left for his cousin's at Petersfield and I've saddled up Marquis ready for you. He's in the usual place, just behind the three oaks.'

'Good girl,' Jane smiled and bent to plant a kiss on Beth's cheek, fondling one breast familiarly as she did so. She felt Beth tense and let out her customary low moan, her eyelids flickering closed and then open again. 'Later, my sweet,' she cooed. 'Be in my bed and make sure it's nice and warm for when I return, eh?'

'Yes, miss,' Beth smiled widely, her green eyes sparkling

with anticipation. 'And I'll warm a bottle of brandy for you.'

'Warm it between your bubbies then, my little dove,' Jane grinned. She reached for the frock jacket that hung across the foot-rail of the bed, and Beth immediately took it from her, holding it up so that her mistress could slip her arms into the sleeves the more easily. Then, as Jane sat upon the edge of the bed, Beth knelt to slip her feet into the sturdy riding boots, lacing them and fastening the three additional buckles on each.

'You be careful tonight, mistress, please?' Beth said, standing up again and straightening her skirts. 'There's talk that Lord Grayling has been onto the magistrates to get army patrols on the roads at night. Too many people complainin', especially the coach companies. Fair crippling their trade on the overnights, so they say.'

'Lord Grayling hasn't been at the Hall these past six months,' Jane chuckled. 'He's in the Indies, they say, looking for new ways to line his deep pockets.'

'But the son is still here, mistress, and they do say as how he's a harder nut than his pa, so they do.'

'There's no nut that can't be cracked, if'n it's hit right,' Jane retorted. 'And Roderick Grayling is no exception to that rule,' she added, with a malicious grin. 'He's no threat to our little game, so don't you worry that fuzzy little head of yours with such nonsense.'

Beth looked unconvinced, but she turned, opened the closet and took out the long black cape and held it up for Jane to put on and fasten the neck clasp. The tricorn hat completed the outfit and Jane returned to the mirror for one final inspection. Yes, she thought, in poor light and especially once she donned her mask, she would pass easily enough for a man, and besides, the only people close enough to make any objective judgement would be too busy looking at her two things than her face.

The two pistols were a pair, bought during a visit to London, from a gunsmith who had assured Jane that they were of a unique design, handmade by a craftsman in India and designed so that although they fired a smaller ball than was usual, their accuracy surpassed any other hand weapon he had ever tested. And he had not been misleading her, Jane knew, for she could drop a rabbit at fifty paces with either weapon; no mean feat in an age when firearms were still very much at the stage of hit-or-miss.

Carefully, Jane hefted the beautifully balanced pistols, weighed them lovingly for a moment or two, and then tucked them through the specially adapted belt.

'Right then, my little kitten tongue,' she said, regarding Beth kindly, 'I'm off to the hunt, or I'll be late and my friends will start worrying, knowing them as I do. Make sure the side door is unbolted once everyone else is asleep, and don't forget my warm brandy. The nights are growing chillier out there now and I'm sure I'll be needing something to drive away the cold, eh?'

Sarah Merridew's schooling had not extended to biology, and she had no idea of just how many bones there were in the human body, just that now, she thought, there seemed to be an awful lot and every one of hers ached from the constant jolting of the coach. The small square of blanket she had earlier folded and placed carefully beneath her bottom did little, if anything, to cushion the repeated impacts, and how she now wished she had been able to afford the extra two shillings it would have cost to travel in one of the more luxurious coaches that plied the route from London to the coast.

She sighed and turned to look out of the window, into the gathering gloom of the imminent night. Two shillings extra – it was scandalous. Men in London worked two or three weeks to earn that much, and heaven alone knew her funds were now sparse enough. Medical bills, funerals – four of them – bribes to no end of officials, bribes to get her out of that area of the city in the first place, new clothing to replace everything she had been forced to burn…

A small tear welled up in the corner of one eye and threatened to spill onto her pale cheek, but she swallowed hard and steeled herself against giving way now. After all, she told herself fiercely, there were hundreds – no, thousands – of people in just as bad a situation as herself, many of them far worse, for the plague outbreaks had more than decimated some areas of the great capital city and some families had been wiped out entirely.

She had to consider herself lucky, that's what her father, rest his soul, would have told her. He had been the last to die, following her mother, her brother and her older sister, all in the space of just a few weeks. Fortunately, the unseasonably heavy rains had served to dampen down the spread of the disease, but Sarah paid men to burn everything nonetheless. Informed opinion was that infection was carried in the very fibres of clothes, and fire was the only certain way to end it.

She shook her head sadly. So much education and science in London and still something like that had been allowed to happen, and everyone powerless to stop it. It was inconceivable that such a thing could wreak so much havoc in a modern world like this. After all, this was 1659 and mankind had surely left the dark ages far in the past by now? At least, she told herself, it was unlikely she would see another such outbreak in her lifetime.

The coach rattled on, the wooden bench seat seemingly becoming harder and harder with every mile that passed beneath the creaking wheels, and she wondered how much further, how much longer, before they stopped for another change of horses and the blissful opportunity that would give for her to stretch her aching limbs, if only for a few minutes.

Outside it was just about dark, which meant it was around seven o'clock. Had they really only been on the road for less than three hours? It seemed like thirty-three and there were still another seven hours to go, at least. It would be past two in the morning before they reached the *Black Drum* inn and, although the clerk at the coach office had assured her there would be a room available for her, even at that hour, somehow Sarah felt it a very un-christian hour to be arriving anywhere.

'At least there will be a bed,' she murmured. She turned from the window and looked across at the only two other occupants of the coach, a pale looking young man, possibly not much older than herself, whose mode of dress suggested he was a cleric of some kind, and a homely woman approaching old age, who sat huddled and swathed in several layers of cloaks, a worn bonnet pulled down over her head so that it obscured most of her face. A nanny, an old servant, maybe a housekeeper, Sarah surmised. Another unfortunate who could not indulge to the extent of an extra two shillings' worth of comfort, though at least her matronly figure meant she had more natural padding between her bones and the uncompromising oak boards.

The *Black Drum*, the clerk had assured Sarah, was a very reputable inn, with good food, comfortable rooms and even – a rarity, even in London – hot water available at any hour of the day or night. For a total of ninepence ha'penny – a special concessionary rate for passengers of the coach company – she would be assured of everything she could possibly want and then the following day, once she was properly rested and replenished, it was but two miles from there to Barten Meade and the sanctuary of her uncle, Oliver Merridew's house.

She sighed again and turned back to look out into the night. At least, she thought, she had left behind no loose ends. She had little money, true enough, but her uncle made it very clear in his letters that she should be more than welcome. It would be quiet after the city, she knew, but at least it would be safe there with the last dangers now many miles behind her.

The countryside, she thought dreamily as she closed her eyes and tried to ignore the bruising jolts, the countryside would be so peaceful after life in the big city…

- III -

The overseer, Adam, was deliberately tormenting her, Kitty realised, making her beg for what they both knew she now craved so desperately, but refusing to sate her desires fully. Several times he used his devilish whip to bring her to a writhing frenzy, but then, just as she thought she was approaching the orgasm for which her every nerve ending was screaming out, he stopped, standing back to watch her frustrations with a disdainful leer on his handsome face.

With her hands still cuffed to what these people referred to as her slave training harness belt and her elbows pulled tightly behind her until they all but touched, Kitty was helpless to help herself, protect herself, or do anything save dance to the tune played by the whirling thongs, and the sheen on her inner thighs bore witness to how his ministrations had succeeded in keeping her on the very precipice.

'Enough,' Adam said at last and folded the whip away. 'I think you've learned what you needed to learn; that you're just a slave and therefore fit to be done to and with as your masters decide. You earn everything now for nothing is free, especially not you, Titty Kitty.'

Kitty hung her head and said nothing, while her breasts rose and fell in time with her laboured breathing. She dared not look at him again and did not raise her eyes, even when she heard the sound of something heavy being scraped across the floor.

Matilda groaned and rolled over onto her back, her eyes screwed tightly shut against the pain across her shoulders, and then immediately twisted back onto her opposite side, regretting the movement that had placed such rough pressure on her stinging flesh.

Crawley's whip had not cut her skin – he took great delight in explaining that he had no wish to mark her permanently – but the flat hide strip sent searing fire throughout her entire body and she could still feel the heat, even two hours after the beating had stopped.

With a great effort, for her wrists were still manacled to the broad leather belt, she managed to roll over and rise onto her knees, at last opening her eyes and peering around the darkened chamber. From somewhere high above a strip of lamplight filtered through a narrow crack, not enough to see anything clearly, but sufficient to confirm that her latest cell was empty.

Her mouth felt dry and her throat sore and, when Matilda's eyes picked out the vague outline of a bowl set in one corner, it was all the incentive she needed to move further. Slowly, her knees scraping against the cold stone floor, she inched her way towards it, fearing all the while that it would prove to be empty and heaving a sigh of relief when she saw the liquid shimmering darkly in it.

Tentatively she lowered her head, sniffing, and then carefully dipped her mouth and chin. Water – clear fresh water. She lapped greedily, ignoring it when the liquid splashed up her nose, stopping only when there was barely enough left for her to submerge her lips again.

She straightened up, sitting back on her haunches, water dripping from her chin and splashing down onto her naked breasts which gleamed ghostly pale in the near darkness, contrasting starkly with the distended nipples. Matilda peered down at herself, between the valley formed by her bosom and down to the now hairless crease between her thighs, and shuddered at the memory of the wickedly glinting blade as it took away her little pubic bush to leave her most intimate treasure as exposed as her shaven head.

So far, neither Crawley nor his cronies had touched her there apart from with the razor, but she knew it was only a matter of time and she cringed at the images that crowded into her mind. It would almost certainly be Crawley who violated her first, but his two henchmen had made it only too clear that they, too, would take their turns with her.

Matilda felt herself beginning to tremble, for the thought of being used thus, as a common whore or even worse, was more than she could bear, and the way the men, Silas and Jed, treated her was little different from the way stockmen would treat cattle or sheep. To them it seemed, she was less than human, just an object or animal, with no mind nor will of her own.

If only James would come for her, she prayed. He would soon put a stop to this barbaric nonsense. To accuse her of witchcraft and heresy was ridiculous, the sort of superstitious hokum that was supposed to have died out with Matthew Hopkins, the dreadful and dreaded so-called Witchfinder General, who had thankfully disappeared into obscurity at least a decade ago, before Matilda had been old enough to understand the tales that she heard in the big city, tales of torture and hangings, cruelty and petty spiteful revenge turned to madness in the hands of a man who people had since come to understand had been at least partially mad.

People in London, at least, Matilda reflected as she eased her position and tried to sit against the rough wall without rubbing against her sore shoulders too badly.

But people in London were more educated and informed and not like the people here. Apart from the likes of James Calthorpe and his father and a handful of others, the villagers and farm folk were largely ignorant and still wrapped in traditions and superstitions that dated back centuries.

Even the local priest, Father Wickstanner, preached of

demons and imps, who waited in shadows to catch the souls of the unwary and of a God who exacted terrible retribution from unrepentant sinners. As a result, the offerings plates were kept well topped by a congregation that might otherwise not have enough coins to feed their families, and it was not Simon Wickstanner who walked through Fetworth village with patched and darned clothing.

Matilda closed her eyes and thought back to her girlhood and to Father Mucklewhite, the Vicar at St Giles on the Heath Church, where her parents had taken her every Sunday from the time she was old enough to walk. A scholar and a true Christian, the kindly old cleric had preached of love and forgiveness and of a God of Salvation and Hope, not spouting the venom and hatred that seemed to be Wickstanner's only message.

Wickstanner! Matilda's top lip curled even at the thought of his name, picturing the greasy-haired little priest, with his close-set, pig-like eyes and thin, sneering lips, the little gob of spittle that always seemed to be present at one corner of his mouth. And the way he always looked at her and at the other young women as he passed them by, frequently summoning them to speak with him under some pretext or other.

Several times, since Matilda had moved in with her grandmother, Wickstanner had approached her, giving broad hints that he would not be averse to something other than just a liaison, talking cautiously around a possible marriage, though without ever directly mentioning the word. Matilda rebuffed these overtures, politely at first and then less delicately when he continued to pursue her and now, she reflected, this was probably partly his way of taking his revenge upon her.

Only Wickstanner could have summoned Jacob Crawley to Fetworth and, even had he not approached the self-proclaimed witchfinder, Crawley would not have dared try

41

to exercise any authority in the village without the direct acquiescence of the local priest. Crawley would have to hold warrants signed and sealed by a bishop, appointing him to his office, but he could not operate within the jurisdiction of a church without the consent of the incumbent, that much even Matilda knew.

She knew, too, of the stories of how Matthew Hopkins had managed to abuse such warrants, taking his supposed authority far beyond the diocese in which they were originally drawn up and terrorising whole areas of rural England, his name synonymous with fear and death wherever he went during a reign that had seemed far longer than the two years or so that it in fact occupied.

So dreadful had been the atrocities inflicted by Hopkins in the name of the Church, that the bishops in London had decreed that witch hunting should be curtailed, but although Hopkins himself disappeared from view, apparently the appearance of Crawley suggested that there were still those who disagreed with this view.

'Oh, James,' Matilda whispered, tears forming in her eyes. 'James, where are you? Please God that you come for me soon.' Her plaintive voice echoed back from the featureless walls, seeming to mock her in her pain and desolation, and now the tears began to flow freely.

The three shadowy riders waited between the trees, sitting astride their mounts well back from the road, so that only someone expecting them to be there would be able to see them. Someone, that is, like Jane Handiwell, who turned her mount off the track and trotted steadily towards the trio.

Her waiting companions were dressed in similar fashion to her, but the voices were unmistakably feminine, for there was no need to make any attempt at disguising their true genders as yet. When that necessity arose, Jane and Mary

Watling would do such talking as was required, both of them able to pitch their voices down, so that with the muffling effect of the kerchiefs they would draw over their mouths, their frightened quarry would not think twice that they were being robbed by anything other than a marauding gang of men.

'It's getting late,' said the nearest of the three, Kate Dawson. She, like Jane, was tall and angular, but without even a pretence towards any feminine beauty. 'We were beginning to think you might not come tonight.' There was accusation in her tone, but Jane was used to her irritability and well aware that Kate also resented Jane's position as leader of the little band.

'There is still plenty of time,' she replied coolly. 'The coach will not reach the crossroads before three at the earliest, and it is rare enough for it to be even that close to time.'

'There are new rumours that the coach companies are adding extra guards to the night runs,' Mary Watling growled. Even her normal voice was deep and rough and her heavy body muscled like a man's. Fifteen years labouring in her father's fields had honed what nature had given her, until she was a match for most men in strength and the mistress of many.

'There are always new rumours,' Jane replied easily. 'But rumours are rumours because they are seldom true. Only this evening I spoke with two officials in the *Drum* and they became quite garrulous in their cups.'

'Aided, no doubt, by you?' Ellen Grayling, the fourth member of the group laughed. Jane smiled back in the darkness.

'A little,' she agreed. 'Their ale was, shall we say, just a little more potent than they would have expected.'

'You and your potions,' Mary said gruffly, but with good humour. 'So what did these fine gentlemen confide in you?'

'Only that there are few enough passengers willing to take the night coaches without them having to pay good coin for extra guards, the same reason the patrols are now less frequent, for the army does nothing for nothing and the offer of rewards is no guarantee of filling soldiers' bellies.

'There is a patrol out this night but twenty miles north of here, close to where we stopped the coach last week. Not only that, but there are only four troopers and a corporal up there, even so. The pending trouble with the Dutch has meant that many troops are being called to muster down along the coast, so that all that are left for such duties up this far are young boys and old men.'

'Your father's inn is a good source of intelligence, and no mistaking,' Ellen Grayling said. 'My brother was saying much the same thing at breakfast this morning.'

Ellen was the youngest of the women, still in her teens and the daughter of Lord Grayling. As such, she had no need of the money that the foursome gained from their misadventures, but the danger and excitement appealed to her such that it had been she who originally mooted the idea that the night coaches were an easy source of money – and more.

'Your brother still has to pay us for the Irish wench we sent him two weeks since,' Jane retorted. 'I trust you reminded him of that?'

'I did, indeed.' There was a faint chink-chinking of metal coins in the darkness. 'I have our bounty here now. I shall divide it when we are done, unless you would prefer to share it out now?'

'No, later will do,' Jane confirmed. 'For now, I think we should be on the move. And,' she added, wheeling her horse back to face the road, 'if my information is correct, we may well have another little filly for your brother's stables this night.'

44

Harriet Merridew could not sleep at all, though the hour was now well past midnight and she had been hard at work since first light that morning. The stories she heard in Fetworth were more than just disconcerting; if true, they meant there was big trouble afoot.

She had not ventured right into the village itself, neither had she seen the man, Jacob Crawley, with her own eyes, but John Slane, at the smithy, told her what he had heard, and his daughter, Mags, confirmed it was true, a man had arrived at the village, proclaiming he was a hunter of witches and heretics, appointed by some bishop in the west country and now authorised by the Reverend Wickstanner to conduct an investigation into allegations of witchcraft concerning Matilda Pennywise, the granddaughter of old Hannah, who had lived in Fetworth since birth.

'That's ridiculous,' Harriet had retorted. 'Matilda Pennywise is no witch, though London has definitely given her a broader outlook on life than many around here. Who has made these allegations against her?'

'The fellow, Crawley, has not said,' John Slane replied, 'only that he has testimony, signed and witnessed. Someone said one of his witnesses was old Paul Horrocks.'

'But Paul Horrocks died nearly two weeks since,' Harriet protested. 'His horse kicked him in the head and he was dead before they got him to the physician in Leddingham.'

'Rumour has it that he signed his testimony beforehand and that the accident was no accident and that his horse was bewitched by Matilda in revenge at his making his complaint about her.'

'Rubbish!' Harriet snorted. 'I doubt Horrocks ever set eyes on Matilda a handful of times, for he seldom came in from his farm and Hannah's cottage is set away from the main village. Besides, old Paul could not read nor write.'

'Wickstanner recorded his testimony, I've heard,' Mags said, 'and Paul made his mark to the document.'

'And then conveniently died,' Harriet mused, but then decided it wisest not to pursue her train of thought. Simon Wickstanner was no friend of hers, nor she of his, for she had not that long since been forced to tell him, in no uncertain terms, that his continued pestering and advances were loathsome to her, although she had not quite gone so far as to use that word directly to his face.

Now, as she sat alone in her bedroom, high up under the eaves of Barten Meade, Harriet sensed that Matilda Pennywise might only be the first to stand accused of crimes against the Church. Jacob Crawley had surely not happened upon the village by chance, which meant that Simon Wickstanner was the instigator in this affair and that the choice of Matilda as the target of these allegations was also no coincidence.

The greasy little priest's eyes roved over every presentable female he came across and it was therefore quite possible – probable even – that she had succeeded Harriet as his main prey. Matilda's London upbringing gave her, so rumour had it, more than just a wider knowledge than the other local girls, but also a quick wit and a ready tongue and Harriet could imagine what sort of rebuff she would have given the piggy-eyed cleric.

'You little swine,' she breathed, barely out loud. 'This is your way of getting back at her, isn't it?' Harriet swung her legs off the bed, stood up and paced across to the window, drawing aside the curtain to peer out into the blackness beyond. 'And then will it be me you turn your dog on?' she mused.

Her breasts rose and fell beneath the thin shift she wore and she remained rooted for several long seconds, her mind filling with so many thoughts that it became too crowded for any semblance of order.

'I think, Master Wickstanner,' she said, opening the window and leaning out into the cool night air, 'that you

46

are quite possibly evil enough to do anything, for all your clerical garb and air of piousness.' She furrowed her brow, thinking furiously and trying to banish the images that swirled around inside her mind.

'No,' she whispered, 'it shall not be, for I know one man who will stand against you and your foul lies. Let us see how you fare when confronted with education, shall we?'

Kitty sat astride the curious rocking horse, groaning and trembling as the device lurched back and forth, the long phallus from the saddle embedded deep within her, the cunningly contoured edge rubbing up and down her swollen clitoris with every movement.

Adam had lifted her onto the devilish seat, strapping her ankles to the rigid iron stirrup extensions and adjusting their length so that her legs were held stretched, thus preventing any chance of the hapless girl lifting herself clear. With her arms still strapped behind her to the training harness, all she could do was remain upright, unable even to prevent her weight shifting, nor to defend herself against the periodic slashing of his whip, which guaranteed that her convulsive movement would set the beastly contraption into another cycle of to and fro rhythm and renewing the stimulation that was even now threatening to launch her into an oblivion of abandonment.

'Nice horsey, eh, Titty Kitty?' Adam stood alongside her, leering into her face, savouring the effect of his insidious torture routine. 'Nice horsey cock in your little cunny getting you all hot, eh, Titty Kitty?' He tweaked her right nipple, sending a fresh spasm of heat searing down through her spine.

'N-n-no, m-master!' she stammered, barely able to control her tongue. 'P-please, I b-beg y-you!'

'You beg me?' Adam chuckled. 'Then beg me the way I told you and we'll see, eh?'

Kitty swallowed hard and cleared her throat of the spittle that was threatening to choke her. 'P-please, master,' she began again, making a tremendous effort to keep her voice steady. 'Your slave, Titty Kitty, she begs you t-to spare her from this punishment cock and punish her with her master's fine cock instead.'

'Better, Titty Kitty,' Adam nodded. He tweaked the nipple again, but this time maintained his grip on the swollen teat. 'Perhaps you are deserving of a good fucking now, after all.'

'Yes, m-master,' Kitty whined. 'I'll be a good girl, I s-swear it!'

Adam laughed, a malicious rumble. 'I think another ten minutes, to be on the safe side,' he taunted her, suddenly slapping her naked flank which set the horse rocking faster again. 'And let's see you ride your fine steed on your own, eh? Show me how good you are and then we'll see about giving you a mount of a different kind!'

Simon Wickstanner entwined his fingers nervously and stared across at his guest, who sat in the high-backed chair on the opposite side of the huge rectory fireplace to the chair that Wickstanner habitually occupied.

'You will not harm the girl permanently, Master Crawley?' he said, not for the first time. 'I wish her no permanent ill, you understand, simply that whatever devils are within her be expunged and that she see the error of her ways and return to the Mother Church.'

'And to the protection of your own good offices, no doubt,' Crawley said, only the flickering of one eye betraying the irony in his statement. He leaned back, held up his wine goblet to the light and pursed his lips.

'Mistress Pennywise will come to no permanent harm, not if you are willing to accept her confession and bestow the Lord's mercy upon her,' he said. 'But I suggest that we do not rush these things. A few more days spent in the crypt chambers beneath the church will do her soul no harm at all, and then I shall parade her through the village, as a warning to other would-be heretics.'

He extended his goblet as Wickstanner picked up the wine decanter and leaned forward to offer it.

'Of course, in the old days she would have been hanged on the green,' he said, 'after a public flogging and a day at the stake to reflect upon her sins. Nowadays, of course, their lordships, in their wisdom, prescribe a far more merciful approach, though whether mercy in this life is any sort of blessing to the soul that eventually faces heavenly judgement is a moot point, in my opinion.'

'Erm, well, yes,' Wickstanner agreed, topping the wine in his own goblet, 'but Mistress Pennywise's sins are not such as they cannot be atoned for in this life, I am sure. She simply needs to see the error of her ways, as do so many modern young women.'

'No discipline,' Crawley sneered. 'No respect, not for their God, their saviour, nor for their elders and betters. For my own sins, the Good Lord has seen fit to bestow upon me the task of restoring the discipline into their ungrateful lives.'

'I heard you whipping her,' Wickstanner said, 'and I know that you have shaved her hair completely.' His tongue ran along his top lip and his eyes twitched.

'All sources of pride must be taken from or beaten from one such as she,' Crawley said, his voice flat, as if repeating a litany. 'Remove a woman's clothing and jewellery, remove her hair even, and what is there to remain proud of? And the lash scourges unclean and unworthy thoughts from within, baring her soul as surely as we have bared her flesh.'

'I understand, Master Crawley,' Wickstanner nodded. He paused, seeming to reflect for several seconds. 'You, ah, enjoy your work, Master Crawley?' he ventured at last.

Crawley fixed him with a long hard stare. 'My enjoyment, or otherwise, is of no account, priest,' he growled. 'I go where God bids and do as he sees fit to direct me. I seek out sin and abomination and first punish and then, by his good grace, expunge it.'

'Of course, Master Crawley,' Wickstanner agreed hurriedly, 'I was not suggesting otherwise, simply that maybe the Good Lord has seen fit to grant you a sense of pride and achievement in your crusade against his enemies?'

'Aye,' Crawley said, 'he has seen fit to grant me that, 'tis true, for without that, He in his Almighty wisdom, knows that I should not be able to serve him as well as I humbly pray I now do.'

The two men fell silent again; a silence that lasted perhaps two minutes and was eventually broken by the witchfinder.

'You have sent a message to the wench's grandmother, as I instructed?' he said.

Wickstanner nodded. 'I sent the verger's boy to her cottage, telling her to be here at sunrise tomorrow.'

'And you think she will pay a tribute to our Lord, in return for His sparing of her mortal body?'

'I believe she will, yes.' Wickstanner rose stiffly and moved to the low dresser that ran half the length of the room. 'She has money aplenty,' he said, examining the remaining row of decanters, 'for I know how much she receives each quarter day and she never seems to spend any of it. She will argue, though, for even I know enough of her to know that she is a strong-willed old harridan, despite her years.'

'Then perhaps I shall see her myself,' Crawley said, in a tone that removed any hint of a suggestion in the statement. 'I am sure I can convince her and one sight of her sinful granddaughter will make sure that she understands what I am telling her.'

He rose in turn, holding up a hand and shaking his head

when Wickstanner finally decided upon a wine and turned to bring the decanter back to the fireside.

'No more, Father Wickstanner,' he said, turning to retrieve his cape from the high chair back. 'I shall return later to sleep, but I must return to the church and continue in my efforts with the heretic. The whole village must see what consorting with evil means and then, mayhap, when we come to the others you have listed, perhaps we shall not have to resort to such extreme measures.

'Besides,' he added, throwing the long black cloak about his shoulders, 'their families are not in such a position to offer as good a pecuniary recompense to the Church, eh? So we don't want to waste unnecessary time and effort on lesser sinners, do we, my reverend friend?'

The pistol shots sounded like cannon fire in the quiet night air, jerking Sarah Merridew from the half sleep into which she had fallen. She saw immediately that the pale young man opposite had now become even paler in the faint light from the interior lamp and the old woman, though she did not move from her huddled corner, looked all about with darting and frightened eyes.

'What is it?' Sarah hissed, sitting forward and almost pitching headlong as one wheel of the coach hit a particularly deep rut.

'Highwaymen,' croaked the woman, almost without opening her mouth. 'Bin gettin' a bit active along these roads of late, so I hear tell.'

'Highwaymen?' The clerical looking young man now looked almost transparent, his watery eyes huge and round. 'But I have nothing of value.'

'Me neither, dearie,' the old woman snickered, 'so they can wave their pistols about as much as they like, for all I care.' She closed her eyes, feigning indifference, but the tone of her voice told Sarah that she was just as frightened

51

as any of them.

From outside came the sound of a cracking whip, loud shouts from the driver above and the sound of two more shots, followed by a loud cry of pain, presumably, Sarah thought, from the driver or his mate. Almost immediately she heard the shouts to the horses and the coach began to slow.

Desperately Sarah delved into her purse bag, took out the few coins that remained there and tucked half of them inside her bodice, praying they would not slip through and fall out onto the floor. The remainder, all small denominations, she returned inside the wash-leather and drew the string closed again.

'Best hope they don't want to get too fruity with you, lass,' the old woman cackled and turning, Sarah saw that her eyes were wide open again and that she had been watching her every action.

'I have so little,' Sarah whispered defensively. 'All our money went after the last plague outbreak.'

The old woman nodded. 'None of us has much nowadays,' she said, and then a small smile spread across her wrinkling features. 'Don't worry, dearie, I shan't say anything,' she promised, soothingly. 'Just stay calm and give them that ring you're wearing and what's left in the purse. Anyone can see you ain't exactly nobility. Besides, they'll be more interested in the post box up top, I reckon.'

Sarah stared down at the plain gold band and for a moment was tempted to pull the ring off and place that inside her bodice, too. 'This ring,' she said hoarsely, 'it was my mother's. It is all I have left to remember her by.'

'A ring is just a ring,' the woman said bluntly. 'You got your mother up here.' She tapped her forehead. 'Give 'em the ring and the coin and let them get on their way. No sense in bringing more trouble.'

Sarah sniffed, opened her mouth to say something else

and then closed it again. She began to ease the ring free, blinking back a tear that threatened to fall as she did so.

IV

Breathing heavily, her cheeks burning, Kitty walked slowly towards Adam, who now stood waiting for her, naked from the waist down, his organ rampant. She saw the look of triumph in his eyes and the almost dismissive look of contempt on his face and new that he had succeeded in achieving exactly what he had set out to do.

Between her legs she now felt wet, as well as hot, her swollen labia parting to reveal the pink tunnel in which the memory of the leather covered phallus was only too recent and too real. She clenched her buttocks, contracting her vaginal muscles, aching to have her hands free, but knowing that her bondage was all part of the scenario. Without the use of her hands there was only one source of final relief available to her, and that now stood to attention before its gloating owner, seemingly beckoning her towards it.

'Come on then, Titty Kitty,' Adam taunted, 'let's see you mount this saddle.' She was almost to him now and she could feel the heat from his breath. Slowly, she pressed up against him, rubbing her lower stomach up and down the length of his shaft, moaning quietly as she did so. His hands came up, cupping her breasts, and she shuddered.

'Good girl, Kitty,' he whispered, his lips close to her ear. 'Now tell your master what it is you want.'

'I want,' Kitty grated, grinding her teeth in a mixture of lust and humiliation, 'I want my master to fuck me for the worthless slave whore I am.' She leaned into him, nuzzling into his neck as she raised herself onto tiptoes. His hands left her breasts and moved downwards, slipping behind her until they cupped her buttocks.

'Time to mount, then,' he leered, and she felt herself being lifted clear of the floor, his throbbing member sliding further down, until it slipped between her parting thighs. With a small squeal she lifted her legs, wrapping them about his waist, preying he would not lose his hold on her, but he was clearly a powerful man for he supported her easily, even freeing one hand in order to guide himself into her sex.

'There, Titty Kitty,' he said, 'can you feel that now, just inside your hot little cunny?'

'Oooh, yes, master,' she gurgled, surprised at how much his weapon was stretching her, for the phallus on the rocking horse had seemed big enough. A moment later she let out a shriek as he once again gripped her with two hands and forced her down, impaling her fully with one thrust.

'Nicely filled now, slave slut?' he laughed as her eyes rolled wildly. Kitty nodded, trying to speak but simply gasping instead. She tried to focus on his face, but his features simply blurred and floated before her in a curious kaleidoscope.

'Yes, indeed,' she heard him say as he began slowly to lift and lower her, 'I think you'll fetch a fine price by the time I'm finished with you, eh girlie?' But Kitty was no longer paying any heed to him, nor did she any more care about what the future might hold, for the first wave of orgasm had already risen up to wash over her and now she was in danger of drowning in the lust he had aroused within her treacherous body.

Matilda said not a word as Jacob Crawley placed the iron collar about her throat and clicked the locking mechanism shut. She did not even look at him directly, keeping her eyes lowered and half closed.

'Well, my little devil's bitch,' he rasped, clipping a length of rope to the heavy ring set into the front of the collar, 'now we have you suitably leashed, let's take you for a little walk, shall we?' He gave a tug on the coarse hemp and Matilda stumbled forward, falling into step with him as he led the way towards the open doorway.

Once through, he turned left into the arched passageway and strode casually along, his boots echoing hollowly on the ancient flagstones, whilst Matilda's bare feet made merely the softest of pattering sounds. They walked what Matilda guessed had to be the entire length of the church above and then, finally, Crawley stopped before a heavy, studded timber door.

'I found this chamber earlier,' he said, taking a crude key from his belt. 'Even the priest had no idea it was here. See?' He pushed open the door, which groaned on little used hinges and stepped back, thrusting Matilda in ahead of him.

Two lanterns already burned inside, hanging from hooks set in the ceiling and, by their light, she saw the hideous looking structures that must have lain here unused for many years, though there was evidence that someone – either Crawley or one of his henchmen – had made a recent attempt at cleaning away the layers of dust that must have accumulated on them meantime.

Matilda recognised the heavy stocks immediately, as she did the pillory, but she had to peer closer before she recognised the crude rack for what it was. There was also an iron-ribbed cage, shaped in roughly human form, standing propped in the furthest corner and, on a wide bench, several other implements had been laid out.

'This will do to start with, I think,' Crawley said, leading her towards the bench and selecting something that looked, at first sight, like a leather bag. 'The hide was a bit stiff, but it had been wrapped in oilskins and Silas has been dubbing it well this afternoon.'

Before Matilda had time to react he had drawn the hood – for that was what it was – down over her head, pulling it about her neck and thrusting the lower edges between the iron collar and her flesh. For a few moments Matilda started to panic, the heavy odour of leather and whatever it was that Silas had used to make it more supple again filling her nostrils, so that she thought she would suffocate.

However, as Crawley moved behind her and began to draw laces tight, the hood began to mold itself to the contours of her shaven head, eyeholes slipped down so that she could once again see and two smaller apertures were drawn up beneath her nose, so that whilst the aroma from the foul garment was still all pervading, at least she was once again able to breathe some air. In addition, she realised, there was also a small slit level with her mouth.

'Now you cannot even use your pretty witch features to beguile God fearing men,' Crawley rasped, turning her around so he could look at her now featureless face. 'And now we should do something about stilling your vile tongue.'

The metal contraption was an old scold's bridle, something Matilda had only previously seen in picture books at her former home. The iron bands were dull, but any rust appeared to have been removed and the hinges showed traces of having been oiled. Her initial reaction was to draw back, attempt to resist having the cruel device placed upon her head, but she quickly realised that such an action was futile and likely only to earn her even more dire retribution.

A few moments later she stood there, the bridle heavy upon her, the vicious pronged tongue flange thrusting in through the small mouth opening, pressing down so that it rendered even the most primitive speech attempts painful in the extreme.

'Very fetching, witch whore,' Crawley snickered. 'And now for your feet. Such dainty toes might tempt the chastity of even the most devout man, and it is well known that witches move silently to come upon the unwary.'

The boots were heavy, like farmer's boots, except that

the thick leather appeared to have been reinforced with metal strands and the soles, as Crawley explained, were made of solid iron. As he stooped to lace them up Matilda's slim calves, she realised that as masculine as they appeared, they had been made to fit a female foot and shuddered as she wondered how many other unfortunates had been made to wear these awful things in the distant past.

'They used to call these penance boots,' Crawley told her. 'An unfaithful woman would be made to wear these for a week and every day would have to walk the bounds of the parish, which is what you will do either tomorrow or the next day, depending.'

He laughed harshly. 'And the iron is good, as iron imprisons the powers of evil. The more iron you wear, witch whore, the less your powers to resist will become. See here,' he added, picking up two circular iron bands, the inside edges of which were serrated like saw blades, 'let's see if you can work out what these are for.'

With a gurgle of horror in her throat Matilda tried to pull back, for there was only one purpose for which these things could be intended, but there was no escaping and soon her distended nipples were clamped painfully within the two circles and a length of chain hung between them, dangling coldly against her breastbone.

'That should hold you, devil whore,' Crawley sneered. 'Now, let's see whether you're hiding any marks upon this witch body, shall we?'

Sarah's screams were brutally stifled, by the simple expedient of someone thrusting a wadded rag into her mouth and tying another strip of cloth to prevent her from expelling it. Then, as hands dragged her from the coach, a sacking bag was thrown over her head and drawn closely about her neck. Her hands were dragged behind her, tied securely and tightly with thin rope and then she felt herself being lifted and thrown over a horse.

Hardly a word was spoken during this, but dimly she was aware of orders being given to the driver to throw down the post box. Hoping her captors might be temporarily distracted, Sarah tried to heaver herself clear, but found herself grabbed again and felt more ropes being tied over her and about her kicking ankles. Finally, as she began to realise the futility of further struggle, a hand slapped down on her upturned bottom, causing her to squeal with pain and surprise through the makeshift gag.

'Keep your arse still, girlie!' a gruff voice said, speaking close to her ear. 'You ain't goin' nowhere and you'll only tire yourself out.'

A few minutes later Sarah heard the sound of jingling harnesses, accompanied by muttered grunts and followed almost immediately by the sounds of more slaps and then whinnying and hooves clattering forward and quickly fading into the distance. Even in her terrified and shocked state she understood what was happening – the highway robbers had unhitched the team from the coach and sent it galloping on its way, obviously with the intention of delaying the rest of their victims from raising the alarm.

'Right then, girlie,' the same voice said again, 'we're going for a little ride, so you just stay still and you won't hurt yourself.' The horse moved and dipped beneath her as the rider mounted behind Sarah and, as it began to move off, to her utter shame, she realised that she was wetting herself in fear!

Roderick Grayling leaned back in his deep armchair and raised the brandy glass to his lips, half closing his eyes as he savoured the sensuousness of the moment. Between his splayed and naked legs, the diminutive black female slave knelt dutifully, her thick lips working steadily up and down the length of his rampant member, her tongue caressing the straining flesh with its usual skill. With his free hand he reached out and patted the shaven head and smiled as the two huge eyes rolled upwards to regard him.

'Good girl, Popsy,' he whispered. 'You earn your juices well.' He smiled contentedly to himself and closed his eyes, relaxing into the near trance that his well trained slave could always manage to induce in him, congratulating himself on the decision he had made, two years since, to keep the young African twin sisters for his personal diversion. The Arab trader demanded a high price for the pair, but it had proven money well spent, Roderick now considered.

Less than five feet tall, Popsy and Topsy, as he named them, had slim, well muscled bodies, with wide hips, prominent buttocks and well developed breasts, all features which had matured since their arrival at Grayling Hall, for they could have been little more than seventeen or eighteen years old when he first set eyes upon them.

Unlike the white slave girls, the twins had no false modesty about appearing naked and, except during the really cold months, habitually wore nothing except the gold decorations Roderick placed there – gold collars, gold wristlets and anklets, gold nipple rings and tiny gold rings through their elongated clitorises, plus heavy gold pendants dangling from their earlobes.

The gleaming yellow metal contrasted beautifully with their dark coffee skins, as did the pale white paint they used upon their eyelids and the rouge they wore on their lips, in imitation of their European counterparts, was echoed on their nipples, giving an overall effect that Roderick found more erotic than anything else he could imagine.

In addition, they had proved easy to train and any use of the whip on their gleaming bodies now was purely for Roderick's enjoyment, for he knew how the kiss of the lash could reduce either girl to the level of a lusting animal in seconds. Not that they ever appeared to need much encouragement, for they both worshipped their aristocratic master and vied with each other for the prime position in his affections.

As Popsy now redoubled her efforts, Topsy rose from her squatting position before the fireplace and padded seductively across the thick oriental carpet, swaying deliberately from side to side, cupping her full breasts and lifting them in a gesture of deliberate supplication. Through slitted eyes Roderick watched her approach and nodded.

She drew closer, leaned across him and guided one nipple towards his lips. With a stifled growl he drew the teat into his mouth, sucking upon it greedily, groaning again as he felt her soft hands tracing lines on his chest and then circling his own hardened nipples.

Suddenly his back arched and his head flew back and his thick shaft began to buck, pumping his semen into the willing mouth that held fast to it still, sucking furiously, eager to accept every drop of what Roderick knew both girls considered magic strength.

'Good girls,' he moaned. 'My two good girls.' He closed his eyes again, his head lolling onto his shoulder and, as the brandy glass slipped from his fingers and dropped onto the thick pile, he fell instantly into a drunken, sated slumber.

'This is getting ridiculous!' Thomas Handiwell stormed, banging his fist down on the bar counter. The young army officer, his ridiculously young features creased with a mixture of concern and embarrassment, shuffled his feet uncertainly and cast a sideways and hopeful glance towards the door, as if eager to escape the coming tirade – which he was.

'Scandalous!' Handiwell barked, and this time punched his left palm with the balled fist of his right hand. 'Look man, look, for God's sake!' He pointed vigorously to the corner bench, where the wounded coach driver was being tended by two of his maids. 'You reckon this sort of thing should be allowed to continue, lieutenant?'

'Er, well no, sir.' Lieutenant John Scarisbrooke took a deep breath. 'But I can do nothing, sir, as I have already said. Sergeant Atkins and myself are simply travelling to Portsmouth, to join our regiment there, ready for embarkation. I have no jurisdiction here.'

'Jurisdiction?' Handiwell cast his eyes heavenwards and let out a dramatic sigh of frustration. 'Jurisdiction, man? You think these highway robbers have any jurisdiction on these roads, do you?'

'No, of course not, sir, but I understand that the patrols on the highway here are under the command of Captain Digwell-Short at the Hindhead garrison—'

'And a lot of damned good they've been so far,' Handiwell cut him short. 'This is the seventh coach robbery in less than two months, d'you know that, sir? And where are Captain Digwell-damned-Short's troopers, eh? Never there when they're needed, that's where!'

'Sir,' Scarisbrooke said, raising a placating hand, 'I understand your frustration and I will be sure to convey your thoughts to my commanding officer when I reach Portsmouth. Perhaps he can exert some influence.'

'He could send us a couple of companies of redcoats, that's what he could do,' Handiwell rumbled. 'There've been troops in Portsmouth waiting to embark for these past six months, to my certain knowledge. Instead of leaving 'em to carousing the ale houses of that den of iniquity, why not put a few of them to proper soldiering?'

'I'll do my best, sir,' Scarisbrooke promised, though both men knew that the likelihood of even a score of troops being sent back up from the coast was as remote as the Indies in the New World. Handiwell conceded that he would be wasting any further efforts on the young officer and turned away, striding across to stand over the injured coachman and his two fussing attendants.

'You're lucky, Dick Willett,' he muttered, seeing the small
lead projectile lying on the adjacent table. 'The fellow is
still using that small shot. A normal pistol ball would have
ripped your arm off at that close range.'

Willett, grimacing as one of the women began tightening
a bandage about his upper arm, nodded. 'Aye,' he agreed,
'but it hurts nonetheless, and it still made plenty of blood.
Damn me, but I should have halted when he first called
out. He was far enough back that I didn't think he had that
much chance of hitting me.'

'Sounds like the same fellow as shot George Cosworth
last month,' Handiwell said. 'Took him in the shoulder from
fifty paces – damned good shooting, with a pistol and in
the dark. There were four of them again, too, so it seems
like the same gang.'

'Lucky neither of us was killed,' Willett growled.

Handiwell narrowed his eyes. 'I doubt there was that much
luck involved,' he said. 'I don't think this fellow is out to
kill, otherwise he'd have put a ball straight through your
chest, which is a far bigger target. No, he's no murderer,
though he'll swing anyway, when he's caught.'

'They took the woman,' Willett said. 'Grabbed her and
bundled her over a horse, all trussed up like a package.'

'So I hear.'

'Not that she was really even a woman, from what I saw
of her,' Willett continued. 'Not much more than a slip of a
girl. Didn't hardly look old enough to be travellin' alone.'

'She's Oliver Merridew's niece, so I'm told,' Handiwell
said. 'Lost her family in the last plague outbreak and had
nowhere else to go.'

'You mean Major Merridew, as was?' Willett said. 'Him
over at Barten Meade?'

Handiwell nodded. 'Aye, that's him,' he said, 'though
the Good Lord himself knows Merridew can barely feed

the mouths he already has there.' He paced across to the bar counter, paused there for a few seconds and then turned back.

'Will you be able to drive the coach on today?' he asked.

Willett shrugged and tried to sit upright, wincing again as he moved. 'Maybe,' he said. 'Give me an hour and a couple of long brandies, unless you've got any laudanum in the place? Young Francis can take the traces anyway and I'll just keep my eye on him. As long as we goes steady, he'll be all right.'

'Then wait a pair of hours,' Handiwell suggested. 'I'll take your place on the box and hitch my horse behind, so I can ride back. Maybe if I go to Portsmouth I can get some sense from the military there.' He slapped his hands together again, frustration and anger showing still. 'But first, I think I'll ride across to Barten Meade.

'If these swine have taken Oliver Merridew's niece it's a fair bet they'll be wanting a ransom, and that poor sod couldn't afford to ransom a church mouse.'

Sarah Merridew had passed beyond terror and into a state of shock so deep that she now appeared to be viewing events through a veil of smoke, unable to believe that what was happening was actually happening and regarding herself as no more than an observer.

Her captors had ridden for what seemed like hours, with Sarah being jolted about even more painfully than she had been on the coach, her breath driven from her lungs on several occasions so that, with the foul rag stuffed in her mouth, she feared she would suffocate inside the sacking hood.

Eventually they halted and, after a short pause, she heard the sound of voices, but it was several minutes before she really understood what she was hearing. There was a new male voice, surely enough, but now there were female voices and, as she strained to hear what they were talking about she realised, with astonishment, that the female voices had to belong to the four masked figures who had waylaid the coach.

Unbelievable as it might seem, the truth was inescapable; the four highwaymen were, in reality, highway*women*! For an instant hope surged in Sarah's breast, but it was immediately dashed as she felt a hand clapping across her backside again and one of the females addressed her.

'Well, my dainty little sweet,' the woman laughed, 'I hope you enjoy your new life. Let's have you down so this tight-arsed swine can see the goods he's paying for.'

Ropes were loosened, but not those that were biting savagely into Sarah's wrists, and more hands bundled her to the ground. Fingers tugged at the cords that secured the sack and then the dusty hood was pulled clear. Sarah blinked, but there was little light to startle her eyes, for they were standing outside what appeared to be a large barn and the only illumination was a flickering lantern held in the hand of a youth, who stood just behind and to one side of a tall and imposing man.

'Get that light closer, Pip,' the dark-haired fellow instructed and the younger male dutifully stepped forward, lifting the lamp higher as he did so. His master – for that was clearly what the older man was – peered into Sarah's startled face, studying her with a detached air, before stepping back and giving a curt nod to the semi-circle of dark-robed highwaywomen.

'Not bad,' he drawled, 'but two guineas is a high price for an untrained wench. We'll need to feed her whilst we break her and that all costs.'

'Two guineas is a bargain, Adam Portfield,' one of the women snapped, 'and you know it. Look at her, man; fair-haired, fair-skinned, pretty face and a nice slender figure, though still with a bosom any man'd pay well for.'

'Or woman, eh, Jane?' Adam leered. The dark-haired first speaker drew a pistol from her belt and levelled it at him, her aim unwavering.

'Want an extra ball down there, Adam Portfield?' she said quietly, and the man raised his hands, his smile fading slightly.

'Janey, you know my humour,' he replied. 'And you know I have a fancy for you, regardless. T'was just my little jest. I meant nothing ill of it.' Slowly, the pistol lowered again. The woman replaced it carefully and gave a little snort.

'That's one fancy you'll never realise,' she said, 'and we both know it. The man who ever takes me won't live to enjoy the feeling.'

'Aye, well, there's a shame to it, but each to our own, eh, Janey?' Adam lowered his hands and then raised two fingers of his right hand and touched them to his lips. 'My loss, bonnie lass, but I'll always be here, if ever'n you take a fancy to change your mind.'

'In your dreams, Adam Portfield,' Jane retorted, already turning away. 'Just take your goods and see to it that his high-and-mightyship gets our two guineas to us quicker than he paid for the last wench, else it'll be two guineas and a half he'll be paying. Just because we're females he'd better not think he can take advantage of us!'

Adam stepped forward, taking a hold of Sarah's upper arm. 'No one who knows you would ever think that, Janey,' he said. 'Not in business, nor in any other way.'

When the four women had mounted and ridden off into the darkness, Adam turned again to Sarah, studying her as he had before, but this time displaying a lot more interest and apparent pleasure.

'Yes, pretty one,' he said as he thrust her towards the barn, 'you are worth every groat of the asking price. A week or two's work with you, and I reckon you could fetch twenty times that price, to the right buyer.'

Kitty was astonished at how many other girls and women there seemed to be in the place, for this was the first time she had been allowed to see outside the two or three rooms within the barn-like structure, where she had spent all her time since first arriving here.

Still with her arms strapped securely to either side of her training harness, and now with a broad collar of leather about her neck, which forced her to keep her head abnormally erect, she was led out by one of the youths who formed the core of Adam's assistants, thin chains attached from her collar to the collars of similarly un-attired females in front and behind her and then, when two coffles of ten girls each had been formed up, they were made to trot around the perimeter of the large meadow that stood behind the barn.

The young handlers used whippy canes to make sure none of the girls tried to slack, ensuring they maintained a brisk pace in the early morning sunshine and that they all remained silent throughout, though Kitty could not help noticing that four of the girls also wore thick gags. She assumed this additional indignity had been imposed as some sort of punishment and resolved that she, at least, would not incur any displeasure.

Memories of her encounter with Adam were still very fresh in her mind and, as she recalled the events of the night before, she felt herself becoming first warm and then wet. She shook her head, trying to block out the images, not wanting any of the younger men to see the evidence of her wantonness, but one in particular, a fair-haired lad whom the others called Daniel, seemed to have singled her out for particular attention.

Falling into step alongside Kitty, he flicked at her bouncing breasts with the tip of his cane and then flicked it against her buttocks.

'So you're the one Master Adam calls Titty Kitty, eh?'

he laughed. 'I can see why; such a lovely pair of bubbies and so nice and firm, too.' He stretched out one hand and stroked her right breast, which was nearer to him. Kitty felt herself trembling at his touch.

'Well, Titty Kitty,' he said, 'when the morning exercise is over I shall take special charge of you; see if you're as good a poke as my cousin reckons.' Kitty looked sideways at him, an expression of surprise and alarm on her face. Seeing this, Daniel sniggered.

'Oh, thought you were cousin Adam's private property, did you?' he cried. 'Well, you'll soon learn that things don't work like that here. All you wenches are common property once Adam's had first poke – all except the two little piccaninny wenches, and they're reserved for his lordship.

'Mind you, that won't stop him tupping you, too, not once he sees you, Titty Kitty,' he added, leering. 'So you'll get yourself a mouthful of aristocratic cock meat before you're sold on, don't you worry about that.'

'Sir,' Kitty panted, lowering her eyes as she trotted, 'may I ask a question?'

'Well yes, you ask away, Titty Kitty,' Daniel said agreeably. 'What can I tell you, slave girl?'

'I'm to be sold, I know that,' she said, still not looking up at him, 'but when will that be?' She trotted another couple of paces. 'And where shall I go?'

'Ah well,' he replied after a few seconds, 'that's a fair question, but the answer will depend. With those nice bouncing boobies his lordship will probably hold out for a good price, so I doubt you'll be shipped out to the Indies with the next major consignment.

'On the other hand, whoever bids best for their disposal might well decide to pay a decent price for you as an extra, so who's to say? Or you could end up going east, to the Orient. The Bey's agent is due quite soon, I believe, and he'll be interested in a fair rose like you, I'm sure.'

'An Arab, you mean?' Kitty said plaintively. 'You mean I am to be sold into a harem?'

'Not a harem as such, I shouldn't think,' Adam told her, 'though you may be lucky and have the Bey take you for one of his wives or concubines. Usually the girls we send go into a sort of stable, mostly for the Bey's favoured guests, once they've had their clitties cut off, that is.'

'What?' Kitty's eyes were round with horror at this revelation, but her tormentor simply laughed.

'Oh yes, probably. The Bey will sample you himself first, and he won't mind having a writhing little eel as his bed partner, but after that it'll be the knife. They don't think their women should enjoy being tupped, you see. Don't understand it myself. I prefer my wenches hot and panting, the way cousin Adam says you were last night. Seems a great waste, turning a panting whore into a plank of wood, but then that's their business. Once they've paid, why should we worry what they do, eh?'

V

James Calthorpe recovered consciousness slowly. His head felt as if it had been crushed by a huge rock and he felt sick in his stomach, almost vomiting when he finally opened his eyes and made to sit up. Gasping, he fell back, closed his eyes again and waited, trying to control his breathing and clear his thoughts.

There had been two men, that much he could remember, two men on horseback who had ridden towards him on the hill road, talking to each other as they approached, seemingly not interested in him at all, other than to raise a hand each in salutation as they parted to allow him to guide his own mount between them.

James, deep in thought concerning a treatise he was currently reading, had barely acknowledged them and so had had no warning of what followed. The back of his head felt as if it had exploded in a ball of fire, bright lights flashed before his eyes and he felt himself falling, but he must have been already unconscious before he hit the ground. Either that, or they had grabbed him and held him in the saddle.

How long ago the attack took place, how long he had been out for, he had no idea. It was mid-morning then, that much he remembered, and the thin shafts of light filtering in through the timber building in which he now lay suggested it was daylight still, but whether he had been out for merely a few hours or whether even a night had passed in between, he had no way of telling.

Groaning, he opened his eyes again and looked around, confirming what he had seen the first time. He was in what appeared to be a small wooden hut, built from roughly hewn and ill-fitted planks, with a single window over which sackcloth had been nailed, and one rustic door. There was dirty straw over half the floor, covering the packed mud from which it had been made.

There was no furniture, just a broken wooden crate turned upside down to form a makeshift table, on which stood a pewter flagon and an earthenware bowl in which lay three or four pieces of plain bread. To one side of this stood an iron bucket and James did not need telling its purpose.

From one side of the hut to the other ran a heavy chain, secured to the timber uprights at either end by robust staples. From the centre of this chain ran another, which had been wound around his right ankle and fastened with a sturdy lock. He did not need to experiment to know that the amount of movement this allowed him would be insufficient for him to reach either end of the first chain to even test the efficacy of its fixings.

At length he tried sitting up again, his hands clasped to his temples as he did so and gritting his teeth in an effort to ignore the fresh waves of pain his movements triggered. Slowly, he inched his way towards the crate and reached out for the flagon, lifting it and sniffing cautiously. Satisfied that it contained only water, he raised it further and placed it to his lips, first sipping and then, having doubly confirmed what his nose had told him, gulping greedily.

The water tasted fairly fresh and the bread, when he tested that, likewise. Replacing the flagon carefully, for he had no way of knowing when it might be refilled, he hauled himself unsteadily to his feet and looked around, peering towards the larger gaps in the timbered walls in an effort to see what might lay beyond his immediate prison.

When this experiment yielded nothing, he paused, holding his breath and listening intently, but save for the distant cry of a bird he could not identify, all about was silent. With a sigh, James sat down again, took another sip from the flagon and tried to think.

Matilda shuffled wearily across the bare chamber to where the water bowl stood on the recessed ledge, dragging the heavily weighted boots at every step. She stood for several seconds, considering the tube that Crawley had fixed to the crude wooden frame that now sat across the bowl and then carefully lowered her face towards the top of it, manoeuvring carefully to push the stem in through the slit opening in the leather mask, alongside the awful prong of the bridle she still wore over it.

The act of sucking to draw liquid into her mouth kept forcing her tongue against the sharp point, but her mouth and throat had become so dry that she forced herself to ignore the pain until she had drunk maybe a quarter of a pint of the musty water.

Finally, standing erect again, she turned and surveyed the empty room, as if by some miracle something might have changed in it while she was drinking. How long since Crawley had brought her back here she had not the slightest idea, though confined and bound as she was, it seemed like a lifetime.

That, she realised, was all part of his strategy. Pain and boredom combined to break her spirit, probably even more effective than any rod or whip. Here she was alone, anonymous, silent, listening only to the sounds of her own laboured breathing and the steady pounding of her heart, the thick leather hood magnifying these two noises out of all proportion.

In the end, she knew, she would be reduced to begging for release, willing to offer anything, including her grandmother's carefully nurtured nest egg, in order to escape this silence and to once again become a living human being, surrounded by noise, lights, colours and sounds, and free of the nagging pains that the clamps around her tortured nipples kept sending throughout her body, reminding her, as if she needed it, of her total abject helplessness.

In the end, perhaps, this oppressive desolation might even drive her so far as to welcome even the return of the man who was responsible for her tortured plight…

What now, mistress?' Beth looked up at Jane Handiwell, her huge eyes adoring. Jane smiled back at her, cat-like, and chuckled.

'Now, Beth,' she replied, 'I settle Harriet Merridew's nonsense, once and for all.' She thrust back her shoulders, stretching her muscles, knowing that her nakedness excited her maidservant all the more when she displayed it so brazenly.

'I could hardly believe my luck when the message arrived here to reserve the room for the cousin,' she continued smugly. 'It was almost too good to be true – an opportunity that t'would have been a crime to have missed.'

'But I heard your Pa tellin' as how he would put up the money for any ransom demand,' Beth said uncertainly. 'An' surely, that'd mean that Mistress Merridew would maybe feel she had to accept his offer of marriage, wouldn't it?'

'Aye, she probably would, the stiff-necked mare,' Jane confirmed. 'Far too proud for her own good, but then she'd have probably accepted the old fool eventually in any case. They're struggling at Barten Meade, Beth, and no mistaking, plus her father is sickly worse than ever. She wouldn't take my father normally, of course, but she's the kind who'd marry a toad, if'n it meant she felt she was doing her daughterly duty.'

'Then surely, mistress, this will only hasten her to your pa's bed?'

'Aye, well my big-titted and small-brained little sweetmeat,' Jane laughed, 'it would, if'n I were to leave her on the loose to decide, but then that's not in my plans, be sure of that. And, whilst my moonstruck pater is away to Portsmouth, trying to drum up a few soldiers to chase his own daughter though he doesn't know it, the time is right to strike.'

'This brazen whore has already confessed that she's a witch and in league with the Devil himself,' Jacob Crawley sneered, looking around the dozen or so villagers assembled in the churchyard. They were mostly men, their eyes staring at the abject, naked figure on the end of the chain leash he held, and Crawley had selected the small group after careful consultation with Simon Wickstanner. The self-styled witchfinder smiled to himself; their reactions were so predictable.

'She has already placed her mark to a full confession,' he continued, 'and so it is possible that the Lord will decide that we should be merciful with her.' There was a low murmur among the small assembly. 'However,' Crawley continued, holding up a hand for silence, 'I must first pray, for He has not yet revealed his wishes to his humble servant.

'In the meantime, you should return about your business, but let it be known throughout the village that the whore, Matilda Pennywise, will be set upon the green, as you see her now, tied to a stake and set about with iron, that all may see how heretics, blasphemers and witches shall come to shame.

'And further,' he added, raising his voice, 'let it also be known that it is known to the Holy Church that there are others in this community whose sins against the Lord are scarcely less dreadful and that they, too, shall be exposed, as this whore now stands exposed before you.'

This was greeted by another murmur of discomfort and the hooded figure of Matilda hung her head, as if in shame. After a few seconds one of the villagers, a large fellow of middle years, named Septimus Brody, stepped forward.

'Master Crawley,' he said carefully, 'I would speak with you in private, if you please.'

74

Harriet regarded the scrawny youth suspiciously.

'You're Ned Blaine's lad, aren't you?' she said. The boy nodded.

'Yes, mistress,' he confirmed. Harriet paused, considering the scrap of parchment he had given her.

'And you say this fellow just gave this to you and bade you bring it here – to me?'

'Aye, mistress,' Toby Blaine replied. 'He said it were real urgent, and gave me thruppence for my trouble.'

'Did he now?' Harriet mused. 'Well, three pence is quite a lot of money.' Probably more, she thought, than young Toby had ever had in his grubby little hand at one time. 'And you say you don't know who this man was?'

Toby shook his head emphatically. 'Never seen him before, mistress,' he said. 'I was sitting out in the yard at the *Drum* waitin' for me dad to come out and this cove just comes up to me and asks me whether I knew the way to Barten Meade. I starts to give him directions, but then he says no, he just wants me to deliver a message paper to you, mistress.'

'To me?' Harriet repeated. 'Not to my father?'

'No, he says for me to give it to Mistress Harriet Merridew,' Toby said, with an air of total certainty. 'Asked if I knew you by sight, even.'

'And where did he go then, this man?'

'Into the inn,' Toby replied. 'Said he had a thirst and wanted to eat, too.'

'And you haven't read what's written on this?' Harriet brandished the piece of parchment between them.
Toby shook his head. 'Can't, mistress,' he said, almost apologetically. 'Can't read nor write, same as I told *him*.'

'Ah, I see.' Harriet looked down at the few lines again, considering. 'Well, Toby,' she said at last, 'how would you like to earn a whole shilling for yourself?' The lad's eyes lit up immediately.

'A shilling, mistress?' he echoed. 'Most certainly, mistress.'

'Well,' Harriet said carefully, 'I'll give you sixpence of it now and the other six in two days' time, when I know you've done as I ask. There may even be another shilling in it for you, depending upon how clever you can be, young man.'

The air inside the hut was becoming more and more oppressive as the sun continued to climb towards its zenith, and James Calthorpe had long since removed his jacket. Now he loosened the front of his shirt, pulling it open and clear of his throat and settled back, laying his head on his folded coat.

There was, he reflected, little else he could do. The chains by which he was secured were new, looked well forged and heavy enough to hold a team of oxen and, though the rustic hut appeared crudely constructed, its timbers were healthy and sturdy, with no signs of rot that might have given him cause for hope.

Whoever was responsible for his abduction and imprisonment had chosen the place well, he realised, and had made careful preparations for his incarceration. As to their identities, he was still no closer to answering that question. The men who attacked him on the road had, from what he could recall, seemed nothing out of the ordinary; just two travellers riding easily, dressed in common enough clothing.

They had not been gentlemen, judging by their garb, but neither had they the appearance of ruffians, or James would have been more on his guard. It had been he realised, a clever subterfuge.

'Well then,' he whispered, staring up at the timbered roof, 'if not who, then why? Ransom, mayhap?' It was the only reason James could conceive of, for his father, whilst not a very rich man, was certainly affluent enough, especially when compared with the average villagers in the area and would be easily enough able to lay his hands on a few hundred guineas, which to some would represent several years' hard work.

Yes, ransom had to be the motive, James concluded, and who was behind it was of no great importance. What mattered was that his father paid whatever demands were made and then he could get out of this oppressive little shack and back to his studies. Prolonged inactivity did not come easily to James and the lack of even the most basic material to read was beginning to affect his mood, even more than the plain fact of having been attacked and imprisoned.

The trouble was, he knew, that too few people had the advantage of an education to be able to appreciate the value and beauty of books. Perhaps one day society would change and schooling would be made available to all, though James could not see now the poorest peasantry would ever be able to afford that for their children. Perhaps the rich, the nobility, the state even, could fund the basics, though right now, according to what he was hearing from London, the state was in little condition to pay for anything.

The war between Parliament and the late King had brought the economies of entire regions to their knees and now, just when things should be looking up after more than a decade of true democracy, a combination of civil unrest and the looming troubles with the Hollanders meant that yet again money was flowing out of the state coffers far quicker than it had any chance of flowing in again. And long before Parliament ever thought about diverting money to the educational needs of the poorest, there would be other priorities for it to consider.

The capital city itself, James thought, that was a prime example, with old buildings rotting, the streets and the Thames river awash with rotting debris, excrement and rats, children running around in rags and bare-footed, with open sores and untreated cuts. No wonder there were constant outbreaks of plagues and fevers; it was a miracle that they had been contained as much as they had.

One day soon, James thought bitterly, there will be an outbreak such as hasn't been seen since the days of the Black Death and London will be reduced to a city of corpses and ghosts within days. Why no one in authority seemed capable of realising this, he could not imagine, but then, as he knew only too well, there was little imagination in authority.

Authority worked for only one end, it seemed, to create and keep even more authority for itself and its own ends. Power, James was only too well aware, had a nasty habit of nestling itself into the hands of those least fitted to handle it properly and too much power in the wrong hands inevitably led to grief, confusion, pain and tragedy.

No one in the village could say, for sure, what age Hannah Pennywise really was, only that she was at least seventy years old and could be as old as eighty-five or six. Even Hannah was not certain, for her father had kept no proper family records and the old parish register disappeared from the church many decades since.

However, no matter which estimate of her years was correct, an observer would have to say the old woman was fit and sprightly for it and she walked with the step of which most women of forty would have been envious; back straight, striding purposefully, her only concession to age being the hazel stick she carried in her right hand.

Pushing aside the low wicket gate, she marched boldly up the short path to the house next door to the church and, ignoring the heavy iron doorknocker, raised her cane and used it to pound loudly upon the thick oak planks. After several seconds of this activity she lowered the stick and took a half pace backwards, waiting patiently, but with a look of grim determination set upon her wrinkled features.

Several more seconds elapsed and then the sound of footsteps came from inside, followed by the rasping sound of a bolt being drawn back. Then, slowly and accompanied by a groan of protesting hinges, the door swung back. Simon Wickstanner blinked and peered out into the bright sunlight.

'Mother Pennywise,' he said. 'A long time since this house, or God's for that matter, has had the pleasure of your society.'

Hannah's top lip curled back, revealing a set of surprisingly even teeth. 'Stow your sarcasm, Simon Wickstanner,' she snarled. 'You know damned well why I'm here, for I sense your hypocritical hand in this matter. Where's my granddaughter? I warn you, you harm one hair of her head and I'll make sure you live only long enough to regret it and not a moment more!'

'Have a care, woman,' Wickstanner said. 'Threatening a minister of the Lord will do your granddaughter's case no good. Quite the opposite, in fact.' His words were intended as bold, but the slight tremor in his voice betrayed his uncertainty. There had been stories in the parish for years concerning Hannah Pennywise and, although there had never been any solid evidence to back these rumours, most folk tended to treat the old woman with deference, on those few occasions she ventured from the sanctuary of her cottage.

She raised her stick and pointed it at Wickstanner, aiming the tip directly over his heart. 'Stow your tongue, you muddy little worm,' she hissed. 'Just tell me what it is you want, eh? As if I can't guess.'

'I assure you, Mother Pennywise,' Wickstanner said, trying to draw himself erect, 'that the matter lies not in my hands. Evidence was laid before me and I, as I am bound to do, laid that in turn before one of the Church's experts in these matters.'

'The one they call Crawley, I suppose?' Hannah retorted acidly. 'Oh yes,' she snapped, seeing the uncertainty suddenly reappearing in Wickstanner's eyes, 'I've heard all about that one. I hear all manner of things, as it happens.' She grimaced and stabbed the tip of her cane onto the ground with such force that Wickstanner jumped visibly. 'Well, where is he, this Crawley fellow?' she demanded. 'Lurking in there, I suppose?'

Wickstanner swallowed nervously. 'Um, no, he's not,' he replied, 'not at this moment, anyway. He is about the Lord's business.'

'The Lord's business! Pshaw!' Hannah hawked up a gob of spittle and launched it squarely into the centre of the stone threshold. 'More likely his own business – and yours too, I'll wager. Well then, if he's not there, where's my Matilda?'

Wickstanner swallowed, even harder this time, his piggy eyes darting from side to side as if he was expecting for some sudden intervention.

'Uh, I presume you did not come to this house by way of the green?' he began, his voice on the verge of cracking. 'Perhaps you should return to your cottage via that route.'

Crawley's henchmen had set the stake deep into the ground and packed the earth firmly about its base, for as she stood against it, her wrists shackled behind her and about the heavy timber, Matilda tried both pulling and pushing, leaning back with all her weight, neither effort producing even the slightest movement from the embedded timber pole.

Before leaving her Crawley fastened cords about each of Matilda's ankles, drawing her feet apart and fixing the lines to sturdy pegs that had been hammered into the ground for this purpose, forcing her to stand with her legs splayed obscenely, displaying her denuded sex for every passing villager to see. It was curious, she reflected, as she stood there helplessly as the hours passed, how many of the male population seemed to have business this day that necessitated them crossing the green so frequently.

Not that they did more than look, however, for Crawley had set smaller iron posts about his prisoner, so that they formed a rough circle of perhaps ten paces in radius, and within this boundary, he had made it very clear, no villager was permitted to stray. It was, he told them, for their own good, for even with the iron he had set upon the witch, her powers could still harm those whose thoughts were not entirely godly and only the iron picket protected them from her evil influence.

'She must yet be scourged publicly,' he announced. 'She must atone and serve a penitence and I await the Lord's decision as to the number of lashes she shall receive and the time she must stand here before the eyes of other sinners.'

It was all so ridiculous, Matilda thought, as she stared out through the eye slits in the leather hood. The man was so obviously a fraud and yet these ignorant country folk hung upon his every word, as though he were Moses and was quoting to them from two tablets of stone. How they could believe him and his vile and wild allegations she had no idea; even though they were largely uneducated, surely no sane person could accept such puerile lies?

Fear played a large part, she understood; fear that they, or one of theirs, would be the next to stand accused. That was what prompted Septimus Brody, for he had three teenaged daughters and he was clearly terrified that one or more of his girls would be next to be paraded in this degrading fashion.

Matilda had heard his words when Crawley led him aside to speak privately, for the witchfinder had led her with them, apparently unconcerned that she would overhear.

'And they do say that the Merridew girl concocts all manner of potions and that she uses them to keep her poor father in his bed, that she might further continue with her devilish rites without that good man's knowing,' Brody said.

'I see,' Crawley said impassively. 'And no doubt she also uses her powers to take advantage of his fortune and use it in her foul work?' For a few seconds Brody looked nonplussed, but eventually he seemed to understand what Crawley was hinting at.

'Well, I don't know anything about that, Master Crawley,' he said slowly. 'I do know that the major has fallen upon hard times, for 'tis common knowledge hereabouts that the pair of them near starved last winter and the girl was selling off stock to make ends meet.'

Hardly, Matilda thought grimly, the last resort of someone supposedly in league with Lucifer and supposedly endowed with supernatural powers, but this blatant anomaly seemed lost on Brody. Not so, she saw, on Crawley, for he dismissed his would-be informant after just a few more words and then turned his attention back to her.

However, as he led her across the grass to where preparations had been made for her public humiliation, she understood that it was not the evidence of Harriet Merridew's innocence that concerned Crawley, merely the fact that if there was no money in the family, there would be little point in persecuting her. The man was a fraud, a blackmailer and a vicious sadist, yet no one else in the village seemed capable of seeing through him.

James, she thought again, where in God's name are you?

VI

Naked and harnessed with her arms useless at her sides, Sarah Merridew stared about her, wild-eyed, still quite unable to grasp the scenes she was witnessing.

There seemed to be at least forty females here, all dressed – or undressed – in the same fashion, all bound, some with their mouths cruelly gagged and all being treated no better than the animals one would expect to see in a meat market. The handful of young males whose task it was, apparently, to exercise and control them, strutted around with an air of arrogance and total unconcern, hardly, it seemed, even aware of so much blatantly displayed femininity.

The other girls, in their turn, seemed also to have accepted their situation, moving with docile obedience to the crack of whip, or bellowed command, trotting in lines with breasts bouncing or jiggling, depending upon their proportions, thrusting back shoulders to display their charms even more crudely, eyes looking straight ahead.

The young man who had brought Sarah out from inside the barn kept a firm hold on her upper arm, but seemed in no hurry to push her to join in with the activities in the meadow. Rather, it seemed, he was content just to let her watch, knowing she knew that soon enough she would become just one more part of this herd of humanity.

'We like to keep our stock healthy,' he said. His name was Ross, Sarah knew, for she had heard one of the other handlers calling out to him earlier. He was tall, willowy in build and had wispy, sandy hair. His features were too narrow for him to be called truly handsome, but there was something about him that, in different circumstances, Sarah thought she might have regarded as pleasing.

Now, however, she could but regard him as a brute, for he had lost no time in applying his springy crop whip across her unprotected buttocks, and just to demonstrate to her that he could and would, for she had been still too dazed to make any show of resistance or rebellion.

He leaned across her and placed one hand flat on her stomach. Sarah started back, letting out a small gasp of alarm, but the fingers of his other hand gripped the soft flesh of her upper arm even more fiercely. He laughed, a scornful harsh sound without humour.

'We'd better get you over that, I reckon,' he sneered. 'And your belly is too soft, as well. Need to sharpen up the muscles there, slave.' He paused and Sarah, regarding him with a covert glance, saw that he was now watching the display of naked women with an air of detachment, as if his mind was suddenly somewhere else.

Suddenly he seemed to come to a decision.

'Down there,' he ordered, jabbing a finger along the line of the nearest boundary hedgerow. Sarah followed the direction in which he was pointing and saw that the grass and earth there had been beaten much flatter than in the rest of the meadow, forming a rough pathway.

'Walk ahead,' Ross instructed, 'and don't get any queer ideas about running. You'll only end up tripping and falling and, without your hands, you'll just smack straight on your face or titties and this ground is harder than you'd think.'

Obediently, Sarah began to walk, all the time looking down at where she was putting her feet, for she new the lad was quite right. The ground underfoot was far from even and, every here and there a twisted root appeared above the grass, coiling around in an ensnaring loop before disappearing beneath the earth again.

They followed the line of the hedge for several minutes until the sounds of the slaves exercising had faded, first to a low background buzz and then altogether, so that only the sounds of the insects and the few birds circling overhead disturbed the peace of the still morning air.

Eventually they came to a narrow gap in the hedge and Ross, with a sharp tap of his whip, indicated for Sarah to turn left through it. They were in another field, but here the grass was wild and much higher, reaching up in places almost to shoulder level, with many wild flowers growing to similar proportions. However, it appeared that they were on a fairly well trodden path, for a narrow track meandered through the overgrown wilderness.

At last the narrow pathway opened into a wider space, at the far end of which stood a small stone hut with a thatched roof. In front of the small building the earth had been compacted to bare mud, with only the odd weed breaking through the otherwise barren surface. In the middle of this area Sarah saw the pillory, a heavy timber structure shaped like a letter T, the cross beam hinging in two sections and with apertures for neck and both wrists.

In addition, she noticed as they drew closer, there was a second structure set just above ground level, like a second pillory, but turned over so that the board surface faced vertically, rather than horizontally. As soon as she saw the row of round holes the two sections again formed, she understood its use: the unfortunate victim of this contraption could have his or her ankles secured and, dependant upon which of the three pairs of holes were used, be forced to stand with their legs drawn apart to differing degrees.

Ross guided her forward and stooped to push her ankles into the middle hole on either side. Even so she found that, as he closed the backboard to imprison her lower limbs, the position was stretched to no little discomfort. A few moments later Sarah's discomfort was complete, as her captor deftly unbuckled her wrists from the harness and bent her forward, placing her neck in the central stock and her wrists in the nearer, smaller apertures to either side.

She winced as the top section of the pillory banged down and shivered as she heard the securing pin being thrust home.

Bent almost to the point where her back was parallel with the ground, Sarah could only look downwards and sideways, and ahead slightly only by forcing her head painfully back. However, she did not have to see to know what Ross was doing and, when he walked back around in front of her, presenting her with a close up view of his rapidly thickening penis, she was not at all surprised.

'I thought, sir,' she said, her voice dry and unsteady, 'that you would prefer to keep me virgin for the moment. Surely I would command a better price at whatever foul market you conduct your vile business?' It was a desperate ploy, but it was all Sarah could think of. Unfortunately, her only reward was a harsh laugh from the young handler.

'That's none of my problem, wench,' he sneered. 'No one has listed you as virgin, so I have only your word for that. Besides, my wages are the same whatever price you eventually fetch, so why should I care?'

He reached forward beneath the cross board, and cupped one of Sarah's breasts in each of his hands, feeling their weight as they hung down and gently kneading the soft flesh. To her horror, Sarah realised her nipples were beginning to tingle at the contact and would, she knew from her private pleasure moments, be already engorging and stiffening.

The effect of his manipulation was not lost on Ross, either. She heard him chuckle, as he transferred his grip to one finger and thumb of each hand, rolling the elongated teats with relish so they grew even more.

'For a virgin,' he sniggered, 'you have the most responsive bubbies and teats I've ever handled. Mayhap your cunny will be a little hungrier, too, eh?' Sarah groaned and gritted her teeth, but she could already feel herself becoming warm and moist, even though the thought of what was to come was so abhorrent to her.

'A lovely rump, too,' Ross commented, as he released her nipples and moved slowly around and behind her. She felt his hands on her buttocks, stroking the full globes and running down either flank, as if testing her flesh for firmness. 'Yes, another pair of prize peaches,' she heard him mutter and then she gasped, as one hand slid between her widespread thighs and cupped her mound, lifting slightly so that she was forced to raise herself on tiptoe as far as the timber ankle shackles would allow.

'Get used to it, slave girl,' he whispered, leaning over Sarah's back. 'This little purse will see plenty of service in the future, believe me, even if it's never tasted a length of man meat till now…'

'Ah!' Sarah gasped as one long finger parted her labial lips and entered her, stopping as it felt the constriction of her unbroken hymen.

'So, the wench spoke true, eh?' Ross chuckled. The finger slipped back a little, resting and pressing upon the little swollen button. Sarah squealed and shivered instinctively, as a small wave of detestable pleasure ran up and down her spine.

'Please, sir,' she moaned. 'I beg you, don't do this to me.'

'No?' His tone was mocking and he rubbed her clitoris, eliciting more tremors and several more strangled gasps from her. She bit into her lip and screwed her eyes tightly closed, trying to fight back the animal lusts his practised actions were stirring inside her. 'You might as well enjoy it, girlie whore,' he whispered, leaning forward and running his tongue up the length of her backbone. 'Mmmm, such deliciously tender flesh,' he said, straightening again and using his free hand to prise her buttocks apart.

She felt a finger pressing against her other opening and

instantly her sphincter muscles contracted against the threat of another invasion. At the same time the walls of her vagina spasmed, gripping his finger reflexively and sending yet another fire wave surging through her.

'No!' she wailed, but he had no intention of stopping. Patiently, deliberately, he played with her, taunting and teasing her nubbin, her nipples and the entrance to the tight little rosebud hole that her position left so invitingly displayed. Sarah fell silent, apart from her laboured breathing and the low groans his wickedly skilful ministrations continued to force from her.

'You bastard,' she cried at last, opening her eyes wide. A terrible, anguished wail tore itself from her throat, soaring into the tranquil, late summer air and sending a nearby flock of starlings rising skywards in noisy and angry confusion.

'Yes, I probably am,' Ross giggled, but he knew he had prepared her as far as any man possibly could. Now he positioned the head of his burgeoning shaft against her labia, using his fingers to part them as he began to push into the entrance to her virgin tunnel. Sarah tried to twist away, but he had already transferred his grip to her hips and held her fast with seemingly little effort.

Sarah closed her eyes again and let out a long sigh. She was undone and she knew it. Held so helplessly by the pillory and Ross's far superior strength, the inevitable was about to happen. 'Well,' she gasped as he stood there, his cock barely in her, 'what are you waiting for, you beast? Take me if you will, like some damned animal. Do your worst, for after this there will be nothing with which you can frighten me… Oh!' she shrieked, as he immediately thrust, the thin membrane within her tearing easily before his onslaught. 'Ohhhh!' She felt his full length sliding into her until she thought she would be rent asunder, but her cries, as they began to come in time with his steady pistoning motion, were not entirely of horror and protestation.

'I sympathise with your problems entirely, Master Handiwell.' The grey-haired army colonel leaned forward, steepling his fingers together beneath his chin. 'However,' he said, 'there is little I can do to help you under the present circumstances.'

'Can't do – or won't do?' Thomas Handiwell growled. 'Seems the army is happy enough just to sit on its backside until there are war spoils to be had.' He clapped his hand to his knee and shook his head.

Colonel Brotherwood shrugged, and shook his head in turn. 'Sir,' he said, weighing his words carefully, 'my hands are tied. I receive my orders from London and can do little without a direct authority. Surely you must realise that?'

'Colonel,' Thomas said, fixing him with a steely gaze, 'men have claimed orders as an excuse for centuries now and I daresay they shall still be doing much the same three hundred years hence, but I speak now of true humanity. Our roads are terrorised by these foul villains, decent folks are frit to venture out after dark and you sit here, with not only your garrison, but also some ten thousand idle troopers waiting to embark to a war that may or may not happen.

'Sir, if you fear God and love your fellow man, I beseech you. Just one score of horse soldiers and one good officer is all we ask. The Hollanders will not miss that small a commitment, of that I am sure. And I ask this not for myself, I urge you to understand, but for the honest citizenry of this realm.

'I have told you my story and you have listened, that much I will grant you, but ask yourself this; should any blackguard be permitted to rule through terror and threats? Did this country not fight a war within itself to prevent such a situation, eh?

'I have told the lady, I should be more than glad to furnish whatever it takes to ensure the safe return of her cousin, and that I shall surely do. But what then? More villainy, more abductions? And what if the ransom cannot be paid, what then? No sir, I tell you, a stop must be put to this.'

'I agree, Master Handiwell,' Brotherwood said, with a heavy sigh. 'But this matter should be taken up in London. However,' he added hastily, 'I have a compromise that may help, albeit in a small and temporary fashion.' He rose stiffly and walked around the large desk, moving towards the window and looking towards the harbour and the forest of masts.

'I cannot,' he said when Thomas made no comment, 'act in any official capacity, you must understand that. Nevertheless,' he continued, still looking out of the window, 'I have one officer who is overdue a leave. He has recently suffered a tragic personal circumstance, his brother and father having died in the latest plague outbreak in London and his closest friend killed when a runaway cart crushed him.

'I could order him to take a week or two away and I could further authorise his orderly to accompany him. I could also, given the intelligence you have just brought me, authorise a travelling guard of, say, four troopers and a sergeant to accompany him.

'However,' Brotherwood said, at last turning back to face into the room, 'I could not countenance a leave of absence beyond, shall we say, two weeks? I should also have a problem with their lordships if I had to justify too great an expense for this leave, if you take my meaning?'

Thomas leaned back in his chair and smiled. 'Colonel,' he said carefully, 'as a loyal subject of the Commonwealth Protectorate, I should consider it my duty to offer the freedom of my humble establishment to such a worthy servant of our country. How long before this officer and his little entourage can be ready to ride?'

Toby Blaine approached the old mill buildings cautiously, his eyes darting from side to side, his ears keened for any unexpected sounds. Fifty yards from the stone bridge, which stood itself fifty yards downstream from the main construction that housed the huge water wheel itself, he halted and stepped off the road to duck into the undergrowth between the trees.

The going here was much tougher and he was forced to thrust his way through tangles of brambles, gorse and weeds, all the time conscious of the need to move as quietly as possible. He gave thanks to his father for the tough leather jerkin he wore, though he also wished he'd had the foresight to go back home first and find a pair of leather gloves, for the thorns clawed at his hands mercilessly.

However, the promise of the extra sixpence Harriet Merridew had promised him and the feel of the six pennies in the pocket of his breeches already spurred him on to ignore the little cuts and abrasions and, before long, he found himself crouching behind one of the massive old willows that ran along the riverbank, a position from which he could watch the bridge without fear of being seen himself.

Beneath the bridge, he could see the small wooden boat moored to the side of the narrow walkway that passed under the outer arch span on this side, exactly as Harriet had told him the letter said it would be. Her instructions – the written instructions he had so innocently carried to her – had stated that she was to take the demanded ransom money to the boat, board it, cast off and drift with the little craft downstream, until she came to the place where the river widened and passed to either side of the small islet known as Priest's Rock.

Here she was supposed to guide the boat aground and place the gold coins – the writer had stipulated gold and not silver – inside a small chest that she would find hidden among the bushes on the western end of the small sliver of land, after which, the note finished, she was to get back into the boat and continue downstream until she reached the bridge at Wareholt Crossing, from where she should return to Barten Meade on foot, a journey of some five miles.

If she was unable to raise the money immediately, she was instructed to take two white napkins, tied around with a strip of coloured ribbon or cloth, and place this in the dinghy, casting it loose to drift on its own. This would be taken as a signal that the money would be paid within the following twenty-four hours and she would find the dinghy moored in its present position, at the same hour the following day.

Toby did not possess one of the new fangled timepieces that he sometimes saw the gentry use, nor could he have used it had he one, but the passage of the sun overhead told him all he needed to know. He had arrived in position a little after four in the afternoon, the same hour Harriet was supposed to either start off with the ransom, or leave her sign and cut the boat free. He opened the front of his jerkin, withdrew the two napkins tied around with a length of red cloth Harriet had torn from an old underskirt, and sat back to wait.

His youthful senses soon detected the sound of hooves coming towards the bridge from the north, and he was immediately on the alert, pressing himself against the tree trunk and peering round and through the trailing fronds, but as the rider came into view he slowly relaxed again, recognising the rider as the daughter of Lord Grayling, dressed, as was her habit when riding, in black breeches, a pale green open-necked shirt and with her long hair tied back at the nape of her neck.

Whoever he was supposed to be looking out for, Toby thought, it most certainly wasn't Ellen Grayling. He sat back waiting for her to continue on her way, but to his surprise she reined her mount off the track the moment she crossed the bridge, slipped from the saddle and scrambled down the embankment. Toby's brow furrowed and he stood upright, trying to see what the girl was doing.

She stopped by the water's edge, appearing to look towards the moored boat and even took a couple of steps towards it, but then after a brief hesitation she turned away, crouched by the water and scooped up a handful towards which she dipped her face. As she climbed back up towards her waiting horse, wiping her damp hands on her breeches, Toby relaxed for a second time.

The next to cross the bridge was a heavy farm cart, drawn by a pair of sturdy horses and driven by a middle-aged man Toby knew to be Jeth Moore, one of the three brothers who ran a farm that had been in their family for as long as anyone could remember. The Moores were respectable, almost gentry and certainly not likely to be involved with any of this, Toby thought.

Traffic over the bridge, both pedestrian and mounted, was sparse, as the road north led to little more than a handful of farms and one small hamlet, the latter being so close to the main road as it swept around towards London that few people came this way, rather than using the back route. It was therefore a further half an hour before Toby saw any further sign of life, and that was just two of the mill hands leaving for their respective homes.

By now the sun was getting low in the west and the bridge and the water beneath it were in deep shadow. Flexing his stiffening knees, Toby rose, moved down to the riverbank and began moving cautiously upstream, all the while watching and listening intently.

He reached the little boat without incident, dropped the little napkin package onto the stern seat, untied the painter and pushed the craft out into the current. It swung around once in the eddies that the nearer span support created, then steadied itself after a fashion and began to drift downstream, gradually picking up speed as it moved towards the bend from which Toby had been observing.

He stood, hidden under the bridge itself, until the boat was out of sight and then, jingling the coins that already nestled in his pocket, he grinned and began climbing back up the embankment.

By the middle of the day, the *Black Drum* was usually a hive of activity and this day was no exception. As she walked across the flattened mud and gravel that formed the forecourt of the inn, Harriet saw there was a regular coach standing to one side, near to the stables block, presumably in readiness for a fresh team of horses, and another two coaches, evidently private vehicles, standing just off the road, the horses all contentedly working their way through the contents of the nosebags they wore.

The two rails were also half full of saddled horses, their owners, no doubt, inside enjoying a break from travelling and a meal, or ale to quench the dust from the highway. No wonder, she thought, as she approached the side door, Thomas Handiwell could afford to loan money and offer to support not only her, but her father and their ailing farm as well. Trade was good for an inn with a favourable reputation and the *Black Drum* was certainly that.

The small side entrance that led, Harriet knew, to the kitchens, was opened to her knock by a village woman whom she knew, Anne Billings, wife of George Billings the shoemaker. Only a few years older than Harriet she was aging badly, her complexion mottled and pale, a legacy of many hours spent in the steam filled kitchens of the inn since the age of thirteen or fourteen.

'I need you to find out something for me,' Harriet said, when she had slipped inside and the door was closed behind her. Briefly, she explained about the stranger who had given Toby the ransom note and Anne, who had heard about Sarah's abduction, nodded. She guided Harriet through to a small parlour at the back of the wing and left her to wait, while she went through to the bar area. A few minutes later she returned, shaking her head.

'Mary Ellison remembers the fellow,' she said. 'He ordered bread and stew and a pint of dark ale, but he didn't hang around once he'd finished. She remembers him, because he paid with a silver florin and gave her tuppence for her trouble, she says, but he was gone long before it started to get busy.'

'Did Mary see which way he went?' Harriet asked, though without much hope.

Anne shrugged. 'I asked her,' she confirmed, 'but she reckons she don't bother none about what they do after they go out the door and she doesn't have time to stand at windows gawping.'

'Well, she'd have no reason to,' Harriet replied. 'I don't suppose he was that much different from twenty other men who come in here every day.'

'Apart from his eye, of course,' Anne said, and Harriet looked puzzled. 'Mary reckons he had a glass eye,' Anne explained. 'Said it was a good piece of work 'cos, she reckons, you had to look pretty close to see it weren't a real 'un. Cost a pretty penny for something like that, I reckons.'

'Yes, probably,' Harriet agreed, 'though that doesn't get me any closer to finding out who he is and who's behind him, if he's not the ringleader himself, that is.'

'Heard tell there was four of them buggers,' Anne said, nodding. 'An' I reckons they've gotta be pretty local, if you asks me.'

'Oh? Why so?' Anne wiped her hands on her apron and perched on the arm of an empty chair.

'Well,' she said, 'I may not be educated, but I keeps my

ears open an' we gets a lot of the drivers and coachmen around in the little back snug, where they can get a cheap meal and soak their feet while their guv'nors eat in the main bar. A body gets to hear all manner of things, especially when she's only supposed to be ladling up soup and fetching ale.

'So, Miss Merridew, I can tell you where and when every one of these coach robberies has taken place, and they're spread out pretty even over the road both north and south of here. Not only that, but a couple of times there's been soldiers happen upon the coaches, just after they bin robbed and they've ridden after the thieves only a few minutes or so behind.

'An' yet,' she concluded smugly, 'they've never caught 'em, have they?'

'So you think these robbers know the back roads and tracks, is that it?' Harriet said.

'Stands to reason they must,' Anne confirmed. 'One time I know for sure, the soldiers rode south in pursuit and met up with three naval officers riding north, for London most like, and they reckoned no one had passed 'em in near on two hours.'

'Have you told this theory of yours to anyone else?' Harriet asked.

Anne smiled lopsidedly. 'Like who?' she demanded. 'No one's going to listen to a simple kitchen hand, are they? I tried tellin' my George a couple of weeks back and even he told me to leave such things to them as knows about 'em, so no one else is going to take much notice of what I might think, are they?'

'Well, I'm listening,' Harriet said quietly. 'Tell me, Anne, what time do you finish here? Only there are a few more questions you might be able to answer and maybe we can work something out on this between us.'

'Well, I'm not due to finish till six, Miss Harriet,' Anne

said, with a crafty look on her face, 'but if you likes – an' if you can cover what I'll lose – I'll tell cook I've got a bad head and cramps in here.' She rubbed her lower stomach meaningfully. Harriet smiled and thought of the few coins still in her purse. Some things, she thought, were more important than others and besides, there was always the chance she might be able to get her cousin safely back without having to be in Thomas Handiwell's debt.

'All right,' she agreed. 'As long as it's not more than a shilling.'

The water in the stream was bitterly cold, but Sarah did not care. Under the watchful eyes of four of the handlers she joined a group of eight other girls, all freed temporarily from their bondage in order that they might wash themselves in the swirling current, splashing themselves thoroughly to remove dust and mud and, in Sarah's case, the smears of blood and dried semen that had stained her thighs by the time Ross had returned her to the main group of slaves.

He had then, apparently, lost all interest in her, turning her over to another handler, a balding older fellow named Travis who, to Sarah's horror, seemed to be very fond of applying his crop across the girls' naked rumps for no other reason than his own enjoyment. She received half a dozen random cuts herself, before the girls were finally allowed to rest and then brought to the stream to perform their ablutions.

Alongside Sarah, a girl of about her own age was cupping water and allowing it to splash over her large breasts and, despite herself, Sarah found herself watching her out of the corner of her eye. After about a minute the other girl noticed her interest and grinned.

'Not many of these to the stone, eh?' she laughed, but keeping her voice low and her eyes mostly fixed on the running water.

Sarah felt herself going red. 'I – I'm sorry,' she began, but the girl made a shushing noise.

'Keep your voice down,' she warned. 'We're not really supposed to talk to each other, and if they hear us,' she added, with a jerk of her head to indicate where the four men stood talking in a group at the top of the grassy bank, 'they'll like as not string us up and give us a good thrashing.'

'Have – have you been here long?' Sarah asked, scooping up water and throwing it back over her own breasts. She cast a furtive glance backwards, but their minders seemed little concerned with the bathing party, and the general noise of the water and the bathers splashing about would mask any whispered conversation.

'A few days,' the other girl replied. 'You only arrived last night?'

'Yes, I'm Sarah Merridew, by the way. What's your name?'

'Miranda,' the girl grinned, 'but here they call me Kitty. Titty Kitty.' She sniggered. 'I reckon you can guess why, eh?'

'But that's so degrading!' Sarah exclaimed. 'Don't you hate it?'

'What's in a name?' she retorted. 'And anyway, same as you seemed to notice, they are big and, with luck, they might save me from being shipped off to some foreign hellhole. Master Adam seems to have taken a bit of a fancy to me and my dugs!'

'Who's Master Adam?' Sarah asked.

'Only one of the big nobs around here,' Kitty said. 'He's not actually the top man, but he ain't far off it and he's hung like a donkey and handsome with it. I could do a lot worse, lovey, believe me. I'm playing up to him for all I'm worth.'

'I can't believe they really intend to sell us off like cattle,' Sarah whispered.

'Not cattle, dearie,' she said. 'We fetch a lot more than cows.'

'But we get treated no better,' Sarah retorted indignantly. 'One of the bastards took me off, fixed me down in some frame thing and then just had his way with me, like I was a brood mare, or something. I still can't quite believe how callous it all was.' Neither, she reflected, could she quite believe how she had reacted, writhing and groaning in the heat of the perpetual stream of orgasms Ross's thrusting pole and devilish hands had induced in her.

'You have to get used to that sort of thing,' Kitty replied, almost nonchalantly. 'Whatever becomes of us if and when we leave here, one thing's for certain; we're intended for regular rogering, not for our wit and conversation.'

'That's just so horrid!' Sarah was beginning to shiver again and her legs, immersed in the stream up to her shapely knees, were starting to feel numb. She ducked her head into the swirling current and shook it, resurfacing with a gasp.

'I think,' she said, as she spat droplets and snorted water from her nostrils, 'that I'd rather drown myself here and now – only I don't think I have the courage for that.'

'Well, where there's life, as they say,' Kitty murmured. 'And given the choice between killing myself and getting soundly fucked every few hours, I know what I'd choose!'

- VII -

The Billings's cottage was set to one side of George Billings's workshop, on the eastern side of the green, some half a mile from the crossroads where the *Black Drum* stood. The two women had to cross one edge of the open space and they were halfway across before Harriet looked up to see the bizarre figure at the stake set in the centre, some seventy or eighty yards away.

'By all that's holy!' she exclaimed, halting in horror. 'What foul business is this?' She started to turn towards the naked display, but Anne grasped her arm and drew her back.

''Tis better not to venture over there, Miss Harriet,' she whispered urgently, looking around as if scared that she might be overheard. ''Tis claimed that she's a witch and the witchfinder is purging her. Anyone goes near, folks may get to thinking they're in league with her and they'll end up just like that, too.'

'What stupid nonsense!' Harriet retorted, but she held back, staring in disbelieving fascination. Suddenly the rumours she'd heard the day before came flooding back and she realised who the poor victim was. 'That's Matilda Pennywise!' she gasped, and Anne nodded. 'But Matilda Pennywise is no witch! If the fools had accused her grandmother, then maybe I could understand it for the old woman has some peculiar ways, but not Matilda. What have they done to her? My God, but that's barbaric – and what has she on her feet?'

'I heard tell earlier that they're called Penitent Boots,' Anne replied.

'Penitent Boots?' Harriet said. 'Yes, I've heard tell of

100

them, but they haven't been seen nor used in more years than the two of us have been on this earth put together, probably longer. And that's a scold's bridle – I thought they were outlawed more than a hundred years since.'

'Apparently not,' Anne said quietly. 'According to what the witchfinder fellow told people earlier, iron shackles a witch's powers and weakens her. Once she's properly drained of her evil powers she's to be flogged, so they say.'

'Oh, the poor wretched girl!' Harriet cried. 'What agonies she must be suffering. We can't just leave her there, surely?'

'We'd best do just exactly that, miss,' Anne said, 'unless you fancy suffering the same fate as she, which I most certainly don't. The way I hear it, people are already starting to make wild accusations about others just to protect their own hides. No point in drawing attention on ourselves, I say.'

Harriet turned to her, about to argue the point, but stopped when she saw the look of sheer horror in Anne's eyes. The shoemaker's wife had a point, she had to concede, for she was only too well aware that ignorance could be fanned into suspicion and hatred by the simplest and most innocent of gestures. Visions of herself tied to a stake, her most intimate secrets bared for all to see, swam before her eyes. Besides, she reasoned, she had problems of her own to deal with and she would be of no help to her cousin Sarah if she herself became embroiled in something she could as easily avoid by walking away.

'Master Handiwell will have something to say about this cruel folly when he returns,' she muttered, 'but for now, perhaps you are right, Anne. Let's deal with one problem at a time.'

Sarah was surprised when Ross handed her over to the older Adam, who slipped leashes to her collar and Kitty's and led both girls off into the depths of the huge barn. They padded along in his wake, side by side, exchanging glances behind his back but not daring to say so much as a word to each other, as he drew them through the long passageway that bisected the building and then turned into one of the partitioned rooms at the farther end.

'His Lordship has a special guest for dinner this evening,' Adam said, closing the door behind them, 'and special guests get special entertainments. In this case, the special entertainment is you two.' Kitty and Sarah stood stiffly, their wrists once again strapped to their harnesses, their damp hair hanging down their naked backs.

'For tonight's little performance you will be rather differently dressed,' Adam continued, 'but for now, we'll just have an undressed rehearsal. Sarah, or whatever your name is, get your legs further apart and stand straighter, or I'll put an elbow brace on you.'

Without thinking, Sarah moved to obey, sliding her feet to the side and drawing back her shoulders, so that her breasts jutted even further. Adam nodded.

'Better,' he said curtly. 'Now, Titty Kitty, let's have you on your knees in front of her.' He grasped Kitty by her collar, thrusting her downwards to emphasise the order, and with a startled whimper she dropped to the floor.

'Now,' Adam said, 'you can get that little Kitty tongue of yours busy on this slut's cunt. Find her nubbin and work her good and thoroughly. I want to see her wriggling like an eel, but be warned...' he took his crop from his belt and jabbed the end into the valley between Sarah's breasts, '...one movement of either foot and I'll whip your arse with this, understand?'

'Yessir!' The words tumbled from Sarah's lips instinctively, even though the prospect of what was about to happen was so appalling to her, to have another woman touch her down there, let alone with her mouth. But then the alternative, of being thrashed by the powerful overseer,

102

was even worse. Adam grinned at her.

'Don't look so damned horror-struck, girl,' he said. 'It's not so bad and probably just as good as having young Ross's prick up you. Oh yes,' he laughed, seeing the look of surprise register on her face, 'I know all about that. I followed the pair of you earlier, just to see how you'd react.

'Ross has a slightly crude technique and a girl can hardly resist in those stocks, but it's usually a fair indication of what a wench is made of. From where I stood, you ended up riding him as much as he was riding you. Ever had a tongue in your pussy?'

'No, master.' Sarah lowered her eyes, blushing.

'Well, if Kitty doesn't do a good job on you, then maybe I'll have to do it myself, eh? Mind you, Kitty, if *I* have to tongue the slut, I'll lace your hide with a few stripes. Now get going, girl. Let's see how good – or otherwise – you really are.'

Kitty leaned forward and Sarah instinctively drew her hips back, but was rewarded instantly by a sharp cut across her rump from the swishing crop. She let out a startled yelp, although the blow had not been as hard as it might have been and her body arched forwards again, thrusting her sex straight into Kitty's hungry mouth.

Immediately the big breasted girl's lips closed on her, tongue thrusting into her warm slit and then, as it located her swelling clitoris, clamping onto it with a ferocious suction that sent a column of fire shooting throughout Sarah's body.

'No-o-oo!' she groaned, but another light tap from Adam's crop kept her thrusting forward, pushing harder still into the hot mouth. At the same moment Kitty began to squirm forward on her knees, arching her back and neck until she was almost beneath her target.

'Press down, slut!' Adam barked, and pressed on Sarah's shoulder to reinforce the command. Sarah felt her knees weakening and her weight settled onto Kitty's face, but rather than distracting the kneeling girl this seemed to serve only to encourage her to redouble her efforts.

Her probing tongue flickered in and out, her lips sucked thirstily on the juices her attentions were stimulating, and Sarah could only stand, splay-legged and wide-eyed, unable to believe either what was being done to her nor the effect it was having on her.

'Tongue fuck the little bitch,' Adam chuckled. Then, to Sarah, 'Grind those hips girlie, and start looking like you're really enjoying yourself.'

'Please, m-master,' Sarah stammered, but the rest of what she was trying to say became lost in a gurgling babble, as he moved behind her and cupped his hands around in front to toy with her breasts.

'Not as big as Kitty,' Adam whispered, his mouth nuzzling Sarah's ear, 'but nice and firm and such lovely teats.' His fingers and thumbs rolled her nipples together and another wave of desperate lust swept over her. She heard him chuckle again and writhed in her bonds, but now her writhings were less an attempt to get free than a reflexive response.

Suddenly a new sensation; she felt the rigid heat pressing up between her buttocks, the head of Adam's burgeoning erection probing for that other orifice, and automatically she clenched her muscles, determined to resist this final humiliation. But in the moment of ultimate struggle, a scream tore upwards from her stomach, as Kitty's cunning ministrations brought the reward of a first orgasm and, as any thoughts of focus or concentration were banished in the same instant, to her horror Sarah felt the pulsing phallus beginning to penetrate her.

Anne Billings brought chalk and a flat piece of board from her husband's workshop, laying the latter across the top of

104

the crude kitchen table.

'You'll mebbe think me presumptuous, Miss Harriet,' she said, 'but I'll draw you a chart as best I can and that'll make things easier for you to understand.'

'Please do,' Harriet replied. 'And I'll not think you the least presumptuous. The fact that you're a woman lies well enough with me. These past two or three years I've had cause enough to know how little import men place in the intelligence of women.

'We start here as equals, Anne,' she continued, 'save that you've had time to put some thinking to this. Pray, continue and show me your theory.'

Anne leaned over the board, the chalk shard scraping across the timber surface, talking as she drew.

'This here is the crossroads, by the *Drum*,' she explained, 'and this line here is the main highway between the coast and London, you see?' Harriet murmured that she understood. 'And here, here, here, here and here,' Anne went on, 'are the places where these four beggars have been stopping the night coaches. See,' she said, marking another line and adding three more crosses, 'these are the others, best as I can remember and here…' she jabbed the chalk at the line denoting the main road, '…is where that robbery happened when the soldiers rode up but a few minutes earlier.

'The robbers were riding south along here, and those naval fellows were coming up here.' She added more chalk marks. 'So, between here and here they must've left the main highway.'

'There are very few side tracks there,' Harriet observed. 'There is a very poor lane that leads north and crosses the road before the lane that leads to our own house. As far as I know that has been so little used of late that it's completely overgrown, but I suppose mounted men could push a way through.'

105

'Aye, horsemen can go where wagons may not,' Anne agreed, 'and if they turned east when they got here,' she added, marking again on the board, 'they would be in Sepley within a half hour. But,' she said, straightening up, 'there are other possibilities. The road up to Grayling Hall lies between where they stopped the coach and where the troopers met the tars.'

'And there are plenty of woods around the hall,' Harriet mused. 'A good place for our thieves to hide out for a few hours, no doubt.'

'Always supposing they knew the lie of the land,' Anne retorted. 'But t'wouldn't be the sort of place to go riding in the dark, not if a body didn't know the area.'

'So, where else might they have turned off?'

'Well, Miss Harriet,' Anne replied slowly, 'I'm not the best authority, but I have lived around these parts all my life and I don't reckon there's anywhere much else. Which means, same as I said, that whoever's robbing these coaches must live very close to Fetworth – or one of the beggars must, at least.'

'I think you could well be right,' Harriet said carefully. 'They were quick to contact me, seemed to know where and when it would be easiest to collect ransom money without being overlooked and were close enough, I presume, to be able to set up certain things.

'I'll know more when Toby returns, assuming he's not let himself get into trouble, but there's something else, too. Whoever has taken my cousin must be holding her prisoner somewhere close by, always assuming they do intend to return her when the ransom is paid. It would have to be somewhere safe from prying eyes, well away from the chance of being stumbled over, yet close enough.'

'Well, there are a few old cottages and huts in the woods, though I'd not want to use any of them for living in, but I reckon they'd serve well enough in the short time.'

'Yes, they would,' Harriet agreed, 'but I just have this feeling that whoever is behind this, they wouldn't risk something as unreliable as a derelict forester's hut. For some reason I cannot explain, I just think they have a base of operations which is far more secure and trustworthy.'

'But where, Miss Harriet?' Anne demanded, pointing the chalk at her rough map. 'There's Fetworth village itself, the church, your own house – which we can forget, of course – and Grayling Hall itself. And I can't imagine four mounted thieves, not when they're carrying a captive woman, risking riding through this village in the dead of night. Even if they did, someone would have seen or heard something and we'd have known about it by now, for sure.'

'Quite,' Harriet agreed. She stood for several seconds, staring down at the chalk-marked board. 'And that, unless we think that Wickstanner would risk church involvement in something like this, which is even more absurd than what he and this awful Crawley creature are doing now, leaves only one other possibility.'

Few people knew the woods, paths, streams and the river in the area as well as Toby, and he was able to take a much more direct route to a spot opposite Priest's Rock than the little boat. Even so, he wasted no time, loping along at a steady pace, determined to find a vantage point in good time before the craft arrived.

However, as he drew closer to his destination he slowed to a walk, stopping occasionally to listen. Whoever was waiting for the boat, be it carrying Harriet and the ransom or just, as was the case now, the sign that the ransom was to be paid next day, would likely be somewhere close by, probably with another boat on hand. Toby paused again, considering what he would do in their shoes.

Grinning to himself, he swung around in an arc, heading for a point slightly upstream from the islet, a sheltered nook from which he had fished many times in his young life. Sure enough, as he slid down through the reeds and bushes, he saw the dark shape of a boat lurking beneath a curtain of willow branches, barely thirty paces from where he was now hidden and about fifty paces upstream from the islet itself.

Whether or not there was somebody in the craft he could not see, for the foliage screened it from the gunwales upwards, but Toby was unconcerned by this. If the boat was empty, whoever intended to use it would not be far away, for as soon as the messenger boat appeared they would need to get out into mid-stream to intercept it and, when that happened, he would have a perfect view of them.

The sun was beginning to set, it was true, but by Toby's calculations the drifting boat would arrive well before darkness fell and, as he looked up at the clear sky and across to where the pale orb of the moon was already becoming visible, he knew that even darkness would not disguise whoever appeared when the time came.

As the sun finally dipped behind the distant hills Matilda began to feel cold, her naked flesh quivering in the light breeze that had sprung up from the south east. She pressed herself tight against the stake and closed her eyes in silent prayer, willing Crawley to return and release her, to give her the chance to move her stiffening limbs and maybe even remove the weight of the iron scold's bridle from her head.

At the same time she knew his return would probably mean the start of the next phase of her suffering, for he had made it clear to the villagers that she would be publicly flogged. Around the edges of the green small groups of people continued to meander slowly, staring across at her naked display, but few wanted to make it obvious that they were looking at her and fewer still approached even as close as the circle of iron pickets.

Only her grandmother had come that near, and she walked right through Crawley's supposed 'safety zone' markers and right up to Matilda, her wrinkled face white with horror and anger, her eyes blazing. Seeing the bridle and recognising it for what it was, the old lady immediately tried to remove it, but the lock held firm and she very quickly realised the futility of her efforts. A further cursory check convinced her that she could not release Matilda from the rest of her bondage, either.

'He'll pay for this!' Hannah hissed. 'By damnation he shall and so shall that lapdog, Wickstanner, or my name is not Hannah Pennywise.' She grasped Matilda's upper arms and hugged her granddaughter.

'Courage, my pet,' she whispered. 'I know what needs to be done and, by all the powers, it shall be done!'

And with that she was gone, hurrying off across the green in the direction of her cottage with her familiar stiff-backed gait, banging her cane into the ground at every other step. Alone again, in her enforced silence, Matilda began to weep, her tears soaking into the inside of the leather mask.

It was beginning to grow dark quickly and a mist forming, its icy droplets settling on Matilda's exposed flesh, so that very soon she was wet from neck to feet and the cold and damp brought on an attack of violent shivering. Hungry, thirsty and tired, she felt herself beginning to drift into a state of near delirium, but knowing, even as she did so, that if they did not come for her soon she would probably die.

Crawley, she thought vaguely, would not be pleased if that happened...

'So, you couldn't see who was in the other boat?' Harriet could not keep the disappointment from her voice and Toby looked downcast.

'I'm sorry, miss,' he said morosely, 'but that big cowl covered his entire head and he had his back to me all the while. Just used a gaff hook to catch hold of the first boat and then paddled back in under them willow branches.'

Standing in the shadows of the stables, behind the *Black Drum*, Matilda pursed her lips in momentary thought, but it was Anne Billings who spoke first.

'If I understand this rightly,' she said, 'then one of 'em has got to row that there boat back up to the bridge by the mill. All we needs to do is keep a watch and see who brings it back.'

'But that could be almost any time,' Harriet pointed out. 'There are only three of us and you, Anne, have a husband and two children to attend to, whilst I need to get back to see to my father 'ere long. He is particularly sickly at the moment – so much so that I dared not tell him about Sarah, for fear the strain might make him worse. All I ventured to him, when he asked, was that cousin Sarah had not been on the coach when it arrived here, which is truth enough.'

'I could get some help,' Toby volunteered, but Harriet looked dubious.

'It could be dangerous,' she said. 'For one thing, we have no way of telling who might be in league with these villains.' She looked at Anne, whose emotionless expression suggested that she was sharing the same misgivings. 'You see, young man,' she continued, 'since you went off upon my errand we have had reason to suspect that someone – maybe more than one person – from this village is involved in these robberies.'

'Well, certainly ain't me,' Toby asserted firmly, 'and I knows it wouldn't be either Matt Cornwell nor Billy Dodds, so I'll take them along with me to share the watching.'

'But they're only children!' Harriet exclaimed, and Toby looked suddenly offended and puffed out his chest.

'Matthew Cornwell is only a week or so younger'n me, miss, and Billy will be fourteen afore Christmas. We're not kids no more, Miss Harriet, and we knows these parts

110

better'n most.'

'I could speak with my husband,' Anne offered, 'and see if he would go along with the lads. I know for certain sure that he's no highwayman.' Her face became troubled as she spoke though. 'Problem is, I saw him going along with several other men as we walked back here just now.'

'Going to watch that poor creature being whipped, no doubt,' Harriet muttered, and Anne set her mouth in a firm line and said nothing more.

'I heard 'em all sayin' as how Matilda Pennywise is a witch and the ugly looking cove in the black cape an' stuff was goin' to whip the devils out of her,' Toby said, round-eyed. 'Is that right, miss?'

Harriet snorted and shook her head. 'Pay no heed to such nonsense, Toby,' she spat. 'Matilda is no more a witch than I am, and I'm nothing to fear, am I?' Toby looked a little more than uneasy and shuffled his feet awkwardly. 'Toby?' she probed. 'You're not afraid of me, are you? Is there something I should know?' For several seconds, the youth looked as if he was about to turn and run, but Anne stepped forward and seized him firmly by the shoulder, shaking him with surprising roughness.

'Cat got your tongue, Toby Blaine?' she demanded. 'Don't you try foolin' with me, either. Something's going on in that head of yours, or I'm not a mother of two boys myself! You answer Miss Harriet's question, my lad.'

'Well,' he began hesitantly, 'it's nothing, not really – just that I also heard someone sayin' as how word is that you, Miss Harriet, that you was also maybe a witch and as how the Crawley cove was maybe goin' to come after you next!' He looked almost as sheepish as he did worried. 'Not that you bein' a witch would worry me, miss,' he added hastily. 'My gran always told us there were more good witches than bad 'uns anyway!'

Even in the darkness Matilda recognised the burly forms of Crawley's henchmen, but they were not working alone and, as she peered out through the eye slits in the leather hood, she was able to identify most of the half dozen or so other men who were bringing armfuls of wood to the steadily growing mound.

She shivered, cringing against the stake, recalling the images she had seen in the books in her uncle's house, of women condemned as witches being burned alive. True, even Matthew Hopkins had not burned his victims, for the burning of witches in England had ceased hundreds of years since, but then this man Crawley seemed capable of making his own laws.

However, instead of piling the kindling about Matilda's feet, the shadowy figures seemed quite content to stack it in a pile some ten or more paces away, and to stack it in a fashion that suggested they had no intention of moving it again. The reason was not long in being revealed.

'Set the fire!' The harsh voice scythed through the darkness and Matilda felt her stomach lurch as she recognised Crawley's harsh tone. The men grouped around and she heard the sound of flints being struck, sparks lighting up the night, before at last a small flame was kindled. One man stepped forward, a pitcher in his hands and bent over the flickering light. Seconds later the spluttering little fire leapt into renewed life, as the oil caught and then the dry twigs succumbed in their turn.

'Turn the devil's spawn whore!' Crawley commanded. 'Let the light see her back.' The man Matilda recognised as Jed stepped forward, his original companion, Silas Grout, but half a pace behind him. They moved behind her and she felt their hands upon her as they unlocked the chains that held her, but the respite was short-lived.

Unceremoniously they spun her about so she faced the stake, hauling her arms around it and chaining them again, except that this time they attached a length of rope to her bonds and hauled her wrists high above her head before tying it off, so that now she was stretched fully, the weighted boots preventing her from even standing upon tiptoe in order to relieve the strain.

Meanwhile the flames were beginning to grow higher, throwing the scene into a dreadful blood-red light and, at the same time, dark figures began to approach from all sides of the green. It was, Matilda realised, a gathering of ghoulish fascination: men especially, but some women too, who had not wanted even to approach as far as the iron ring perimeter during the hours of daylight, now used the cloak of darkness to embolden them into watching the impending spectacle.

Straining to turn her head from side to side, Matilda peered into the shadows, trying to identify Simon Wickstanner, certain that he would not miss the chance to witness her further pain and degradation, but most of the faces were remaining just far enough back so that they were not illuminated by the fire sufficiently for her to recognise them.

The crowd was growing more quickly, the less adventurous of the villagers taking their lead from the early comers, and even through the leather hood and above the crackling of burning timber Matilda could hear the ambient buzz of whispered conversations increasing by the minute. She closed her eyes and prayed for strength, knowing that the moment could not be far away now…

- VIII -

Adam finally left the two girls alone in a bare timber-walled store to rest, bringing in two blankets, which he threw over a heap of straw.

'We'll wash you again and dress you properly before this evening,' he said, turning in the doorway. 'Our visitor likes to have his ladies elegantly attired in the French style, so I'm told, so we've got you your own personal maids in attendance later.' He chuckled again and stepped outside, banging the door shut, and they heard the sound of the wooden locking bar being dropped into place.

'I'm sorry, Sarah,' Kitty sighed, lying back across her half of the rustic pallet. Sarah, her eyes already closed, sighed in turn.

'Don't be,' she said, wriggling to make herself as comfortable as possible, though the fact that Adam had left them both in their leather harnesses, with their wrists still cuffed at their waists, did not make this an easy matter. 'You did what you had to do, that's all.'

'Maybe I did more than just that,' Kitty murmured.

Sarah opened one eye and turned her head to where her recent 'lover' lay. 'Oh?' she said quizzically. 'And how was that?'

'I should be shamed to tell you, but I think I ought.'

'Tell me what?'

With an effort, Kitty struggled back into a sitting position. 'I think I should tell you fair,' she said, 'seein' as how we'll be expected to do the same again this evening, by all sound of it.' She pursed her lips and half lowered her eyelids. 'An' the fact is,' she continued, 'that I for one am lookin' forward to it.'

114

'You are?' Now Sarah's eyes were wide open. 'But surely—?'

'Surely I can't be?' Kitty cut her short. 'Well, that's where you're wrong, my pretty Sarah. I'd dip my lips to your sweet honeypot anytime, any day and without no threat of the whip to urge me on.'

Sarah hesitated, unsure of what she should say.

'Yes, because I prefer the soft feel of another woman to the brute coarseness of most men, though I confess I'm not completely averse to a good tuppin' now and then.' Kitty grinned, almost shamefacedly, though not quite, Sarah thought.

'But why do you feel the need to confess this to me now?' she asked. 'Whatever is planned for this night will happen one way or the other, for neither of us would much relish the thought of being whipped. Almost anything would have to be preferable to that. Even what that swine Ross did with me earlier, though I never thought I'd ever hear myself admitting to such a thing.'

Sarah laid still for several seconds, studying Kitty's naked body, her eyes drawn to her incredible breasts and their still swollen nipples. 'Do you think I shall be expected to do the same to you tonight?' she asked quietly.

Kitty shrugged her shoulders. 'I shouldn't wonder at it. Does it worry you greatly, then?'

Sarah felt her cheeks slowly beginning to burn and she averted her eyes again, staring up at the ceiling beams instead. 'Well,' she said hesitantly, 'I've never done any such thing before, and I assumed you had not, either. Have you done it often?' She heard Kitty give a barely stifled laugh.

'Often enough, or not, depending upon your point of view, I suppose,' she said. 'And had the favour returned, too. My first time was with a friend, before I was taken the first time.'

115

'First time?' Sarah said, turning to look at her companion once again. 'How do you mean?'

'Well, I was taken by men while I was walking along the shore, near where I lived,' Kitty said. 'It was early in the morning and I was collecting driftwood for the fire in our cottage. My brother usually came with me, but this morning he was stricken with an ague. I saw the boat drawn up in the shallows, but thought little enough of it for there were always fishing boats offshore. One of the men called out to me and I went closer, thinking he was asking me for the name of our village, for there had been some high winds the night before and, for all I knew, they had been blown off course.

'But then, as I came close by, two of them sprang from the boat, bore me to the ground and bound me with ropes. I was thrown into the boat and they set the sail and drew away from the beach with all speed. I quickly discovered that most of them were French or Dutch, only the one who had hailed me was English.

'They were mostly navy deserters, pillaging on both sides of the water, wherever they could steal – goods, money, or people, it was all the same to them. A week later we had sailed south, so the English one told me, and were heading close in shore to Spain, where I was to be sold to Moorish traders, probably to end up in some wealthy Arab's harem, they said.'

'You poor thing!' Sarah gasped, her voice no more than an awed whisper.

Kitty smiled thinly. 'By then I was half past caring. The crew numbered some nine or ten and each of them had his way with me several times, despite the fact I was often half dead with exhaustion. The thought of being only one woman of several and only one man to worry about, that came as a blessed relief, believe me.'

'But you didn't get to a harem, I presume?' Sarah said.

'Otherwise, even I know you would never have come back here.'

'No, more's the pity,' Kitty said, a tinge of sadness in her voice. 'All those other women,' she continued, a wistful look in her eyes.

'So, what happened?'

'The crew were betrayed by a Spaniard they'd hired to negotiate for them,' Kitty continued. 'We were all taken to this great warehouse by a trading dock and there more Spaniards fired upon them, cutting them down before they could defend themselves. At first, once I'd finished being terrified out of my wits by the musket fire, I thought I'd been rescued, but I was soon put to rights on that, believe me. The Spanish leader – he spoke quite good English – told me I'd be added to a group of women being sent north again, into France, again on the coast. From there, he said, I'd probably be sent to the east.

'For a few days I thought again I should end up in some harem, but again it was not to be. Twenty of us were taken to a house just outside of a French port and there they held an auction. Four of us were purchased by one man, apparently acting as an agent for a French nobleman in the north, for that's where we were next taken.

'There was a big house – a chateau, I was told they called it – and we were locked in a cellar room, but then we were all brought up again and handed over to this Englishman. Apparently, he had won us from our supposed new owner.'

'Won you?' Sarah demanded uncomprehendingly. 'How was that?'

'On the turn of a card, so we heard,' Kitty retorted. 'Why we were given as the stake, I didn't know, nor do I now, but the outcome was that we finally travelled all the way back to England, landed by night in some deserted cove and then, a few days later, ended up here.'

'What a terrible tale,' Sarah said softly. She wriggled

117

herself closer, so that her head was level with Kitty's bare knee. 'How you must miss your home and family.'

'Huh!' Kitty tossed her head back, her hair swirling about her shoulders. 'What is there to miss? My mother and father died when we were both small and we lived with a man who said he was our uncle, though I doubt he ever was by blood.'

'He treated you both badly?'

'Both?' Kitty laughed harshly. 'He treated my brother well enough, took him for the son he never had, but I was nothing more than a burden to him. Well, apart from being used as a bed-warmer and more, once I was old enough. Even my brother turned against me as we grew, though the good Lord knows I never gave him cause.

'No, Sarah, I was well enough rid of all of them and would have gladly found myself in some harem, believe me.'

'Well,' Sarah whispered, looking up into her eyes, 'perhaps you someday still may.' She continued to stare into Kitty's face, quite unsure of the palpitations overcoming her entire body. The big breasted girl stared back for several seconds and then, as if understanding, turned slightly, moving her knees further apart, revealing the mouth of her sex.

'There's no need,' she whispered hoarsely. 'Not yet, anyway.'

Sarah smiled. 'Maybe there is,' she whispered, inching closer. 'Maybe there is, at that.'

From the corner of one eye Matilda saw Crawley as he approached her, carrying a wicked cat-o'-nine-tails. Instantly the murmuring in the crowd fell away and she could sense, rather than hear, several of their number moving slightly closer.

'This woman stands accused of heresy and witchcraft,' Crawley began, his voice carrying on the still night air like

118

a scythe through ripe corn. 'I have examined the facts and testimony carefully and find her, by the powers vested in me by the Holy Church, guilty as charged, and have since spent many hours in meditation and prayer seeking the guidance of Our Lord and Saviour.

'God is merciful!' He cried, raising his voice higher still, and there was a generally ragged chorus of muttered 'amens' from the darkness. 'God is a merciful god,' he said, speaking more quietly again, 'and he sees fit to spare the life of this whore of Satan, if she will once recant her sins and save her soul.'

Suddenly Matilda felt hands about her head and heard the rasping of metal upon metal. A few moments later, to her relief, she felt the awful iron bridle being lifted from her, though no attempt followed to remove the leather hood.

'Speak, Matilda Pennywise,' Crawley ordered. 'Speak now and repent ye of your sins and your penance will be a merciful one.'

'Go to hell!' Matilda hissed through clenched teeth. 'I'll not dignify your ignorant barbarity with a single word. Listen well, all of you!' she shouted, her voice sounding cracked and harsh. 'Listen well, for this man is no servant of God, rather he serves his own lusts and his own purse!'

'Silence!' Crawley roared and at the same instant, Matilda heard the dreadful hissing as the nine leather thongs cut through the air. A moment later the night was torn asunder by her scream as the braids seared into the unprotected flesh of her back.

'Repent!' Crawley barked and again the lashes found their mark. Matilda screeched again and bucked and writhed. Through a buzzing haze of agony she was vaguely aware that Crawley was once again addressing the assembled villagers.

'The whore will repent, good people, of that I can assure you,' he cackled. 'And in her repentance and by her blood,

so shall her wickedness be purged from her soul forever.'
He paused, turning slowly, peering into the darkness as if
he were searching for someone in particular. Gasping,
Matilda realised who it was he was expecting to see, but
knew her grandmother would not be there without coming
forward to try to intervene.

Without warning Crawley swung the whip again, this time
twice in rapid succession, and Matilda danced and screamed
in her agony, so that even in her near delirious state she
knew that the sound of her suffering would carry easily to
their cottage.

'Repent!' he growled, coming closer yet again. 'Repent,
or suffer as you please.'

Matilda, her weight slumping so that she hung almost
entirely by her wrists, peered out from the mask through a
curtain of tears. 'Repent of what, you animal,' she gasped.
'I have done nothing to repent of, as God is my witness and
my judge!'

'Wrong, devil whore,' Crawley sneered. 'We have the
testimony of your witness and the Lord has appointed me
to be your judge, or would you rather swing from a gibbet
tomorrow noon?'

'I doubt that would serve your purposes, Master Crawley,'
Matilda muttered, 'nor the purposes of that slug,
Wickstanner. Calls himself a man of the cloth, yet I see he
is not here to witness the results of his foul plotting.'

'Very well, Matilda Pennywise,' Crawley said, stepping
away again, 'if that is your choice then so be it. My men
can erect a gallows soon enough, but you shall certainly go
to the next life with your body purged, if not your soul.'

Again the terrible hissing, followed by the excruciating
firebrands, but this time, as if by some merciful intervention,
Matilda scarcely felt them, as she passed away into a dead
faint.

Although outside the day itself had been no more than warm, inside the cramped hut the heat had risen to an almost unbearable level. James had early on divested himself of his torn and muddy jacket and quickly followed that expedient by unbuttoning the front of his shirt, but the stifling humidity continued unabated and, by the time darkness began to fall outside, bringing with it a welcome but slow decrease in the interior temperature, he realised he'd all but finished the water supply his unknown captors had left behind.

He prayed they would return soon, for he knew that another day like this would be more than he could face with only the meagre dregs of liquid that now remained. Moreover, the hours of enforced activity were beginning to take their toll.

Over and over he tried to find a reason for his abduction, other than the most obvious one that his assailants would approach his father with a ransom demand. That, he knew, made sense, yet throughout the day, as he lay sweating in the straw, he could not escape the nagging thought that it might just be something more than that…

Adam returned for the girls accompanied by yet another handler, this one being a little older than the majority of the younger grooms, together with a woman who was clearly fast approaching middle age, though her fine-boned features still bore more than just traces of her former youthful beauty.

'This is Master Robin,' Adam announced, after stirring the two dozing female forms with the toe of his boot. 'And this lady is Miss Prudence. She will prepare you for your evening performance and you will obey her, as you would obey me, or I'll have the skin off your pert little bottoms before the sun rises again.'

As Sarah and Kitty scrambled to their feet, they realised that Miss Prudence was abnormally tall for a woman, standing equally as tall as Robin and only an inch or so less than Adam. Although not heavily built, she was certainly well boned and muscled and probably, Sarah thought, quite capable of dealing with an average female without any male assistance.

In addition, she wore a pair of men's breeches and what was almost certainly a man's shirt, though the front of it bulged considerably, thanks to a generous bosom. Her long neck was tanned and bare, with her brown hair pinned up clear of it, and she had brown eyes that hardly seemed to blink at all.

'You will both follow me,' she said in a quiet yet very firm voice. 'There will be no talking and you will follow all my instructions immediately. If I ask you a question, you may reply to it and you will address me, at all times, as mistress. Do you understand that?'

'Yes, mistress,' Kitty replied immediately.

'Yes, mistress,' Sarah added in a low whisper, dropping her eyes.

To the surprise of both girls, they were led to where a closed coach and pair stood waiting and helped up inside. The journey was not long but would, Sarah guessed, have taken perhaps half an hour on foot. When the coach finally stopped the door was opened by a liveried footman, who held up a hand to assist each of the bound girls to step down and who, if he was at all surprised to be confronted by a pair of naked females, did not betray the slightest sign of it.

Looking up, Sarah saw that they were at what she took to be the rear of a large country house – a very large country house, in fact. There were three main floors stretching towards the night sky and small dormers projecting from the roof. Whoever lived here was not short of money, she guessed.

Inside, they were taken through a series of passageways

and up a flight of narrow stairs, until eventually Prudence stopped before a panelled door and took a small key from her breeches pocket.

'Inside,' she said curtly, stepping back as the door swung open. 'Everything is ready for you.' Everything, Sarah saw to her amazement, included two large porcelain baths set a few feet apart from each other on a marble tiled floor. Both had been ready filled and with hot water, for steam curled off their surfaces and the room was heady with the scent of oils.

'Now,' Prudence said, confronting the pair of them, 'I am going to remove your harnesses and you will not wear them again this night. But be warned, if you even think about trying to take advantage of that situation I have an even more stringent form of harness that you will find yourself in. And just in case,' she added, 'you need further convincing, I shall show you what I mean.' She clapped her hands together loudly. 'Jasmine!' she cried. 'Get your unworthy arse in here – now!'

As the two girls looked on, a curtain against the right hand wall moved aside and a tall dark-skinned female walked awkwardly through it – awkwardly because she was perched on the most incredibly heeled shoes either Kitty or Sarah had ever seen before and because her arms appeared to have been folded double up her spine and were cuffed to a wide collar that forced her head at an almost impossibly erect angle.

'This is Jasmine,' Prudence said. 'She is my own personal maidservant, but an incorrigibly lazy little bitch at times. Therefore, I dress her as you now see for two hours each evening, just to encourage her to work a little harder during the rest of the day.' The girl – she had to be Arabian, or maybe even Indian, Sarah thought, approached and they could see the thin strap running across her face and between her lips.

123

Her raven hair, hanging down her back to her waist, had been arranged so that it concealed most of the strap and her full lips had initially disguised its purpose, but now, as she halted a few paces in front of them, Sarah realised that it served to hold something in place inside her mouth. Prudence's next words confirmed this observation.

'You will see that Jasmine is also gagged,' she said. 'Not that she would ever dare to speak without my permission, but it amuses me to discomfort her further during her punishments, doesn't it, Jasmine dear?'

The dark girl nodded briefly and made a sort of gurgling sound by way of reply. Prudence nodded, apparently satisfied, and turned back to her two newest charges.

'If either of you give me cause,' she said menacingly, 'then you will be dealt with exactly as you see Jasmine now, except that it will not be for two hours. More like twenty-four or even thirty-six without food or water, and with a sound flogging every four hours in addition.

'Right then,' she went on brusquely. 'I shall now release Jasmine and she will release you and help you bathe. I shall be in the next room, preparing your costumes properly. The door to the corridor is locked, and there are bars at the windows behind those curtains, so please don't trouble your sorry little heads with thoughts of escaping.'

The adjoining room was a large bedroom, the centrepiece of which was a massive French, four-poster bed, draped in luxurious deep red velvets. Prudence, it seemed, had been busy, for there were several items laid out in two identical rows, one along the top of each side of the bed.

There were also two padded stools, set a few feet apart at the foot of the bed and Sarah and Kitty were instructed to sit upon these, still wrapped in the huge towels Jasmine had given them as they emerged from their baths.

Immediately Prudence began to work on Sarah's hair, brushing it out while it was still damp and Jasmine turned her attentions to doing the same with Kitty. No one spoke and the silence in the room, with its heavy wall drapes and thick piled carpet, was eerie, broken only by the sounds of the stiff brushes as they did their work.

Sarah closed her eyes, trying not to shiver, for although the room was warm enough the thoughts of what might be to come, together with the memory of her most recent humiliation, threatened to start her trembling with apprehension. Beneath the towel her pubic mound felt cold and very exposed, now that she, like Kitty, had been expertly shaved by Jasmine and the soothing oil the Asian girl had massaged in to the newly bared flesh had left a mild tingling sensation that could not be ignored.

'We will finish your hair when it is drier,' Prudence announced, tossing her brush on the end of the bed. 'It is pointless trying to pin it up in its present condition.

'Now,' she continued, 'let's see if we can turn you into an acceptable pair of courtesans. The gentleman you're entertaining this evening has given very precise instructions and his lordship is eager to impress him.'

They began with garments that neither girl had seen before, stiffly boned corsets that reached from beneath their breasts to just on the top of their hips and, as Prudence picked up her one, a stunning emerald green and black concoction trimmed top and bottom with black lace, Sarah let out an involuntary gasp.

'You think it looks too small for you, I suspect?' Prudence said.

Sarah swallowed and nodded. 'It does seem so, mistress.'

Prudence laughed and began unhooking the front busk. 'They're from France, girl,' she said, 'as are most of these things. The women there cherish small waists – or rather their menfolk do – and the fashion is spreading to London. Now, stand up and fold your arms behind your neck.'

Reluctantly, Sarah rose to her feet and unwrapped the towel

that had been her protection these past few minutes.

'Just drop it at your feet for the moment,' Prudence instructed. 'Jasmine will take care of it later. And stand up straight, you little slut.' Sarah pulled herself to attention, her breathing shallow and rapid, and Prudence wrapped the confining garment about her and proceeded to refasten the row of tiny hooks.

As she worked her way down Sarah gave out a series of stifled grunts, for the wickedly boned confection compressed her stringently. However, as she quickly discovered, this feeling was as nothing to what it would become, for immediately prudence began drawing in the back laces, reducing the girth even further.

A few feet away Jasmine was performing the same operation on Kitty, whose cheeks were already a bright red from the exertions of breathing, but Sarah had to admit that the corset was producing entirely new contours on her new friend's body, shaping her figure dramatically, so that her hips and especially her stunning breasts were made to look even more prominent. She peered down and saw that her own corset was having a similar, if less marked effect.

'Not bad,' Prudence said eventually. Kitty could not have said anything much, even if she had dared to, for it was all she could do to draw enough air into her lungs to prevent her from fainting away completely.

'Breathe from up here more,' Prudence said, jabbing a finger between Sarah's breasts. 'And forget about breathing deeply – you can't, not now. Come on, sit again and let's get you both into some stockings and shoes.'

The stockings were pure silk, green in Sarah's case and pink in Kitty's, to reflect the colour of their corsets. They reached to just above the knee and were fastened in place by matching lace garters, except that the colour of these matched the darker hue of the respective corset, rather than the paler shade of the stockings.

126

Sarah's eyes almost rolled in her head when Prudence produced her shoes. Made from soft deerskin-like leather, they encased the foot to the lower ankle, drawn snugly about by a row of tiny glittering metal buttons, which stood out from the darker green like myriad stars. But it was the heels that Sarah could not believe, for they forced her instep into such a cruel arch that she felt certain she would not be able to stand in them, let alone walk.

'French again,' Prudence chuckled, detecting the consternation in her subject. 'Most impractical for walking any great distance, but then we are not concerned with practicalities and you are not expected to walk far. All the same, you will have a little time in order to practice and I can tell you, they do make a girl's assets wiggle most provocatively, which I assume is the idea.'

Gloves came next, deep green satin gloves for Sarah, which smoothed up her arms almost to her shoulder and were then buttoned tightly at the wrist, stretching them so that they shone like a second skin. This task completed, jewelled collars were added about the two girls' throats, row upon row of paste stones, but fixed to a leather backing which was hidden from view, yet ensured that the wearer was forced to hold her head high and, supposedly, proudly.

The two women now turned their attentions to the girls' faces, powdering, painting, rouging, working deftly and assuredly. Sarah felt the various cosmetics as they dried upon her features: her face began to feel as if it was now a mask and she began to wonder exactly what she must look like.

However, there seemed to be no mirrors anywhere in the room and her only clue was when she sneaked a sideways glance at Kitty, who was receiving the same treatment at Jasmine's hands. What she saw made her all but gasp out loud, for the face she now saw bore little resemblance to the original Kitty, who now looked like an ornate and passive doll, complete with a bright carmine, cupid bow mouth.

The final touch, before the question of their hair was addressed, were large earrings, heavy diamanté pendants that screwed tightly to each earlobe.

'Very good,' Prudence declared, walking around to a position roughly between the two sitting girls. 'All we need now is to take care of your hair and pin in the necessary pieces. Don't worry, they'll be quite secure once we've finished.'

The finished effect, from what Sarah could see of Kitty and feel upon her own head, was almost ridiculous, for the additional hair pieces were like small cages, covered in hair themselves but which, once the girls' own hair had also been piled up, arranged and pinned, seemed to become part of the original, producing a high display that glittered from the heads of the various pins securing it.

'Stand up, both of you,' Prudence ordered. Shakily, Sarah got to her feet and immediately almost toppled face down as the elevated heels threw her weight forward. She staggered, flapping her arms in panic, but managed to regain some semblance of balance just in time.

'Bring your knees together, girl,' Prudence ordered. 'You're standing like you've already got a cock up your hole. And you,' she added, turning to Kitty, who was faring little better. 'Now keep your knees straight, that's it. Well, Jasmine, what do you think of them?'

'They're very pretty, mistress,' Jasmine replied, her features totally impassive. Prudence approached Sarah, who was astonished to find that she could now almost look her straight in the eyes; so much height had the awesome shoes added to her.

'All that remains, little slut girl,' she said, 'is to teach you how to walk without falling on your pretty face and bruising your pretty titties, eh?' Without warning, her right hand shot out, her fingers thrusting between Sarah's thighs, one digit forcing itself between her denuded labia. Sarah let out a squeal of surprise and almost fell again, this time backwards, but Prudence's cruel grip drew her back close again and she found herself with her painted mouth only inches from that of her tormentor's. Prudence held her gaze for several seconds and then her thin lips curled into a devious smile.

'Later, little one,' she whispered, 'I shall have the pleasure of what I have created for myself. Your little friend shall join us too, though I confess her udders are a tad large for my tastes. Perhaps I shall give her to Jasmine for whatever remains of the night, as a reward for all her endeavours.

'But for now,' she went on, raising her voice, releasing her hold and stepping back, 'we have work to do. Before the clock strikes the hour we must have you walking properly. We must serve up an attractive dish for the guest, must we not?'

Hannah Pennywise ground her teeth and closed the door of her cottage, trying to block out the sounds of Matilda's screaming, which carried clearly on the gentle night breeze. Tears stung her eyes but she shook her head fiercely, forcing herself to remain firm, for she knew that if she once gave way Wickstanner and the despicable Crawley would not only have won, they would almost certainly use their victory to enable them to prey upon yet more victims.

'Be brave, little one,' she whispered, as she turned to the heavy old table that dominated the centre of the room. On it were laid out a variety of curious and mundane objects; pieces of greenery, some small nuts, what appeared to be a handful of crumbling, dried mud, and three small dark green glass bottles, sealed with worn wooden bungs.

Hannah bent over the tabletop and began to arrange its contents into a different order.

'We'll see who is sorriest when this evil is brought to its conclusion,' she muttered, picking up the wickedly gleaming knife that lay waiting. 'The wolf should beware of the lamb he seeks to devour, Master Crawley. Witchcraft indeed!' The knife scythed downwards, slicing through one of the little mounds of leaves, the sound echoing loudly in the confines of the cramped kitchen. Hannah picked up one of the cut portions, held it to her nose and sniffed.

'Witchcraft indeed!' she repeated, her voice dripping with scorn and hatred. 'You don't know the half of it, you murderous charlatan, I promise you!'

Matilda stood against the cellar wall, her arms held wide by the thick cords with which Crawley's men had bound her to two of the heavy iron staples. Her back felt as if it were on fire and she fought to keep her raw flesh clear of the rough stonework, but her legs trembled, threatening to buckle and she knew it was only a matter of time.

The witchfinder stood regarding her thoughtfully, stroking his chin, his eyes glinting in the semi-darkness. Matilda peered through the slits in the hood, trying desperately to focus on his image, for he seemed to be shimmering, almost unreal, as though he were merely some part of a dream.

'Your grandmother will come around to being sensible,' Crawley said, after a lengthy silence. 'I think she will not stand by and watch us hang her only relative, do you?'

'My grandmother, sir,' Matilda gasped, fighting to get the words out, 'will not be intimidated by the likes of you, nor would I expect her to yield to your blackmailing threats.'

'But they are not empty threats, Matilda, my dear,' Crawley hissed. 'I shall surely dangle you on the rope tomorrow if she does not agree to paying the tithe the Church demands for your forgiveness and salvation. Under the circumstances, it is a modest sum.'

'The Church demands?' Matilda snorted. 'I think the Church plays little part in all this, Master Crawley, save that it offers you a blanket from beneath which to crawl. You shall not get away with this, for if you hang me, it will be murder and you know it as well as I!'

'Murder?' Crawley chuckled. 'I think not, for I have all the proper warrants and authorities, all quite legally and properly signed. Mr Wickstanner has seen and validated them.'

'Signed by whom?' Matilda sneered. 'Some drunken, avaricious old bishop whom you probably bribed or blackmailed in turn? Or do you send him a portion of your evil spoils, Master Crawley?'

'Have a care, wench,' Crawley growled. 'I could have that spiteful tongue cut out of your head in an instant.'

'It will matter little,' Matilda replied, gasping as her shoulder rubbed against the wall behind her. 'Tongue or no tongue, you'll be hanging me tomorrow noon whatever, for I know my grandmother will not pay you a ha'penny.'

'Then the manner of your execution should be of great interest to you,' Crawley leered, 'for I shall take it upon myself to make sure that you go to face eternal judgement with your mortal soul as scourged as can be. What you suffered tonight was nothing. I had hoped the old biddy would see sense and therefore I cut short your intended flogging. Twelve lashes was all you received, but it could have been fifty, or even a hundred. Tomorrow I shall not be so lenient, for I see I have made a mistake. My Christian charity has been perceived as weakness, I think.

'I cannot allow that misconception to persist, of course,' he continued. 'Therefore, tomorrow I shall give you a full one hundred lashes and you will be revived whenever you fall into a faint, I promise. You shall feel every kiss of my lash, you proud little bitch, and then you shall dance at the rope's end.'

'You'll do your worst, I am sure,' Matilda whispered, fighting to keep her voice steady, for now she had no doubt that Crawley meant every word he said. He would indeed kill her, but hers would not be a merciful death. 'God will spare me from my sufferings,' she added defiantly.

'Then let's see if he will spare you this,' Crawley chuckled. He had removed his cape earlier and now he stooped to remove his boots, his breeches following them in swift succession. Deliberately he stood posing before her, massaging the length of an organ that was already beginning to swell and grow.

Matilda gave a harsh laugh. 'Are you not afraid of sticking that rod into a devil's whore, as I believe you think me?' she said. Evidently, she realised, he was not, even if he believed what he said, which she doubted, for his shaft stood

132

up straight and proud and, even in the poor light, Matilda could see the tiny veins straining against the near translucent flesh.

'My faith keeps me from sin, whore,' Crawley snickered. He stepped closer, so close that she could feel the warmth and foetid sweetness of his breath and the pressure of his cock against her lower stomach. She shrank back automatically and immediately groaned as her back pressed against the rough surface.

'You'll moan some more, ere I'm through with you,' Crawley said viciously. 'And don't think to talk of this on the morrow, for you'll go to your death with a nice fat gag in your heathen mouth.'

He stooped slightly and Matilda felt him probing with the engorged head, seeking out her defenceless sex, his hot flesh beginning to force an entrance. She closed her eyes, drawing in a deep breath. 'Go ahead then, you vile bastard,' she grated. 'Take your pleasure of me if you will, for the Lord knows I cannot stop you. But know this, Jacob Crawley, with every thrust of your foul pole you surely commit your own soul to a fate far worse than any even you could conceive for me.' She gasped again as his entire length slid into her and then opened her eyes wide, fixing his with an unflinching stare.

'So fuck me then, you spawn of a diseased cunt!' she hissed. 'Fuck me as long as you want, though I doubt that will be very long, will it?'

'You cannot hang her, Master Crawley!' Simon Wickstanner's face was a dark shade of purple. He stopped his pacing, grasped the marble mantelshelf and banged his fist against the chimneybreast. 'Good Lord, man!' he exclaimed. 'Where is the sense in that?'

Jacob Crawley, who had been sitting in the padded window seat, rose slowly and walked to the centre of the room. He stood motionless for a few moments, a sardonic smile upon his drawn features, and then shook his head slowly, a gesture that was more dismissive than anything else.

'Priest,' he said coldly, 'you have no subtlety whatsoever. Neither, I fear, are you any judge of human nature. You assured me the old biddy would be forthcoming long before we reached this evening's stage, did you not? Well then, where was she, eh?

'I tell you this, she was out there somewhere, yet despite her granddaughter's screaming, did she come forward? No, we both know she did not. So, we must believe her gold means more to her than blood, except that if that were true, then everything I have learned about human nature would be proved false.

'Yes, she seems capable of allowing the wench to suffer – mayhap the supposed suffering is nought but an act, for all we know – but will she see her swing at the end of a rope? I think not.'

'But what if she will?' Wickstanner snapped. 'What then? Will you hang the girl?'

'It shall not come to that, priest, that much I do know,' Crawley said. 'At least, I doubt it, though there are those who can yet surprise me. The grandmother is the only family, you say, so I cannot see her permitting events to go that far. Did she not give you any indication?'

Wickstanner's expression was wooden. 'The only indication she gave me was that she would ensure that I paid for this for all eternity.' For a moment his sunken cheeks and hollow eyes were close to betraying his true feelings, but he fought to regain his self-control. 'Of course,' he expostulated, 'I took no heed of such empty threats, but the problem is, as I see it, that if the old woman holds true to such beliefs, then she may not be forthcoming.'

'Then we hang the wench and have done with it,' Crawley

said. 'As far as I am concerned, it is a simple case of cutting losses. My warrant guarantees me twenty guineas for every witch or heretic I execute, so my journey down here will not be totally wasted. Besides, we already have murmurings against two more of the village women. There may yet be fruit to be gathered, priest, so hold firm. We do the Lord's work, the Lord's bidding, so have faith. He shall provide.'

After half an hour's careful scouting, Toby was finally satisfied that there was no one else watching the bridge. The mill, long closed for the night, was in total darkness and the Calthorpe cottage showed only one lighted window, probably as the miller and his wife ate a well earned supper before bedtime.

The main barn and the smaller outbuildings were all shut and bolted from the outside with heavy timber bars, so if there was anyone inside any of them, they were in there for the night. A rapid check through the woods behind the mill revealed nothing, either. He grinned; whatever happened next, they had the advantage of what he had heard soldiers call 'early ground', which meant they would also hold on to the element of surprise.

The *Black Drum* was a regular overnight stop for military personnel travelling between London and Portsmouth and, on the summer evenings, the young officers often sat at the benches outside, drinking and chatting among themselves and, more often than not, quite willing to regale Toby, or any of the other youngsters from the village, with stories of their campaigns, real or imaginary.

Toby had long since decided that he, too, would be an officer in the army, travelling the world, fighting the enemies of the Commonwealth, seeing sights he could never hope to see if he remained stuck here, the way his father and grandfather before him had. Of course, he realised, not being able to read or write would be something of a drawback to this ambition, but he had practised sword fighting with a wooden sabre he'd fashioned himself and he was a dead shot with the musket his father kept for rabbiting and foxes.

Maybe his lack of literary skills would be overlooked. Or maybe, he thought, as he made his roundabout way back to where Billy was still sleeping, he could ask Miss Harriet to teach him. Maybe he could offer to help her on their farm, in exchange, for he knew she was hard pressed, what with her father being so ill all the time.

And she would surely understand his wish to be an officer, for hadn't Oliver Merridew himself been a major in the King's army, before the war between the King and Parliament? Of course, Major Merridew hadn't fought in that war, because he was wounded before it ever started, but he had been a soldier, an officer and a gentleman, which was why Miss Harriet was such a lady, even if she did have to help milk her own cows, which not many...

'Holy shit!' Toby gasped, stopping dead in his tracks and his thoughts and clapping one palm to his forehead. 'Holy bloody shit!' he repeated. 'Of course, that's what was wrong.' He shook his head and crouching down, ran the last few yards to where Billy still laid snoring, pouncing on his friend and shaking him awake unceremoniously.

'Wassamadda?' Billy yelped, his eyes flying open wide. 'Wassup?'

Toby placed a finger to his lips and the other on Billy's. 'Not so loud,' he whispered. 'Nothing's up. The boat wasn't there yet and no one's come, either. There's also no one else about, 'cause I've just checked, but I've just thought of something.'

'Oh yeah?' Billy struggled to sit up, rubbing his eyes. 'Like what? Like maybe we should be home in our beds instead of trying to sleep against some mouldy old tree?'

'No, you oaf,' Toby snapped. 'Like try this.'

'What?'

136

'Well, let me ask you something,' Toby said. 'Matthew pretended he needed a drink from the river, so he could sneak a look under the bridge, right?'

'So what? It was a good ruse.'

'Exactly,' Toby concurred. 'No one watching would think anything suspicious about a lad getting himself a drink from the river, would they?'

'Course not,' Billy said. 'I've done that a few times myself, though the water isn't as sweet here as it is from the well, nor from the little stream over by Harper's Wood.'

'No and I reckon only the likes of us would bother drinking here, wouldn't we? And only then if we didn't have a water flask with us.'

'Well, I ain't got a water flask anyway,' Billy said.

'Me neither,' Toby said. 'But all the nobs have them, don't they?'

'So what? Nobs are nobs and they have everything, because they're nobs,' Billy said. 'That's what bein' a nob is all about; you can have whatever you want.'

'Like Ellen Grayling does, you mean?' Toby said, grinning.

Billy shrugged. 'Well, she's a nob, ain't she? Her pa's got so much money he could probably buy her anything she wanted.'

'Like that horse of hers she rides about on?' Toby said. 'That big bay, with the white blaze?'

'She's got that other one, too,' Billy reminded him. 'The roan – the one they reckon her pa had brought from the Arab countries especially for her birthday.'

'Well, it don't matter where it come from,' Toby said. 'What does matter is how she rides it – either of 'em, for that matter.'

'You means she rides like a man,' Billy said. 'Yeah, my mam reckons it ain't proper for a lady to ride like that, nor to dress the way she does. Why?'

'Well, think Bill, think 'ard. You seen her ridin' around hereabouts as many times as me, right?' Billy nodded. 'Well, just try and picture her in your head. She uses a military saddle, yes?'

'And she wears them boots with the little spurs,' Billy added.

'And what does she have on her saddle?'

'Dunno,' Billy said. He screwed his eyes tightly shut, trying to concentrate. 'There's a little thing on one side, where a soldier would carry a musket, maybe, but she don't carry a musket in it.'

'No, she don't,' Toby agreed. 'But what else does she have on that saddle?'

'Well… nothing really, except that leather water bag thing, the same as the soldiers carry with them on their horses.'

'Yeah, that's *right*,' Toby cried triumphantly. 'She carries a water bottle and I've even seen her drink from it, when she's stopped on the village green to water her horse at the trough there.'

'So what?' Billy demanded. 'Nothing unusual in that, is there? I mean, it maybe ain't the right way for a lady to carry on, same as me mam says, but then that Ellen Grayling ain't like most women, so everyone reckons.'

'No, that she ain't,' Toby said. 'But that ain't my point. What I'm wonderin' is this: if she's got that water bottle, why would she want to stop and have a drink from the river down under the bridge over there?'

'You mean she's been here tonight?'

Toby shook his head. 'No, not tonight,' he said, 'but she stopped here this afternoon, while I was watching the place. Went down to the edge, just like Matt did an' scooped up some water. I thought she was havin' a drink, but why would she, eh?'

'Maybe she just wanted to splash her face?' Billy suggested, after a moment's consideration. 'Gets pretty dusty on the roads this time of year.'

'Yeah, well, she could have,' Toby conceded, 'but I don't reckon she did either. I knew something was wrong earlier, when I watched Matt, but I couldn't figure it out to start with. Then it hit me, when I was thinking about Miss Harriet.

'To start with, why would a lady – even a lady like Ellen Grayling, drink from a river, unless she really had to? And even if we suppose her bottle was empty, if she drank using her hands or even if she just wanted to splash her face, she'd wipe her mouth, her eyes, or whatever. Only, now I think back to it, she didn't. All she did was wipe her hands on her breeches and get back on her horse.'

'So what?'

'Well, think about it, Bill.' Toby sat back, regarding his friend. 'What I'm saying is this,' he continued, when no further comment was forthcoming. 'Ellen Grayling didn't drink down there, nor did she wash her face.'

'So what was she doing there?' Billy demanded obtusely, and Toby's grin threatened to split his face in two.

'That's a fuckin' good question, Bill,' he retorted. 'An' right now, though it seems a bit mad, I can only think of the one answer. An' also, if'n I'm right, it's made me start thinkin' of another possible idea, though you ain't gonna believe me, no more than anyone else round here would!'

For several minutes Hannah Pennywise stood in the middle of the woodland path, poised as if she were listening for something, but the only noises on the night air were the faint rustling of leaves in the canopy above and the occasional plaintive hooting of a distant owl.

High above, just visible through the narrow gap in the foliage immediately above the track, the sky was clear and dark, a smattering of stars winking or shimmering. The moon had settled beyond the hills and in the woods, between the trees and among the bushes, it was very, very dark.

The ghost of a smile flickered over Hannah's gaunt

features and she sniffed the breeze and nodded. She bent to pick up the wicker basket laid at her feet, squared her shoulders and began to walk, her ever-present cane sending a hollow tap-tap echoing among the black, sentinel tree trunks.

George Billings had indeed gone along with almost every other male in Fetworth and young Toby Blaine did not seem at all worried about continuing the adventure without his stewardship, and so it was that the three youths approached the bridge by the water mill at shortly after nine o'clock in the evening.

Matt Cornwell, a stocky boy with square pugnacious features, volunteered to go and make sure the rowing boat had not already been returned to its former station. 'I'll just wander along to the bridge and slide down the bank, as if I'm getting meself a drink,' he said.

'Yes,' Toby agreed, 'and then carry on walking over the bridge and up the lane a-ways. Don't come straight back over here, in case someone's watchin'. Right?'

Matt nodded, grinning in the darkness. He laid a hand on Toby's shoulder. 'It's right rum, this, ain't it?' he said. 'You reckon someone will come along this way?'

'Sure to,' Toby affirmed confidently. 'Stands to reason; they got to get the boat back here, ain't they? And what better time to do it than at night?'

'There's a lot of night ahead of us,' Matt pointed out. 'Could be almost any time, if'n they do come.'

'Which is why there are three of us,' Toby said. 'We can take it in turns to watch and to nap, if we start gettin' tired.'

'Well, I'm tired now,' Billy Dodds, the third member of the trio complained.

'Then you settle down against that tree trunk there,' Toby said, pointing to a horizontal bough that had clearly fallen at least a couple of years before, 'and you get yourself a catnap now, see. I'll wake you if'n I start gettin' tired an' you can take over my watch. In the meantime, once you've checked under the bridge, Matt, I'm going to scout a bit. I'm going around the back of the mill buildings just to make sure there ain't anyone there looking out, like. I'll give you a little while to walk on up the lane, then you sneak back and get in among those bushes on the other bank. From there you'll be able to see anyone who comes upstream in a boat.'

'An' what if there's a boat already there?' Matt demanded. 'You want me to come straight back here instead?'

Toby considered this for a few seconds before shaking his head. 'No,' he said. 'If the boat is already there, could be that whoever put it there is watching out, so we need some sort of a signal.' He paused again. 'I know,' he said, 'if'n the boat's there, you stop halfway across the bridge and throw a couple of stones into the water.'

Without further discussion the plan was put into operation. Matt Cornwell backtracked through the undergrowth, to a point where he could emerge onto the road without being seen from either the bridge or the mill and then began to saunter back again, whistling tunelessly as he went, apparently without a concern in the world.

Just before he reached the bridge he stopped, half turned and looked up at the night sky. Then with an elaborate show of wiping the back of one hand across his mouth, he turned back again and moved towards the top of the gently sloping embankment. He slid down the grass incline easily, stood upright at the water's edge and then knelt, stooping forward to cup his hands into the cold current.

At last, after taking several scoops of water, he straightened up once again, wiped his mouth with both hands and climbed back up the slope to the road. Watching from his hidden vantage point, Toby waited with bated breath to see if Matt stopped on the bridge to give the signal, but the lad made no attempt to stop. Still whistling, he carried straight on across and strolled slowly out of sight.

Toby turned to Billy, but even in the darkness he could tell his friend had already fallen asleep, for the muffled snoring sounded unnaturally loud in the otherwise silent night. 'Lotta use you're going to be,' Toby muttered to himself. Silently, he began to count, though only to ten each time, for beyond that he had never been sure of the sequence of the numbers. However, he did know that ten times ten was a hundred and so, each time he reached ten and restarted, he folded down one finger. If he counted to a hundred this way and counted slowly, he reasoned, Matt would have enough time to sneak back and watch the bridge, while he reconnoitred the rest of the area on this side of the river.

However, as he counted something started working somewhere in the back of his mind, a little questioning niggle he could not quite put his finger on. There was something curious, something he knew he should try to get to the bottom of, but what exactly he wasn't at all sure.

'Bugger it,' he whispered. 'What the hell is it? I know you're missing something, Toby Blaine, and I just feel it in me water that it could be important.'

The final touch to Sarah and Kitty's costumes was added just before Prudence allowed them to see their reflections in the long mirror that had been hidden behind one of the wall drapes. Wide, jewelled bracelets were snapped about both girls' wrists, a hidden locking mechanism clicking into place.

Staring down at hers, Sarah saw that there were two cunningly concealed fitments, one on each, the left wrist shaped like a projecting socket, the right a grooved prong. The one, it was clear, fitted into the other, no doubt locking as securely as the bracelets themselves; though extremely

142

decorative they could obviously also be used as a means to manacle the two wrists together.

Similarly, the jewelled collars they wore had small but sturdy rings set in among the fake gems, to which fine chain leashes could be attached and this Prudence did. Satisfied that the clips were secure, she gave a sharp tug on both leashes and walked the teetering girls over to the mirror.

Sarah stared at her reflection in sheer disbelief and her hands went instinctively to cover her denuded crotch. She had felt less naked when completely unclothed and certainly now, she saw, the bizarre way in which they were both attired served simply to make them look nothing more than objects for sexual gratification.

The two white faces, with their painted eyes and painted little pouts of mouths, gazed back in an almost bland fashion, the high piled hairstyles, with their glinting array of pins, were nothing more than mockeries. Standing perched upon their high-heeled shoes, their stockings gartered in froths of ribbon and lace, their waists pulled impossibly small inside the breath-taking corsets, arms sheathed in smooth satin, the two girls, with their bared breasts and rouged nipples had been prepared for one fate, and one fate only.

Slowly, Sarah turned away from the mirrored tableau and stared at Prudence, who was watching them both with a peculiarly crooked smile on her face. The older woman stood motionless for several seconds and then began to chuckle mirthlessly.

'Such sweet little confections,' she mocked. 'Good enough to eat, as you will shortly find out.'

- X -

'My dear Grayling, I must congratulate you on an excellent dinner.' Lord Henry Soberton, seventh Earl of Heckham, distant cousin of the late King Charles, sat back in the hugely padded chair and raised his glass to his host. Balding and now well into middle age, Henry Soberton did not let his lack of physical attraction worry him one jot – with his wealth, there was no need to.

The Heckham estates were vast, both in England and in the New World, thanks entirely to inherited wealth and the unceasing efforts of the men he paid to run them, for Soberton was not an industrious man by nature, preferring to spend his time enjoying the fruits rather than husbanding them.

His earlier cautious approach and coded overtures had come as a surprise to Roderick Grayling, but a prospective new client was always welcome, especially one with Soberton's resources.

'I know what I like, Grayling,' he had said, finally, when each man finished sounding out the other and they cut to the chase. 'Need a couple of pretty English fillies, obedient and properly trained. None of this foreign stuff. Wouldn't believe what some people will try to do, I can tell you. You on the other hand, my young friend, come highly recommended.'

'I'm glad to hear that, Lord Henry,' Roderick replied easily. 'I have taken a great deal of trouble to ensure that the goods we offer are of the finest kind available anywhere in England. If I offer you an English rose, then you can be sure that's what she is.'

Soberton looked pointedly across to where Roderick's

two little black slaves squatted on cushions in one corner of the room. He raised his glass towards them and grinned, revealing teeth that were blackening in many places. 'Yet I see your own tastes are a little more catholic,' he said.

Roderick twitched one eyebrow. 'Variety is the spice of life, Lord Henry,' he replied. 'Popsy and Topsy are utterly devoted to me and will do anything I require of them, without question and without hesitation.'

'Very nice, I'm sure,' Soberton leered, 'but I trust you were aware of my own preferences?'

'Indeed, milord,' Roderick grinned, 'and I have several prospects for you to view, but that can wait awhile. First, I have arranged for some entertainment for you – for both of us, in fact. I instructed George Hawkin to have Adam select from among our newer arrivals.

'Neither girl has been here for very long and as such they are far from properly trained, but this may give you some idea of the effectiveness of our methods. What you are shortly to see will, I am confident, astonish you, so imagine what you get when we have completed the regime on a girl, eh?'

'I hear a horse!' Matt Cornwell hissed. 'More than one, too.' He had finally rejoined Toby and Billy, reporting that the far side of the river, like this, seemed deserted.

In the darkness, Toby nodded. 'Keep well down,' he said. He nudged Billy with his foot and the youngest member of the trio, who had been threatening to fall asleep again for some little time, grunted and muttered an oath under his breath. 'Get up a bit and use your eyes,' Toby said, ignoring the insult.

'Yeah, look, a rider!' Matt whispered, pointing back down the road that led from the village. 'Only one though. That's funny, I could have sworn – no, he's leading a second horse, look!'

'You mean *she* is,' Toby corrected him. 'That's a woman on that horse, or I'm a fucking papist!' The two horses and rider were now no more than seventy yards from them and although there was now no moon, the starlight showed them an unmistakably feminine silhouette.

'Ellen Grayling again?' Billy asked, peering over Toby's shoulder for a better view. Toby pushed him back.

'No, it's not her this time,' he said. 'Not sure who it is, not from this distance.'

'I am,' Matt said. 'That's Kate Dawson, from over Hepping Hill Farm. I'd know her anywhere, even in the dark and from back here. It's the way she rides, bobbin' up and down like that, all stiff and upright. My brother John tried courting her a year back, but she wasn't interested. Thinks she's a nob herself, that one.'

'Well, she keeps company with the nobs at times,' Toby said. 'I seen her out riding with Ellen Grayling more than once. They go over by Thatcher's Ridge and over towards Butser way, right out in the wilds. I seen 'em when I bin that way lookin' fer rabbits.'

'Doesn't mean anything,' Billy grumbled. 'I reckon we're just wastin' our time an' I'm gettin' hungry.'

'Maybe not, but – look!' Toby hissed urgently. 'She's left the road, down there between them yew trees, see? There's a little clearing just behind, ain't there?'

'Yeah,' Matt nodded, 'but what's she up to? There's nothing else there.'

'Well, if you ask me,' Toby smiled, 'I'd say she was waitin' for someone, wouldn't you? Why else would she have a spare horse with her?'

'Ah!' Matt exclaimed, the light of understanding dawning in his eyes. He turned and nodded towards the river. 'You mean whoever is rowing the boat back upstream?'

'Almost surely,' Toby said. 'I did wonder. I thought maybe whoever brought the boat back might have another one in

146

tow and go back that way, but rowin' one boat up against the current is hard work enough, without havin' to haul a second one.'

'So now all we have to do is wait for the boat?' Matt said.

Toby nodded. 'An' I don't think we'll have to wait much longer, either.'

Sarah did not need to be told which of the two men was Roderick Grayling, the man ultimately responsible for the horrors of the past hours. Hours? Was it really only hours, she thought, amazed as she realised how short a time had elapsed since her initial abduction.

Grayling looked almost exactly the way she had pictured him from the first time she learned of his existence. He was tall, dark-haired, slim, but well muscled and handsome in a disdainful way, as if he knew he'd been blessed with better than average looks, but really did not care either way.

His companion, on the other hand, bordered on being downright ugly and Sarah's heart sank at the thought of what she might be expected to do. It had been bad enough having to suffer at Ross's hands, but at least the young handler had something about him which might have attracted her in different circumstances, but this fellow was not just plain, fat and with bloated features, he was old enough to be her father.

'Titty Kitty and Sarah, your lordship,' Prudence announced, leading the two girls across the polished wooden floor towards the rug on which the two armchairs had been set for the men. 'Sarah has not been renamed yet, as she's only been with us a matter of hours.'

'No need to ask which one is which,' the fat man said, laughing. 'What a fine pair of melons you have, eh, Titty Kitty?' Kitty lowered her eyes, but Prudence immediately slapped her hard across her naked buttocks, making her

147

head jerk upwards again.

'His lordship asked you a question, Kitty,' she snapped. 'Answer in the way you have been taught.'

'Yes, my lord,' Kitty demurred. 'I trust this humble slave girl's titties meet with your approval?'

The man threw back his head, roaring with laughter. 'Capital!' he exclaimed. 'By God, Grayling, I tip my hat to you!'

'Master Adam has told me all about you, Kitty,' Grayling said, leaning forward in his chair. 'Seems you like your little cunny well reamed and have a taste for the tongue, eh?'

'Yes, master,' Kitty replied quietly. 'I am a slave slut.'

'But a pretty one, Titty Kitty!' Grayling's companion roared again.

'And what of you, Sarah?' Grayling asked, turning his attention from Kitty. 'Are you a slave slut, too?'

'Indeed, sir,' Sarah replied, hating herself, but knowing that she would face a whipping if she did not answer as she had been instructed, 'I am becoming one, if I were not already.'

'Ah,' Grayling said, 'I detect perhaps a sign of some education and breeding in you, slave Sarah. Are you book read, girl?'

'I have had some education, yes master,' Sarah said. 'My father was a scholar and we had a fine library in our London home.'

'London, eh?' the fat man cried. 'Capital! Really capital, har-har!' He laughed raucously at his own joke, slapping his thighs repeatedly and Sarah cringed. The thought of such a creature even touching her with a single finger was more than enough to make her stomach turn – the thought of anything else was dreadful beyond anything she could compare.

However, it quickly became apparent that neither she nor

148

Kitty had been brought here for Grayling's guest's personal gratification, rather to repeat what they had done in their stall cell earlier, this time with additional spectators. Grayling clapped his hands and the two black girls – unnoticed by Sarah until this moment – rose from their cushions, pattered across the floor in their bare feet and drew aside a curtain that had been hiding a deep alcove.

From this they drew out a large square mat, or so Sarah thought it, until they dragged it across to the centre of the polished wood surface. Now, she saw, it was more than just a mat; rather it appeared to be some form of thin mattress, two large squares of thick velvet sewn together, one atop the other and stuffed with something soft.

'Now, my two little coquettes,' Prudence whispered, as she led the two English girls back to stand behind the mattress, at a point where the two men could not hear her instructions, 'I want you to act as though you're both enjoying this, which I suspect you will anyway, from what I've heard. I want to see those little tongues in those honeypots, lapping hard. I want to see those pretty red lips sucking those pert red nipples and I want to see those painted fingers working all the time. Their lordships will know if you try faking and if they don't whip you – which I suspect they will – then I'll do it myself.

'Now, get down there my painted jezebels, and let's have a performance worthy of the name. If not,' she hissed, drawing their heads closer to hers, 'apart from the whipping, you'll probably end up with the fat pig there poking the pair of you. And I doubt,' she added maliciously, 'whether you much fancy that, my pretties, mm?'

'This is getting beyond a joke, Captain Hart!' Thomas Handiwell fumed. The young captain of horse looked a little sheepish; behind him the line of soldiers, all now leading their horses, did their best to pretend they were not listening to the conversation between their officer and the innkeeper.

'I don't see what else I can do, Master Handiwell,' Timothy Hart said. 'We now have three horses lame at the same time. We cannot possibly ride them further, surely you must see that?'

'Of course I see that, man,' Handiwell said curtly. 'I saw that ten miles back, when we passed through by the *Boar's Head*. I said then that those mounts looked the worse for wear and that we should have asked if there were replacements available.'

'Yes, I know you did,' Hart admitted. His thin face looked even more drawn than it had when Colonel Brotherwood first introduced Handiwell to him in Portsmouth. The strain of his recent losses had been evident then and now, as what should have been a straightforward journey of a few hours threatened to disintegrate into a farce, it was plain that he was not coping at all well.

'The problem is, Master Handiwell,' he went on, 'that these horses are the property of the government. I am not authorised to simply trade them in against fresh mounts. There is no way of knowing just what sort of horseflesh we might be getting in exchange.'

'The sort that can carry a rider more than ten miles without breaking down!' Handiwell snapped. 'No,' he said, his tone softening slightly, 'it's not your fault, man, I know that. But look ye here, at this rate we'll not make the *Drum* before midday tomorrow. I don't know about you and your men, but I can't walk all night.'

'Then what are you suggesting, sir?'

'I'm suggesting,' Handiwell said firmly, 'that we still have five good horses between us, so five of us should ride on. Once we get to my inn one man can ride back with three fresh horses. At least that will leave four of us to try to find out something about these villains who have taken my niece.'

'I cannot leave three men on the road on their own,' Hart insisted. 'It's completely against regulations.'

'Then don't leave them on their own. Have your sergeant swap his good horse for one of the lame steeds and leave him in charge of two of your troopers. Surely that's not against your precious regulations?'

'Well, no,' Hart admitted, 'though Sergeant Riley is supposed to be in charge of my safe passage, as you know.'

'Damn your safe passage!' Handiwell's voice rose alarmingly and the younger man flinched. 'What about my niece, Sarah? What about her safe passage. You'll still have three of your men, plus myself, so what are you frightened of? Feared some ghost is going to jump out and make off with you, is that it? Strike me in the saddle, but I thought you were supposed to be a soldier!'

'Of course, Master Handiwell,' Hart said. He shook his head, but it was clear he did not have the stomach for a further confrontation. He turned and called back to the line behind them.

'Sergeant Riley,' he instructed, 'let Fuller have your mount, man. The three of you with lame horses will proceed on foot, with all possible haste. We shall send a rider back with fresh mounts for you as soon as possible.'

Sarah groaned, but there was no fighting the wave of lust that kept washing over her. As she lay on her back, legs akimbo, with Kitty crouched over her, offering her own sex to Sarah's lips as she buried her face in Sarah's soaking orifice, she knew she was about to climax yet again and dug her fingers fiercely into the soft flesh of Kitty's pendant breasts and let out a piercing wail.

Immediately Kitty lifted her head, pivoted on her knees and pressed her lips to Sarah's, her tongue forcing entry so that Sarah was able to taste her own juices plainly. By the fireplace, the two aristocrats watched the performance with differing reactions: Roderick Grayling seemed only mildly amused, whereas the fat Henry Soberton leaned forward in his chair, his eyes bulging as he relished every intimate contact.

'By Jove, Grayling,' he said hoarsely. 'They're a splendid pair of fillies and no mistaking. I simply must have them. Name your price, man. Name your price!'

'I'm afraid these two aren't for sale, milord,' Grayling drawled. 'Not just yet, at any rate. They show too much potential and they could be worth a ransom by the time their training is finished.'

'Damn your ransom,' Soberton snapped. 'I'll pay you your price, here and now.' Kitty, as her orgasm subsided, became vaguely aware of this exchange and her entire body stiffened.

'It's not just a question of money,' Grayling replied easily. 'These two have a potential value even if I decide to keep them here. See how well matched they are, apart from the one Kitty having larger breasts? And see how there is also an affinity between them? Such a pair of beauties could provide untold entertainment for my more valued guests here,' he explained. 'You don't need to sell a girl outright in order to turn a profit on her, y'know.' He clapped his hands.

'Prudence, have them stop now before their juices soak the rug. I have a mind to reward those sweet little rumps personally. Get them in position, please. Topsy,' he called, looking to where the two black girls squatted in the corner, 'fetch master's little crop, there's a good girl.' He held his hands up, palms inwards, about two feet apart. One of the girls leapt instantly to her feet, padded across the floor and opened the front of the heavy oak chest that stood in the window bay.

'And I think, milord,' Grayling grinned, 'that we shall

make this a bittersweet experience for them, to reward them for their enthusiastic display, eh?'

Hannah stood watching the shadowy figure in the clearing for a few minutes, before finally revealing herself. She smiled as she saw how the girl crouched over the pot as it simmered on the small fire, dropping things into the steaming water from time to time.

'It's not just the ingredients, Jane Handiwell,' she said at last, stepping from behind the tree from where she had been observing the ritual. 'It's the skill of the cook that counts.' Jane swung around with a start and rose to her feet, her face even paler than usual.

'Mother Pennywise!' she gasped. 'What brings you here?'

Hannah grimaced and walked over to her, stopping a few paces away and leaning heavily on her stick. 'Not choice, missy,' she snapped. 'No, I'd as soon leave you and your daft friends to play your little games here, but I need some help.'

'Help?' Jane echoed. Her eyes narrowed suspiciously. 'What help could you possibly want from me?'

'The use of younger legs,' Hannah retorted. 'The miller's boy has disappeared and I need his education and commonsense to help me stop the nonsense that's going on back in Fetworth.'

'What nonsense?' Jane demanded.

Hannah smiled mirthlessly. 'You mean you ain't heard? You ain't heard what that weasel of a minister and his new crony are doing to my Matilda?' Jane looked genuinely bemused and Hannah quickly outlined the situation.

'So they want money from you, or they hang your granddaughter?' Jane said, when the old woman had finished.

Hannah nodded. 'That's about the strength of it, yes. But I'll see myself burn in hell afore I give so much as a penny piece to the likes of them.'

'You'd rather see Matilda under the lash, is that it?'

'No I fuckin' wouldn't, you stupid little slut!' Hannah's eyes blazed. 'But what would happen if I paid 'em, eh? There's already rumours that they're thinkin' of tryin' the same thing with other gals, an' if I give in, who knows where it'll stop, eh?'

'If Wickstanner's involved,' Jane mused, 'then maybe he'll be after Harriet Merridew next.'

'That's one story I've heard, yes,' Hannah confirmed.

'Well, t'would serve the hoity-toity little bitch right, I say,' Jane sniggered.

'You're too fast with your judgements, Jane Handiwell,' Hannah snapped. 'Besides, you ain't exactly on safe ground yourself. You and your three friends. Wickstanner and this Crawley pig might be interested in hearing about what the four of you get up to, out here in the woods nights, as well as in your bedchambers.'

'There's no proof we ever did anything, old woman,' Jane snarled. 'Besides, do you think they'd listen to you?'

'Maybe they would, maybe they wouldn't,' Hannah conceded, 'but how sure can you be, young lady?' Jane reached under the folds of her dark cape and Hannah saw the glint of metal as she withdrew a wicked looking blade.

'I can be very sure,' Jane said quietly, 'if I slit your old gizzard here and now.'

'"If" is a small word, but a big difference,' Hannah said smoothly. 'You could no more stick that thing in me than you could let a man stick his cock in your cunt, you silly little girl.' As she spoke she fixed her gaze on Jane's eyes and lifted her free hand slightly. A curious expression appeared on Jane's face and, a moment later, the knife slipped from her grasp and dropped onto the grass with a soft thud.

'Now, Jane Handiwell,' Hannah said, speaking very

softly, 'I'll tell you how this is going to be, right? You came to me once, some years ago, when you were nothing but a child and I tried to help you, to advise you. Yes, you do have some of the powers and I tried to advise you how best to use them, but did you listen? No, of course you didn't. Instead you used them to satisfy your own cravings, and draw those other three stupid mares into your web, didn't you?

'Well, what goes up your hole b'ain't none of my business, I reckon, but there's a responsibility goes with power and now it's about time you realised that. Whatever you may choose to do after this night, that's your affair, but you'll give me what I ask, else I'll show you what real power is about and no mistaking.'

'If you have that much power, Mother Pennywise,' Jane replied, 'then why not turn it directly on those who have your precious granddaughter? What do you need me for?'

Hannah shook her head dismissively. 'Shows how little you know, you young fool,' she said. 'Wickstanner and Crawley both wear the sign of the cross about their foul necks. Maybe – more'n like, I dare say – they despoil their damned faith, but the symbols have been blessed and hold a power nonetheless.

'Besides, they both lurk in their lair in that church, which is like having the wall of a castle about them. Maybe my powers would be enough anyway, but I don't know for certain, so we'll use other more earthbound methods to begin with. Those idiots in the village are like children, so we have to fight their ignorance. Your father will help stop all this stupidity, but they tell me he may not be back until the morrow, by when it may well be too late. The miller's boy will make them listen, I know, so we have to find him.'

'Perhaps he's away, too?'

'No, that he ain't,' Hannah said. 'I bin askin', dearie, and he's missin', that's all. Very convenient that, in certain quarters, if'n you get my meaning?'

'You think Wickstanner and this Crawley fellow have got him out of the way?' Jane asked. 'How can you be sure they haven't just killed him?'

'Oh, I'm sure,' Hannah said confidently. 'Same as I said, there are powers you've not even begun to understand, let alone master.'

'So where is he then, if you know so much?'

Hannah chuckled. 'Somewhere in these woods,' she replied. 'Exactly where, I can't be sure, which is why I need your help. Your help, and the help of your daft friends. Your young legs can move a sight quicker'n mine and besides, you've got horses.'

'What makes you think I can get my friends to help in time, old woman?' Jane said caustically, and Hannah tapped the side of her nose with one bony finger and looked meaningfully at the simmering cauldron and crackling fire.

'You were thinking of spending the night out here by yourself, then, was you?' she cackled.

XI

'That's Mary Watling,' Matt Cornwell whispered, as the three boys watched the dark figure climb up the riverbank from beneath the bridge. 'There ain't no other woman round hereabouts is that big!'

'Yeah, that's her all right,' Toby agreed. He squatted down, thinking furiously. 'So that's three of 'em,' he said, 'if'n I'm right about Ellen Grayling. Three women, Matt. Women, not men.'

'So what you sayin', Toby?' Matt Cornwell was far from slow, but he did not possess his friend's reasoning powers.

'Not sure what I'm sayin', not yet,' Toby admitted. 'But think of it this way – everyone's gotten into their head that there are these four men who keep stopping the coaches down from London, right? God knows how many they've done so far, yet no one has ever got the slightest idea about who they are.

'Now, I ain't no magistrate, sheriff or nothing, but if I were, I reckon I'd be thinkin' as to which four men in the area were known for bein' seen in each other's company a lot, see? You can bet the soldiers've bin askin' around all the villages for several miles both ways.'

''Spect so,' Matt agreed, 'but I still don't see what you're geddin' at, Tobe.'

'Well, think about this,' Toby said, as Mary Watling strode past them at a distance of no more than fifty yards, 'with the rewards the coach company is offerin', you'd think someone would've talked, even if just to say that these blokes and these blokes were all pals, or whatever.'

'So?'

'Well, my pa spends a lot of time in the *Drum*, an' he

gets to hear most things, but he ain't said nothing, which means that no one's bin' able to point a finger at four men as might be likely robbers, yes? But then, they wouldn't, would they?' Mary Watling drew level with the trees where the boys had last seen Kate Dawson leave the road and turned into the woods herself. 'Not if the robbers was mostly women,' Toby concluded.

Matt's eyes grew very round. 'You ain't suggestin' that…?' He shook his head. 'No, that's daft, Tobe. Ellen Grayling is a nob, for a start.'

'So? Maybe she just fancies a bit of extra loot, Matt.'

'Well, yes, I suppose—'

'Maybe she's in love with the man who's leading them all,' Billy suggested, breaking a silence he'd maintained for more than a quarter of an hour. 'Perhaps he's poor an' she's tryin' to help him get enough money so she can marry him?'

'Perhaps,' Toby said, but without enthusiasm or conviction. 'And then again, perhaps not. Then again, still,' he said, grinning anew, 'who says the fourth robber has to be a man?'

The second part of the 'entertainment' for Lord Soberton was prepared with careful elaboration, beginning with the reappearance of Adam and Robin, each man carrying an elaborate and curious looking contraption made from sinister black iron bands and rods.

These they placed in the centre of the room, spaced a foot or two apart, so that they resembled two four-legged animals, with spindly legs, long thin necks and circular bands where the heads should have begun. Looking at the two stands, Sarah realised immediately that the circular bands were intended for hers and Kitty's necks and that the strategically placed smaller bands on each of the four legs were intended to secure wrists and ankles.

Her instinct, when Robin placed his hand upon her shoulder, was to try to resist, but the sight of the wicked crop dangling from his belt was enough and she allowed him to lead her demurely behind the nearer of the two stands and dutifully shuffled her feet wider, so that he was able to cuff each of her ankles to the respective back legs.

Facing her, Adam was carrying out the same procedure with Kitty and both girls were pressed forward at the same time, so that their stomachs and chests rested on the near horizontal flat band that formed the back of the 'animal', their breasts hanging on either side of it and their arms drawn down the forelegs and cuffed in the same way as their legs had been.

Next, the two circular neckbands were opened and the girls were required to lay with their necks inside the lower halves. The top semi-circles were then swung closed and locked by means of a simple catch. Finally, two broad leather straps were produced and buckled about the girls' waists, pinioning them even more firmly.

'I say, Grayling,' Sarah heard Henry Soberton chuckling, 'what a splendidly ingenious idea. Like a couple of little ponies, just right for the mounting, eh?'

'And equally as well presented for a little rump warming,' Grayling said, and from the corner of her left eye Sarah saw the young aristocrat approaching, but he stopped short, at a point roughly level with the gap between the two helpless prisoners.

'Bit them, Prudence,' he said, flexing his crop, which appeared shorter and lighter than the implements carried by the other two men. 'Let them share this together, as they shared earlier.'

Without warning Sarah felt her lower jaw being gripped and dragged wide open and she had barely enough time to see what looked like a leather phallus being presented to her gaping lips, before it was forced deep into her mouth and a stout strap buckled at the nape of her neck, ensuring she could not eject it.

She fought against the gagging reflex, snorting air in through her flaring nostrils, her eyes widening as she saw that a second cock – in reality an extension of the one that filled her mouth – was jutting from her face on the end of a short metal tube that was perhaps six or seven inches in length. Where the bar joined the leather phallus the two ends of another strap hung down, their purpose unquestionable.

Adam and Robin took hold of the frame over which Kitty was stretched and began dragging it closer. At the same time, Prudence took hold of the projecting leather organ in one hand, using her other to prise Kitty's jaws apart, as she had just done with Sarah.

Wide-eyed, Kitty nonetheless made no real effort to resist and, at such close range that it was difficult to focus her gaze on her, Sarah was treated to the spectacle of her friend slowly swallowing the twin half of the foul-tasting member. When the leather strap to this was likewise buckled tight the two girls were held, heads pulled awkwardly erect, sucking noisily on opposite ends of the beastly gag.

'What a superb tableau, Grayling,' Soberton said, his voice hushed with complete awe. 'Would that I could have a painter record the scene.'

'Perhaps I could arrange that, milord,' Grayling chuckled. 'I do know a couple of aspiring brushmen who can be trusted to keep their own counsel as to what they might see here. The commission would not be cheap, however,' he added.

'Hang the money, Grayling!' Soberton exclaimed. 'Some things in this world transcend mere gold.'

'I agree, sir,' Grayling said, 'and you shall see many more of them before you leave here.'

When he had finished with her, Jacob Crawley added a thick leather blindfold to the outside of Matilda's hood, blocking out even the dim light in the cellar and plunging her into the most complete darkness she had ever known. With her hearing already dulled by the thick hide stretched over her ears, she now felt awfully isolated, cut off from the last vestiges of reality.

She could hear Crawley's laboured breathing and the sound of something heavy being dragged into the room, but then, after several minutes – which could almost have been hours – the chamber became completely silent yet again. With only the rasping sound of her own breath and the dull, thump-thump of her heartbeat echoing inside her skull, Matilda waited.

Her ordeal was far from over, she knew. Crawley had said nothing, but the vicious iciness in his eyes when she had simply stood motionless as he had her, told that he needed to be able to reduce her to a state of total surrender and that his failure yet to do so had kindled in him a burning hatred for her in particular.

As for women in general, Matilda thought, it was almost certain that this brutal animal had hated the female sex for a very long time. Behind the blindfold, she closed her eyes and fought back the tears that threatened to overwhelm her once again.

'Damn!' Matt Cornwell gasped, staggering to a halt and leaning against a tree at the side of the roadway. Toby Blaine stumbled up behind him, panting heavily and dropped to his haunches, wheezing noisily. From somewhere behind them they could hear the uneven and now faltering footsteps of Billy Dodds, who had been falling back almost since the trio first set off after the mounted women.

'S'no good!' Matt wheezed. 'No way we can keep up with 'em on foot.'

'No,' Toby agreed. 'I didn't think they were riding that fast, not at first. D'you reckon they heard us?'

Matt shook his head. 'Doubt it,' he said, turning to slide down with his back against the trunk. 'They'd not have heard our boots, not over the sounds of their horses' hooves. Besides, we was runnin' along the grass verges most of the time, wasn't we?'

'Too late now, anyhow,' Toby said. 'They're well ahead, though it ain't maybe quite so bad as it seems. Only one place they could be headed for now, unless they're intendin' to ride towards Winchester.'

'Well, there's a few more places between here and Winchester,' Matt pointed out, 'but I know what you're gettin' at. Grayling Hall is over this ways, ain't it?'

'Yeah, 'bout a mile and a half up the lane and then turn off,' Toby confirmed. 'Makes sense, I s'pose. If Ellen Grayling is involved they'd do worse than hide Miss Harriet's cousin somewhere on the Grayling Estate. It's big enough.'

'Ever bin in there?' Matt asked. His breathing was slowly returning to normal and he used one sleeve to wipe the cooling perspiration from his face.

'Only once,' Toby replied. His features clouded at the memory. 'Went lookin' fer rabbits, about a year back now. Took me dad's old crossbow so's not to make any noise to draw attention, like, but there was a couple of keepers, skulkin' in the woods like they was poachers themselves. Fired on me, they did,' he added indignantly. 'Maybe not aimin' exactly for me, but too fuckin' close for comfort an' they wasn't firing buckshot. One ball took a branch clear off only about that much above me head!' He held his hands about a foot apart to demonstrate the closeness of the unknown man's aim. 'Yeah, damned nearly shit meself, I did.'

'So, you don't fancy takin' a little look around the

Grayling place now, I s'pose?' Matt said, and Toby gave him a disdainful look.

'Not a chance,' he replied firmly. 'Besides, what's the point? Like I said, it goes on for bloody miles in all directions. We could walk around all night and find nothin' at all.'

As he finished speaking the shadowy figure of Billy came limping up, slumping down into the soft grass at the edge of the roadway and collapsing into an exhausted heap.

'So what now?' Matt demanded, ignoring the younger lad.

'Go back and tell Miss Harriet what we seen and what we think,' Toby said. 'Then she can tell whoever she needs to and maybe send for the soldiers.'

'To search Lord Grayling's place?' Matt all but shrieked. 'You got to be jokin', Toby Blaine! They wouldn't dare!'

Roderick Grayling, Sarah quickly realised, was not a man who liked to be hurried in anything he did, yet his outwardly languid demeanour hid a ruthlessly efficient nature and a meticulous attention to detail.

Having allowed Henry Soberton a few minutes in which to appreciate the aesthetic delight of the way in which he'd had his people position the two girls, he returned to the fireside, unstoppered one of the wine carafes that stood on the side table there and poured fresh glasses for himself and his guest. Soberton, clearly very excited at the scene before him, took his drink almost absently, reluctant to turn away from the sight of the two girls so blatantly displayed and presented.

'What next then, Grayling?' he asked impatiently. 'Do we tup the little beauties?'

Roderick laughed and lifted his glass to his lips, sipping with exaggerated appreciation. 'Certainly not, my dear fellow,' he said at length. 'Wouldn't do for a member of

163

one of the oldest families in the land to be dipping his wick in the posy of a rough flower. No, these little rosebuds need careful cultivation before they'll be ready for the likes of us.'

Hearing these words, Sarah heaved an inward sigh of relief. Almost anything, she told herself, was better than the prospect of being abused by the fat nobleman – even the whipping it was now obvious they were both going to receive. She closed her eyes for a few seconds, steeling her nerves and wishing it would be over, but Grayling was still unrushed.

'It amuses me,' he said, strolling back across to resume his position almost between the two spreadeagled girls, 'to watch a pretty pair like this being brought back to the boil with finesse – finesse and a little cut and thrust. The trick is,' he continued, pausing to sip his wine yet again, 'to try to bring both wenches to a climax at the same time.

'You see how they've been placed, so they cannot but gaze into each other's eyes? Of course, they can close their eyes as this one has now.' He tapped Sarah lightly on her left buttock with the tip of his crop; it was the lightest of blows, but Sarah nevertheless jumped, pulling instinctively against her bonds.

'However,' Grayling continued, running the end of the crop delicately up Sarah's spine, 'it is my experience that, after the first few lashes, they find themselves unable to continue like that. Perhaps they derive a little comfort from watching their friends suffering the same sweet agonies, I don't really know, but you will see that they will gaze intently at each other as the moment of their final surrender approaches.'

'I must say,' Soberton observed, waddling over to join his host, 'that their expressions are truly delightful. Those fat cocks in their mouths seem to do something for them, eh?'

'Indeed,' Grayling chuckled. 'A gag in a woman's mouth always produces such a sweet look of what could best be described as surprise. See how the eyes appear so large and so round.'

'Not half as large and round as this one's bubbies,' Soberton said crudely. He stood almost over Kitty, staring down at her with evident lust and, as she reopened her eyes, Sarah could not but notice the huge bulge in his tight breeches. 'Would you mind, sir?' Soberton stooped, his free hand indicating Kitty's right breast, which hung so invitingly below her.

'Be my guest, milord,' Grayling replied blandly. 'But don't titillate her too much just yet.' Greedily, Soberton bent further, his hand cupping the heavy breast and kneading it without any thought for its owner. Kitty groaned and writhed as far as her bondage allowed, the sudden motion of her head tugging Sarah's head with it, much as Sarah's earlier convulsive reaction had caused Kitty's head to mirror her own movements from side to side.

Sarah stared into Kitty's huge eyes, seeing her friend blink several times, her features etched with the strain of trying not to respond to Soberton's clammy touch, but although the gag had the effect of dulling her face's ability to display emotion, it was clear to Sarah that Kitty's large mounds tended to take over any natural reticence.

'I think that will do now, my friend,' Grayling warned quietly. 'We don't want to pre-empt anything now, do we?'

With obvious reluctance Soberton yielded his prize and stood back. 'So what now?' he demanded.

Grayling inclined his head slightly. 'We leave them awhile,' he said. 'Allow them a short time for contemplation and anticipation. Meantime, you mentioned earlier the possibilities of a painting, so I thought you might like to come and view my own private gallery. Come, there is much to see and these two little coquettes won't be going

165

anywhere in a hurry, will you my pretties?'

Laughing lightly, he delivered a dismissive swat to each pair of raised buttocks in turn and then, lifting his wine glass, quaffed its remaining contents in a single draught.

Matilda was left in her enforced isolation for what seemed to her to be yet another lifetime. Lack of proper sleep, combined with her continuing ordeal, had left her so exhausted that she actually slept, rather than dozed, hanging by her wrists and totally oblivious to the acute discomfort this caused.

How long she slept she had no idea, but she was eventually awakened by the sounds of voices and the scraping noises of something heavy being dragged across the floor. For several seconds she had to concentrate to make sure that she was actually awake again, for with the blindfold still securely in place her world remained as dark as pitch.

Confirmation was not long in coming. She gave a small gasp as rough hands cupped her breasts, hefting them indelicately and then she felt warm breath upon the top of her chest, as her latest assailant leaned in closer.

'Nice to see you're still with us, missy.' Immediately she recognised the voice as belonging to one of Crawley's henchmen; Silas she guessed, though it scarcely mattered, she conceded, as his hands continued to rove all over the body she was helpless to defend.

'What do you want?' she hissed, realising it was a superfluous question. She heard his harsh laugh, echoed by another, similar, though coming from slightly further away.

'Well, we thought as how you might like some company,' Silas leered, 'seein' as how this is almost certain to be your last night on earth, like.'

'My last night?' Crawley had made the threat clearly

166

enough, but even now Matilda found it difficult to believe he would carry it through. She heard the second man – presumably Jed – snicker to himself in what seemed the far distance, but it was Silas who continued speaking.

'Well, missy,' he breathed, 'unless your granny pays the tithe for your absolution, which she appears not willin' to do, then I'm afeared we'll have no choice, see? We'll have to hang you on the green, same as Master Crawley said.'

'Aye,' Jed joined in, moving closer, 'we've brought the wagon around to the green, with all the timber for the gibbet. Only takes a while to bolt it all together and then it's as strong as if it was built to stay there all the while.'

'But don't you worry too much, missy,' Silas said, ''cos this ain't no normal gibbet. You won't dance at the rope's end like most do, oh no. We drops you, see, and the rope snaps your neck.'

'Usually,' Jed added ominously. 'Depends if we get it right, with the rope length, I mean. If not, well, then you chokes to death, just like they normally does.'

'It's a bit difficult to be sure, like,' Silas continued. 'Not many people as knows just how the thing should be done properly. It's a technique they uses in some places in the east, apparently.'

'Yeah, they ain't all as barbarian as some people would have us believe,' Jed added. 'Master Crawley learned of the idea from some Arab, or Jew, or something like that. Not sure.'

'And you say this method kills a person straight off?' Matilda asked tremulously. She had seen hangings in London and the pictures of the miscreants writhing on the end of the ropes like stranded eels were still vivid in her mind, as were the strangled squeals and gasps that had accompanied their protracted demises.

'Humane, Master Crawley calls it,' Silas said. 'But then he's a man of God and he wouldn't want a body to suffer 'out of hand.'

'Is that why he flogged me?' Matilda snarled. 'Is that his idea of not making someone suffer?'

'But that's different,' Jed said calmly. 'That's to purge your sins. And he'll purge them again tomorrow afore we hangs you, but if you're lucky, at least you won't suffer on the gibbet. We just knocks out the board and wallop!'

'Snap!' Silas said.

Matilda shuddered. 'Why are you telling me all this?' she demanded, trying to steady her voice.

There was a short silence, before Silas spoke again. 'Well, we just thought of how you'd like to know as how we really only has your best interests at heart, like,' he said. 'Thought you might take some comfort from that and also be grateful for us coming here to comfort you now.' Matilda felt a hand on her breast again, but this time she did not start from it.

'I see,' she replied evenly. 'What you mean is, if I offer you a little comfort in return, then you'll see to it that my end is a quick one?'

'Well, them wouldn't quite be my words,' Silas said, and she could imagine that he was grinning widely.

'And what about the flogging Master Crawley intends to give me first?' she said. 'Am I to believe you'll dissuade him from that intention?'

'Hardly, missy,' Jed chuckled. 'Master Crawley don't get dissuaded from his course by no one—'

'But we do have a potion we could offer you,' Silas interrupted. 'A little something that will dull the pain greatly. It won't knock your senses cold, but I promise you, you'll scarce feel them lashes.'

'I see.' Matilda hesitated. 'And just what am I expected to do in return for such charity?' There was another short silence and then Silas began to speak again. In blunt words he explained in graphic detail, and Matilda felt her stomach lurch.

'No,' she whispered, when he had finished. 'No, I'll not debase myself such. Do whatever you wish, for God knows I cannot stop you, not like this, but as I told your master before, you'll find me cold fare.'

'Cold fare maybe,' Silas leered. 'But with a warm purse.' His hand suddenly grasped her sex, one finger forcing its way between her labia and Matilda groaned. 'Yes,' he repeated, 'a nice warm purse indeed.'

'It sounds most unlikely,' Harriet mused, 'but then why not? In some ways it all makes perfect sense.' She regarded the three boys across the kitchen table in Anne Billings's cottage. 'You're sure of who they were?'

Toby Blaine nodded. 'Yes, miss,' he replied sombrely. 'I'd swear to that on me mam's grave.'

'Better wait till she's dead first,' Anne interjected, pouring broth into the three mugs she had lined up on the hearth. The two women had waited in the cottage for the boys to return; George Billings, having returned from the spectacle on the green, had shown little interest when they tried to explain to him and left again immediately, heading for the *Black Drum*.

'The problem is,' Harriet continued, 'what to do now. The boys are right when they say that no magistrate would dare order a search of the Grayling estate. Besides, Roderick Grayling is a proxy magistrate while his father is abroad.'

'The nobs all look after each other, right enough,' Anne agreed. She began placing the bowls of hot broth on the table and the boys pounced upon them eagerly. 'I reckon the best course is to take what we know to Master Handiwell. He'll know what to do.'

'If he's yet returned,' Harriet pointed out. 'For all we know, he may have decided to stay in Portsmouth overnight.'

'That I doubt,' Anne said. 'From what you say he'll not

leave you alone with this for longer than he has to. Besides, you'll need his money to pay these scoundrels, won't you?'

'Aye, that I shall,' Harriet replied thoughtfully.

'And that, I think,' Anne continued, 'will be our best chance of catching them. Pay the ransom as agreed and set a trap for whoever comes for it.'

'It all sounds too easy,' Harriet said dubiously. 'Whoever they are, male or female, they'll know we've had an extra day to work out a plan. I can't see them being so foolish as to walk into any trap.'

'Well, they've got to collect the money somehow, haven't they?' Anne persisted.

'Of course,' Harriet conceded, 'but I've been wondering why they wanted me to go with the money in the boat. Why not just wait downstream for it, as they did today?'

'In case someone else sees it driftin' and hooks it into shore, miss,' Toby interrupted, lowering his bowl. 'I was thinkin' about that earlier, if you don't mind me sayin'.'

'No, not at all, Toby,' Harriet said, smiling at the lad. 'That's a good point, in fact.'

'Not only that, miss,' Toby continued, 'but I had another thought.'

'You have too many thoughts, if you ask me,' Anne chided, but the smile on her face was full of warmth.

'Well,' Toby continued, 'I was thinkin' about how I'd get the money, and without anyone catchin' me. I mean, yesterday they probably knew you'd not have time to do much, not with how little time you had to go to the boat, or even send me. That's why they weren't too careful, I reckon, though whoever was in that other boat kept their face well hid, like I said.'

'And anyway,' Anne mused, 'there's no crime in intercepting a drifting boat. No way anyone could make any accusations.'

'But tomorrow,' Toby said, 'they'll expect something – I

170

know I would, if it was me.'

'So how would you go about making sure you weren't caught, Toby?' Harriet asked encouragingly. 'You've clearly been giving the matter some thought, as you said.'

'Well, miss,' Toby proffered, his young features creasing into an expression of thoughtful concentration, 'I reckon, what I'd do is this. When you gets to Priest's Rock in the boat, you ain't gonna find anyone waitin' there for you. It'd be too easy to trap them there, see?' Harriet and Anne nodded in unison. 'So what I reckon,' Toby continued, 'is that, if it was me like, I'd leave you a message there, see?'

''Cept you can't write,' Matt pointed out, and Toby gave him a sideways look that said more than any words could have.

'*If* I was them then I'd be able to write, all right,' he said scathingly, 'so I'd leave you a message, nailed up somewhere so you couldn't miss it.'

'What sort of message?' Harriet prompted, though she thought she was beginning to understand where Toby was going. He really was, she thought, a very bright lad.

'It'd say somethin' like go to somewhere else,' Toby said. 'Probably you'd have to take the boat on down the river, maybe to where it goes through Kings Woods, 'cause it'd be hard to follow the river on foot through there. The trees are really close and the undergrowth is too tangled to get through. I know, 'cos I've been down there before.'

'And after that,' Harriet said, 'I suppose I'll be expected to go ashore and go to wherever they tell me on foot?'

'That's what I'd do, anyway,' Toby said, looking very pleased with himself.

'I'll bet you would, too, Toby Blaine,' Anne said, shaking her head. 'The Good Lord preserve us from the likes of you ever turning to crime!'

XII

Roderick Grayling continued his meticulous preparations only after he and Soberton had returned from viewing his dubious collection of art. Meantime, Sarah and Kitty were left in their enforced mutual silence, spread lewdly over their respective frames, unable to do anything but stare into each other's eyes and attempt to give some sort of communicative support by means of that eye contact.

Kitty, Sarah thought, seemed curiously calm about the entire situation, but then, with the previous experiences she had suffered, maybe this scenario held few terrors for her. Perhaps she too would come to accept such indignities and humiliations as commonplace: certainly, if she remained here for long, she knew it was more likely than she would ever have thought possible only a day earlier.

In one way, she had to admit, resignation made complete sense. After all, what use was there in trying to resist, what point in self-blame or deprecation? None of this was her fault, so why should she feel any shame, save that which was natural when a woman was forced to display herself in such wanton fashion?

Perhaps, she reasoned, the real root of the pangs of guilt that kept assailing her had nothing to do with any of that, but rather with the way she had so easily been brought to a point where she actually derived some pleasure out of her abasement. She was a virgin before being brought here and had no experience of sex as such, but her natural curiosity led her to some little self-experimentation, so that she was only too well aware of the magnitude of the orgasms her base treatment had triggered.

Did that mean, she demanded of herself as she sucked

upon the awful penis gag, that she was, in truth, the sort of slut and whore these people habitually addressed her as? Could every woman be so simply subjugated and controlled, not just controlled by means of chains and straps, but controlled on a deeper level? Or was it just her?

No, she thought, looking at Kitty, not just her. Maybe women *like* her, but then what were women like her, exactly? Could she really be held responsible for the reflex actions of her body? Should she have the spirit, the determination, the strength of will and character to resist these primal urges?

Whether Prudence knew what sort of thoughts were going through her mind or not, the older woman soon gave Sarah further cause to doubt herself, for having at first left the room in the wake of the two noblemen, she now returned and, seeing that Adam and Robin had similarly departed, wasted no time in availing herself of the opportunity.

She moved behind Sarah, one hand reaching out to trace a delicate line down the length of her spine. Sarah shivered and her back arched as far as her stringent bondage would permit. Prudence chuckled, a throaty, animal-like sound.

'You see?' she whispered. 'You cannot help yourself, can you?' Fingers moved again, this time cupping Sarah's naked vulva, though gently, supportively, pressing hardly at all. Sarah made a small mewling noise and closed her eyes, unwilling to look at Kitty.

'Such a sweet little puss,' Prudence crooned. 'And such a shame it should be stuffed with tasteless man-meat, mm? Such delicacies should be tongue-savoured, not gorged like pigs.' One slender finger prised Sarah's nether lips apart and slipped inside a tunnel that was very moist and warm.

'Open your eyes, little miss,' Prudence said softly. 'Don't hide your shame so. Look at your friend – she has no false modesty, do you Kitty? She yearns for Prudence to play with her pouch. Well, fear not my little sweetmeats,' she sighed, withdrawing her hand, 'I'll take care of you both later, when these oafish men have had their fun. With luck there'll be no cock for either of you this night, for his lordliness won't stoop to poke a slave wench. Oh, he'll bury his pole in your mouth maybe, but he'll not sully himself on seeding the lower classes, just in case some undetected offspring of his ends up in a slave colony on the far side of the world.

'No, unless he decides to keep you, you'll not taste that particular rod between your legs and dear Roderick's rod could *never* be sullied in your alternative hole, though there are many here abouts who are not half as choosy. No, my guess is that you'll have a far more tender night, though tender will these lovely moons be, too.'

Sarah quivered as cool hands moulded her upthrust buttocks. Strangely, she found this touch even more intimate than the earlier one, for Prudence's fingers lingered long, stroking, massaging and etching light lines with the edges of their nails.

'Ah,' Prudence declared suddenly, breaking the contact, 'I think I hear footsteps returning.' She stepped back. 'Now, let's see how right I am, mm?'

A moment later the door swung open and Roderick Grayling strode in, with Henry Soberton, redder still in the face than even before, hard on his shoulder. Seeing Prudence, Grayling's features twisted into a devious smile.

'Preparing the dishes for serving, Prudence?' he chuckled. Soberton, who was beginning to look far the worse for drink, stared from his host to Prudence with a total lack of comprehension. Grayling's laugh became harsher.

'Ha!' he exclaimed. 'No matter, dear Prudence. You shall have the two little lambs for your supper when I am done with them here. You see, milord,' he continued, turning to address his guest, 'we have found that there is a great market for a certain type of wench and these two here, though

174

they'll ride a cock as well as any, I'd wager, show inclinations towards being that particular type of slave of which I speak.'

'Ha, sir, you speak in riddles, methinks!' Soberton exclaimed, trying very hard to focus his eyes. 'A maid'll either ride a cock well, or else she's an old maid, surely?'

'Yes... and no,' Grayling smiled. 'Both these have had a good poking or two since they got here and both ended up squawking like stuck chickens, I'm told, but earlier you saw a different side to both, did you not? Well sir, 'tis not only we fellows who would give well for a pretty bird and a good fuck, eh Prudence?'

Prudence said nothing, but the inference remained lost on the drunken aristocrat. Grayling opened his mouth as if he were about to elucidate, hesitated, appeared to realise that further words would be a waste of time, and then shut it again. Instead, he turned away to where his two African girls waited in their corner and clapped his hands.

Immediately the diminutive creatures sprang up, their unfettered breasts jiggling freely as they ran a cross the room to flank their master, sheer adoration shining from their huge eyes. They seemed to know exactly what was expected for them, for having paused long enough just for Grayling to tweak a nipple each, they suddenly dropped to their knees and slid beneath the two bound white girls, squatting on their haunches, facing the feet of their respective woman, their upturned faces mere inches away from the two bared sexes.

'The kiss of the whip is one thing,' Grayling purred, 'the kiss of the tongue is another. Put the two together and we create a thing of pure beauty.'

'I don't follow, man!' Soberton exclaimed. 'Just what are you getting at?'

'Well, my lord,' Grayling said, 'prepare yourself for a new education. My two little Nubian beauties here have

175

tongues the like of which no white woman has ever been possessed. Why, I suspect they may even be descended from the serpent in the Garden of Eden itself.' He clapped his hands again and made a flickering movement with his tongue.

Immediately the two black girls stuck out their own tongues and Soberton gave a cry of astonishment, for both girls easily curled their tongues in great loops, so that their tips touched not just the tips of their noses, but the very bridges themselves.

'Good God, sir!' Soberton exclaimed again. 'But they are a pair of little serpents and no mistaking!'

It was a good analogy, as Sarah and Kitty quickly found out. Another signal from Grayling and the crouching girls went to work. Sarah gasped, her startled moans forcing their way past her gag as the warm appendage pushed its way inside her, parting her labial lips easily and penetrating almost as far as Ross's member had earlier.

Almost immediately her girl's fulsome lips seemed to clamp about Sarah's swollen clitoris, sucking it out to an unbelievably distended length and sending fiery currents of desire swirling throughout her every nerve ending. She was dimly aware of Kitty's eyes growing even larger above her gagged mouth and realised that the other girl's tongue was having just the same effect upon her.

'Excellent,' Grayling said with quiet satisfaction. 'You see, milord, how they can work a cunny, eh? Every bit as good as they are at sucking a man's cock, I can tell you.' He laughed and continued to pace up and down, stooping every so often to study the girls' progress.

'See here, milord,' he invited, bending down to examine between Sarah's splayed thighs. 'Have you ever seen a nubbin stretch to such length? Hold Topsy, loose your devilish little grip for a moment.' He clicked his fingers and Sarah felt her clitoris sliding from between the soft

176

lips. At the same time, Soberton moved around to see for himself.

'By Jove!' he wheezed. 'Damn you, Grayling, name me a price for *her*, at least. You'll still have the one with the big titties, for heaven's sake!'

Hannah Pennywise halted less than a hundred yards on from the clearing where she had left Jane Handiwell. A fallen tree, long dead and rotted and victim of the previous winter's storms, lay half across what there was of the track she'd been following and she eased down onto it, sighing heavily.

'Well, little Miss Janey,' she said, voicing her thoughts out loud, 'a lot of use you intends to be, unless I'm mistaken, which I knows I ain't.' Her eyes narrowed and her wrinkled forehead furrowed even deeper in concentration.

'I reckons you've got more to hide than just your tomfoolery efforts at witchin',' she mused. 'But one thing's for certain, you ain't got nothing to do with Wickstanner's wicked doin's and you don't know what's happened to the lad, neither.'

Pausing and straightening somewhat, Hannah lifted her head, sniffing the breeze. She remained thus for two or three minutes, her eyes half closed, yet not blinking, her breathing barely noticeable. At last, she relaxed again.

'Ah,' she whispered, 'so that's it, is it? Well, you're closer than I thought, my lad, and at least you're more than just alive. And what's this?' She stiffened again, her head inclining to one side, a cunning smile spreading across her weathered features.

'Well, well,' she hissed, her knuckles whitening as she gripped her cane even more tightly. 'So comes the keeper, eh? And fresh with the smell of his devilish excesses, too. Well, we'll soon see about this, won't we?'

With a stifled grunt, Hannah pulled herself back to her feet and then, with one curious glance back towards where the clearing was now hidden by trees and bushes, she manoeuvred around the rotting tree and began to move even deeper into the woods.

The two women and the three lads walked together along the lane towards the crossroads and the *Black Drum*. Late though the hour now was, they knew the small taproom at the rear of the inn would still be open, for although most of the travellers who were staying overnight would like as not have taken to their beds by now, there were always a few local men happy to drink on into the night and ever the chance that there would still be others on the road, seeking shelter and refreshment for a few hours.

Sure enough, as Harriet pushed open the door a dozen pairs of eyes – male, apart from Lizzie Eldridge, who was performing her usual late serving duties – turned towards her. Ignoring the men, Harriet made for Lizzie, only to be told that Master Handiwell had not yet returned from the coast. Harriet thought for a few moments, considering the possible courses of action that remained open to them. They were not many.

'Mistress Jane,' she said eventually, 'is she at home?'

Lizzie looked blank. 'I'm blessed if I know, Miss Harriet,' she said. 'We don't hardly see her down here. I can pop up and see if Beth, her maid, is awake, though it's quite late, you know.'

'Yes, I do know,' Harriet said apologetically, 'and I should not be here at this hour, were it not a matter of great importance.'

Leaving Anne to deal with any more orders for ale, Lizzie disappeared through a curtained doorway. Anne drew closer to Harriet and whispered in her ear.

'Why ask for Jane?' she asked urgently. 'You surely can't expect her to be of much use? She's a queer one, and no mistaking.'

'Maybe so,' Harriet replied, 'but I've been thinking since we left your cottage and something has been eating away at me. Jane Handiwell has no time for me anyway, but I just have a feeling that something here is sitting all wrong.'

A few minutes later Lizzie reappeared, shaking her head.

'Beth reckons Miss Jane is fast asleep and has been these past two or three hours,' she informed them. 'Reckons it's more than her job's worth to wake her, whatever the reason.'

'I see,' Harriet replied thoughtfully. 'Well, I thank you, Lizzie.'

'Would you like to wait for the master?' Lizzie suggested. 'The little parlour is empty and I could fetch you something, maybe some wine?'

'No, thank you all the same,' Harriet replied, smiling. 'Perhaps we shall return in a while, but for the moment I think I need some air and a little exercise. The thought of just sitting in the one place would drive me to my wits' end.'

The three boys were waiting for them outside, Toby not wanting to risk entering the taproom in case his father Ned, an habitual late night drinker, should be inside. He greeted the news that Ned had not been present with some surprise and not a small amount of sarcasm.

'Probably started early and gone off to sleep it off,' he muttered. 'There's a few comfortable ditches hereabouts.'

'You hold your tongue, Toby Blaine!' Anne snapped. 'Show a bit of respect for once.' She turned to Harriet. 'So, what next?' she asked.

Harriet pursed her lips thoughtfully. 'Toby,' she said, 'you were saying earlier about Lady Ellen's two horses?'

'S'right,' he agreed. 'Know 'em both well. Both fine beasts.'

'What about Miss Jane's horse? Does she always ride the same one?'

'Mostly,' he said. 'That big bugger, Marquis. Black as

179

the night, he is.'

'You know him well, then?'

'Pretty much, miss, yes. We all sees her out riding. She's often over towards the downs.'

'On her own?'

'Um, mostly, yeah,' Toby said.

'Seen her riding with Kate Dawson a couple of times,' Matt Cornwell offered.

'And with Lady Jane,' Billy Dodds added, 'though only the once, I think.'

Anne looked closely at Harriet's face, but Harriet's expression remained impassive.

'You ain't thinkin' what I think you're thinkin', are you?' she asked quietly. Harriet let out a long, low breath.

'I'm not sure what I'm thinking,' she replied. 'Too many unexplained things, too many possible coincidences. However,' she continued, looking meaningfully towards the boys again, 'there's one thing we can check out for certain.

'Toby, I want you to go around to the stables, if you please. Tell whoever is on duty in there that I wish to discuss the possibility of hiring a mount until the morning. Tell him I am waiting here, under the light. Then, when he comes around to see me, I want you to sneak inside and see if you can see this Marquis.'

'No need for that, Miss Harriet,' Anne interrupted before Toby could move. 'Master keeps his three mounts and a couple more, including Marquis, in the smaller stables, over there, under them trees by the paddock, see?' She pointed towards a low, darkened building about fifty yards from the main stable block.

'It'll be locked for the night, then, surely?' Harriet said.

'Surely it will,' Anne said, 'but I knows where they keeps the key. Give me a couple of pennies to slip Lizzie and I'll go fetch it for you.'

Sarah felt as though she were in the midst of a dream, drifting weightlessly on clouds of lust and desire, the long tongue thrusting in and out of her taking on a life of its own, coaxing from her some inner self that she would never have believed existed. Oblivious to everything but the warm, wet little invader and to the eager and nimble little fingers that now teased her nipples, she sucked languidly on the penis gag, groaning and writhing gently in her bonds.

The stinging cut of Roderick Grayling's crop, as it hissed across her raised buttocks, brought her screeching out of her reverie, bucking in agony, her teeth clamping on the leather that held them apart, Kitty's head writhing in time with her own. A second later she heard the sharp crack of leather on flesh again, but this time it was Kitty who howled and jerked.

All the while the two black slave girls remained at their tasks, tongues lapping and probing, lips massaging and sucking.

'Pain and pleasure,' Sarah heard Grayling say. 'Such bittersweet harmony, I always think. See, Soberton, how even the kiss of my lash does little to dull their desires. In fact, you will see that, if anything, a well-placed stripe or three will actually serve to heighten them. See here!'

He moved back behind Sarah as he spoke and again the braided crop fizzed through the air. The report seemed to echo inside Sarah's very head, yet, though her anguished cry was scarcely stifled by her gag, the fire in her ravaged nether cheeks seemed merely to merge with the furnaces already burning within her.

As the crop descended upon Kitty for a second time Sarah let out a long wail, her back arching and stiffening like a board, her stomach tightening like a bow-string and then releasing, as an orgasm of the greatest proportions drove everything else from her consciousness. She was not even aware that in front of her, joined to her by their communal gag, Kitty too had finally surrendered to her body's demands.

And neither girl, each as helpless to resist as the other, either heard, or cared, as Roderick Grayling chuckled evilly to himself and Henry Soberton, his hands pressed tightly to his crotch, ejaculated madly inside his fine silk breeches.

'Would anyone else ride Marquis?' Harriet asked Anne, after the boys had returned from the paddock stable with the news that Jane's big black stallion was not in any of the stalls there. 'How about her father? Might he have taken the horse to go to Portsmouth?'

'He's got his own two favourites,' Toby replied, not waiting for Anne to respond. 'There's Lightning, the one with the funny looking blaze and then there's Quicksilver, the grey. Lightning's not in there either, in case you was going to ask.' He grinned impishly and Harriet could not help but smile back at him.

'I think I chose well when I recruited your help, eh Toby?' she chuckled. 'So,' she continued, looking up into the moonless sky, 'we can assume that Thomas has not ridden to Portsmouth on Marquis.' She pondered silently for several more seconds.

'Which begs the question,' she continued eventually, 'as to where the beast might be. And I can think of only one logical answer.'

'Me too,' Toby said smugly. 'She's gone out a-ridin' somewhere and don't want anyone to know. That Beth would say anything she was told to say. She dotes on Miss Jane like a soft puppy dog.'

'Well,' Anne said cautiously, 'maybe we'd best not go too far down that road, but Toby's right: Beth would do anything for her mistress.'

'So, we have two of our three ladies definitely out and about this night,' Harriet said, 'and possibly a third one.

182

Ellen Grayling we don't know about, but we can assume that she's somewhere in the vicinity of Grayling Hall, which was the direction these lads last saw Mary Watling and Kate Dawson riding.'

'You think Jane Handiwell is mixed up with them three, then?' Anne asked, doubt in her tone but eagerness in her eyes.

'I don't know,' Harriet admitted. 'None of us does. As I said earlier, there are just coincidences, nothing more, and nothing less. But I do know one thing for certain, I most certainly cannot suggest such to Master Handiwell, if and when he returns.'

James Calthorpe came out of his fitful sleep with a start, the hairs on the back of his neck bristling. Laying motionless in the dark, he listened keenly, certain that it had been some unexpected noise that had awakened him. He did not have long to wait.

From beyond the door of the hut he heard two sharp snapping sounds, as unwary boots fell upon dry twigs and then, muffled, but nonetheless recognisable, the sound of an oath and a low groan. After a few further seconds of silence another twig snapped, and then came the sound of heavy boots on the dead and dried leaves that carpeted so much of the forest floor this late in the season.

Slowly, James levered himself up into a sitting position, tensing himself, though he was only too well aware that his fettered ankles made any effective attempt at confrontation most unlikely. Halfway to rising to his feet he hesitated, considered his situation, and sat down again.

A moment later the door swung open, revealing a rectangular patch that was only marginally less black than the rest of the interior walls and a barely distinguishable silhouette that quickly filled it.

'Who are you? Speak man!' His voice sounded too high,

183

even to his own ears, but James was determined to voice his indignation. His only immediate reply, however, was another muttered curse, followed by a succession of sparks as the newcomer, whoever or whatever he was, struggled with a tinderbox. Finally the wick spluttered into flame, the flame was brought towards the lamp the man had brought with him and then, at last, the hut was bathed in light again.

Staring up, James studied the fellow and was not heartened by what he saw. The man was perhaps in his late thirties, or early forties, with weathered face, large rough hands, and powerful shoulders. His clothing was serviceable and of reasonable quality, but his shirt looked grimy and his fingernails, as he reached out to place the lantern alongside the now near empty water flagon, were encrusted with dirt.

'Who are you?' James demanded at last, his voice now nearer its normal pitch. 'I demand to know and I also demand to know why I have been kept prisoner here?' The fellow straightened up, placed his hands on his hips and grinned, revealing teeth that were uneven and badly blackened.

'Don't matter who I am,' he said. His accent reminded James of London, and his attitude was all too reminiscent of the villainous underclass that frequented the taverns around the docks. Up close it was easy to see – on the road, James realised now that he had not been so astute, for he was certain that this fellow had been one of the two riders who assaulted him. 'What matters, mister,' the man growled, 'is that I've brought you food and water, so mind your manners or I'll tip the lot outside and the foxes can have it, see?'

'Then at least tell me,' James persisted, though in a tone he hoped sounded more reasonable, for the importance of fresh water was not lost on him, 'why I am being held against my wishes.'

'Because his nibs says to, that's why,' the man replied carelessly. 'And that's all I'm going to say, so you just rest easy, right. You'll be set free again soon enough, so long as you don't give no trouble.' He turned, stepped outside the hut, reaching for something, and a moment later ducked inside again, clutching a small sack.

'See here,' he laughed, reaching inside the bag, 'I even brought you some meat tonight. Fresh cooked at that inn and very nice it is, too.' He set down a hunk of pork and followed this with half a loaf. The final item was another pewter flagon, the twin of the one in which James had discovered the water earlier.

'There was a lump of cake, too,' the man said, grinning, 'but my mate wolfed that, gutty pig that he is. Still, we could have just let you starve. If it had been up to me I wouldn't have bothered. It's a fucking dangerous ride through these woods at this time of night, I can tell you.'

Ignoring the original flagon and bowl he folded the sack and turned towards the door, from where he looked back, still with his foul-toothed grin.

'I'll even leave you the lamp, see?' he said. 'No use to me out there, 'cos his nibs said not to show a light, but it'll be all right in here. Mind you,' he added, 'I'd turn the wick down some, if I was you. There ain't much oil in the bugger.'

'When will you be back?' James asked hurriedly.

The man paused and shrugged. 'Depends,' he said. 'Tomorrow night. Maybe earlier. Way I hear it, it all comes down to whether the old baggage pays the tithe. If not, we hangs the wench at midday and that's an end to it.'

'What old baggage?' James demanded, more alarmed than ever now. 'And what wench are you to hang?'

The fellow shrugged again. 'Does it matter? You ain't in no place to do anything about it, which was the general idea, of course.'

185

'It's Matilda!' James gasped, the sudden realisation hitting him like a rock in his stomach. 'You're talking about Matilda! Ye gods, what have you done to her?' The fellow started to laugh and then, to James's surprise, his features took on a quizzical look, the rough laughter turned into a sort of choking sob and then, as blood began to spray from his mouth, he pitched forward face first into the straw at James's feet, knocking the makeshift table and its precious contents flying and only just missing the spluttering lamp.

'More a case of what the bastids haven't done to the poor child.'

James looked up again in sheer confusion, but there was no mistaking that voice, a voice he had heard many a time throughout his young and formative years.

Hannah Pennywise stood framed in the doorway, her cane gripped now in her left hand, in her right a long, thin and very sharp looking knife and, as James continued to gawp, slack-jawed, she carefully began to wipe its blade in the folds of her skirt, removing from it the last traces of blood – the same blood that even now was beginning to seep out from beneath the lifeless body which lay between them.

Thomas Handiwell sat and listened very carefully as Harriet related what the boys had discovered, though she carefully avoided mentioning his daughter Jane, or the fact that she might, in any way, be involved in Sarah's abduction. When Harriet had finally finished the innkeeper sat back, gnawing lightly on his knuckle, considering the implications.

'It's a delicate situation, Miss Merridew,' he said at last. It was curious, Harriet thought, how he still refrained from using her Christian name, even though he had several times hinted heavily at the possibilities of a marriage between them. 'Young Ellen Grayling is an odd one, of that there's no doubt,' he continued, 'and I'd definitely not discount the chances of her being in some way involved in this. The

186

Graylings have ridden roughshod over people in these parts for as long as I can remember and even before that, but then that's so-called noble blood for you.

'On the other hand,' he said, 'we have nothing beyond the observations of a village lad and nothing to connect Lady Ellen with the other two wenches.' He sat back, stifling a yawn, his features looking pale and drawn, a clear indication of fatigue, for it had been well past two in the morning when he finally returned.

'I suppose Captain Hart could arrest the other two and see what they have to say for themselves,' Thomas suggested at length. 'We do, after all, have three witnesses that can place them at the scene where the boat was left, but that is no more than circumstantial and I'd wager the wench who returned that boat has some sort of story ready, in case she was seen.'

'Whatever we do, Master Handiwell,' Harriet said carefully, 'we must act quickly. I am supposed to take the ransom money, and the boat, and there are only a few hours before I must leave. I presume your offer is still open?'

'Yes, of course.' Thomas nodded. 'I have the money here, so there is no problem. However, I do not like the idea of you taking it alone. Ned's boy is quite right in his reasoning. They will not be at the original rendezvous this time and anything could happen to you.'

'I don't see that I have any choice in the matter,' Harriet replied. She shook her head slightly, blinking eyes that were becoming heavy and sore from her own lack of sleep. 'I have to deliver the money. Also,' she added, 'I have to return and make sure my father is all right. Besides, there are cows to be milked at first light.'

'Forget the cows,' Thomas said. 'Young Matthew and Billy can take care of the milking. We'll maybe have use of Toby, however. A sharp lad, that one, and no mistaking.'

'He is certainly intelligent,' Harriet agreed, 'and he knows the woods well.'

'Aye, he probably knows more than is good for a lad of his tender years, too,' Thomas said. He paused, considering again. At last he rose stiffly, stretching his leg muscles with some care.

'I think,' he said, nodding, 'that I have an idea. Let's have young Toby in here and see what he thinks, eh?'

- XIII -

Simon Wickstanner stood quietly in the cellar doorway, studying the figure sprawled against the far wall. Her face and head still tightly enclosed in the leather hood, Matilda lay, legs splayed, her feet still encased in the ugly, heavy penance boots, arms once more cuffed to either side of the broad leather belt, oblivious now to her surroundings or sufferings.

Crawley's two henchmen had used her for several hours, Wickstanner knew, for he had ventured down on several occasions during the night, mostly listening to the sounds of their abuse from the security of the darkened passage and eventually, when he could control himself no longer, pushing open the door to the chamber and watching through the crack.

Eventually the two men had tired, and the minister retreated further down into the vaults, waiting for them to leave, and then returned again, but Matilda was by then exhausted and even the sound of his voice failed to stir her.

That had been two hours or more ago and still the wretched girl showed no sign of regaining consciousness. Wickstanner moved closer, raising the lantern he carried and stood, unmoving, his eyes roving over the display of naked female flesh, his tongue running lightly back and forth over his dry lips, beads of cold perspiration forming on his forehead.

Matters had not progressed the way he originally envisaged, and he was uneasy. He had been sure that the old woman, Matilda's grandmother, would pay up a sizeable sum for her granddaughter's release and absolution and that, in addition, he would have been able to set a further penance that would have placed Matilda in his power for at least a year.

Twelve months, in which the memory of her ordeal at the hands of the witchfinder would have been fresh in her mind, and Wickstanner had been confident that she would have come to view his petitions in a different light, probably turning to him as both confessor and confidante.

What he had not anticipated was the debauched approach Jacob Crawley and his minions had taken with the girl. Scourging with the lash was quite acceptable – it had been for centuries – and even the treatment of stripping her, shaving her hair and parading her naked before the village, but what had been happening here, in the vaults beneath the church itself, went far beyond what Wickstanner considered acceptable.

Then why, the voice of his conscience pricked him, had he not done something to stop them earlier? Why had he simply stood back, listening and eventually even watching, his entire body shaking uncontrollably? And why had he found himself imagining that it was he, Simon Wickstanner, who was thrusting himself in and out of the helpless girl's sex?

He groaned, aloud this time and bit his lip, drawing blood, which mingled with the sweat now running down into the corners of his mouth. The time was long past for him to turn back. If he was not damned in the eyes of his Church, Wickstanner knew he most definitely was damned in the eyes of his God.

Shivering, his stomach aching, he turned away, stumbled towards the door again and there, as he lurched into the passageway beyond, he was violently, noisily sick.

Jane Handiwell sat staring into the crackling flames for a long while after Hannah Pennywise had gone on her way again, her thoughts wandering as the sparks floated up from the slowly burning wood and the smoke drifted in small coils on the night breeze.

At last, as if breaking out of a trance, she snapped upright, her eyes darting around the perimeter of darkened woodland and then travelling upwards, to where myriad stars twinkled in the moonless sky. Pursing her lips she shook her head and smiled grimly.

Let the old woman attend to her own problems, she thought. After all, her granddaughter, Matilda, was nothing to her, just another young woman she would sometimes see walking through the village or out along the country lanes. Why, Jane thought indignantly, they'd never even exchanged more than a couple of polite words in passing, so why should she put herself out now?

Of course it was ridiculous, what was happening back there in the village, but someone would be bound to stop things before they got too far out of hand, probably her own father once he returned from the coast. Matilda Pennywise a witch? The idea was laughable and Jane snickered to herself at the thought.

Now, if Wickstanner and this Crawley fellow had accused Hannah herself, well then, Jane smiled, that would have been an entirely different proposition, though to actually describe the old harridan as a witch? Well, she did have some curious powers, that much Jane knew at first hand, but then Jane herself was capable of picking up emotions, feelings, signals and also quite expert now at using her own powers in order to persuade certain, more susceptible people, to do what she wanted them to do.

Hannah Pennywise, for all that air of mystery with which she liked to surround herself, was probably not any different from herself, Jane thought. Certainly, when Jane had first begun to experience the unsettling feelings, to feel the auras that surrounded some people, Hannah had been quick to notice that there was something wrong with the then gawky teenage girl and she had, true, taken her aside and tried to explain, but that did not give her the right to demand things of her now, surely?

Except, Jane mused, she had the uncomfortable feeling that the old woman knew a bit more about her than she was letting on. No. Jane shook herself mentally. No, that was ridiculous, there was no way Hannah could know anything about what she and her friends were doing, save that they met out here in the woods each month and…

Well, if people wanted to think of that as some kind of witchcraft, then let them. In truth, they were nothing more than simple rites that came from centuries in the past and meant nothing whatsoever. Jane and Ellen Grayling had only started it in the first place as a dare, when Ellen, then only fifteen and seemingly as innocent and naïve as a puppy, had looked up to the older girl with whom she romped in the woods.

Then, one night, when they had both sneaked out to rendezvous in the darkness, giggling, nervous and rapidly becoming drunk on the bottle of rum Jane had liberated from her father's cellar, Kate Dawson stumbled across them, and the twosome became a trio after that. Quite why Kate had been out here, in woods that were part of the fringes of the Grayling estates, they never did discover, but it mattered not, for she quickly proved herself a loyal and trustworthy friend.

It had been Kate who introduced them to Mary Watling, the near giant of a girl who could wield axe or pitchfork to match almost any man and whose stature had first given Jane the idea that the four of them might dress up and pass as men in order to rob the coaches on the London to Portsmouth road.

Not that either Jane or Ellen needed the money that their nefarious enterprise brought them; indeed, rather they did what they did for the pure excitement, for the feeling of power it gave and for the sheer joy of being able to thumb their noses at so-called masculine controlled authority. It was also the same, though to a lesser extent, for Kate and Mary, though in their respective cases an extra few guineas every now and then did not come amiss.

No, Hannah couldn't know anything about that side of their lives, or she would surely have said something by now, Jane was certain. She laughed, this time out loud.

'So, why should I help you, Mother Pennywise?' she cried, her voice echoing back from the circle of trees. 'Think you can scare me, the way you manage to scare most of the other poor fools? You want to find your precious granddaughter's beau, then you go right ahead. Don't expect—'

She stopped suddenly, her brow furrowing deeply.

'Except...' she breathed, her eyes gleaming brightly. Except, she thought, that maybe there was a way in which she and her friends could help the old baggage save her granddaughter and, at the same time, deal with Jane's other little problem. Of course, the fact that it would also discredit that bumbling fool Wickstanner and that awful creature Jacob Crawley at the same time, that was indeed a bonus!

'Indeed a bonus,' she repeated, in a harsh whisper. She looked up at the night sky again, trying to calculate the probable hour and how much time remained before daybreak. The timing would be tight – very tight – but then maybe it would be possible to persuade Crawley to delay his planned noon deadline. A guinea, maybe two?

If he could be made to think that the money had come from Hannah herself, as a gesture of good faith, and that the rest of his demanded tithe might yet be forthcoming, Jane felt confident he would agree. Slowly she rose to her feet, dusted the seat of her breeches and turned to walk back to where she had left Marquis.

By the time Sarah recovered her senses sufficiently to take stock of her surroundings again, she found herself laying on a massive, canopied bed, alone and in a room that was different and far larger than the one in which Prudence and Justine had dressed her and Kitty earlier.

Sitting up, Sarah examined herself morosely. She still wore the corset, stockings, boots and gloves, and the stiff lined collar was also still about her neck, but her hair, which had been so meticulously prepared earlier, now hung about her shoulders in a tangled mess, damp with her sweat and cold on her naked shoulders.

Tentatively she swung her legs over the side of the bed, lowering her feet to the thick rug and stood up, swaying slightly at first as blood rushed to her head, so that she was forced to reach out for the nearest upright bedpost for support. Closing her eyes, Sarah tried to breathe in and out as deeply as the strictures of her corset would permit, and slowly the dizziness passed.

She opened her eyes again and looked about, studying her latest surroundings. It was, as she had first noted, a very large bedroom, the walls draped as elegantly and fussily as the earlier bedroom, dark rosewood furniture, including two chests and a long dressing table upon which stood an ornate gilt framed mirror.

Slowly, wobbling on the unaccustomed heels, Sarah swayed across and leaned forward, studying her reflection and wincing as she saw the picture she now presented. The earlier powders and paints, so skilfully applied at the time, were now a sad wreckage, black smudges beneath both eyes merging with the white foundation to form various grey rivulets that had, mercifully, dried.

Sarah groaned, not so much at her appearance, but at how that ravaged countenance reminded her of what had happened to produce that effect and more so because of the memory of how she responded to her mistreatment. She closed her eyes again, unwilling to face the travesty of what she now imagined she had become, and turned away, feeling blindly back towards the bed.

'I see you are back in the land of the living?' The new voice, female, aristocratic, youthful and also mocking, brought Sarah up short. Her eyes flew open again and she stopped short, staring at the newcomer in a mixture of guilt and shame. The girl, seeing this reaction, smiled crookedly and stepped further into the room, closing the door behind her.

She was, Sarah realised, even younger than herself, slightly smaller in build though scarcely less tall, once the height of Sarah's heels was discounted. Her long, strawberry blonde hair was tied back into a loose ponytail, revealing a face that was lightly freckled, pretty and surprisingly innocent looking, with wide, unblinking green eyes.

Her mode of dress was curious for a female; tight male riding breeches, a pale blue silk shirt, unbuttoned to display the beginning of her modest cleavage, and soft black kid leather, wrist length gloves. Over her left arm she carried a black velvet jacket and Sarah realised, suddenly, that she was actually wearing an outfit designed for riding, though she had discarded her boots somewhere and her feet were bare.

'Who are you?' Sarah said, eventually finding her voice when it became clear that the girl was in no hurry to break the silence that had descended between them. The girl smiled again, crossed to stand on the opposite side of the bed from Sarah, and carelessly tossed the jacket onto it between them.

'My name,' she said easily, 'is Ellen Grayling, and this house belongs to my father, Lord Grayling, though the way my dear brother acts you would think it were he that owned it.'

'That terrible man is your brother?' Sarah gasped. 'But I

thought he was Lord Grayling!'

'No, my papa may be getting on in years and totally disparate, but he is not yet dead, at least not to my current knowledge,' Ellen Grayling said. 'However, the servants all address darling Roderick as if he were already the viscount and he does nothing to discourage them, but then such is the vanity of men.' She sniffed disdainfully and then the smile returned once again.

'You are Sarah Merridew, I suppose?' she said. Sarah nodded, but said nothing. 'You look a little different from when I last saw you, but then it was dark then and you were attired, shall we say, a little more modestly. I must say, however, that you really do have a perfectly splendid body, though your make-up does leave a little to be desired right now.' She giggled and Sarah felt herself blushing.

'Oh, don't be such a silly and modest little goose,' Ellen said scornfully. She began walking around the end of the bed. 'I know exactly what goes on here whenever Roddy brings a couple of slaves up to the house. Those two little heathen serpent bitches of his can't wait to get their snake tongues into fresh fanny!'

She stood only a foot or two away from Sarah and was once again looking her up and down appraisingly, a superior yet softening expression on her youthful features.

'I'll say one thing for my brother and dear prudence,' she said at length, 'they do know how to present woman flesh to its most appealing advantage.'

'I find little appealing in my current state of dishabille,' Sarah returned softly. 'And I doubt whether you would, either, if the boot were on the other foot.'

Ellen gave a little sigh and reached out a tentative hand. Sarah's immediate instinct was to recoil from her touch, but at the last moment she held her ground. The soft gloved fingers stroked her left breast gently, a feathery, butterfly wing caress. 'Not as big as your little friend's,' Ellen whispered, 'but then I never have had a taste for overly big boobies.' With her other hand she flicked open two more buttons on her shirt, pulling the front apart to reveal her own unfettered breasts, smaller than Sarah's by some way, but with firmly pointed nipples.

'Small titties are so pretty, don't you think?' she whispered, staring straight into Sarah's startled eyes. 'Wouldn't you just love to take my teats into your pretty mouth and suck on them?' Suddenly she broke the contact and stepped back, pulling the front of her shirt loosely together again.

'First, though,' she said, 'I think we should wash your face and make it pretty again.'

Unlike the hapless Sarah, Kitty had survived their joint encounter whilst retaining most of her senses, though when the time finally came for Prudence to release her from the fiendish horse contraption, her legs did feel very weak and unsteady. As she stood meekly, while her wrists were strapped behind her back, she looked down at the unconscious figure still on the second horse and wondered which of them was better off.

Prudence had made them both some thinly veiled promises as she supervised their earlier preparation, but it was perfectly clear, at this moment, that Sarah was in no fit condition to carry on with anything. The prolonged excesses visited upon them had taken a heavy toll of her lesser experience and she would be of absolutely no use for anything the older woman might have in mind.

Roderick Grayling stooped over the motionless form, bending further to look at her face and shook his head. Turning to the two black girls he clapped his hands and made a series of signals, which they seemed to understand, for they immediately began unstrapping and unlocking Sarah's bonds and, as soon as they had freed her, lifted her easily between them and carried her towards the door.

No such reprieve was forthcoming for Kitty however, although at least, she realised, any chance of the despicable Lord Soberton being given the freedom of her body had been averted, if indeed it had ever existed. Instead, after a hurried and whispered conversation between Grayling and Prudence, the latter turned back to Kitty and pointed in the direction the two girls had just taken Sarah.

'Come along, my big-titted little cherub,' she leered, 'let's get you tidied up some and then I have a few more little surprises for you. I had hoped to entertain the both of you, but now you'll just have to work twice as hard, won't you?'

Looking at Ellen Grayling, especially from the perspective of the extra height her heels gave her, Sarah began to wonder if she might not be able to overpower the girl, for she looked to be several pounds lighter and had clearly been drinking. However, hardly had the thought entered Sarah's head than the younger girl seemed to read her mind. Tossing her jacket across the end of the bed she turned, folded her arms across her chest and planted her bare feet firmly.

'You can try it, if you like,' she said softly. 'You wouldn't be the first and neither would you be the first to end up flat on your back. I may look small, but I am very strong and I have been taught well in the arts of unarmed fighting. I have always believed that just because one is born female, one need not assume the sweet little girl role that men seem to take for granted.'

'I expect, then,' Sarah said, 'that you fight like street urchin.' For a few seconds the two of them stood confronting each other, and then Ellen burst out laughing.

'Aye, that I do, pretty girl,' she said. 'Only I'd give any of the village urchins more than a run for what little money they have. So, I can assume you will be sensible then? Otherwise I'll ring for a couple of footmen and have them

198

truss you like a chicken first.'

'First?' Sarah echoed. 'And what then?'

Ellen grinned impishly and threw herself back to loll on the bed, crossing her legs and leaning back on her elbows. 'Well then, pretty,' she giggled, 'I should have to thrash that splendid little bottom of yours, after which you would be begging me to let you do the very thing I want you to do now anyway, do you understand?'

'Yes,' Sarah said simply. Yes, she did understand. Whatever the older Prudence had intended to do with her once Roderick Grayling was through, his young sister clearly intended to do instead. Ellen's eyes had not left Sarah's near naked body since she entered, and now they seemed actually to be devouring her.

'Furthermore,' Ellen continued, her lips suddenly forming a grimly set line, 'if you are wilful and disobedient, or if you displease me in any way whatsoever, I shall have the grooms hang you from one of the garden oaks by your pretty little ankles and whip you until you think you have gone to hell itself.

'On the other hand, if you please me well, I may decide to ask my brother to let me keep you as my personal bed slave. You are certainly pretty enough for my tastes.'

'Your *slave*?' Sarah gasped. 'I am no slave, whatever you people may like to think – not in the eyes of the law, at least.'

Ellen studied Sarah's indignant expression and then gave a derisive snort. 'Let me tell you something,' she said, her voice dropping so that Sarah could barely hear her words, 'and it would be the better for you if you learn from it – and quickly. This estate is very large – the grounds stretch for miles in all directions – and there are keepers with dogs patrolling to keep away unwanted interference from the local people. As for anyone else, my father is a powerful man and my brother now likewise.

'This is not the only place in England where you will find slaves, and there are plenty of other rich and powerful people who will ensure that always remains so, despite the worst efforts of those drab Puritan oafs in London.

'So you – Sarah, isn't it? – had better get this into that pretty head. Here you are a slave and here you will remain, with me, for as long as it pleases me. Either that, or you will find yourself aboard a ship bound either for the Indies or for the east. Whichever it is, I would not envy you, for a slave girl in either place would not expect an easy life, nor would she expect a long one, understand?'

Sarah lowered her eyes and nodded. She knew enough to accept that what she said was largely true. Parliament may well have dethroned and executed a king and even humbled many of his former supporters, but wealth still remained in the hands of the privileged minority and wealth had always bought power and influence.

On the surface, no doubt, the pampered aristocracy would appear to be conforming, but underneath, away from the public eye, in places like this, the old ways would die hard – if at all.

'Good,' Ellen said. 'Now, come over here and remove my shirt and breeches and then you can use that sweet little tongue to help me relax for a little while. Later, perhaps, we may go riding, though we shall have to find you something a deal more suitable than what you are wearing now, delightful though it looks on you.'

'They wouldn't dare!' James Calthorpe expostulated, still struggling to unfetter himself with the rather crude key Hannah had taken from the dead man's pocket. 'Would they?' He looked up at her, his features strained with doubt. Hannah, her eyes narrowed, looked deathly pale in the flickering lamplight.

'I reckon they would,' she replied quietly. 'That bastard

Crawley holds all the proper warrants. Wickstanner may be lower than a cockroach, but he'd not dare try anything like this, not unless everything was all legal.'

'But all that witchcraft nonsense was ended six or seven years ago,' James protested. 'After that maniac Hopkins disappeared Parliament passed a law.'

'Which half the Church doesn't recognise still,' Hannah said. 'And besides, laws are only good when there are people around to see them upheld. From what I saw back in Fetworth, there ain't a body dares to raise a voice against this wicked stupidity.'

'What about my father?' James demanded. 'Or Thomas Handiwell?'

'Your father has neither said nor done diddly-squat,' Hannah said scornfully. 'And I know for a fact that he was there, on the green, standing in the crowd, goggling along with all the rest of them stupid fools, while Crawley flogged my poor Matilda.'

'Handiwell, then?' James persisted.

Hannah shook her head. 'Master Handiwell apparently had urgent business elsewhere.' Briefly, Hannah summarised what she had learned of the coach robbery and Sarah Merridew's abduction. 'So, he went a-tearin' off down to Portsmouth before anyone really knew what was happening with Matilda.'

'But he'll be back, surely?'

'Aye, he'll be back, boy,' Hannah agreed, 'but with more on his plate than just our troubles to concern himself with.'

'Then I must talk with my father, get him to talk to some of the other men in the village. This cannot be allowed to continue.'

'That it can't,' Hannah agreed. 'But it'll not be as simple as you seem to think, my lad. Your father's money has bought you a good education and you know a thing or two about the world, same as I do, though my learnin's been of

201

a different school.

'Those fools back in the village are a different kettle, James Calthorpe, a different kettle of fish altogether. Wickstanner is a cretin, a spineless little weasel and worse, but to them he's still the Church and they'd not dare to raise a finger against him. And Crawley – well, the same goes for him.' She looked down at the corpse at her feet.

'The Church rules by a creeping terror,' she said. 'The likes of Wickstanner frighten people with tales of what damnation awaits their souls, if'n they turn against the teachings and rule of the Church. Crawley's kind terrorises differently; they shows people just what hell on earth is like.' She prodded the dead man with the toe of her boot.

'At least,' she growled, 'he's got one less hell spawn bastard to help him now. But,' she added darkly, 'he now has an entire village to do his bidding, so the loss of this swine will hardly weaken his hold.'

- XIV -

Ellen lay back across the edge of the bed, her legs wide apart, the pink mouth of her sex inviting from beneath a carefully tonsured triangle of pale pubic hair. Sarah knew exactly what was expected of her. Stiffly, she began to kneel on the floor; as she did so Ellen stretched out her two hands, entwining them in Sarah's elaborate hairstyle, gripping with astonishing power.

'Lick gently, my little kitten,' she whispered hoarsely, lifting her legs so that she could lower them again and rest them on Sarah's bare shoulders. 'Kitty lap some milk,' she cooed, with a scarcely stifled giggle. Obediently, and guided by Ellen's insistent pressure, Sarah brought her mouth to the waiting orifice, first pressing her lips gently against the outer labia, then slowly sliding her tongue into the moist warmth within.

Above her she heard Ellen groan and gasp and then, as her tongue located the hard bud of the girl's clitoris, she felt her entire body stiffen and arch.

'Oh, yes – yes!' Ellen's fingers gripped tighter still, her nails digging into Sarah's scalp and Sarah winced, but knew she dared not stop nor complain. Closing her eyes tightly she began to lap and suck, tasting the curiously bittersweet juices that were now flowing so copiously that she was forced to swallow them.

'Beautiful, kitten!' Ellen sighed, and began to gently rock to and fro on her buttocks, thrusting against Sarah's face so that her nose was buried in the neatly trimmed bush, and then withdrawing slightly before thrusting yet again. Quickly she began to build up a rhythm, all the while mewling and groaning so that Sarah was certain she must reach her climax without further ado, but then, just when she seemed on the verge, she stopped, pushing Sarah's head away and sitting upright, brushing a few rogue strands of hair from her very flushed face.

'Sit back,' she ordered hoarsely. Sarah looked up at her uncomprehendingly, and Ellen seized her shoulders, thrusting her further away until she was, indeed, squatting back on her haunches. Ellen gave her a curious little smile and slipped forward, lowering her bare feet so they were one either side of Sarah's stocking-clad thighs and her crotch poised a few inches above Sarah's upraised face.

'Diddle yourself, pretty,' she said, and once again Sarah looked blank. Ellen grinned again and placed the middle finger of her own right hand inside her sex, gently rubbing it against her swollen bud. 'Like this, silly,' she said, and Sarah felt her cheeks beginning to burn even more. After all she had been put through in such a short space of time, this was, unbelievably, the worst humiliation of all. To kneel, dressed like a cheap court harlot before this chit of a girl and to be told to do... *that*... to herself. She shook her head and tried to protest, but all that came from her mouth was a whimper, and suddenly everything seemed to explode before her eyes and her ears rang and resonated. As the tears cleared and the sounds began to subside, the burning pain in her left cheek became almost unbearable.

'You want me to slap you some more?' Ellen hissed, and blinking to clear her vision, Sarah saw that the girl was already holding her hand with open palm.

'No,' she croaked. 'No, please.'

'Please, *mistress*,' Ellen said, deliberately.

'Mistress,' Sarah repeated dutifully, and Ellen lowered her hand.

'That's better,' she whispered. 'Now, get your fingers down there and start diddling. I want to see you make yourself come, understand?' Miserably, Sarah nodded again.

'And when I see you are growing close,' Ellen continued, thrusting her crotch forward obscenely so that it brushed against the tip of Sarah's nose, 'I'm going to squat my pussy right over your open mouth and you're going to drink everything I give you from it, like the good little slave girl you're now becoming.'

'Never mind postponing it,' Simon Wickstanner said, 'I should rather you cancelled the idea altogether, Master Crawley. It was never in my mind that you would actually hang the wench.'

'I dare say it was not,' Jacob Crawley replied, testily, 'but then you, priest, take only the narrow view, don't you?' He paced slowly across the floor of Wickstanner's study and stopped before the window. 'If I show even the slightest sign of weakness in these matters,' he continued, without turning round, 'then what do you think would happen with the next heretic or witch?

'There'd be almost no recanting, no absolution tithes paid, nothing, that's what! Oh yes, there'd be a few creatures would confess and beg forgiveness under the lash, I know, but let us be brutally honest here, priest. This goes beyond the saving of souls for both of us, does it not? The Lord shall provide, for it says so in the good book, doesn't it?' he turned back to face into the room again, his silhouette dark against the window and the early morning sun beyond it. 'But it also says that the Lord moves in mysterious ways, and who is to say what those ways might be?

'So, if the Lord chooses to provide for me by placing sinners in my way, I cannot but accept that manna that he bestows upon me, can I?'

'I am still not at all easy with the idea of taking another human life,' Wickstanner said, shifting uneasily and averting his gaze. 'We have the one testimony, it's true, but

Matilda has not yet confessed to her guilt, despite your best efforts.'

'And what if I were to tell you that she has, eh?' Crawley snapped. 'To me, in the privacy of the church building itself – what then?'

'And has she?'

Crawley grimaced and turned back to the window once again. 'I'm sure my word and the oaths of my two men would suffice to satisfy anyone who queried the matter, wouldn't you agree?' he said smoothly.

Wickstanner stared at him, his jaw slack. 'You would *lie*, on oath?' he all but shrieked.

Crawley regarded him from the corner of his eye. 'No,' he replied quietly, 'I would not lie on oath. Not at all.' A low chuckle escaped his lips, which twitched with what Wickstanner realised was purely evil amusement. 'Would you, Master Wickstanner?'

The witchfinder's features suddenly became totally immobile, only the slightest movement of his eyes indicating that his face was anything but an inanimate mask. Wickstanner opened his mouth to reply, to deny that he would ever commit such a damnable sin, but found no words would come.

'Anyway,' Crawley said, relaxing again, 'with any luck and the Lord's blessing, there will be no need for us to hang Matilda Pennywise. I received a messenger an hour since, offering me two guineas to stay the execution and with the promise of paying the full amount by nightfall.'

'This messenger,' Wickstanner said, 'was he from Hannah Pennywise?'

'He didn't say he was, nor did he say he was not,' Crawley replied. 'It matters not to me, either way. I can tell you this, however: I do not think he was from the village, not the village itself, anyways. I had never set eyes on him before, and his clothing was just a little more refined than most to be found around this backwater.'

'Perhaps Mother Pennywise has found a benefactor?' Wickstanner suggested.

'More likely the granddaughter has,' said Crawley. 'After all, she was quite an attractive wench, particularly when she had hair.' He chuckled harshly. 'And she will be again,' he added, 'just so long as the tithe is paid by tonight.

'But don't worry yourself, priest,' he went on. 'The two guineas will ensure she gets a painless enough death, should it come to it. My men are very good with the rope, you know. They learned a few little tricks from an Italian traveller we met in Norfolk some years ago, and now their victims only dance if they want them to.'

'I still say you should let me take the money in your stead,' Thomas Handiwell urged Harriet. 'It is madness for you to go yourself, let alone unaccompanied.'

The pair stood outside the back door of the house at Barten Meade. Upstairs, Harriet's father still lay in his bed, the latest fever abating, but still far too weak and vague even to realise what was going on. With him now was Lizzie, from the inn, whom Thomas had brought to tend the former soldier, while the Merridew's young general maid, Biddy Lathwell, took a well-earned break after an unbroken nursing stint nearing twenty-four hours.

'You read the note, Master Handiwell.' Harriet remained adamant. 'If I do not take the money myself, alone, they threatened to kill my poor cousin.'

'And what if they then take you, as well? What then? They will have the money, your cousin and you.'

'I cannot see that two women will be of much use to them,' Harriet retorted. 'Who will be left to pay a further ransom then?'

'Yes, who indeed.' It was not a question. Thomas could see that nothing he could say would dissuade Harriet from her purpose and that his only option now was to reduce the element of risk as far as possible. To that end, Harriet herself, together with young Toby Blaine, had already concocted a rough plan, but it was still dangerous and relied too much on an element of chance, for Thomas's liking.

'Whatever happens,' he said, 'you must use every effort, every tactic, to delay your eventual encounter with these villains, male or female. If that youngster is correct – and I have to say he makes a lot of sense for one so young – then there are only so many other places where you will be able to leave the river, so you must give us time to catch up to you, whatever else you do.

'Remember, my dear Harriet,' he urged, all pretence at formality now banished, 'it would break my heart if anything ill were to befall you. I know you remain determined not to take me, but you will always remain very close to my heart and a dear friend, too.

'Would that we had more resources for this, too,' he continued, before Harriet could think of a suitable reply, 'but all we have is young Captain Hart and his handful of men, which is nowhere near enough given the size of the area these scoundrels have at their disposal. If we had even twenty men, then we could disperse several patrols to throw some sort of a cordon about those woods, but as it is we are forced to rely on being in the right place at the right time – and upon the element of surprise,' he added grimly.

'The odds are not good, Harriet, and I do not like this at all. I just wish you would let me talk you out of it, but I see you will not. Perhaps just another few hours – maybe send the boat downstream with another message?'

'No, Thomas.' Harriet used his christian name for the first time in all the years since she had known Handiwell. 'They would know it was most likely a ruse, for sure. I cannot afford to put poor Sarah's life at risk in that fashion.'

'Then so be it,' Thomas conceded. 'And let us all pray

that the Good Lord chooses to look kindly upon our endeavours.'

Sarah opened her eyes, blinked and turned onto her side, trying to focus her thoughts through the blur of fatigue that still held her in its grip. She had slept, but she had no idea for how long, although she remembered, vaguely, Ellen talking to someone at the door and then returning to the bed and stretching out alongside her again. Now, however, there was no sign of her.

Groaning, Sarah sat up and, as her head slowly cleared, began to look about. The bedroom was much as she remembered it from the night before, except that now, through the heavy curtains at the window, chinks of bright sunlight cast thin shafts of brilliance across the thick carpets. Ellen's riding garb of the previous evening still lay in a crumpled heap next to the foot of the bed, the ornate oil lamp on the high chest still flickered and the bottle of wine that Ellen had produced to refresh them during their prolonged encounter lay empty and discarded in the middle of the floor.

Stiffly, Sarah swung her legs over the side of the bed and rose unsteadily to her feet, barely noticing, as she did so, that they were still firmly encased in the ridiculously high-heeled shoes. Wobbling precariously, she made her way slowly to the door, gripped the gold plated handle, turned it and pulled.

Nothing happened. With a sigh of frustration she tried again, but she knew, even as she did so, that the door was not going to open, not until whoever had locked it – presumably Ellen – returned with the key. For several seconds Sarah stood there, her hand still gripping the handle, her thoughts in total disarray.

At last, for want of a better alternative, she turned, teetered across to the window and drew back one of the curtains, shying away from the sudden brilliance of the morning sun. Shading her eyes with one hand she peered out through the latticed glass, noting the broad expanse of manicured lawn, the carefully shaped miniature trees and what appeared to be a large stone-edged pond, some distance from the house and just before the cultivated area gave way to a screen of much higher trees.

The windows were secured by means of simple catches, but as soon as Sarah swung the first one open, she realised escape via this route was impossible. Peering over the cill she saw that the bedroom was on the third storey and that the lower two were, if anything, higher than the one she was now on. Below her was a sheer drop of at least thirty feet, possibly more, straight down onto a broad expanse of paving that ran along the entire length of the building.

'I shouldn't even think about it.' The sound of Ellen's voice made Sarah jump and the little squeak of surprise was out before she could prevent it. She turned guiltily, facing her self-appointed mistress, her cheeks already beginning to burn again. 'If the drop didn't kill you,' Ellen said evenly, 'it would most certainly cripple you for life.' She now wore much more feminine clothing, though even so the cut of her new outfit was decidedly severe. The black velvet skirt was much straighter than was currently fashionable, the waist drawn in by a wide belt, booted ankles and feet just visible below the lower hem.

Above this she wore a simple blouse of a lemon coloured silk, over which a tightly fitted jacket to match the skirt was open fronted, cut away in a Spanish bolero style. It was, Sarah decided, feminine and yet masculine, both at the same time and Ellen, with her hair newly drawn back and up and her make-up freshly and meticulously reapplied, looked stunning.

'I – I was just getting some fresh air,' Sarah offered plaintively. 'I felt a little dizzy. It must have been the wine.'

'Yes,' Ellen smiled knowingly, 'it must have been. Well then, my pretty Sarah, I think the best thing for you will be a nice bath. We have a furnace house here and plenty of hot water, so I've instructed the servants to fill my own personal bath for you.' She held out a hand. 'Come along, pretty, let's get you nice and fresh and then we can find you something more suited. Can't have you sitting a horse like that, no matter how delicious you'd look. It'd be no way to greet your cousin, especially as I understand you've never met her before.'

Simon Wickstanner stood once more in the doorway of the little cellar room, staring at Matilda's motionless figure, now huddled in the furthest corner. Her head and face were still enclosed within the leather hood, her arms and wrists still pinioned to the harness she had now worn since Crawley and his men had dragged her here. Her feet remained locked inside the heavily weighted boots and, as he studied her, Wickstanner was finally forced to face up to the enormity of what he had done and to the monstrous atrocity that had been committed in the name of the God he was supposed to be avowed to serve.

He saw again the red welts on her back, buttocks and thighs, and shuddered at the memory of the way in which the poor creature had been flogged, and at the way the assembled villagers had witnessed the scene with an air of what could only be described as relish. The way the men in particular had shuffled closer, their eyes almost glazing over, had haunted Wickstanner ever since and he had not dared to close his own eyes in sleep all night, for the devils of darkness waited just such an opportunity to come and avenge themselves on him.

Tears welled up in his eyes and his entire body began to shake, so that he was forced to grip the doorframe in order to remain upright. For several minutes he stood thus, unable

211

to enter, unable to leave, as he fought with his conscience in an unequal struggle that could have but only one outcome. He knew what he had to do, but first he needed to summon the strength to do it.

At last, breathing heavily, he forced himself to release his supportive grip and stumbled forward, hesitating as he reached Matilda and then forcing himself to kneel beside her and shake her shoulder, before what little resolve he had managed to muster could dissolve again. Matilda moaned quietly and then, as if in slow motion, turned her head to look up at him.

Her eyes stared out through the narrow slits in the mask, but the hatred in them was unmistakable.

'Matilda?' He reached out again and touched her lightly on the top of her arm, expecting her to cringe from the contact, but instead she remained motionless, her glittering stare unwavering and unblinking.

'What do you want?' she demanded flatly. 'Come to gloat, have you?' At last she stirred, rolling onto her back, the sharp intake of breath and the single wincing blink of her eyes indicating that the skin there was still raw. 'Well, reverend Wickstanner,' she hissed, 'gloat all you want. I'm past caring now, believe me.' Shamefacedly, Wickstanner averted his gaze and looked down at the stone floor beside her. Matilda let out a harsh, dry cackle.

'What's the matter, little man of God?' she taunted him. 'Afraid you'll be damned if you look at me? Well, you'll be damned all right, so go on, dear Simon, you might as well look. After all, who's here to bear witness against you, eh? Not me, that's for sure, for when they take me out to hang me, Crawley's made it quite clear I shan't be able to speak, but then, he's probably told you that, hasn't he? The old scold's bridle will ensure I can't say a word about what's been going on here and the rope will make certain it stays that way.

212

'So,' she rasped, raising her head slightly, 'look all you like. It must be morning by now, so you don't have a lot of time left. They'll be coming for me soon, you know.'

'No, they won't,' Wickstanner said quietly. 'Not today, anyway. Master Crawley has postponed everything until tomorrow.'

'So he can spend another night screwing me, I suppose,' Matilda spat.

Wickstanner shook his head. 'No, that's not the reason. A small sum of money has been paid towards your absolution tithe and the rest is promised for either tonight or tomorrow morning.'

'From my grandmother? I don't believe you! She wouldn't give in to that sort of blackmail, not even to save my skin.'

'I don't know,' Wickstanner admitted. 'Perhaps you have another friend?'

'Friends, yes,' Matilda grunted, 'but not with that sort of money.' he saw her eyes narrow. 'Is this some sort of trick?'

'No. At least, none that I am party to. With luck you'll be free of all this, come this time tomorrow. Believe me, if I had the money myself I'd pay Master Crawley and get you away all the sooner.'

'Oh, is that so?' Matilda's tone was worse than scathing. 'Am I supposed to feel grateful for that, reverend dear?' She snorted. 'Don't think I don't know it's you who's responsible for me being here in the first place.' With an effort she managed to sit up and half turn the upper portion of her body away from him.

'See, reverend, that's all the gratitude you'll get from me, you godless bastard.'

Wickstanner stared, as though transfixed, at the criss-cross pattern of welts. Matilda remained thus for several seconds and then slowly turned back to face him again.

'If you think I'd ever be grateful to you, then think again,

213

you evil little worm,' she said. Her voice sounded as if it had been coated in ice. 'I think I know your game, *reverend* Wickstanner. Well, forget it. There's no way you'll ever get what I think it is you want from me, always supposing I ever do live long enough.

'So, you might as well take it now, eh? Come on, *reverend*, what are you waiting for? See? I'm totally helpless, so why not just shuck your breeches and do what you've wanted to do ever since you first set eyes on me. C'mon, get your holy prick out, why don't you? Why should I care, eh? Your prick, Crawley's prick, those other animals—'

'Stop!' Wickstanner leapt to his feet, covering his ears with his hands. 'Stop! Stop, please! Please, I beg you!'

Matilda stared at him for a few seconds and then began to laugh, a sound that seemed to start from deep within her stomach and grew and grew until, in Wickstanner's tortured mind, it was ricocheting around the walls of the empty chamber like the sound of battlefield musketry.

With a supreme effort she managed to climb to her feet. With her wrists and arms pinned to her sides her breasts were thrust out and unencumbered, and she deliberately shuffled her heavily weighted feet until she stood with legs spread.

'C'mon, mister priest man,' she hissed. 'C'mon, let's have your prick inside my devil cunt to rot with all the others I must have had in there.' As she spoke she began to inch towards him.

'Nooo!' Wickstanner retreated towards the door, but instead banged hard against the wall a few feet from the opening. Covering his eyes with one hand he held the other up between them, as if to ward Matilda off, but she stopped just short of it, breathing hard.

'Pathetic little bag of shit!' she exclaimed. 'Can't even take a woman when she's neatly plucked and parcelled for you. Or did you want that I should come sweetly and beg your love?'

'No!' Wickstanner's denial came out like a rush of winter wind. Slowly he lowered the hand from before his face, which Matilda saw had gone even paler; so pale, indeed, that he looked almost transparent. 'No,' he repeated. 'No, I beg only that you forgive me.' Tears welled up in his eyes and coursed down his puffy cheeks like two streams. 'Please, Harriet, forgive me, for I know now that I have sinned greatly and offended the Lord.'

'Oh, is that so?' Harriet drew her legs slowly together and squared her shoulders. 'You've offended the Lord, have you? Well, deary, deary me, how terrible for you.' She paused, but only for a brief instant. 'How terrible indeed. But pardon me if I say that I don't give a shit how offended your so-called God is! If he were half a god I doubt he'd countenance the likes of you as his servant, let alone let you get away with the sort of atrocity you've committed here in his name!

'So don't come snivelling to me, Wickstanner, because it'll be a cold day in Hell before I offer you any forgiveness. You ragged, useless, spineless little turd – I'd have thought more of you if you had just come in here to finish what you started, but I see now you can't even manage that.

'I'd rather be flogged and hanged than give you the satisfaction. Take your guilt and suffer it. Who knows, little man, you might even achieve martyrdom and sainthood. From what I've seen of your church, it wouldn't surprise me!' She turned her back on him, almost tripping in the cumbersome boots as she did so and stared at the blank wall.

'Go on!' she growled. 'You ain't got it in you to fuck me, so why don't you just fuck off, eh?'

- XV -

The bath certainly left Sarah feeling refreshed and a lot more alive than when she had first woken, but the relief she felt at being released from the strictures of the tight corset and the shoes did not last for very long afterwards. Prudence's curious servant, Jasmine, now attired in a brief Greek style robe, helped her from the water, towelled her briskly and then guided her back through the door that connected the bathroom with Ellen's bedroom.

Ellen was sitting propped up on the bed, still fully clothed, even to her boots. On a table alongside the bed sat a strange glass bowl-like contraption, half filled with what seemed to be water, a brass container set atop it, a flexible tube rising from its side. The other end of this tube Ellen held, periodically raising it to her lips and sucking upon it, causing a stream of bubbles to rise to the surface of the clear liquid inside.

'It's called a water pipe, or hookah,' Ellen said, seeing Sarah's look of puzzlement. 'The Arabs invented it. Very pleasant and most soothing. Come, try some.' She held the mouthpiece towards Sarah, who after a momentary hesitation, padded forward uncertainly. The ivory end felt cold between her lips and again she hesitated.

'Suck gently, pretty,' Ellen whispered encouragingly. 'I know you can do that.' She giggled and laughed even louder when, as Sarah tried to obey, the sudden inhalation of smoke sent her into a spasm of coughing that brought tears to her eyes.

'Don't worry, pretty,' Ellen chortled, 'you'll soon get used to it, same as you'll soon get used to a lot of things around here. Try it again, only take it into your lungs more slowly

216

and let it just drift out again.' Sarah blinked, wiped her eyes with the back of her free hand and did as she was told.

Once again the cool smoke felt harsh in her throat and mouth, but at least she managed to take it down without choking this time. However, as she slowly exhaled a curious feeling of detachment began to creep over her. She struggled to focus again, concentrating all her willpower on trying to stop Ellen's image from wavering.

'That's a good girl,' Ellen said softly. 'One more now, and then we'll get you into your nice new corset.'

When Sarah stood for Jasmine to wrap the heavily boned stays about her, she was actually swaying rather than standing properly, and she was barely aware of the steady tightening as the servant girl began to draw in the laces at the rear. By the time her head began to clear again she was suddenly and acutely aware that whatever drug was in the smoke was quite a powerful painkiller, for as its effects slowly began to abate, she realised this latest corset was even tighter than the one in which she had spent the night and her ribs felt as if they were being crushed in a vice.

On the outside the shimmering black satin looked so elegant, so feminine with its lacy trimmings top and bottom, but as Sarah stared down at her rapidly reducing waistline, she realised that appearances could be totally deceptive and that the inner lining, whatever it was made from, combined with the vicious whalebone stays that were hidden inside the fabric, formed a cage in which she was now held rigidly.

'I just adore the way the French couturiers design their undergarments, don't you?' Ellen said. 'Such a tiny waist you have now, pretty Sarah – one could almost believe one could snap you clean in two.'

'P-please!' Sarah gasped, fighting for breath. 'Please, mistress, have some charity. I shall surely suffocate in this terrible garment.' Ellen, however, did not seem at all disposed to heed Sarah's protests.

'Nonsense,' she cried dismissively. 'In a little while you will grow quite used to be laced so snugly and you will even thank me for making you look so elegant. You wouldn't believe me if I told you how much that beautiful corset cost.'

Mercifully, Jasmine conceded that she had closed the corset as far as was humanly possible and began knotting off the laces, slicing away the spare end lengths, which were by now very long, with a small knife. Sarah groaned, realising that, with the way the laces had been tied, there would be no way for her to release the pressure herself.

'Black stockings, Jasmine,' Ellen instructed. 'The long ones if you please, and those really wide garters that came from Spain earlier this year. She has such pretty legs, doesn't she? It seems a shame to cover them with skirts, but then that need not be for very long, I suppose.' She grinned at Sarah, but Sarah was more concerned with trying to inhale sufficient air to prevent herself from passing out.

Once the stockings were in place – beautiful spun silk of the finest quality – long gloves were produced, once again in black, this time satin, to match the corset. Jasmine drew them up the full length of each of Sarah's arms in turn, employing a small button hook to close the wrist openings and the small open darts just above each elbow, thus ensuring a perfect, unwrinkled fit.

'You look delicious, pretty,' Ellen murmured. She stepped forward and cupped both Sarah's barely supported and mostly uncovered breasts, using her thumbs to stimulate the already erect nipples. 'These are such sweet bubbies, too, not great melons like that Kitty creature has. No, these are just right, aren't they?'

Sarah had expected to be forced into more high-heeled shoes, but was surprised when Jasmine took a pair of long boots from one of the closets. They too were black and fitted right to the knee, lacing up the entire front to give a fit as tight as everything else Sarah was wearing, and the heels were every bit as drastic as those of the shoes from the night before.

'You'll find these a little easier to walk in,' Ellen said, as if anticipating Sarah's possible protestation. 'The leather supports both ankle and calf, reducing the chances of you stumbling and breaking a bone.' She said this last with the air of someone who clearly thought she was bestowing a tremendous favour, rather than the reality of the situation, which was to reduce Sarah to an almost puppet-like state in which she could walk with only the tiniest of precarious steps.

'The boots will also prevent your stockings from ripping when you are in the saddle,' she added, as Jasmine completed the lacing of the second boot. 'And you will have a pair of specially adapted stirrups, from which, once your instep has been placed in it correctly, it will be all but impossible for your foot to slip. And then,' she continued, 'there is even a special heel strap, so even the tiniest element of chance will be removed.'

Once again, a diamante decorated choker was produced and fastened about Sarah's throat like a collar, the stiffened inner lining forcing her to resume her previous posture with head held as though proudly erect, and then heavy earrings were screwed to each lobe, as they had been before.

'Excellent,' Ellen declared, walking slowly around Sarah, who stood perched almost on tiptoe, feeling like a helpless doll in her new finery. In truth, she realised, that was almost exactly what she had now been reduced to, for this new costume made what its predecessor had inflicted seem almost like total freedom in comparison.

Even the gloves were more stringent, their tightness restricting her ability to bend her arms at the elbow by more than a few degrees and the fingers holding her own fingers almost rigidly within their grip. Her arms and hands, Sarah saw, were now of little use beyond decoration and a slight aid to her balance when she attempted to walk.

'Perfect,' Ellen said, stooping and kissing each of Sarah's nipples in turn. 'Well, almost,' she added, with a crafty little smile. She turned to Jasmine.

'You can pierce her teats now, Jasmine,' she said, 'and put in those nice thick gold rings I showed you earlier. They'll be the best to use, at least until the piercings heal properly. Then, pretty,' she continued, turning back to the horror-struck Sarah, 'we shall have a new, heavier pair for you and have the goldsmith braze them shut permanently!'

The churchyard behind St Matthews seemed deserted as Jane Handiwell approached it from the narrow back lane, but she paused for a few minutes, watching from the clump of ash trees, fingering the heavy key Ellen Grayling had given her. At last, satisfied that there really was no one else about, she pushed open the narrow wicket gate and made her way quickly along the path to the ornate stone structure that dominated the rows and clusters of tombstones and crosses.

The Grayling family vault had stood here for more than two centuries now, the bodies of seven generations incarcerated in the depths below, Grayling family money ensuring not only its continuance but at least half the cost of the upkeep of the old church itself.

Pausing only to check again that no one was watching her, Jane jiggled the key into the solid looking lock and turned it, surprised at how easily the wards moved beneath her hand. The door, too, opened quietly and smoothly, testimony to regular maintenance, though inside the dust suggested that no one had been here since the death of the previous Lord Grayling, some quarter of a century earlier, though Jane knew the truth of the matter was quite different.

Slipping in, Jane closed the heavy timber structure behind

her, inserted the key from that side and locked the door once again. The only light now came from four shallow window openings, set just beneath the vaulted ceiling but, as she allowed her eyes to become accustomed to the gloom, she found she could see easily enough to find her first priority.

The lantern was tucked away in a small alcove, to the left of the door and with it sat a tinder box, just as she remembered from when she had come here with Ellen, four or five years ago now, she realised. She smiled, the image of the willowy young aristocrat girl, standing naked in the centre of this surface level chamber, her budding breasts pert, her rosebud nipples stiffening with a mixture of cold, anticipation and even fear, Jane suspected.

'Ah, my sweet little Ellen,' Jane whispered, checking there was oil in the lamp. 'How much you've changed in some ways – how little in others.' The wick flared into life and Jane had to adjust it before replacing the glass. Now, as she lifted it, moving towards the inner door just a few steps away, shadows danced along the walls and the scampering of small feet betrayed the sudden retreat of what was either a rat, or a very large mouse.

The steps down into the vault proper were smooth but even, so little use over the decades ensuring that they still looked as square and level as they must have done when the place was first built, when the first Grayling to be buried here, Lord Edmund, whose mummified corpse sat in the long alcove just at the foot of those same stairs, had ordered its construction.

Ignoring the rows of deceased Graylings on either side of the tunnel shaped vault, Jane moved quickly towards the far end, passing the six or seven alcoves that stood empty for future family members, until she reached another door set into the end wall. Much smaller than either of the doors through which she had passed so far, it was nonetheless heavier, for it was constructed entirely of iron.

Using the same key Jane unlocked it, placed the lamp down on the floor and, using both hands, pulled with all her strength. Slowly, with a slight murmur of complaint, it opened and Jane, first listening for any sounds of movement from beyond, finally stepped through and stood again, looking to right and left into impenetrable darkness.

It had to be at least four, if not five years since she and Ellen had last used this door and before that it was unlikely that anyone else had opened it for another twenty years. In fact, according to Ellen, it was also unlikely that anyone else now even knew of its existence, apart perhaps from Roderick and his father, for this was a way back into the crypt of the church, a quite unique feature in itself.

Once, probably, it had been used for family members, or the priest, to pass from the church into the burial chamber without having to brave whatever elements prevailed outside, but now, Ellen had assured Jane, no one ever used it for that purpose and even Wickstanner probably had no idea it existed, for it emerged into a small side passage that was now frequently flooded by the underground spring that ran close by and there was no key to it anywhere but in Grayling Hall, the key Ellen had given her this morning.

Today, however, the uneven stone floor was dry underfoot and, taking up the lantern again, Jane began to make her way stealthily in the direction of the main crypt, stopping every few paces to listen out again. At the end of the passageway stood another door, this one unlocked; turning the lantern as low as it would go without extinguishing it, Jane turned the wrought iron handle and eased it open the merest fraction, placing her eye to the crack.

The main passageway beyond stood empty, illuminated by a single lantern that hung from a bracket further down, giving just enough light to see by, but leaving pools of shadow alongside each supporting pillar. Smiling to herself,

Jane pulled the door further ajar and slipped through, pushing it to after her.

'Now then,' she said softly, 'let's see where they're keeping you, Matilda Pennywise – and just what it'll take to get you out of here when the time comes.'

It was not difficult to guide the little boat ashore on Bishop's Rock, for years of the swift flowing current parting around it had worn the upstream promontory so that earth, sand and rocks had crumbled into the water to form two small embankments and a narrow, flat beachhead into which the little craft drifted at Harriet's lightest guidance.

As it grounded she stood upright, jumped easily over the side and splashed ashore, grasping at the gunwale by the prow to pull the boat further in. Breathing heavily from her exertions, Harriet looked about and then down at her boots, discoloured as far as mid-calf by their immersion.

For this venture Harriet had discarded even her most practical gowns and chosen, instead, a pair of man's riding breeches, something her father had brought back from London for her several years since, before his wound and subsequent illness had reduced him to the mere shell of a man he now was. The breeches had been one of his jokes and were far too big for her then, but now they came in very useful and Harriet often wore them when working with the cows.

She raised her eyebrows slightly, sighed and wondered just what she should do now, where to start looking, or even whether she should just wait. If Toby's theory was correct the kidnappers would not be here in person, but if they had left further instructions, where in heaven's name were they?

Bishop's Rock was, in fact, several great slabs of rock, all clustered together in midstream, upon which, over the centuries, a sparse soil had somehow collected, into which

223

had rooted a dozen or more trees and a haphazard selection of bushes and grasses. From end to end it was about sixty or seventy paces, assuming that one could actually pace a straight line along its length, which the tangled undergrowth almost certainly precluded. From side to side at its widest points it was little more than half that, at its narrowest, almost in the middle of its length, it was less than half that distance again.

In all, Harriet concluded as she stood turning slowly, despite the ground cover the little island was too small to be concealing much. So what was she supposed to do now?

And then she saw it, a small leather satchel hanging from one of the lower branches of the nearest tree, its dark colour ensuring that it would not be seen from either bank, yet here, up close, quite visible to anyone who knew they should be looking for something out of the ordinary. Her heart beating, Harriet stepped forward, pushing her way through grass that she now saw had been previously flattened by whoever had placed the bag there.

'It says to continue downstream to a place called Platt's bridge,' she said, studying the rectangular parchment that was the satchel's only content. 'No, keep your head down.' She raised her own head just far enough to see Toby's eyes peeking out over the gunwale of the boat, the rest of him hidden beneath the cape that Harriet had seemingly so casually discarded upon boarding the craft beneath the bridge by the mill.

'There's a sort of map drawn here, with a cross marking the spot,' she said, keeping her voice low so as not to carry to anyone who might be watching from either bank. 'But I don't remember any bridge down there.'

'Is it where the river loops right around on itself?' Toby hissed. Harriet nodded, almost imperceptibly, and Toby's eyes bobbed up and down as he mirrored her action.

'That's about a mile the other side of where Kings Woods

ends,' he said. 'There ain't no bridge there any more, just a few piles of stones. Must have been washed away in a flood, or something, and no one ever bothered rebuilding it.'

'But why build it there in the first place?' Harriet demanded. 'There aren't any roads crossing the river anywhere near that.'

'Not now, no,' Toby agreed, 'but there used to be. I bin down there, fishin', cos the water's really shallow on the left bank, see, and you can scoop the little beggars out dead easy. There's a road all right, but no one uses it no more, not since I known it, anyway. But then that's hardly surprisin' when you thinks about it, Miss Harriet. That's part of the Grayling estates there and that road was the one that used to lead out to the north, towards where Hogarth Green used to be. The Graylings chucked everyone out of the village years ago, me dad said, and then they closed off the road completely. There is another track into the estate from that side, but it's narrow and there's usually a couple of keepers wanderin' around with dogs. Not that we'll need to worry about them today, not with Master Handiwell's soldier boys and their guns.' Toby's face shone with excitement and it was obvious he was relishing the prospect of seeing a real conflict of arms.

'I see,' Harriet said, trying to ignore the way her pulse had suddenly started racing. She studied the crude drawing again, noting how, as Toby had said, the river ran around in a wide sweep and trying to imagine the scale of the map in her mind. Yes, she saw, Toby was right. The river there ran deeply inside the boundaries of the Grayling lands as she knew them, but then, as Toby had also said, that fact should not have surprised either of them.

'Right,' she said, replacing the map inside the satchel, flipping it closed and looping the strap over her shoulder, 'as I get back in, you roll out over the other side. The little embankment there will keep you hidden from anyone

225

watching from that side and I'll pick up my cape and pretend to shake it out and fold it again, so it'll make a screen on this side.'

'Right you are, miss,' Toby grinned, peering up at her. 'But I shouldn't worry too much about anyone watching. They won't be here, same as I said. Too risky. Probably had someone watchin' for you further upstream, somewhere from where they could ride off easily, take the news to whoever's waitin' for you at the other end.'

'Now then,' Harriet said, as she finished replacing her cape and began the task of pushing the boat back out into the water, 'you know what you've got to do, don't you?' Crouching among the reeds, waist deep in water, Toby nodded.

'Sure, miss,' he replied, raising one thumb. 'Don't you worry about me. Just you make sure you use them oars to slow you down, not the other way round. It'll take me a few minutes to swim ashore and a good ten more to run back down the road and find Master Handiwell and them soldiers, and we'll have to ride right round about three extra miles to find that track I said about.'

Jasmine spent even more time than before on making up Sarah's face and arranging her hair. Once again, Sarah was forced to sit as the Asian girl worked away in silence, painting her cheeks, her eyes, her lips, teasing her locks back and pinning them so that a small tail was left hanging down over the nape of her neck. The final touch was the addition of a neat velvet covered riding bonnet, with black ribbons trailing from the rear and a jaunty rim surrounding it. Long pins secured this in place and, when Sarah was finally permitted to see her reflection in the full-length mirror, she stood and gaped at the erotic spectacle she now presented.

Totally formal from the neck up, from the neck down she

still wore only the tight underwear and gloves and the high boots, affording a contrast that was not lost upon her. The addition of the gold rings through her newly pierced nipples simply enhanced this effect, the steady, throbbing soreness reminding her of their presence with every heartbeat. Ellen, who had returned to her water pipe meanwhile, languished on the bed, smiling at her contentedly.

'You look so lovely, pretty,' she cooed, forming her own painted lips into a lascivious moue. 'I really think, if I am not very careful, that I could fall completely in love with you. Of course,' she said, sighing with mock severity, 'that would never do. After all, you are my slave and I am your mistress, is that not so?'

Sarah, realising that any hesitation on her part might well trigger almost any sort of unpleasant reaction from the drug-hazed girl, nodded quickly.

'Yes, mistress,' she replied meekly, lowering her eyes. The two gold rings, hanging from her almost impossibly engorged teats, seemed to wink back at her, mocking her apparent acceptance of her new status.

'Never mind,' Ellen said lightly, 'I shall still love you as I would love a favourite puppy dog, or as I loved my prettiest dollies when I was small. Come here, pretty Sarah, and I shall kiss those pretty lips.'

She did not, however, mean the lips that Jasmine had not long finished painting, for before Sarah could even attempt to bend – a feat the corset rendered all but impossible – Ellen leaned forward, grasped her by both bare buttocks and drew Sarah staggering forward off balance and placed her own lips full on Sarah's cleft.

Sarah shivered and felt her stomach contract instinctively, as the fiery little fingers pitter-pattered once more up and down her spine. She closed her eyes in mortification, unable to help herself and knowing that she had grown wet immediately upon the contact and that Ellen could not fail

227

to notice the effect of her lewd kiss.

'So sweet a little honeypot,' Ellen muttered, her words sounding slurred. 'So sweet that I think I shall have to taste it some more.' She looked up into Sarah's face, just as Sarah reopened her eyes and Sarah saw that her pupils were now hugely dilated. 'I think you would like that too, don't you?' Ellen whispered. Slowly, Sarah nodded, unable to deny the truth, no matter how shamed she felt by it.

Wickstanner found Silas Grout working beneath the tallest of the oak trees that stood in a roughly circular cluster on the eastern side of the village green. He had drawn the witchfinder's wagon up beneath a sturdy lower limb that was perhaps fifteen feet above the ground, unhitched the two horses, which now grazed idly a few yards away and was busily assembling a collection of pre-cut timbers.

'Good day, parson,' Silas said, looking up at Wickstanner's approach. 'Fine and sunny again, eh?'

'Such a shame you'll not be hanging the girl today then,' Wickstanner replied sarcastically. The sarcasm seemed lost on Silas.

'It'll still be fine tomorrow,' he said confidently, 'all the time the winds stays in the south west, anyway. Besides,' he added, straightening up and letting his hammer drop onto the back of the wagon, 'it'll give us a bit more time to get this little lot ready. My mate usually does this with me, you see,' he continued, by way of explanation, 'only he's gone missing this morning. Probably sleeping it off somewhere, if I'm any judge.'

'Drink is an evil temptation,' Wickstanner said.

Silas seemed unmoved by this observation. 'Maybe it is and maybe it ain't,' he said non-committally, 'but there are some who needs a drop of something now and again.' He nodded towards the structure he was building. 'Always upsets Jed, you see,' he explained further. 'Me too, but then

I always tells meself it's God's work we do.'

'And of course, as Master Crawley tells me,' Wickstanner said, 'the two of you are charitable enough to make sure that most of your victims – I mean charges – are given a quick and merciful death.'

'Aye, that we are, usually,' Silas said, puffing his chest out proudly. 'Master Crawley tells us we're real masters of our craft, that he does.'

'Yes, he did explain the principle in outline,' Wickstanner said. 'Apparently you leave enough slack in the rope so that the prisoner's own weight breaks her neck.'

'That's the truth of it, Master Wickstanner,' Silas nodded. 'An' it's quite an art, too. Heavier prisoners are the easiest, but the lightweights need a longer drop. We needs to find a nice high branch for them.'

'And what if you can't – find a high enough branch, that is?' Wickstanner asked. 'What if the condemned is a particularly light person?'

Silas grinned. 'Oh, don't you worry,' he chuckled. 'We got all that sorted out a long time ago.' He jabbed a finger at a hemp sack that stood in one corner of the wagon. 'See that?' he said. 'That's filled with stones and hung on a belt round her waist. Even the skinniest wench will drop fast with that on her.

'Of course, we've come a long way since we first started dropping 'em,' he added, eager to impress further. 'We started off by taking 'em up a ladder and shoving 'em off, but that was a bit cramped. Then we had two ladders – one for the condemned and one for one of us to stand on, but sometimes they wouldn't climb up, so we had to tie 'em to the ladder first, then raise it up, then cut the ropes that held 'em.

'All a bit complicated, till we thought of this idea. The platform is twice the height of a man and more and there's a set of steps goes up to it from the bed of the wagon, see?'

He pointed to what appeared to be a particularly wide ladder, the rungs of which were broad enough to be classed as steps, just.

'Even if the wench struggles we can walk up that, one on each side of her, get her onto the plank and drop the noose over her head. Usually, once they get up a few steps, they stops struggling anyways, so it's quite quick from then on.'

'Better than a ladder, yes, I can see that,' Wickstanner replied thoughtfully. He remained silent, staring at the rustic steps and then looking up to the overhanging bough. 'Yes,' he repeated thoughtfully, 'I can see the advantages.'

'Master Handiwell, I cannot authorise this intrusion.' Captain Timothy Hart looked extremely distressed, his already gaunt features deathly pale, his eyes watery. 'Lord Grayling is a very influential man and for me to take my men onto his property – well, the repercussions, they could be enormous.'

Thomas Handiwell regarded the young officer disdainfully, while the other members of their small party – Toby Blaine aside – tried desperately to affect an air of disinterest.

'Captain,' Thomas said levelly, 'your remit was to accompany me back here and, whilst officially you are on a leave of absence, if the opportunity presented itself, you were to use your office to pursue these miscreants with what your commanding officer referred to as "every expedience", was it not?'

'It was, indeed,' Hart replied. 'However, this really is the flimsiest of evidence upon which to proceed.' He looked over his shoulder at Toby, who was sitting nonchalantly astride the spare mount Thomas had brought with them for just that purpose.

'I'm certainly not disputing the lad's integrity,' he continued, 'but to go tramping through a private estate without being certain we'll even find the people we're after? They could turn off and leave the Grayling land at any point.'

'Then the sooner we get after them,' Thomas growled, 'the better, wouldn't you say? That young woman has put herself at risk in the belief that we would give her every support and protection and I have no intention of sitting here, arguing with you, when her very life could be in danger!'

The riding habit was, like everything else Sarah now wore, completely black. Made from a woollen cloth fabric, the jacket was tailored to fit snugly, buttoning to the neck and hugging Sarah's constricted waistline perfectly, its frock design flaring out over her hips.

Beneath this the skirt was long, reaching to her ankles and loose fitting beneath the hips, pleated cunningly to disguise the fact that it was in fact split from top to bottom in several strategic places. Seeing Sarah's puzzled look, Ellen, who had now discarded her pipe, offered a brief explanation.

'The skirt is designed like that so you can sit a horse the more easily,' she said. 'The usual fashion for a lady to ride a horse whilst wearing a skirt is, of course, to adopt the ridiculous side-saddle, but you are not exactly a lady and, in any case, I have a far more interesting saddle in mind for you.'

The addition of the top clothing made Sarah feel a little easier; thankfully, she thought, everything was now covered modestly, even if, beneath it all, she knew how exotically she was attired. The tight corset, its boning seemingly intent on piercing her through, was unlikely to let her forget that, but as she stood before the mirror one more time she saw that outwardly, at least, she presented an almost demure image, of a young and fashionable lady dressed for a morning's riding in the park. Even the height of the ridiculous boots was now all but disguised by the swirling skirts.

There was, of course, one more difference, Sarah knew; a critical difference that no observer, casual or otherwise, could possibly have discerned. The tightly fitting gloves, their extreme length now hidden inside the sleeves of the jacket, handicapped her arms and fingers so heavily that without help she would be unable to remove any of the clothing.

Dressed thus, Ellen could take her riding in public and not one person would possibly guess that she was, in effect, a virtually helpless prisoner of her clothing, a strikingly pretty creature who could no little, if anything, for herself and was therefore totally at the mercy, both of the girl who had ordered her prepared in this way and of anyone else into whose clutches she either fell, or was placed.

'Ready for our little ride, pretty?' Ellen asked, reaching for her own jacket again.

'Mistress,' Sarah began hesitantly. 'Mistress, you said you were taking me to meet my cousin? I presume you speak of Harriet, for I have no other cousin, at least none that I know of.'

'Yes, pretty Sarah,' Ellen replied, shrugging into her jacket, 'I was speaking of your cousin Harriet and yes, with luck, you shall see her shortly, for she should even now be making her way to deliver a ransom for your release. She comes alone, of course.'

For a brief moment Sarah's heart leapt, but then, as she saw the expression on Ellen's face and understood the significance of that final remark her hopes immediately fell again. 'And you have no intention of releasing me, mistress,' she said dully. Worse, she realised, though she did not voice her suspicion, Ellen Grayling and whoever else was involved in her abduction originally, would very soon have

Harriet in their clutches as well.

'No,' Ellen confirmed quietly, though Sarah barely heeded her words now. 'No, no intention whatsoever. You would, of course, make a pretty pair, for I can see the family likeness and there is little in age between you, right enough, but I fear there are other plans already made for Miss Harriet Merridew.'

Jacob Crawley stood looking up at the curious structure that stood partly supported on the back of the wagon and nodded. Above him, Silas Grout knocked in the second pivot pin, seized the broad plank in his left hand and lifted it from the vertical to the horizontal, lowered it and raised it again.

'Just the two supporting brackets now, Master Crawley,' he announced, 'but if it's all the same with you and seein' as how we won't now be needing this until the morrow, I'd like to take myself over to the inn for a bit. 'Tis a warm day and this is warmer work, especially for one man on his own.'

'Well, you've done well, Silas,' Crawley conceded. 'Take yourself off and enjoy your ale. None of these peasants would dare touch anything here, that's for sure.' He grimaced. 'And still no sign of that rogue Jed, I take it?'

'Not a sign, master,' Silas confirmed. 'Probably still lying drunk somewhere. He never was too good at holdin' his drink, but I'll wager he turns up again just in time to see me finish here.'

'Maybe,' Crawley said, 'but it's strange, even for him. He's not to know I've postponed the execution and the original time is only a half hour from hence. Unlike him, that, no matter how drunk the oaf tends to get. Come to think of it,' he mused, 'I haven't seen the wretch since he went off to take food and water to the miller's son.'

'Me neither,' Silas began, 'but then...' He stopped, and Crawley saw that he was peering into the distance. 'Damnation!' The oath was muttered half under Silas's breath, but it came down clear enough to Crawley, who immediately stiffened.

'What is it, man?' he demanded, trying to follow the line of Silas's gaze, though a small clump of bushes screened him from the view that Silas's higher vantage point afforded him.

'I think, Master Crawley,' Silas replied, beginning to climb down the framework of the scaffold, 'that we might just be about to find out why Jed ain't here. Less'n I'm much mistook, which I knows I ain't, the old biddy is headed this way and she's got the bloody miller's lad with her. But don't worry,' he said, dropping the last few feet to land on the grass beside Crawley, 'I've got both my pistols here in the wagon and a knife that will cut through three layers of leather at one thrust.'

'Leave the pistols hidden, Silas,' Crawley said, placing a restraining hand on his arm. 'Unless the lad is armed we have no need of them. I have all the protection we need right here,' he added, patting his jerkin beneath his cloak. 'The law is the law, after all, and the authority of the Church is beyond question.

'No need to harm the lad, not unless he recognises you – and then you simply deny having ever seen him before. I can't see any of these villagers siding with him, not once I swear you haven't been out of my sight these past three days. The sight of your gibbet here will be more than enough to still their tongues in their heads.'

Harriet saw the ruins of the bridge as the little boat rounded the second half of the long bend and pulled the oars inboard, while she turned to study the left bank, where she was supposed to land. Nothing seemed to be stirring there, but she had not expected to see anyone standing in full view anyway, so she turned back, hefted one of the oars over the right hand side and began using it as a paddle, guiding the craft gradually in from centre stream.

Steadily, the distance began to decrease and she was able to make out the crumbling chunks of masonry lying half submerged in the water at the bases of all that remained of the original bridge supports. Whatever floodwaters had been responsible for the structure's demise, she thought, they must have been fierce, or else the destruction of the bridge had been assisted by a human agency.

At last she was able to manoeuvre in to the shore and the prow of the boat bumped gently onto the silt and mud beneath the steeper bank. Carefully she stood up, made her way forward and splashed down into the shallows, dragging the boat a few feet further in, before finally pulling herself up the muddy incline to the flatter ground above.

Panting from her exertions, she stood for a moment to regain her breath and looked about. As Toby had said, there was still a road, or lane visible, leading away from the ruined bridge and into the thick woodland, but it was already becoming badly overgrown and she wondered just how passable it would be, even for someone on foot.

Presumably there was a way through, otherwise the kidnappers would not have chosen the place to begin with. As the rise and fall of her breasts slowed she held her breath and listened intently, but apart from a few birds calling from the treetops high above and the musical background from the river waters, which ran slowly at this point, she could hear nothing.

Delay and buy time; that was what Thomas had stressed. She turned, looked back across the water to the pile of broken masonry and beyond that to the barely discernable gap in the trees that marked the line of the road on that side. Not that she expected to see or hear anything from that direction, for Toby had been adamant that the only way for Thomas and the soldiers to reach this side of the river was by making a circuitous approach, crossing the river by another bridge, further downstream and not part of the Grayling lands.

Sighing, Harriet wondered just how long it would take them. The woods around her looked dense, hardly ideal for men on horseback, but then she really had no other alternative and, if anyone was watching her, much more delaying on her part would surely arouse their suspicions.

She swallowed and turned back to the track, doubt beginning to assail her for the first time, for now, as she stood, the safety of the river behind her, the unknown of the woods in front and with no one to help her, possibly not for miles still, Harriet suddenly realised how alone and vulnerable she really was and even the hard lump of the small pistol hidden inside her shirt did little to reassure her.

- XVII -

The confrontation with Crawley had shaken James's confidence badly. Instead of the supposed witchfinder being concerned by being faced with logic and learning, he had simply turned what James had considered as being his strengths and used them against him.

'Your schooling will no doubt have covered a few basic points of the law,' Crawley said, when James had finished trying to harangue him and demanded Matilda's immediate release. 'Therefore, you will be well aware that a warrant signed under the seal of a bishop is not something to be treated lightly.

'Regardless of what you might like to believe, young fellow,' he continued, 'I thank the good Lord that there are still some who are aware of the continued presence of evil in these lands and that they have vested in me the authority to root it out, wherever it lurks. The young woman in question has confessed to practicing the dark arts and to heretical utterings. The law of the Church is quite clear in these cases. Unless the absolution tithe is paid by this evening, she will be put to death in the proscribed manner, tomorrow morning, at eight of the clock precisely. Only the payment of the first two guineas has persuaded me to delay the execution beyond my original intent. The balance must be paid by sunset – no later!'

James had barely constrained himself from leaping forward and seizing the wretched man by the throat, but the lurking presence of Silas Grout, who was both taller and heavier than James, eventually persuaded him that violence would bring no solution. He looked upwards at the strange assemblage of timbers and at the overhanging bough high above them and shuddered.

'It will not happen, Master Crawley,' he said, struggling to keep his voice from trembling with rage. 'It will not happen!'

When they had moved out of earshot, Hannah Pennywise spoke for the first time since they approached Crawley on the green. 'He has the law on his side,' she said, 'no matter how cackafanny that law may be. We cannot go openly against the law. That swine he has with him would break your back in an instant, or else the rest of these fools would fall upon you.'

'But that's just the point,' James seethed. 'He *doesn't* have the law on his side. Parliament changed the laws regarding witchcraft a good few years back now. His warrant, if indeed he has one, must now be out of date and invalid.'

'And I suppose you have signed and attested copies of their new law, eh?' Hannah sighed. 'No, I thought not, and somehow it would appear that news of London laws does not exactly fly to the ears of villagers such as these. And yes, he does have a warrant, for he took great delight in showing me it yesterday, and that's all he needs to sway the simple minds that abound hereabouts.'

'Maybe not all the minds hereabouts are so simple,' James retorted. 'I'll speak to my father.' He paused, recalling that Hannah had said his father had been among the crowd watching Matilda's scourging. 'Better still,' he said, 'we'll go and see Master Handiwell. Whatever else he has on his mind he surely cannot stand by and watch Matilda murdered. He will know about the new laws and he can make that knowledge known throughout the village.'

However, by the time the unlikely pair had walked to the *Black Drum* it was to discover that Thomas Handiwell, in company with the small detachment of troopers that had returned with him the night before, had already left. None

239

of the remaining staff seemed to be privy to actual details, but the word was that they had gone to try to apprehend the villains responsible for robbing the stagecoach and abducting Thomas's niece.

'Damn!' James cursed, pounding his right fist into his left palm. 'There's no knowing what time they might return. If they're chasing outlaws they could end up riding clear across the county. All we can do now is try to reason with Wickstanner. I've never liked the man, but perhaps he will listen to us.'

'Even if he does,' Hannah growled, 'I doubt there's much he can do about it now, not without admitting to all and sundry that he's a liar. It was he who alleged the so-called evidence and accusations against Matilda, accusations that the original so-called witness no longer lives to confirm or deny.

'Besides,' she added, 'Jacob Crawley is now like a snowball rolling down a hillside that grows steeper and steeper. Wickstanner has set him loose upon this village, true, but I don't think he could stop him now, even if he wished it.'

'Then what's to be done?' James all but wailed. 'We cannot just stand back and let them do this foul thing, surely? Perhaps,' he said, halting in his stride, 'perhaps there is yet time for me to ride down to Portsmouth and return with a magistrate or a bailiff, some official who can tell this foolish village that they are living in the past.'

'The hour grows later,' Hannah said sombrely. 'Even if you could make it there before sunset, I doubt you'd find anyone willing to ride back with you tonight. And by morning,' she added meaningfully, 'it will be too late. My Matilda will be swinging beneath yon tree.'

'Then I shall fetch my father's musket and pistol and shoot both Crawley and his hangman!'

'Brave words, young James,' Hannah replied, laying one

skeletal hand upon his arm, 'but foolish. Whatever we may think of Crawley, no matter that his authority is probably long out of date, he remains a vassal of the damned Church and if you kill him, whatever your reasons, whatever you might prove afterwards, they'll hang you for it, mark my words.'

'Jacob Crawley is no true servant of the Church!' James declared vehemently. 'No court in this land would convict me.'

'Perhaps not,' Hannah conceded, 'assuming you lived to face a court. There are plenty here who would shoot you or swing you and they'd swing you alongside Matilda, too. What good would that do, eh?'

'Then what?' James demanded hopelessly.

'For the moment,' she said quietly, 'there is no alternative other than that I pay the bastard what he asks.' She frowned and paused. 'Perhaps that's what I should have done in the first place, but I didn't think he would dare go so far as he has and besides, if I had agreed too quickly, who knows what else he might have demanded.

'As it is, having used Matilda as an example, I suspect he may well inflict his foulness on others yet. We shall have to wait and see, but now,' she sighed, beginning to walk again, 'I must go and fetch his gold. Come with me, James, for I shall need your young muscle, unless I want to spend all night digging.'

She looked up at James and gave him a lopsided grin. 'You don't think I'd leave that sort of money lying around in my old cottage now, do you?' she demanded, seeing the look of bewilderment in his face. 'Indeed no. My gold is well hidden and buried deep, so we must set off without delay.

'One thing still puzzles me, though,' she muttered, as they began to pick up the pace. 'Crawley mentioned the paying of two guineas, unless my old ears are failing me.'

241

'Yes, he did,' James confirmed. 'What of it?'

'Well,' Hannah replied thoughtfully, 'it wasn't me who paid it and it certainly wasn't you. Which begs the question, who did pay it… and why?'

Sarah stared at the saddle in horror, understanding now part of the reason for the particular design of her riding skirt, with its strategically placed slits, for the highly polished leather column that curved upwards from the centre of the seat could only be intended for one purpose.

Ellen allowed her a minute or so to take in the full import of what she was seeing and stepped forward to use a soft cloth to gently buff the gleaming column, her steady up and down hand movements carefully calculated to induce a feeling of awed trepidation in Sarah, who shivered at the thought of what was about to come.

'Mistress, please…' she whispered, her throat so dry her voice cracked and failed her momentarily.

Ellen smiled devilishly and patted the horse's flank. 'You like your new mount, pretty?' she mocked. 'A sturdy beast, wouldn't you agree?'

'I – I can't… possibly…' Sarah struggled to get the words out, all the time knowing that no protestations or pleadings on her part would save her from this newest ordeal. The young groom who held the horse's head steady regarded her with barely disguised amusement and to one side, another groom, who was holding ready a horse that was obviously Ellen's, looked on similarly. A third groom, Ross, who had taken her virginity the previous day, stood next to him, arms folded, affecting an air of utter disinterest.

'Of course you can, pretty,' Ellen retorted. She turned to Ross, raising her eyebrows dramatically. 'Would you say this cock is any bigger than yours, Ross?' she asked, stifling a giggle.

'Perhaps a tad bigger, mistress,' he replied, shrugging

242

his shoulders. Sarah stared at him in disbelief, for there was no way that his weapon, large though it had seemed at the time, compared with this manmade column and she could not imagine that there was a man living who could hope to rival its size. She took an involuntary step backwards, shaking her head.

'No,' she squealed. 'I cannot... I won't!'

'Oh, but you will, pretty,' Ellen purred dangerously. 'You will mount this fine animal and you will impale yourself on this fine cock horse for if you don't I shall strip you, hang you from that tree over there and have every groom and keeper on this estate give you a dozen lashes and a damned good fucking for your disobedience.'

Sarah hesitated, but she could see from the expression on Ellen's face, reinforced by the sudden steeliness in her voice, that this was no idle threat intended just to frighten her into submission. If she did try to resist, the threat would undoubtedly become reality and the thought of having to endure so many whips, let alone so many men ravishing her helpless body, horrified her even more than the prospect of being made to mount and ride the humiliating saddle before her.

'Well, come along then, pretty,' Ellen urged, seeing the rebellion dying in Sarah's eyes. 'We don't have all day you know. Ross, give her a hand up, if you please. The irons have been shortened so she can raise herself sufficiently, but you'll need to position her skirts as she mounts.'

To Sarah, who had not sat such a saddle, even without its bizarre modification, since her early teens, the horse seemed frighteningly large, the saddle itself a long way from the ground. The stirrups, which she saw had indeed been shortened, looked to be far too high for her to lift her foot to, especially with almost no use of her hands to effect any sort of purchase or leverage.

However that, she quickly realised, was why Ross was

243

on hand. Moving swiftly to her side he lifted her easily, placing one forearm beneath her buttocks and, with his other hand, guided her left boot into the peculiarly shaped iron, pushing it down until the lower bar sat snugly between her heel and the underside of her instep.

At the same time Ellen moved around to the far side and as Sarah swung her leg awkwardly over, she guided the right boot into place similarly, so that Sarah was now standing in the stirrups, poised above the saddle, her balance dependent mostly upon Ross's hand which now supported her buttocks, the black phallus standing just before her, its tip pressing gently against her mound through the material of the skirt.

'Lift her skirts out of the way, Ross, if you please,' Ellen ordered. 'Yes, that's right, high and clear so they don't get in the way. Now, pretty Sarah, lift yourself just a little and come forward. Yes, that's right – just a little more and… yes, that's perfect.'

As she spoke, Ellen was using one hand to steady the phallus, gripping it so that she could guide it slightly in whatever direction was required, and Sarah felt the cold, unyielding tip settling between her outer labia. She closed her eyes, drawing in a breath as deep as the unyielding corset would allow and then, surrendering to the inevitable, began to slowly lower herself.

Inch by inch the monster began to penetrate her, aided by the fact – inexplicable to Sarah – that her sheath was already wet and slippery. She whimpered though, as she felt herself being stretched more and more and as the rough forward edge of the stitched seam began to rub against her clitoris. 'I can't!' she gasped, tears of shame clouding her eyes, yet knowing she would have to accept the entire length of the dildo. 'Oh please, no… ooohhh!'

The last three or four inches slid home as she settled her buttocks on the equally unforgiving leather of the saddle and her breath whistled through her nostrils as the horse stirred, sending a sudden vibration via the saddle and up the shaft which now filled her.

'There now, that wasn't so bad, was it?' Ellen stepped back, smiling up at her and, as Ross began to lower Sarah's skirts, gathered those intended to fall that side and began arranging them. Ross meanwhile was attending to matters on his side and these included altering the length of the stirrup leathers, lowering the irons by several inches until Sarah's legs were once again at full length. This, she realised, would prevent any chance of her lifting herself off the phallus.

The penultimate touch was the addition of a short leather strap from one side of each stirrup iron, passing about the heels of her boots and buckling on the outside of each, so that, even should there have been any chance of Sarah's feet slipping accidentally from the stirrups, now she could not even remove them deliberately.

Finally Ross reached up, took her hands and buckled leather cuffs around each wrist, cuffs that were connected by a short length of chain, which he then, in turn, attached to a small metal ring set into the front of the saddle. The reins of her mount, it seemed, were not to be in her own control.

'Perfect,' Ellen declared. 'Thank you, Ross, you may go now, and take these lads with you. Give them a tot of rum for their troubles. I can handle matters from now on.' She looked up at Sarah again and winked.

'Comfortable, pretty?' she snickered. 'Or are you starting to get just a little warm under all that stylish finery?' She took the reins from the young groom and turned the horse towards her own mount. The sudden rocking movement, gentle though it was, caused Sarah to sway in unison, that movement in turn causing the phallus to feel as though it were trying to rotate within her.

She first groaned and then whimpered, trying without luck to clench her useless fingers. Ellen wound the reins around the small pommel of her own horse's saddle and turned back to grin at her over her shoulder.

'Relax, pretty,' she laughed. 'Just wait until we start trotting in a minute!'

Alone in the churchyard, Jacob Crawley perched on one of the worn gravestones and took out the folded parchment again. The two golden guinea coins that had been wrapped in it were now safely in the small money pouch on his belt, beneath his cloak. Carefully he unfolded the document and peered carefully at the neatly written words.

Master Crawley, he read again, *the enclosed is a signal of my good faith, for I would talk with you on a matter of great urgency and must meet you in secrecy.*

Come this night, at eight of the clock, to the bridge by the mill, where you will learn and receive something to your great advantage. You may fear duplicity in this, but be assured you need not and may bring your men with you, if you fear for your safety.

However, you must approach the bridge alone and you will see me clearly at a distance and that I too will come by myself. Meanwhile, beware the old witch's trickery, for she is more than she seems.

Crawley sat pondering this curious missive for several more minutes. The writer, he noted, referred to his men, in the plural. Given that Jed had still not returned and that James Calthorpe had somehow escaped from the hut in the woods, it seemed logical to suppose that something had happened to him, though as yet there had been no opportunity to despatch Silas to investigate. In all probability, Crawley reasoned, Jed was already dead, probably taken by surprise by the old woman, for Calthorpe showed no signs of having been in a struggle.

Presumably Jed had been half drunk by the time he set off for the woods the previous evening and would have been easy game for anyone with sufficient determination. Crawley shrugged. His loss, if he were indeed dead, was inconvenient but not insurmountable; he would easily find another recruit when the time came, possibly even among these stupid villagers and meantime, Silas Grout was as cunning as a fox and surprisingly ruthless for a man who took pride in being able to execute his victims painlessly.

He came back to the reference to 'men' in the plural. Unless the boy and the old woman were far trickier than he thought – a possibility he was not prepared to discount in the latter case – that reference discounted them as being responsible for the note's origins. Besides, there had not been time for them to have written it and arranged for the stranger to deliver it to him.

Another stranger.

Crawley's brows beetled together. The first note and the first two guineas had been similarly delivered, though by a different fellow altogether and the handwriting in each case was different, though both had come from educated hands, he could tell immediately. He reached inside his cloak and produced the first note, opening it out and holding it up alongside the later one. No, they were most definitely different hands, and yet there was something about them that was similar.

He sat for another minute, concentrating, and then he realised what it was. 'Aha,' he muttered, 'I see now.' He chuckled, nodding. 'Both written by women, unless I'm very much mistaken. Hmmm, very interesting... very interesting indeed.' He folded both letters and put them away together and then stood up, shaking the folds of his cloak so that it once again hung straight.

'Well then, little lady,' he whispered, turning towards the churchyard gate, 'I wonder what's so urgent. Perhaps the example I've shown with the Pennywise wench has frightened a few of you more than I expected.'

Simon Wickstanner slumped onto the empty front pew bench, breathing heavily, sweat pouring down his face. He groaned, closing his eyes and tried to find the words of a prayer, but every time he tried to move his lips to form them, nothing seemed to come out right and his tongue seemed to grow thick and stiff.

'Dear God!' he gasped at last. 'Dear God, forgive me!'

He forced his eyes open again and half turned, looking up to where the long ladder stood now, its very top propped against one of the main roof beams high above. It had proved surprisingly heavy to carry in from the small barn that stood behind the church and it had taken all Wickstanner's strength to raise it to its present position, but he had refused to let the task defeat him.

Alongside the ladder, the rope, taken from the tower bell and now with a carefully knotted noose at its lower end, hung down, swaying ever so slightly in the slight draught that always seemed to blow through the building, though in Wickstanner's tortured imagination its movement seemed to be beckoning him, reminding him of what he knew he had to do.

Slowly he forced himself to stand again and, on swaying legs, he moved across to stand by the ladder, reaching up with one hand to confirm that the noose was still at the correct height. With a stifled sob he clung to the ladder, his entire body shaking, his earlier resolve on the brink of disappearing.

Painless, Silas Grout had assured him. Completely painless, like snuffing out a lamp. Snap! Simple. Quick. Painless.

Simon raised his head again, leaning back to stare up the length of the ladder, and began counting the rungs as they appeared to narrow away into the gloomy spaces of the high vaulted roof. Twenty, twenty-five, thirty, thirty-five, thirty-six, thirty-seven, thirty-eight…

Thirty-nine. Thirty-nine steps to where the ladder leaned against the beam, with a few more stretching above that point. He tried to calculate, guessing at the spaces between each of the rungs, but his head would not get itself around the equation. With a cry of exasperation he gave up the struggle and reached inside his coat pocket for the brandy flask.

It had to be more than high enough, he told himself fiercely. Far higher than that cursed tree branch from which they would hang Matilda. He unscrewed the cap of the flask and raised it to his lips, swallowing greedily and ignoring the way the raw brandy burned the back of his throat.

'Damn you, Matilda!' he screeched, shaking the now empty vessel towards the altar. 'Damn you, for you surely are a witch!' He threw the flask violently into the rows of pews where it rattled and ricocheted off the unsympathetic oak, and deliberately drove his forehead against the ladder, welcoming the sudden spearing pain, for he knew well enough that his accusation was groundless.

Damn *yourself*, Simon Wickstanner, a hollow voice echoed, mockingly. He looked up and looked about him, unsure of whether the voice had been real or just his own conscience, but the church was as empty as when he had entered it and the main door was still securely bolted from the inside.

'Yes, I am surely damned,' he whispered, tears dribbling into the corner of his mouth as he spoke. 'Oh dear Lord, what *have* I done? What have I done?'

Suddenly the tears ceased. Blinking fiercely, Wickstanner drew himself upright, turning to look again at the simple wooden cross on the altar. He remained thus, motionless, for several seconds and then, turning, began slowly to ascend the ladder, pausing only to collect the noose and hang it over his right arm as he drew level with it.

Within a very few minutes Sarah found that the persistent movement of the saddle dildo inside her was creating exactly the same sort of sensations her treatment at the hands of Ross and her subsequent experiences with Kitty, the two slave girls and Ellen had produced.

Unable to do anything to prevent what was happening, she was forced to remain seated, outwardly the picture of refined, aristocratic womanhood, inwardly a seething cauldron of rampant sexuality. As her mount trotted dutifully behind Ellen's stallion, the pressures began to rise and every nerve ending in her body was alive with raw desire.

Within the tight confines of her jacket, her breasts and in particularly her newly pierced nipples throbbed mercilessly, her teats feeling as though they had grown to several times their normal size, and between her legs, as the leather shaft slid in an out of her bouncing sex, Sarah could feel herself getting wetter and wetter by the moment.

Ellen cast a look back over her shoulder, grinning at the spectacle she had created. 'Nice and comfortable, pretty?' she called out. 'My, but I must say there's some colour in your cheeks, though you do sit your mount so proudly!'

'I – I can't, m-mistress!' Sarah managed to gasp. 'P-please, I... ooohhh!' The first wave of orgasm drove what little breath there remained from her body, which tensed like a bowstring. Only the cunning bondage prevented her from toppling sideways, while the stout shaft with which she was impaled triggered a reflexive instinct that made her grasp the saddle pommel with her manacled hands.

'Well, pretty one, whatever is the matter?' Ellen asked, giggling. 'That surely is no way for a lady of breeding to behave in public! I shall have to take my crop to your sweet bottom, I can see that now!'

But Sarah did not hear the implied threat, nor would she have cared if she had, for her treacherous body had taken on a life of its own, a life that defied and superseded all the logic, learning and inhibitions she had striven so hard to encompass throughout her young life.

As lights began to explode before her eyes and a roaring of wind and waterfalls thundered and echoed in her ears, she was dimly aware of just one thing and an image of Ross, his erect penis standing before him like a pikestaff, swam before her, taunting her with the one thing she now craved and which, apart from the unfeeling substitute that filled and stretched her, she knew her mistress would not let her have, quite possibly ever again!

The sudden crackle of musket fire was followed almost instantly by what sounded like an angrily buzzing bee, passing so close to Toby's head that he felt the wind from it. He ducked instinctively, but his reaction would have been far too slow to save him had the shot been on target.

Behind him a tree branch exploded into a thousand spiralling fragments and at the same time one of the troopers gave an anguished cry, clutched at his chest and toppled slowly from his saddle, a dark patch of crimson already spreading over the front of the brighter red of his uniform tunic.

'Down men! We're being attacked!'

Even as he slid from his saddle and threw himself beneath the fronds of the nearest bush, Toby could not help but laugh at the stupidity of the young captain's cry. One man already down and another ragged volley of shots was more than enough to render his observation superfluous.

All around him, it seemed to Toby that horses were rearing and whinnying, men diving for cover, leaves and twigs flying as more musket balls slammed their destructive paths through the foliage. From close by two muskets opened up to return fire, but the shots were hurried, badly aimed and in any case, Toby realised, none of them knew from exactly which direction the sudden attack had come.

Another shot, this time the report higher, sharper, as Thomas Handiwell fired his pistol and then, for several seconds that seemed to stretch into hours, everything fell silent once again. From behind a gnarled tree to Toby's right he heard a muttered oath, followed by a raucous cough.

'Keep your heads down, lads!' This time it was the lilting Irish brogue of Sergeant Riley that gave the order. His voice sounded calm, almost detached. 'Reload quickly and wait for the order. No sense in wasting good powder and shot on ghosts. Johnson, where do you think you're going, lad? Get back behind your tree, before one of them blows your fuckin' head off!'

'I only wanted to see how Hollis was, sarge,' the man named Johnson cried. 'He's just lyin' there, look, in the middle of the track, right out in the open.'

'Look harder, Hollis, m'boy,' Riley retorted. 'Ye'll see the lad's dead. There's a hole in his chest youse could put yer hand in.'

'Ah shit!' This was yet another voice. Toby wriggled into a better position and peered out from beneath the curtain of leaves. Glimpses of scarlet showed where three of the soldiers had taken cover and he could see the corpse of the unfortunate Trooper Hollis laying sprawled at the side of the track, about twenty paces in the direction from which they had come, but the rest of the small party were now invisible.

'Toby – Toby Blaine, are you all right, lad?' Thomas Handiwell sounded close, but Toby could see no sign of him.

'Y-yes,' he stammered, forcing the word out with some difficulty. 'Yessir, I'm fine.'

'Good, well keep your head well down and don't try anything silly. Captain, can you see anything?' There was a long pause, before captain Hart finally replied.

253

'N-no, nothing, Master Handiwell,' he called, his voice sounding very shaky. 'Perhaps they've gone, d'you think?'

'They've not gone yet, sorr,' Riley growled. 'I kin see a movement away to the left, up in the treetops. There's at least one of them up there and probably more on either side. Sean Kelly, are you awake there, ye skillipin' liddle bog trotter, youse?'

'Would I be after sleepin' on a fine day such as this, sergeant darlin'?' Another Irish voice, this time from somewhere behind Toby. 'And what would it be that ye're wantin' of me, seein' as how we seems to have a liddle time on our hands here?'

'See those three big elm trees, Sean?' the sergeant called softly. 'See them over slightly to yer left? Well, that's where I'm thinkin' most of these sneakin' English backstabbers are skulkin'. See if youse can get yer idle arse around to the side of 'em and get yerself a clear shot.

'I'm going to count to twenty, slowly – and then I'm going to see if I can't surprise that bastard up above there. The smug bastard probably reckons we can't see him, but he's showin' a bit of leg enough fer me to work out where his black heart oughta be.'

Everything fell silent once again and only the slight rustling of foliage away from the direction where Sean Kelly's voice had come indicated that the trooper was moving to obey Riley's instruction. His lips moving silently, Toby began to count slowly, using his fingers to guide him through the numbers once he reached ten.

Nineteen... twenty. Nothing.

Twenty one... twenty and... two... twenty and...

Crack! The loud report of Sergeant Riley's musket discharging made Toby jump, startling him so much that he felt himself lose momentary control of his bladder, but a strangled cry from the treetops that the Irishman had indicated earlier told that the shot had found its mark and the ensuing crashing and tearing of branches testified to an even greater accuracy than that.

'That's one less, captain, sorr!' Riley cried triumphantly.

'Good shooting, sergeant!' Hart exclaimed excitedly. 'Can you see any more of them?' Almost as the question was out another report, further away this time, followed again by a cry of pain and then answered by three or four more reports, though this time there was no corresponding shout to indicate that Sean Kelly had been hit by the return fire.

'Ah shit!'

'Sergeant?'

'Those last shots, sorr,' Riley called back. 'They were from further across again. I don't think they hit Sean, but it means there's at least a half dozen of the sods out there and they're spread to both sides of the track.'

'Then they have us fairly well pinned here, yes?'

'Well, we can always fall back, sorr, unless they've got in behind, of course, but as to advancin', well, it'd be a foolish move, in my opinion. These buggers know the ground, too.'

'Captain!' Thomas Handiwell's voice sounded strained and urgent. 'Captain Hart, call out and tell these people you are a commissioned officer in the service of your country!'

'Ah, Master Handiwell, sorr,' Riley's voice came back again, 'I'd be after thinkin' they moight well be knowin' that already, sorr. Beggin' the captain's pardon, and yours too, yer honour, I think the best thing we can do here is to fall back, before they do get the idea of gettin' in behind us.'

- XIX -

The sudden noise of the guns sounded frighteningly close behind her and Harriet leapt for the nearest tree and pressed herself against it, staring back down the overgrown track with terrified eyes. Instinctively, her hand slid inside her shirt, her fingers closing over the grip of the pistol, but even as they did so she knew she could never bring herself to use it.

The first shots, which had sent several small flocks of birds flapping and squawking into the afternoon sky, were followed by an almost eerie silence; high above, the disturbed birds circled indecisively, but their indignation was no longer voluble, whilst the faint breeze was barely enough to stir the leaves in the trees themselves.

Her heart pounding, Harriet moved around the tree trunk until its bulk was between her and the noise of the shooting. She knew that whoever it was they were not aiming at her, but she knew enough about stray musket balls to take every sensible precaution. After all, she told herself, was it not a stray ricocheting ball that had felled her father and caused the seemingly endless years of misery and ill health he had suffered ever since?

'Oh, pa,' she whispered, her lower lip trembling, 'why ever did I think I could do this? You have always thought me such a sensible and competent daughter, but how sensible is this now?'

More shots rung out. One single shot, a second single shot and then a fractured volley. Somewhere in the distance Harriet thought she heard an anguished cry, but she could not be certain that her ears were not simply playing tricks on her. The only thing she could be sure of was that her potential rescuers, those on whom she depended for her very safety in this venture, had come under attack, for she was convinced they would not themselves start an engagement, not knowing that she was somewhere ahead of them and alone.

She hesitated, indecision pushing its way through the uppermost layer of trepidation, for if Thomas and the small group of soldiers were being attacked, there was little likelihood of them catching up with her in the immediate future; therefore, if anything went wrong, or the kidnappers refused to hand over Sarah once they had been paid their ransom, Harriet's position would be perilous in the extreme.

How could she have been so foolish and so obstinate? It had all seemed so simple, but here now, alone and a long way from any help, she realised that this venture had been fraught from its very beginning. Whoever they were dealing with – male or female – they were both cunning and ruthless and had the confidence even to take on the state in the form of armed soldiers.

'Cousin Sarah,' she whispered, biting her lip, 'I'm so truly sorry, but I cannot do this, I really cannot!'

Harriet turned, seeking a way into the relative safety of the woods, desperate to find a refuge where she could lie low until it was safe to retrace her steps and, hopefully, rejoin Thomas and the soldiers. As she did so a sudden rustling to her left made her start backwards, but it was too late for the danger lay in a totally different direction and, as she made to run, from behind her the net snaked out, dropping neatly over her and dragging her struggling and screaming to the ground.

Despite his youth and inexperience, it did not take Toby very long at all to work out that the young Captain Hart had almost certainly never been under fire before and that it was the Irish sergeant, Riley, who afforded the small party

257

their best chance of retreating without further injuries or loss of life.

Calling out softly, he instructed the remaining troopers to make sure they were reloaded and to wait upon his word, whereupon, he said, they would fire a volley that would have their unseen assailants ducking for cover. At the same moment Thomas Handiwell, Hart and Toby himself were to make a run for it, back down the track.

Further volleys would enable the soldiers themselves to retreat in orderly fashion, he said, and Toby noted that his supposedly superior officer said nothing to disagree with this tactic. His heart pounding, bowels clenching and unclenching, Toby tensed himself.

'Right-oh, lads,' Riley's lilting brogue came at last, 'on my word, let the bastards have it. And – fire, lads!' The muskets crackled and roared as one and Toby found himself on his feet even before he'd thought about it, but as he sprinted along, bent almost double, something made him forget about his own safety for just long enough to stop by the body of the fallen trooper, scoop up his musket and grab the pouch from his belt that contained his powder and shot.

For a few seconds it seemed to Toby that everything hung suspended in mid-air, that he was surrounded by a curious blue mist and that the two figures of Thomas Handiwell and Captain Hart, as they went past him, were running in slow notion, their legs seeming to float just off the ground as they ran.

He saw Thomas Handiwell turn his head towards him, watched the innkeeper's mouth open and shut and knew the man was shouting to him, but he could hear nothing save for a furious buzzing sound in his head. And then he was moving again, the sounds of crashing branches and snapping twigs all around him and finally he slithered into a shallow ditch, a few feet away from where Thomas was crouching behind a broad elm tree.

'You bloody little fool!' Handiwell cried. 'You could have got yourself killed!' Toby rolled over onto all fours and raised his head to peer back in the direction from which they had come. Everything was quiet again, but a moment later more shots rang out and he saw two red-coated figures come hurtling towards him, only to stop short and duck behind trees on either side of the track.

Immediately, Toby saw, they began reloading their muskets and he understood precisely what was intended. Without thinking he raised the commandeered musket, checked that it was loaded and primed and raised it to his shoulder, steadying himself on one elbow.

'Do you know how to use that thing?' Thomas called across. Toby did not bother to answer, but concentrated his aim in the general direction of where the original firing had come and waiting to add his shot to those of the soldiers, when the moment came. He did not have to wait long.

Shots from ahead were joined by shots from the two crouching troopers and, letting out a slow breath, Toby fired likewise. The recoil was a lot more powerful than he was used to from his father's musket and the barrel of the gun leapt in his hands, so he knew his shot had gone far too high, but the overall effect was more important than actually finding a target and he was rewarded, seconds later, by the sight of Riley and the other Irishman loping back past the first two soldiers.

'Right then, lads,' the sergeant called out, already reloading his weapon. 'Same thing again, only this time me and Sean will duck aside into the bushes. If anyone starts to follow, we'll pot them.'

'What about the horses, Sergeant?' Captain Hart shouted from somewhere behind Toby. 'We can't just abandon them – they're army property!'

'Fuck army property,' Riley growled, just loud enough

so that Toby could hear, though probably not so loud that Hart would understand his words. Louder, he called back.

'They'll start to make their own way back, sure enough, sorr,' he said. 'Once everything goes quiet I'll whistle the beggars. Master Handiwell's horses will follow ours, more'n likely. More important you all get back well out of range in the meantime. Leave the rest to me and Sean. We'll be all right, don't you worry.'

And somehow, Toby knew they would be.

The two men quickly gathered in the net, imprisoning Harriet helplessly within its mesh and then winding a length of rope about her middle, pinning her arms even tighter to her sides. Realising the futility of struggling further, she stopped and stood staring defiantly out at them.

'My name is Harriet Merridew,' she said as calmly as she could manage, though she was acutely aware of the tremor of fear in her voice. 'I have brought the ransom money as demanded, and I should like to see my cousin.'

'Oh, you'll see her all right, missy,' the taller man said. He looked to be aged about thirty, while his companion, a head shorter than he, seemed to be scarcely out of his teens.

'Then I suggest you take me to her without further delay,' Harriet said, trying to sound authoritative, though without much success.

'All in good time, missy,' the older man replied. 'Artie, get a cord about those ankles and get her over your shoulder, lad. Time's getting on and the mistress wants her back and made ready by sunset.'

Artie, the younger man, quickly stooped and looped a stout cord several times about Harriet's ankles, drawing them together and knotting the ends tightly. Then, with a strength that belied his youthful frame, he hefted her unceremoniously up and over his right shoulder, slapped her heavily across her upraised buttocks and began marching along the trail in his companion's wake.

Harriet opened her mouth to protest at such summary treatment, but quickly closed it again, realising it would do her no good. Instead she let herself hang limply, while her fingers, hampered by both net and rope, began to seek the handle of her pistol.

It was the better part of an hour before Sergeant Riley and Sean Kelly emerged from the woods, but they did have with them all the horses, including the dead trooper's mount, with his body tied across the saddle.

'They weren't interested in the horses,' Riley said to Toby, who had contrived to ride alongside him on the remainder of the return journey. 'Come to that, they weren't really interested in us, not once they'd convinced us not to go any further.'

'Couldn't we have tried to encircle them?' Toby suggested, and Riley looked across at him and grinned.

'Well, I suppose we could have,' he replied, 'if we'd had maybe a dozen more men and weren't too worried about losing maybe half of them as well. Like I told the officer gentleman earlier, those woods are their ground and they probably know every inch of it.

'On top of that, me darlin', we had no way of tellin' just how many of the beggars we were up against.'

'I thought I counted about six shots when they all fired,' Toby said.

Riley nodded, knowingly. 'Me too, lad,' he agreed, 'but I'll bet you couldn't tell me if they was the same six muskets each time, eh?' Toby considered this and then shook his head. 'Well, there you have it,' Riley continued. 'There could have been as many as a dozen of them in there.'

'But you and the other trooper got two of them,' Toby pointed out.

'And they may well have got us before we got any more

of them,' Riley retorted. 'If you ask me,' he added, dropping his voice to a whisper, 'this whole bloody thing was asking for trouble. The young captain had that half right, if nothing else. You go blundering into someone's back yard uninvited you shouldn't expect them to make you feel a whole lot welcome!'

'Then what happens next?' Toby asked. 'Miss Harriet is still in there, somewhere.'

Riley wrinkled his forehead and pulled a wry face. 'Not my decision, sunshine,' he said. 'That's for the officers to sort out. We're just other ranks, you and me. Keep our powder dry and our cocks washed and leave the thinking to those as are paid for it.' He winked and grinned. 'Oh, and by the way,' he added, 'I saw what you did back there. Very brave, son. Ever thought of joining the army?'

'Well… yes,' Toby replied, trying to hide the blush of pleasure he could feel welling up.

Riley let out a snorting laugh. 'Well, don't,' he said. 'You seem like you've got too much sense for all this rubbish, so think again, unless the idea of letting some fancy pants get you killed appeals to you more than it should.'

- XX -

The sight of Ellen Grayling, sitting astride her stallion, smirking with her usual superior air, came as no surprise to Harriet when Artie dumped her unceremoniously on the grass before the two horses, but when she sat up again and looked at the young woman on the horse beside Ellen, she felt a strange chill crawl up her spine.

Even with the girl's elaborately made-up face, the family resemblance was unmistakable and Harriet new instantly that this was the cousin she had never met, but there was something more, something about the curiously vacant expression on Sarah's face and the way she sat her horse as if she were not really there, but somewhere deep inside another world, far away and totally cut off from what was happening.

'So, it *is* you behind all this, *Lady* Ellen!' Harriet said, trying in vain to get to her feet. 'Well, you won't get away with this, I can tell you that. We already suspected you were involved and Master Handiwell and the soldiers will soon be here.'

Ellen Grayling leaned over in her saddle and regarded Harriet with a look of malicious amusement. 'Is that so?' she said languidly. 'Well, my dear Mistress Merridew, for your information we have more than two dozen men employed on this estate, all of whom are well trained in the use of arms. No doubt you heard the sounds of musket fire a little while back, yes? Well, I'm reliably informed that Master Handiwell and his sorry little band have now retreated, minus at least one of their original number. I don't think they'll be bothering us any more.'

'They'll be back,' Harriet snapped. 'Master Handiwell

has sufficient evidence to lay charges against you and all your friends.'

'Even his own daughter?' Ellen retorted scathingly. 'Or haven't you told him of your suspicions in that direction? Ah, I see you're surprised I know about that. Well, you shouldn't be, my dear. The walls of the *Black Drum* have very keen ears at times.'

'That little vixen, Beth, I suppose?' Harriet said. She tried to think back, wondering if she and Ann Billings had mentioned Jane's name anywhere where her maid might have overheard them, but her memory refused to focus.

'Among others, maybe,' Ellen replied easily. 'Not that it matters who now, anyway. No, the main thing is that you are here. Say hello to your dear cousin, why don't you? I'm sure she can hear you, though I'm afraid she seems a little distant at the moment.'

'What have you done to her?' Harriet demanded, turning her attention back to Sarah.

Ellen sniggered. 'Nothing she hasn't enjoyed, though I'll admit I didn't give her a great deal of choice in the matter. Arthur, untie *Mistress* Merridew's ankles if you please, and help her to her feet. She'll have to walk back with us, after all. If only I'd thought, I could have furnished her with a mount to match her sweet cousin's.'

As soon as her legs were free Harriet scrambled upright, thrusting away Artie's efforts to assist her. Still enmeshed in the net and with her arms pinioned and all but useless, she stumbled across to Sarah and peered up into her vacuous face.

'Sarah?' she cried. 'Sarah Merridew! Look, it is I, your cousin Harriet. Are you all right?' Sarah blinked slowly and looked down, but her eyes were still glazed, her pupils dilated.

'Harriet?' she said eventually, her voice wavering. 'Ah yes, my dear cousin. Are you well?' Her face at last began to show some signs of animation, a series of peculiar twitches that started in her cheeks, spread to her painted lips and finally reached her eyelids, which began to flutter.

Harriet rounded on Ellen. 'She looks drugged!' she exclaimed accusingly. 'What have you given her?'

Ellen smirked. 'No drug I think you have ever tasted, Mistress Merridew,' she reposted, 'but a powerful one, nonetheless. Here, let me show you.' She wheeled her horse about, almost knocking Harriet sideways as she did so and reached out with her riding crop, using it to lift part of Sarah's long riding skirt up and away. For a second or two Harriet did not understand, but then, as her brain understood what her eyes were showing her, she recoiled in horror.

'Monstrous!' she shrieked, backing away. 'Utterly monstrous! You will surely hang for this infamy, Ellen Grayling. You and your friends!'

'I think not, my dear sweet thing,' Ellen replied, allowing the black fabric to fall back and cover the evidence of Sarah's enforced debauchery. 'Your friend Handiwell will no doubt try to come to your aid, but he won't get farther than the house itself, which will surely be his next approach. My dear brother will undoubtedly send him packing with a flea in his ear and, if he fails to understand the legalities of his position, then he will surely realise that his pitiful little force is sorely outnumbered. By the time he can persuade the authorities to send reinforcements – if indeed he can at all – it will be far too late.

'Besides, even with a hundred troopers he will still need a warrant to search this estate, and our family has more influence than you might imagine and people in high places who rather approve of what we do here. As a matter of fact, your dear cousin met one of those very people only last night, and he was greatly appreciative of the entertainment she helped provide for him.'

'Your terms,' Harriet said, trying desperately to change

265

tack now, if only to buy a little more time, 'stated that you would release Sarah in return for a certain sum in gold. I have that sum with me now, or am I to assume that you have no intention of honouring your word?'

'You're a fast learner,' Ellen sneered. 'Of course you have the money, otherwise why would you have come, mm? But the money is secondary and, if it will make you feel any better, I shall see to it that it's returned to Master Handiwell in good time.

'No, the idea all along was to get you here, and your cousin's arrival was simply a means to effect that. Had she not turned up we should have had to find some other way before too long, and I must say I thought all this was just a mite over gilding the lily, but no matter, you're here now.

'And the timing is quite opportune in another way, too. You, my dear Mistress Merridew, are going to help us deal with another small problem. A certain party has been growing just a little too suspicious for comfort of late, and discrediting him would put an end to his busy bodying interference. Of course, you know our dear Reverend Wickstanner, don't you? A particularly unpleasant little oik, to say the least. Quite useless as a man, of course, but he has an unpleasant talent for snooping around and prying into things that don't concern him and, unfortunately for him, he overheard a conversation between two of our grooms a few weeks ago. Nothing very incriminating, but just enough to whet his appetite, and it's come to our notice that he's been asking around – discreetly, he thinks – trying to find out more. So far, fortunately, he's not gotten very far, but his type are persistent in the extreme and tend not to let go of something once they've got their teeth into it. No doubt you've heard or seen what's been happening to the Pennywise girl? That's Wickstanner's doing, though he's had to call in that so-called witchfinder to do his dirty work for him, the spineless little worm.'

'I don't see what Master Wickstanner has to do with all this,' Harriet declared uncertainly. 'I like him little more than you apparently do, but I have no dealings with the fellow. I have enough on my plate without becoming involved with his business.'

'And not even enough time to attend Sunday services, I hear,' Ellen chuckled. 'Which fact, among a few others he's concocted, would be enough to give him grounds to turn his attentions to you, once he's finished with Matilda Pennywise.'

'He wouldn't dare!' Harriet exclaimed, horrified at the suggestion. 'In fact, he has overstepped the mark already with what he has done to Matilda.'

'Undoubtedly,' Ellen agreed, 'but who is there to tell him so? Maybe Master Handiwell, but he's been preoccupied with trying to save your dear cousin here and now; with you disappearing as well, I doubt he'll give the wretched girl another thought, not until it's far too late.'

'Word is,' Harriet said defiantly, 'that the man Crawley intends to hang her tomorrow morning and Master Handiwell and Captain Hart are well aware of that. Whether I am still missing or not, they will take time to put a stop to that, I am sure.'

'I'm sure that's their intention, yes,' Ellen rejoined, 'but intention and execution are two differing beasts at times and, in this case, I think the execution will be of a different kind to the one Master Handiwell envisages.

'But enough talking; there is work to do and we are two miles from where we need to be to do it properly. Arthur, remove that net, manacle our guest's hands securely and make sure you remove that pistol I believe I can see hiding under her shirt. We wouldn't want any nasty accidents on the way back, would we now?'

'Even the Grayling family are not above the law of the land!' Thomas Handiwell stormed. 'You've had a man shot and killed, Captain Hart, and but for good fortune more of us could have died in that cowardly ambush.'

'Agreed, Master Handiwell,' Hart replied hesitantly, 'but I know what they will say if we do go to the hall and confront them. We have no proof it was Grayling's men who fired upon us, and from the map you showed me earlier, their estate is so vast that these robbers could easily have been there without Grayling's knowledge.'

'I think not, though,' Thomas growled. 'And we cannot just skulk around here and do nothing. It was bad enough before, but now Harriet is almost certainly in their clutches. We have to go and challenge them, perhaps unsettle them enough that they'll release the two womenfolk.'

'If the Graylings indeed do have the two young ladies,' Hart said, 'then I should think the last thing they are likely to do would be to release them so that they are then free to testify against them.'

'Then what would *you* advise, captain?'

Hart chewed nervously on his lip and paced slowly up and down on the gravelled courtyard. He and Thomas were alone by the inn stables, the soldiers all having taken the horses in to rub them down and feed them. Some distance away, Toby Blaine sat perched upon the corner of one of the troughs, a mug of ale clutched in his two hands.

'The only course I can think of, Master Handiwell,' Hart said at last, 'is for one of us to ride back to Portsmouth and lay the facts before a magistrate, first thing in the morning. Perhaps if we went together and, while you arrange for a warrant, I'll talk to Colonel Brotherwood and ask him to let me have perhaps a half company detachment of men.

'Warrant or not, if we march up to Grayling Hall with our present strength they may decide it's simpler to shoot us all down. They certainly seem to have the firepower for it.'

'And meantime,' Thomas retorted, 'they spirit away the Merridew girls and there's no evidence for us to find tomorrow.'

'Certainly, it's possible they might try something like that,' Hart agreed, 'but I could send Sergeant Riley and one man to keep watch on the place. Riley is a seasoned veteran and a former poacher, I understand. There are few men I'd sooner trust for such a mission.'

'He seems very reliable,' Thomas conceded, remembering how the Irish sergeant had reacted so coolly during the ambush. 'But it could be dangerous, sending just two men in there.'

'A lot less dangerous than marching in with a full platoon, yer honour,' Riley grinned, when the suggestion was put to him. 'I'll take Sean Kelly with me and we'll get rid of these red coats, too. They make for too easy targets. Far better something dark, if y'can perhaps do the honours, sorr?'

'I'll find some jackets for the two of you,' Thomas replied. 'Whatever happens, we cannot let them move the women.'

'If yer girls are there, yer worship, we'll find 'em,' Riley promised, 'and dependin' what else we find, we'll maybe even have 'em out of there even afore you and the captain sorr gets back with yer warrant.'

'It may not be as easy as you think, sergeant,' Thomas warned. 'There are probably a couple of dozen armed men up there, maybe even more.'

The grizzled Irishman raised one eyebrow and grinned. 'Sure, and Sean and meself have sorted worse odds than that of a Saturday night in Dublin,' he quipped. 'And if ye've ever been faced with even half a dozen drunken Irishmen, then thirty paltry English lackeys – beggin' yer pardon, sorrs – are nothin' to worry over. We'll be all right, Sean and me, don't you worry now.'

The full implications of what she had walked into only began to dawn on Harriet when the party eventually reached what appeared to be a huge barn and she was hustled inside, pushed into one of what she supposed had once been stalls and forcibly stripped by the two grooms.

Despite her frenetic struggles and attempts to gouge the eyes of the older man, whose name she learned was Nathan, she was soon completely naked and stood, shivering against one wall, desperately trying to preserve what remained of her modesty with her hands. Even that was quickly denied her, for her arms were drawn roughly behind her back and secured there with linked metal cuffs.

'Damn your souls for eternity!' she hissed, spitting at Artie, who simply laughed at her final attempt at defiance. At the same time Nathan stepped forward and delivered a heavy slap to the side of her face, the impact sending her staggering sideways.

'You worry about your own soul, you arrogant little bitch!' he snarled. 'Any more of your filthy nonsense and I'll hang you up by your thumbs while we finish our work.' Blinking furiously, with tears now filling her eyes, Harriet managed to bring his face back into some sort of focus; the expression she saw on his face assured her that his threat was no idle one.

'Now then, Artie,' Nathan said, when he saw that the fight was, temporarily at least, gone out of her, 'let's have that trestle in the middle here and mount the bitch on it. Yes, that one there, the one with the nice fat cock on top.' He turned back to Harriet, leering at her.

'You look like a good cock in your cunt would do you a world of good,' he rasped. Harriet recoiled in horror, seeing for the first time the trestle, from the top of which rose a dark and forbidding looking shaft. Momentarily the horror of what they were proposing to do threatened to overwhelm her and she fell back against the timber partition, her knees buckling so that she would have fallen to the floor had not her senior tormentor caught hold of her arm and pulled her upright again.

'Probably never had a man inside you, eh?' Nathan sneered, with awful accuracy. 'Well, we can't have you staying virgin now – not where you're going to. It'd give the game away for sure. Artie, gimme a hand with her, but oil that damned cock a bit first.'

The younger groom turned away from the trestle and moved to a high shelf on the far side of the cubicle, reaching up to take down a dark coloured glass jar, which he brought back to the centre of the room, unstoppered and dipped two fingers inside. When he drew them out, Harriet saw they were thick with some sort of grease, which he proceeded to transfer to the leather shaft, smearing it liberally and evenly.

When he was done and the jar returned, he came over and took up a station on the opposite side of Harriet from where Nathan stood, still gripping her upper arm. Then, at a quick count of three, both men placed a hand about one of her thighs and, steadying her by her elbows, lifted her high off the floor, drawing her legs wide apart and carrying her the short distance to where the awful contraption awaited her.

'No-ooo! *Please*!' Harriet wailed. 'You surely cannot! Oh, such foulness!' She tried to struggle again, but such was the position in which they held her that her best efforts were to no avail and then they were lowering her, guiding her unerringly, until she felt the hard tip of the phallus pressing against the entrance to her sex.

'Nooooo!' she whimpered. 'Please no… oh God… aaahhh!' She gasped, as they allowed her weight to descend and the unyielding rod began to penetrate her, thrusting its way through the tender necklace of tissue, pressing onward until she finally felt the rough timber beneath her buttocks

271

and knew she was finally and fully impaled.

Such was the height of the horizontal beam of the trestle that Harriet's bare feet dangled just clear enough of the flagstones beneath to prevent her from raising herself up again, so that, until the two brutish men decided otherwise, she was helplessly trapped, unable to free herself and all but unable to move and certainly not the latter without causing the fat dildo to exert pressures in places that Harriet had not, until now, fully realised she had.

'Bring a razor and soap, Artie,' Nathan instructed the younger man. 'Apparently the other wench is shaved down there. I'll tend to the shaving myself, though, otherwise you're likely to nick and cut her and they might notice that.'

Harriet stared at him through eyes grown round with disbelief, hoping she had misunderstood the meaning of his words, but it quickly became apparent that she had not.

'Now then, missy,' Nathan said, when Artie had brought the bowl of steaming water, a brush and some soap, 'this won't actually hurt you, not unless you wriggle about and make me catch your flesh.' He had produced a razor from somewhere and also a short leather strop, which he laid along the top of the trestle in front of Harriet and began sharpening the wicked looking blade on it.

Harriet hardly dared breathe, even when he was simply lathering the soap over her neatly trimmed triangle and, when he finally brought the blade close, every muscle and sinew in her body went rigid. She closed her eyes, partly unable to actually witness the humiliation that was being inflicted upon her, partly because she was too terrified to look, convinced that the deadly implement would slice through her most intimate flesh.

Nathan, however, was true to his word. He worked carefully and methodically and, when the final stroke was complete, not the slightest trace of a cut was to be seen. Harriet now began to shiver, for the sensations from her newly depilated mound were indescribable and seemed to emphasise her nakedness ten times over. What came next, however, was worse still.

Artie passed Nathan a large pair of shears and, after satisfying himself that the blades were properly sharpened, the older man grasped a handful of Harriet's hair and cut it away at a single stroke. Harriet tried to duck away to avoid his next grab, but only succeeded in reminding herself of the size of the silent invader within her and, as she gasped and groaned, another thick lock joined the first one beneath her feet.

- XXI -

Hannah led James deep into the woods behind her cottage, first following a footpath that was so overgrown as to be barely visible and then turning away even from that spartan trail, weaving her way between trees and around patches of unruly undergrowth, so that before long James knew that without her it would take him many hours to find his way back to where they had started.

At last the old woman came to a halt and leaned heavily against her staff. She turned, looked up at James, and sighed. 'Perhaps I should have done this earlier,' she said. 'The money would all have been Matilda's anyway, once I am gone. Whatever was I thinking about, lad?'

'As you said, Mother Pennywise,' James replied softly, 'to give in to such extortion would only open the way for these fiends to pressure other innocents in the same way.'

'Aye, but Matilda should have been my first concern – my only concern, in truth, for these blackguards will wreak their own foul hell on earth regardless and now the entire village has seen what they're capable of doing.'

Gently, James laid a hand on her bony shoulder. 'Don't blame yourself for the wickedness of others,' he said soothingly. 'Let's just do what needs to be done now and what is past let remain so.' He gripped the shovel in his free hand. 'Is this the place?' Hannah nodded and pointed towards a strangely twisted oak tree that stood on its own, even the undergrowth keeping a respectful distance.

'Down there,' she said, 'between the largest of the two roots on this side. You will need to dig quite deep, though the soil should be quite soft.'

The earth between the roots was indeed quite loose,

despite the covering of grass and moss and James realised, as he began to dig, that it could not have been so long since it had last been disturbed. Hannah, presumably, made frequent pilgrimages to the tree to add to her little hoard. After ten minutes, however, James began to form a new respect for the old woman, for even with his jacket discarded the sweat was pouring from him.

At last, when the pit had reached a depth approaching three feet, the blade of the shovel clanked against something hard, something metallic itself. Crouching awkwardly, James began to clear away the soil from either side and, after another five minutes, was able to climb out of the hole, kneel by the side of it and reach down to withdraw the small iron box, its coating of rust evidence enough of the years it had spent going in and out of the ground.

'Fill the hole, James,' Hannah instructed. 'I'll not be needing it again.' She stepped forward and took the heavy casket from his, cradling it in her arms. 'There are those who think of me as wise,' she said, 'among other things, of course. Well, I have today learned a new wisdom.' She looked down at the box and smiled, sadly. 'In this casket, James Calthorpe,' she said huskily, 'is gold to the value of more than one thousand guineas.' James stared at her in disbelief. 'Oh yes,' she continued, seeing his look of incredulity, 'it's a small fortune, I know.'

'A large fortune, more like,' James said, aghast.

Hannah nodded and the thin smile evaporated. 'A fortune, anyway,' she said levelly, 'and yet what good has it ever done anybody, buried deep in the ground? Will it sprout and grow? Will it bring forth green leaves, fragrant blossom or fruit? No, none of those, as we both know only too well.

'And what, pray, if something had happened to me before now, eh? I'll tell you what, James – this little trove would have remained buried where it was until the last tree in these woods had withered and died and probably long after that, useless and forgotten, as most of us shall be in time.

'Come, lad, leave the hole anyway. Nature will attend to her own in time. We have far more pressing business, for the sun is beginning to sink faster even as we stand here rueing my folly.'

'Well, I see they've done an excellent job in preparing you, my dear.' Jane Handiwell stood in the open doorway of the stall, a malicious grin on her face. Harriet, who had been left mounted on the abominable trestle, trying to ease the aching in her hips without causing too much friction from the dildo that filled her, raised her head, her cheeks burning with shame and hatred.

Nathan had finished hacking away her hair quite quickly and then, not satisfied with that, had lathered the remaining stubble and proceeded to use the razor again, so that when he finished Harriet's skull was as smooth as ivory, the cool draught tickling the naked flesh in seemingly mocking fashion.

'Why are you doing this to me?' Harriet whispered. 'I know you cannot face the fact that your father has feelings towards me, but surely you realise I am no threat in that direction, nor ever was?

'Thomas is a fine man, an honourable man,' she continued, 'and a good and trustworthy friend, but that is all and I have repeatedly made my position clear to him.'

'Which will never stop him persisting in his folly,' Jane sneered. She stepped into the chamber and looked down at Harriet's spread thighs. 'He'd give everything he owns to have his cock where that shaft now is,' she leered, 'but I intend to make sure that never happens.'

'It shall not, in any case,' Harriet retorted. 'But I see there is no reasoning with you, not now, nor ever in the past. It is a great pity, Jane, for we could have become friends, I'm sure.'

'That I doubt,' Jane snapped, 'for I know your sort. Sweet and blushing and always so neatly pretty. Butter'd not melt in your mouth, nor even between your thighs.' Her long thin face contorted into a grimace so fearsome that Harriet let out a frightened whimper. 'Well, you ain't so damned pretty now, are you Harriet Merridew? Oh, how I wish there were time to have a picture painted of you just as you now are. I'd make sure that my dear, foolish, gullible pater received it in a gilded frame and be there to see his face when first he set eyes upon it! However, there is no time for that, sadly.

'I have a better purpose for you, my sweet little English rose. Tonight we kill two birds with the one stone – perhaps even three. Nathan!' She turned and called towards the doorway. 'Nathan, bring in that harness I left on the bench out there. Might as well get her as ready as possible here and save ourselves some time later!'

By the time the grooms finally lifted her from the saddle, Sarah had lost all sense of reality and it was some time before she could even begin to take stock of her surroundings again. When she did recover sufficiently to regain some perception, it was to find herself sitting against a fencepost, a little way away from the large barn structure, with her legs stretched straight out before her and a set of manacles locked about her ankles, connected with a short chain.

Several horses stood grazing disinterestedly on the grass nearby, among them Ellen's and the animal on which she, herself, had been mounted, the thick dildo still projecting up from its saddle. Seeing this, Sarah lowered her eyes, a wave of shame engulfing her, but she was not left alone with her thoughts for much longer.

'Well, pretty,' Ellen exclaimed, emerging from the barn, 'that *was* lots of fun, wasn't it? And how like you your dear cousin is. I hadn't realised, not until I saw the two of you together. How I wish there was more time, for I'm sure we could have had so much enjoyment together, the three of us.'

'My cousin?' Sarah tried to concentrate, grasping at fragmented images. 'Oh, yes,' she said, remembering vaguely that there had been someone else there, somewhere back there, in the woods. 'Yes, my cousin Harriet. Where is she? What have you done with her?'

'Now, don't you worry your pretty little head about Harriet,' Ellen giggled. 'She's in very good hands, I can assure you, and she'll be well taken care of.

'Well taken care of indeed,' she added, with another sniggering laugh.

The harness, Harriet realised, was the same design as the one she had briefly glimpsed on the unfortunate Matilda the previous day. It was simple, but very effective, the broad waist belt cinching tightly and the two straps at either side rendering her wrists immobile and her arms and hands useless.

Only when the two men had finished fitting it did they finally lift her from the trestle, and she closed her eyes in shame as she saw that the leather covered phallus now glistened with her intimate juices.

'Take her into the main chamber,' Jane instructed Nathan. 'Put a collar on her and fasten her to one of the posts, facing it. Then I want you to fetch me a length of thin sheeting, soaked in water.'

Very soon, Harriet found herself arranged as per Jane's orders, a wide collar about her throat, a ring at the front of it tied to one of several posts that were set in the ground of the larger room into which they had taken her. As Artie finished the knot, Nathan reappeared, carrying a crumpled piece of greying fabric, from which water dripped steadily.

'Wring it out,' Jane instructed, on seeing this. 'I want it damp, not sodden, man!' It was quickly done and Jane took the sheet from him and placed it carefully over Harriet's shoulders and back, tying two corners about her neck so that it formed a crude cape.

'Not perfect,' she whispered, as she leaned close to Harriet, 'but it will do for my purposes. You see,' she explained, 'I'm now going to whip you and this wet cloth will make the stripes appear less fresh, though I'm afraid they won't lessen your pain.'

'You wicked woman!' Harriet gasped. 'Haven't you done enough to me already? Have you no pity, no conscience?'

Jane stepped back and Nathan handed her a long, whippy looking crop. 'Conscience,' she said smoothly, 'is a luxury I long ago decided I could not afford. I'll take my chances in the next world, if indeed there is one, which I doubt. Now, Nathan, I shall give you a demonstration of the real way to whip a slave and then you and young Arthur can have your way with her, provided you are quick about it.'

With careful deliberation Jane stepped to one side, adjusted her grip on the crop and raised it, drawing it around to the height of her shoulder. Harriet tried to look back at her, but the collar and tight leash prevented her from turning her head more than a fraction, so that the first warning she had was when she heard the low whistle of the braided leather as it scythed through the air.

In almost the same instant a bolt of agonising fire seared across her shoulders and a scream tore from her throat as she writhed helplessly against the post.

'About a dozen in all,' she dimly heard Jane say. 'From what I saw earlier that should look about right.' Vaguely, Harriet found herself wondering what on earth the girl was talking about, but then, as the crop slashed home again, such luxuries as thinking were banished in a second, ear-splitting shriek of agony.

The iron box was very heavy and James had to pause several times on their way back to the cottage, in order to put it down and relieve the strain on both his arms and his hands. Despite her evident desire for haste, Hannah leaned patiently on her staff each time and waited until James felt able to continue once again.

'Gold is more damned trouble than it's worth,' she muttered as they finally reached her gate. 'I think, when this is over, I shall use whatever is left and take Matilda far away from this accursed village.'

'I hope you will permit me to come with you both,' James said, between panting breaths. 'After this I could not bear to let your granddaughter out of my sight.'

'After this,' Hannah growled, pushing open her front door, 'my poor Matilda may not be able to stomach the sight of a man ever again.'

'I hope…' James began, but the words died in his mouth as he saw the figure slumped in the chair by the hearth. 'Dear God!' he exclaimed, his voice rising an octave. 'Dear God, but it can't be!' He stood frozen, staring in disbelief, but Hannah pushed past him, dropping her staff on the floor and knelt stiffly beside the motionless form.

'The bastards!' she hissed through clenched teeth. 'Oh, the bastards! What have they done to you, my sweet? How could I have even thought to let things come so far?' She turned and raised her eyes to James, who still had not moved since first seeing Matilda.

'Go to the cupboard in the kitchen, man!' she cried. 'There's a bottle on the top shelf, bring it to me – quickly! Don't just stand there! Can't you see how badly she's fared?'

As James finally stirred from his frozen shock, Hannah turned again to Matilda, one bony hand stroking her hairless skull, the other clasping her naked arm. Matilda gave a whimpering moan and struggled to open her eyes.

'Grandma,' she croaked. 'Is it really you? Is it over now?'

280

Hannah's own eyes narrowed, but she forced herself to smile back at the semi-conscious girl. 'Yes, my pet,' she crooned. 'Yes, it's over now. They'll not lay another finger on you now, I swear it.'

- XXII -

Harriet stared up through the narrow slits in the leather hood. The two men had now gone, half dragging, half carrying the naked form of Matilda Pennywise, who was still strapped into the leather harness which was the twin of the one that had been put onto Harriet back in the barn.

'You must be mad!' Harriet croaked, fighting to stop her body from trembling. 'Crawley will know I'm not Matilda!'

Jane smiled, her features taking on a spectral look in the flickering lamplight. 'I think not,' she retorted. 'You're about the same build and those stripes on your back and legs now look much like the ones he put on her – like enough to fool him, anyway, for I doubt he'll be looking that closely, not at those parts of you, anyway.' She crouched down, so that her face was level with Harriet's.

'He'll doubtless give you one last fucking, though,' she sneered. 'He's a man, after all. And I find that prospect almost poetic; the first flesh and blood cock inside you will belong to the man who will then take you out and hang you.'

Harriet shook her head. 'He'll know, I'm sure of it,' she said, but with more conviction than she felt. 'The whip marks on me are still too fresh. They might fool him in here, where it's almost dark, but in daylight, in the morning—'

'Except that there won't be any morning for you,' Jane interrupted her. Harriet looked at her in astonishment. 'You see,' Jane continued, 'Master Crawley is going to take you out and hang you at midnight, with three witnesses, as per the law. I might even volunteer myself to be one of them.

'The great shame of it is, though,' she said, 'that as I

understand it you won't feel a thing. Crawley's fellows have this quite unique gallows, from which they drop you and the rope then snaps your neck. Quite painless, they say, but never mind; at least you'll be dead and out of my way.

'And then, afterwards, when they remove this hood to bury you, that's when the people of the village will realise that a great mistake has been made. Crawley will protest his innocence, of course, but it'll do him no good. I doubt whether they'll actually do anything to him, but he won't be able to show his face around here again.

'And the same will hold for that greasy little oik Wickstanner. He'll be considered guilty by association and his damned church will have to replace him here. That'll be one more meddlesome bastard out of the way. Now, I have something for you to drink, before I leave you.'

She held up a small vial and removed the cork from it. Harriet drew back, shaking her head violently, clamping her jaws firmly shut.

'Don't be afraid,' Jane said, her voice sounding like a cat purring over the cream. 'It won't harm you, I can assure you. After all, why would I seek to poison you when Crawley will be hanging you in less than two hours, eh? He's already at the *Drum*, rounding up his witnesses.

'No, this is simply a potion that will relax you, perhaps make you feel a bit groggy.' She leaned forward and seized Harriet's lower jaw through the leather, her thumb and fingers biting cruelly. Harriet let out a muffled squeal and tried to pull back further, but Jane twisted her grip viciously and the sudden pain overwhelmed her resolve.

In an instant Jane had forced the open end of the bottle between her lips, tipping its contents in one go and holding Harriet's head back so that, despite her staunchest efforts, when Jane dropped the vial and gripped her nostril closed with the newly freed hand, Harriet was forced to swallow the liquid, or suffocate.

'There now,' Jane said, releasing her grip and sitting back, picking up bottle and cork and tucking them away inside her jacket. 'That wasn't so bad, was it?' She turned away and, when she turned back again, Harriet saw she was holding the rusting scold's bridle.

'I think I shall put this delightful piece of antiquity on you before I go,' she said lightly. 'If my estimate of Crawley is right he won't bother removing it before you hang, but even if he does, it won't matter. Do you feel your tongue beginning to grow thick yet, mm?'

Hannah gaped at her, for indeed, almost as soon as she had swallowed the potion a curious tickling sensation had begun at the back of her throat and was spreading along the length of her tongue.

'It's a little concoction of my own invention,' she continued. 'I shan't bother you with the details, but I can assure you that it is most effective, especially when used on slaves we don't want to openly gag.

'As I said, it will also make you feel a little groggy, which may, in fact, make what is still to come easier to bear, but its main purpose is that it affects the tongue, deadening it so that it is impossible to utter intelligible speech for three or four hours after it is administered.

'So, even if Crawley does decide to remove this, you won't be able to tell him you're not Matilda, will you? Now, open wide and let's put this wonderful old contraption on you, eh?'

'That's close enough, Master Crawley!' The figure on the far side of the bridge was shrouded in a long cape and cowl, which in the darkness masked its identity totally, but the voice, despite her attempts to deepen it, was most certainly female. Jacob Crawley paused, two paces onto his side of the bridge and leaned casually against the stone parapet.

'I have to tell you,' he said easily, 'that my men are hidden just back in the trees, with muskets trained on you. At the first sign of any treachery they will open fire on you and they are both first rate shots.'

'Is that so, Master Crawley?' the woman chuckled. 'I made it one man only, over there, to the right, unless I am mistaken.' She raised her arm, pointing in the direction where Silas Grout had hidden himself just two minutes earlier. 'The range would be what – seventy paces? I doubt your man could hit a barn door from there, but no matter, there is no treachery here.

'However,' she continued, lowering her arm again, 'there is great treachery in this village, as you well know. Treachery, heresy and witchcraft.'

'Indeed there is,' Crawley agreed. 'Is that what you wish to speak with me about, mistress?'

'It is, Master Crawley,' she confirmed. 'The witch, Matilda Pennywise?'

'What of her?'

'You will hang her?'

'Yes. The absolution tithe has not been paid. The hour specified has now passed. Although, God in his wisdom may yet guide me to be merciful.'

'It has not yet been paid, nor will it be,' the woman said. 'The old witch never did have any money.'

'And the miller's boy?'

'His father would not let him have the money.'

'Then the wench shall hang in the morning.'

'Why not hang her this night and be done with it?'

'What is it to you, mistress?' Crawley smiled to himself in the darkness, sensing that there was far more to this than even he had suspected, for he had anticipated someone might wish to make another accusation, or even, perhaps, to try to buy Matilda's life, for there was still the unresolved matter of who had paid the first two guineas.

'Matilda Pennywise has placed a hex upon a member of

my family,' the woman replied, carefully. 'I cannot give you details, nor can I reveal my identity to you, but I am willing to pay you and pay you well for her speedy execution, for all the while there is breath remaining in her body, her powers are surely killing one who is dear to me.'

'I see,' Crawley said thoughtfully. His smile flickered again. 'And you have proof of this?'

'None that I can show you,' the woman said, 'but I was under the impression that you had all the evidence and proof you needed against the witch.'

'Aye, that I do, mistress,' Crawley agreed, 'but the sentence is to be carried out in the morning, nonetheless.'

'I was under the impression that you had the authority to decide the hour of her execution.' The woman reached inside her cloak and Crawley instinctively stiffened, but when she withdrew her hand there was no weapon in it, only a small dark and almost shapeless object, which she held out and shook. Crawley heard the unmistakable chinking of heavy coins.

'I have here fifty golden guineas,' she continued. 'These I will give to you now.' Her arm whirled and there was a blur as the little bag flew through the air, landing just in front of Crawley's feet with a jingling sound. His immediate instinct was to bend and pick up the bag, but he forced himself to remain unmoving, his gaze set firmly upon her outline.

'You don't want to count it, then?' she asked, a note of surprise in her voice.

Crawley shook his head. 'I am sure there will be fifty guinea coins in there, as you said,' he replied. 'There would be little point in it being otherwise.' He stepped forward and reached out with the toe of one boot, prodding the bag as if he expected it might at any moment spring to life.

'There will be another fifty guineas for you as soon as you have executed the Pennywise witch,' the woman said.

'I shall have the sum delivered to you before dawn's first light.'

'I see,' Crawley said. 'That is indeed a large sum of money, mistress.'

'The same amount, I hear said, that you demanded for her reprieve and absolution.'

'I shan't deny that,' Crawley chuckled mirthlessly. 'You appear well informed.'

'Aye, Master Crawley, that I am,' she said, and he heard a low laugh from within the cowl. 'Well informed enough to know that this is the only way you'll get your money now, and you have to hang the bitch anyway.'

'Aye, that I do,' Crawley said. Slowly, he stooped and picked up the bag, hefting its comforting weight in the palm of his hand.

'Do we have ourselves a bargain then, Master Crawley?'

He let out a deep breath, looked down at the bag, and nodded. 'Aye, mistress,' he growled. 'We have ourselves a bargain. I shall hang the witch at midnight before three witnesses, as the law demands.'

James had found two sheepskins, which he placed in the back of his father's cart and laid Matilda carefully upon them, and drew a thick woollen blanket over her. While he had been gone, Hannah had bathed her granddaughter's raw flesh and helped her into a soft shift, but even so, the pressure upon her back drew a pained groan from her.

'Have courage, my pet,' Hannah urged, as James helped her up to sit alongside Matilda. 'Here, drink some more of this.' She lifted Matilda's head and raised the bottle to her lips. 'It will start to take effect soon, little one,' she whispered soothingly. 'And we are taking you somewhere they shan't find you.'

'Crawley?' Matilda croaked. Her eyes were open, but they were not focussing. 'Crawley... he's...' Hannah lowered the bottle again and allowed Matilda's head to fall gently back onto the soft fleece.

'You don't need to worry yourself about him no more,' she said firmly. Instinctively her hand went behind her, seeking the reassuring lump where she had hidden the old pistol beneath the makeshift bedding. 'That animal won't lay a finger on you ever again, I swear.

'Now drive, James Calthorpe,' she said, looking up to where James had taken his position on the driver's seat in front of them. 'Drive on and let's get her away from here. I don't know what's happening, but there's little point in staying around to find out. Whoever brought the poor child here, I'm willing to bet everything I have in this box that it weren't Crawley and, when he finds her gone, this is the first place he'll come looking.'

Despite her nakedness, Harriet found herself sweating heavily, the tightly laced leather hood stifling her and the weight of the awful iron cage bearing down agonisingly on her neck muscles. The vicious spike raked her tongue whenever she tried to move it, despite the numbing effect of the potion Jane had forced upon her, and her buttocks and thighs were cramping from the pressure of the cold stone beneath them.

In the darkness she began to picture all manner of horrors: every slightest noise, real or imagined, had her stiffening in terror, her ears straining through the thick leather, her mind racing in time with her pulse. She tried to pray, but all the words kept tumbling over each other inside her head and finally, with tears stinging her eyes, she gave up.

It seemed impossible that this was happening to her, but the reality was too stark to deny and she found herself seized in the grip of a paralysing horror. Until now, more concerned with the fate of her cousin than with the other drama unfolding in the village, she had paid the events concerning

Matilda Pennywise and Jacob Crawley little attention, convinced that someone would soon enough bring the village to its collective senses, but now, alone, helpless, naked, she began to understand how truly desperate her position was.

Insane as it had first seemed, Harriet now saw how diabolically cunning Jane's plan truly was. The leather hood hid her true identity effectively enough, the barbaric bridle and the drugged potion combined to prevent her being able to tell Crawley otherwise, and the welts across her back, buttocks and thighs were close enough to the marks she had seen on Matilda's body not to give the witchfinder any cause for suspicion.

Shortly now, if Jane was to be believed, Crawley would return, convinced she was Matilda and, by the time the truth was discovered, it would be far too late.

For the first time Harriet began to understand the nature of true wickedness. Jane Handiwell would be rid of two threats – one real, the one from Harriet herself only imagined – at a single stroke. She would be dead and Crawley, together with Wickstanner, would be driven from Fetworth and probably from the county itself, but only after they had unknowingly done Jane Handiwell's evil work for her.

Harriet's head slumped forward and she began to sob, tears soaking the leather, her naked breasts heaving as she gulped in air, the pains and discomforts now melding into one overall feeling of helplessness such as she would never have believed possible.

And then, through the haze of despair and frustration, she heard the sound of heavy boots scraping on the stone floor of the passageway beyond the door and the blood seemed to freeze in her veins…

- XXIII -

Jacob Crawley reined his horse to a halt and swung slowly from the saddle. Behind him, Silas Grout dismounted likewise and moved forward to take the reins of his master's horse.

'Human nature is a curious thing, Silas,' Crawley mused, looking up at the darkened silhouette of the church. 'Greed, suspicion, superstition – the Devil sows them all in equal amounts, I tell you.'

'Do you know who the woman was then, Master Crawley?' Silas asked.

'Does it matter?' he replied. 'We could doubtless enquire and probably find out, eventually, but why waste time?' His hand went to the money pouch at his belt, hefting the comforting weight. 'The important thing is that she has helped us salvage something from what was in danger of becoming a totally lost cause. Why the old woman was so stubborn I have no idea, but some people behave strangely and these villages breed some curious sorts.'

'So what now, Master Crawley? Shall we hang the wench and have done with it?'

'We'll hang her right enough, Silas,' Crawley said. 'This fifty guineas and the promise of another fifty ensures that, but the thing must be seen to be done properly. You take your horse around to the barn and then go down and see to the girl. I'm sure you can find something to amuse yourself for a short while, eh? But check your scaffold first, in case anyone has sought to interfere with its workings.

'Meantime, I shall ride across to the inn and select three suitable witnesses to observe the execution. It's quite likely there will be more come to see the spectacle, if I'm any judge.'

'What if the old woman turns up with her money?' Silas asked. 'She still might, even though it is well past your deadline.'

'Aye, she might at that,' Crawley said, but his tone indicated that he did not think it likely. 'If she does, then lock her in one of the rooms down there. Whatever's happened to Jed, I'll wager she's responsible and I reckon he must be dead, or we'd have seen something of him by now. So if she does show her face, tomorrow, at first light, we'll go and have a look in the woods and, if we find a corpse, well then, you shall have the pleasure of hanging her too, before we finally take our leave of this place.'

'None of what she's saying is making any sense,' James said. He and Hannah were sitting on a fallen tree trunk that lay just outside the small woodsman's hut where they had brought Matilda. It was only two miles or so from Hannah's cottage, but she assured James that they would be safe enough, for the time being, at least.

'That Crawley don't strike me as being a country fellow,' she said, 'and Wickstanner would have trouble finding his way from one end of the village to the other. No one's used this place these past ten years, except me. I come out here from time to time, when I feels the need of me own company.'

Only partially reassured by this, James nevertheless carried Matilda carefully inside, where he found a clean and comfortable bed, upon which he laid her. A small stove stood in a stone ingle, already laid with kindling and this Hannah soon had crackling away.

'We'll have to damp it down before first light,' she warned, 'otherwise someone might see the smoke, but it'll be all right till then. I'll get some broth going for Matilda, you go move that cart up behind the next lot of bushes and

291

take the horses out of the way. If you go straight past that gnarled old sycamore, you'll find a small clearing where they can graze for a bit.'

By the time James had carried out these instructions Hannah was simmering a small pot on the stove and, while he then walked back along the track, just to make sure there was no sign of their having been followed, the old woman coaxed some of the broth into Matilda. By the time he returned for a second time Matilda was at least partially conscious, though she seemed dazed and her speech was largely incoherent.

Tears sprang to James's eyes as he stared at her shaven head and at the welts that were still visible above the neckline of her shift, and he had to go outside again, not wishing to display his anguish at seeing her in such a condition. Walking back to the cart he reached under the various skins and blankets and retrieved the small case he had placed there just after he first hitched up the horses back at the mill.

Laying it on the tailboard, he opened it carefully and stared down at the two pistols within. There was also a small compartment that held an ornamental powder horn, plus a small wash bag containing several lead balls. Hands trembling, James began painstakingly to load the two weapons and tucked them into his belt, transferring the powder and shot to opposite pockets of his jacket.

'They'll not harm you again, Matilda,' he whispered. 'I'll kill the first man who tries, I swear it.'

Back inside the hut for a third time, James saw that Matilda was now resting much easier, thanks largely, he guessed, to her grandmother's potions. She saw James and seemed to recognise him properly for the first time, managing a watery smile and then trying to tell him something, though little of it made any real sense. Eventually she fell back again, closed her eyes and was soon breathing the shallow, regular breath of the sleeper.

'She'll not wake again for a few hours,' Hannah said, standing up and moving to the small window. She pulled the rough sacking curtain to one side and peered out into the darkness. 'And I don't think we're likely to be disturbed here, either.' She turned back into the room and nodded in the direction of the door. 'Talk outside,' she whispered. 'Leave Matilda in peace for a bit, eh?' They moved quietly outside and settled on the fallen tree trunk.

'Well, she seems a bit confused,' Hannah admitted, when James made his observation, 'but that's only to be expected, seein' as all she's been through.'

'I couldn't really understand anything of what she was trying to say,' James said. 'All that about another girl and the graveyard – I think her mind was wandering.'

'Maybe so,' Hannah conceded, 'but then again, maybe not. Some of it did make a sort of sense, if you picked your way through careful, like. One thing's for sure, she never got out of that church crypt by herself, not in the state she's in.'

'But who helped her?' James demanded. 'And what was all that about another girl and going through a place full of bodies?'

Hannah smiled grimly. 'My guess is that she was talkin' about the Grayling mausoleum. Not many people would know it, but I happen to know for certain that it used to be connected to the church crypt by a tunnel. Whoever brought Matilda out, they brought her that way, I reckon.

'Not only that,' she continued, 'but I reckon they've left someone else in Matilda's place, maybe so Crawley won't realise she's gone straightaway. That's what she was on about when she was trying to say about the other girl.'

'Yes, but *why*?' James asked. 'Why bother to rescue her in the first place, too? Who would care for Matilda enough to do that?'

293

'Well, that's a good question, young James,' Hannah replied slowly, 'but it might not be the right one to ask. I'm not so sure that whoever is behind all this did it for Matilda's sake.'

'Oh? Well, if not for Matilda's sake, then whose?'

Hannah shrugged and looked up at the stars. 'That, my lad,' she answered quietly, 'is a damned good question.'

Jane Handiwell slipped out of the private entrance at the rear of the *Black Drum*, paused in the shadow of the building, her eyes accustoming to the gloom once more and then, satisfied that there was no one to observe her, she quickly crossed the yard towards the stable buildings and made her way directly to the smaller structure.

Inside a single lantern burned in the concourse between the two rows of stalls, and two horses looked out over the lower halves of their doors, turning their heads towards her expectantly as she walked towards them. She patted each of their muzzles as she passed, but did not stop until she reached the final stall on the right, the door of which stood wide open.

As Jane turned into it the shadowy figure rose from the straw and came towards her, and the two women embraced in the darkness without speaking for several seconds.

'Is it done?' Ellen Grayling said, at last.

Jane nodded. 'Yes, the bitch is safely in the crypt. You saw Crawley?'

'Yes, a little while back, at the hour you said. He accepted the money.'

'Of course he did.' Jane's white teeth glinted in the near darkness. 'And of course, he agreed. I've just heard him inside, in the taproom, recruiting his witnesses. No shortage of volunteers.'

'What happens if he removes that mask before he hangs her?'

'I doubt he'll bother,' Jane replied. 'I twisted the knots in such a way that he'll have to cut the laces to get them undone, but even if he does, one bald woman looks much like another in the dark. Crawley's like any other man – he won't see much further than her tits and neither will the rest of those oafs. The only one who'll realise will be my dear father. He so moons after her, it's sickening.'

'And your father?' Ellen said. 'He's not likely to interfere?'

'He probably would, if he were here,' Jane retorted sourly, 'but he and that foppish captain have ridden off to Portsmouth. He's still more interested in looking for Harriet in your woods. I can't wait to see his face on the morrow when he sees his dearly beloved, precious Harriet Merridew dangling from that tree with her pretty little neck snapped in two.'

'The shock may be more than he can bear,' Ellen said quietly.

Jane let out a derisory little snort. 'Unfortunately,' she said, 'I doubt that. And now,' she continued, her tone brighter, 'we have a little while before Master Crawley deals with our problems for us.' She grasped Ellen by the shoulders, stooped and kissed her on the mouth. 'You seem a little warm, my darling friend,' she whispered. 'Why don't you let me help you out of those stifling clothes?'

Jacob Crawley hung the lantern from the iron bracket just inside the door and stood, staring down at the huddled figure in the far corner. Noting that she wore the heavy scold's bridle again, he smiled to himself. Evidently Silas Grout had decided he wanted Matilda silent for her last hours and replaced the rusting device.

Grout was a strange one, that was for sure, Crawley thought. On the one hand the man made meticulous preparations to ensure the swift and merciful despatch of his victims, but on the other, until the final moment arrived, he seemed capable of inflicting almost any form of torture on them.

Crawley shook his head and began removing his cloak. He had long since despaired of trying to work out human nature, as he had also long since ceased questioning his own motives and darker desires. After all, he reasoned, why should he show compassion to people who allowed themselves to remain in ignorance the way most of them did? They deserved everything they got, in his opinion, even if half of them weren't witches.

There was no gratitude, no understanding – Crawley had come to realise that many years since. Once he had felt a calling, known that God needed him to help purge this terrible world of all its evil and he had thrown himself into that vocation with all the energy and dedication a man could offer. And he had been successful, too. Over half the kingdom, as it had then been, people trembled at the mere mention of his name and everywhere he went there had been awe and respect.

Of course, his name then had not been Jacob Crawley; he had been forced to adopt another identity when some of the Church he served so diligently turned on him. Vile accusations had been muttered, falsehoods of the most heinous kinds, rumours, whisperings, machinations by those who had started to fear him and to be jealous of his reputation.

Thankfully, he still had friends and the warnings came in time. He managed to fade into obscurity, travelling to France for a year and a half and only returning when his own carefully seeded rumours convinced his enemies that he was no more.

The war between Parliament and the King had come opportunely for the now Jacob Crawley. Men died in battles, were hanged, were thrown into the Tower and a dozen other prisons, where they rotted and died or simply went mad. Much of what was past became quickly forgotten, much of the so-called 'enlightenment' that had so very nearly proved his undoing, was buried in an avalanche of civil upheaval.

As Crawley, he found it easy and safe enough to travel the countryside and, as Crawley, he could continue the work he had once found so spiritually rewarding, even if now his zeal was directed primarily to looking after his own needs. The end result, he told himself, was near enough the same.

He stooped over the unmoving girl and prodded her in the side with one foot, rocking her roughly until she began to stir. She raised her head and he saw her eyes were wide open, fear shining in them, to be replaced by pain as she tried to speak and the iron prong bit into her tongue.

'Not long now, Matilda Pennywise,' he said softly. 'Another hour and you'll be out of this black hole forever. But first,' he continued, with a harsh chuckle, 'I have a use for you. Come – up on your feet, wench. You'll go on your way with something to remember me by, or my name ain't Matthew Hopkins!'

To be continued…

Author's Note

Before anyone starts writing to me to say that Matthew Hopkins died when and whenever, I should say that I, too, have read various accounts of his death, but that the point is that they do vary, even to the country in which he is supposed to have died, and that none have ever been verified, nor is there any record, or marker, of where his body was finally disposed of.

I appreciate, also, that the 'long drop' method of hanging victims was not introduced officially into England and Wales until nearly two centuries after the time of this story, but there exist accounts of various executioners experimenting with the process long before that, particularly in some regions of Italy and Germany, and there is no reason to suppose that certain individuals might not have brought the idea to England as early as this.

A certain degree of artistic licence should be permitted in the telling of any fictional tale, so I trust you will suspend your sense of disbelief wherever necessary. In any case, the only people who can say for sure who is right and who is wrong are now long dead, including Matthew Hopkins, alias Jacob Crawley.

So, if you want to find out just how *I* imagine he might have met his end, you'll have to buy the concluding volume in this saga – which I think I might just call *The Devil's Surrogate*.

More exciting titles available from Chimera

All **Chimera** titles are/will be available from your local booksho͏ or newsagent, or direct from our mail order department. Pleas͏ send your order with a cheque or postal order (made payable ͏ *Chimera Publishing Ltd*) to: **Chimera Publishing Ltd., PO Bo͏ 152, Waterlooville, Hants, PO8 9FS**. If you would prefer to pa͏ by credit card, email us at: **chimera@fdn.co.uk** or call our 2͏ **hour telephone/fax credit card hotline: +44 (0)23 92 78303͏** (Visa, Mastercard, Switch, JCB and Solo only).

To order, send: Title, author, ISBN number and price for eac͏ book ordered, your full name and address, cheque or postal orde͏ for the total amount, and include the following for postage an͏ packing:

UK and BFPO: £1.00 for the first book, and 50p for eac͏ additional book to a maximum of £3.50.

Overseas and Eire: £2.00 for the first book, £1.00 for the secon͏ and 50p for each additional book.

*Titles £5.99. All others £4.99

For a copy of our free catalogue please write to:

Chimera Publishing Ltd
Readers' Services
PO Box 152
Waterlooville
Hants
PO8 9FS

Or visit our Website for details of all our superb titles
www.chimerabooks.co.uk

Sales and Distribution in the USA and Canada:

LPC Group
1436 West Randolph Street
Chicago
IL 60607
(800) 626-4330

***